VISION OF FIRE
EPHRAIM WRIGHT

Copyright © 2025 by Ephraim Wright

All rights reserved.

No part of this publication may be reproduced, distributed, or transmitted in any form or by any means, including photocopying, recording, or other electronic or mechanical methods, without the prior written permission of the publisher, except as permitted by U.S. copyright law. For permission requests, contact ephraim@bladeandrosebooks.com.

The story, all names, characters, and incidents portrayed in this production are fictitious. No identification with actual persons (living or deceased), places, buildings, and products is intended or should be inferred.

Book cover illustrated by Felicity Wright. Scene breaks and chapter images created by author. All rights reserved.

ISBN: 979-8-9932493-1-5 (paperback)

First edition 2025

To my mother for helping make this dream possible, and everyone who
waited so patiently.

CONTENTS

On Fate — IX

Prologue — XI

Part One: Chasing Dragons

1. The Golden Keg — 3

2. Ambush — 11

3. Servailles's Proposition — 21

4. A Shadow and a Skirmish — 33

5. Up In Smoke — 44

6. Ill News — 55

7. The Chancellor and the Soothsayer — 65

8. The Trial of Winston Servailles — 77

9. Grudgingly Into the Maw — 86

10. Dominus Square — 96

11. The Bookkeeper — 104

12. Tunnels of the Past — 112

13. Blood and Broken Bones — 122

14. The Legend of the Vida Imralta — 129

Part Two: Hope

15. Counsel From the Shadows   143

16. The Streets of Seruvia   148

17. The Acolytes of the Seer   161

18. Heavy Is the Mantle   170

19. Westbound   176

20. The Messengers   183

21. Flight   193

22. A Test of Mettle   199

Part Three: Liberty or Ruin

23. Vision of Fire   213

24. To Topple a Tyrant   219

25. The Cost of War   227

26. Governor Tullin   235

27. The Wolf   243

28. Andre and the Soothsayer   252

29. The House of Endela   258

30. A Question of Trust   266

31. Mask In the Night   275

32. Andre's Accusation   281

33. Ride and Ruin   291

34. Nightmare Under Seruvia   304

35. Crossroads   315

36. The Stakes Are Set   325

37. Caito's Malaise   333

38. The Soothsayer's Warning   343

Part Four: Red Dawn

39. Servailles Victorious   351

40. Storm Over Seruvia   365

41. The Madness of Winston Servailles   376

42. The Lord Artreus   386

Epilogue   399

Acknowledgements   405

About the author   407

"Accept the things to which fate binds you, and love the people with whom fate brings you together, but do so with all your heart."

\- Marcus Aurelius

PROLOGUE

Corynthia

THIRTEEN YEARS AGO, A nation to the south erupted into bigotry as the Holy Voice of Salamoa uttered a declaration that would set the stage for three years of bloody genocide. The persecuted fled, leaving their homes behind to seek safety at the border of the vast empire of Kaval. Alas, no solace was to be found, and the Border Conflict imprinted its stain upon history.

Three long years it raged, immigrants losing lives even as soldiers lost their souls, until one man brought it all to an end.

Winston Servailles, emerging from nowhere, rallied the people of Southern Kaval, the land that would soon become Corynthia, and declared secession from the empire. By uniting their voices against the horror of the Border Conflict in opposition to the imperial rule allowing the bloodshed, he turned the butcher's block into a haven. As the refugees poured tearfully in, Kaval, realizing the evil part it played, withheld its outrage and offered a hand in peace.

Thus was Corynthia, the land of freedom, formed.

However, as with all new, radical endeavors, utopia was elusive. Even after promising democracy, Servailles assumed control of the government as Corynthia rushed to repair the damage wreaked by the Border Conflict. At first, the Corynthians were content—Servailles was regarded as a hero throughout the land—but as months lengthened to years with no sign of change, that sentiment soured, and whispers of dictatorship haunted his good name.

An election hurried to the horizon, and a man named Berling Tench defeated Servailles with alluring promises of wealth and recognition. The new chancellor stepped into his role, and Corynthia settled back into comfortable lull.

Until Winston Servailles was arrested for treason.

Claims of a coup and an assassination attempt swept the land. Taverns burst at the seams as beer flowed and tongues wagged, repeating with dumbfounded eagerness every detail of the subsequent trials. Narrowly escaping execution thanks to a sympathetic court, Servailles was sentenced to exile—banished from the land on threat of death should he return. He and his allies fled into the wilderness.

Then, Berling Tench revealed his true colors. A thunderhead of tyranny descended upon Corynthia, battering them with increased taxes and brutal punishments. Realizing their mistake, the people protested, but it was too late. Tench's iron grip was already strangling the freedom from the land even as he mockingly maintained the ruse of democracy.

The land fell still, free no longer. The Corynthians retreated timidly into their homes, sympathetic politicians silently behind their masks.

The uneasy calm was broken by steel. Armies amassed and marched to the borders, bolstered by arrogant young men who were enticed by promises of wealth and glory. The threatening display led the surrounding countries to draw back and conduct affairs more cautiously.

The continent seemed to be holding its breath—as though preparing for war.

But as freedom suffocated and the shadow of war deepened, rumors of a rebellion in the wilderness began to spread, bringing a spark of hope back to the oppressed people of Corynthia. Yet what drew their attention even more were the whispers of a vision seen through the eyes of a troubled young man.

A vision of fire.

PART ONE: CHASING DRAGONS

THE GOLDEN KEG

R OM STOOD AT THE counter, scrubbing the dirty dishes. A wind storm raged outside like a great beast, and the Golden Keg creaked around him. Wind whistled through the gaps in the closed windows and door, providing background noise to his musings.

He was concerned. Despite its location in the tiny, northern village of Baggot, the Golden Keg was a popular tavern, bearing a reputation for good food and drink, respectable service, and clean rooms. Even though there was an occasional troublemaker, most patrons were respectable and paid good money. The past few weeks, however, only a trickle of people came to dine, almost none to lodge. Just one person purchased a room in the last three days.

He knew it was fallout from the rumors prowling around about the insurgents: The people once so involved in the upbringing of Corynthia who were now public enemies of said nation.

Rom remembered the moment he heard the news that began this mess as clearly as thunder during a storm. A busy Friday evening, the Golden Keg had been full of customers when a traveler burst through the front door shouting that Winston Servailles and a group of his closest allies were in custody for charges of treason against the chancellor.

Needless to say, the messenger's tab was fully paid that night.

Over the next few months, word of Chancellor Tench's growing brutality trickled up to the villagers' ears. The protests and excessive force they elicited gave life to nights of grave gossip around the fireplace in the Golden Keg's dining room. Heads were shaken, speculations voiced, and many a *poor bastards* was solemnly uttered.

Comparatively, in their sleepy village, little changed. The citizens grew most of their own food and made their own clothes, selling goods to travelers that came through and buying what they couldn't provide for themselves. The lack of outside interference meant the village enjoyed an intimate community with no soldiers, no taxes, and no trouble.

Then the rumors started.

Travelers passing through brought claims that Servailles had been wrongfully accused of treason; that he was gathering an army in the wild to take Corynthia back from Tench. Tales were told of groups of rebels pestering the lines of soldiers, then disappearing back into the wilderness.

As though following the stories, Corynthian soldiers appeared in the small village that had known nothing but peace and quiet. Grim-faced men on horseback rode into Baggot, and a group of gaudily dressed officials took up residence in the Muncer estate, forcing its residents into servitude. People disappeared or were arrested openly by the chancellor's men with little context. Those remaining stayed indoors, peeking their heads out from behind drawn curtains at passersby. As suspicion grew, the air became laced with a thin film of fear, and people walked on opposite sides of the road.

Naturally, visitors waned for the Golden Keg. Rom understood why people didn't want to risk leaving their homes (he was brought in for an interrogation once and still cringed at the unpleasant experience); however, the threatening pressure of poverty made his breath catch in his throat whenever he checked his pantry. Another few months of similar business, and he would be in real trouble.

At least there's only myself to provide for, he thought with relief, reaching for a bar of soap. He recalled what happened to Burk the grocer last week.

Late in paying one of the many ridiculous "residential" taxes, Burk was subsequently arrested and carted away to the nearest prison in the port of Clamiera, thirty miles away. His wife and two children were left behind to fend for themselves.

Poor bastards.

Suddenly, the door swung open, startling him. He looked up to see a hooded man in the doorway surveying the empty dining area. The stranger stepped inside, shutting the door behind him.

The wind returned to playing around the edges of the frame as the man approached the counter. He was tall and moved with measured ease. A weathered scarf hid the lower half of his face, and eyes glinted intelligently from under his hood.

Rom set down his mug and pressed his palms into the wooden countertop. "You're not from around here. What's your business?"

"Just passing through." The man raised an eyebrow at his brusque tone. "I'm searching for someone." He shifted, and Rom caught a dull sheen of chainmail at his collar. "I'm wondering if you've seen him."

"I'm not at liberty to share any information 'bout my patrons. You could inquire in town; there's a traveler's checkpoint. They'll know the person you're looking for if they came through." He snorted at the thought. A cat couldn't make its way through Baggot without a guard knowing about it anymore.

"I'm not keen about soldiers."

"Neither am I. I still can't help you."

The eyes narrowed. They were green and cold, like a serpent's. "You're not having much business these days, are you?"

"It's been slow," Rom admitted with a shrug. He didn't care for the traveler's demeanor.

The man reached into his cloak, pulling out a few coins. He placed them on the table and covered them with a hand. With his other, he presented a sketch of a young man with a thin face and short hair. "Have you seen him?"

Eyeing the money, Rom scratched his chin. "Maybe."

He had. The young man arrived yesterday, though he declined to give his name. Rom understood. These were uncertain times.

"Could you point me to his room?"

"How do you know he's at my inn?"

"I have my ways. Which room is his?"

Rom glanced again at the money. This was obviously very important information to the stranger. He wondered how much more he could pinch out of him.

"You're in no position to haggle," the stranger uttered softly, as if he read his mind. He shifted his hand slightly over the coins. "His room, innkeeper." It wasn't a question this time.

Rom considered his options. This man seemed dangerous. He wasn't sure how dangerous, though he certainly didn't want to find out; the stranger seemed used to having his way. He was also right: He really was in no position to haggle. The money presented would buy him a couple months' worth of groceries. If business continued to be sluggish, at least he wouldn't starve.

Relenting, he nodded to the stairs. "Room eight. I can show you to him."

The man returned the sketch to the depths of his cloak. "No, thank you."

Watching the stranger walk to the stairs, Rom swept the coins off of the counter into the pouch hanging from his belt. They rattled inside the purse, and he smiled as the comfortable weight of money returned to his hip. He grabbed another mug from the few dirty dishes on the counter, wondering what the stranger wanted with the man in the sketch.

Normally, he wouldn't consider himself a nosy person; however, this was suspicious activity. The new Baggot "representatives" encouraged the villagers to report *any* suspicious activity, even regarding their neighbors. They might pay him handsomely for the information.

Making a split-second decision, he returned the glass and followed the stranger up the stairwell.

The stairs creaked as he ascended, making him pause and cringe. Shifting his weight to the outside of the steps, he continued upwards. When he crested the landing, he crept quietly to the fourth door on the right, pressing his ear against it. He made out a voice speaking: It was the stranger's.

"Chancellor Tench already has your identity. He visited your home after you fled. Meanwhile, the insurgent has eyes and ears everywhere. I'm sure he knows who you are. He certainly knows what you're capable of. You will be found, if you haven't been already."

"I don't want to be involved. That's why I left."

Rom recognized the voice of the young man who purchased a room a night ago—the one from the sketch. He sounded nervous.

"You can't avoid becoming tangled in this, no matter your feelings," the stranger replied. "You have a gift. They want it. The insurgent has cause; circumstances are against him. Whereas Chancellor Tench... there's not enough power in this world for him."

"I won't let them use me."

"So, you'll do..." the stranger paused, "...what?"

The bed creaked inside the room, and Rom heard footsteps pacing the floor. "I'll keep running."

"Forever?"

"If I must."

There was silence. Rom's breathing sounded deafening in his own ears, and he stifled it with his hand. This was something big. He wondered again who these people were.

As though hearing his thoughts, the young man spoke again, "Who are you? How do you know of me?"

"Oh, everyone knows of you by now. The world doesn't stay oblivious to people like you. I just know a little more than most."

"How much more?" The young man sounded irritated now.

"Enough to help. You cannot hide forever. They want your gift, and they won't rest until they find you."

"Why?"

"Why?" The stranger laughed. "Don't play the fool. You have tremendous power. They think that if they control you, they can manipulate the coming events to their own benefit."

"It doesn't work like that," the young man explained in a tired voice. "I can only see what will come to be. I don't know how it will happen or when. I don't even know what the visions pertain to until afterwards."

Rom's heart pounded as he tried to wrap his mind around what he was hearing. *Could this young man*—he hardly dared to finish the thought—*see the future?*

He had heard stories of Soothsayers: Men and women visited by visions of events yet to take place. He never gave them much stock—they were usually in children's fairy tales. Except now, listening to how seriously the two men talked, he wondered.

As the stories went, Soothsayers appeared around important or calamitous events, carrying vital information. Unfortunately, death and destruction always surrounded them. If the young man *was* a Soothsayer, then this was far more serious and dangerous than Rom could ever fathom.

And the insurgent... The stranger must be speaking of Servailles.

He swallowed as he came to the realization. Servailles was the most condemned man in Corynthia. Posters of his face were everywhere Rom visited, even in Baggot. He needed to step away and forget this ever happened.

He made to retreat back downstairs; however, the stranger spoke again, drawing him back to the door.

"My point remains. You have visions, and both sides desire to exploit them. In the simplest of terms, *you* are a strategic advantage—a piece in the puzzle of victory. With two headstrong leaders like the chancellor and the insurgent, you won't find peace. Even now, they're scouring the land for you."

"Then what do I do?" the Soothsayer pleaded, a desperate edge to his voice.

"Join a side. Spare yourself the exhaustion of running and hiding. You might even find a way to change fate."

There was more silence, followed by the bed creaking again. "They're uncertain."

"What are?"

"The visions. They're confusing, chaotic." The Soothsayer's voice dropped. Rom leaned closer. "Their faces are covered in shadow. I can only see the figures and hear... the screams. I don't know who will be victorious. I can't determine who will die, or who will live—if anyone does. It isn't much help to anyone."

"What have you seen?" The stranger sounded cautious.

"I—I can't say. It's..." the Soothsayer's voice trailed off, lost in misery.

"I understand. It's a burden."

The other heaved a weary sigh. "Who are you? Did Gertie send you?"

Pressing his ear to the door, Rom listened as hard as he could. He was already invested. Might as well learn the identity of the stranger, then he could take it to the authorities for a reward.

"Someone who has your best interests at heart."

"The others don't? From what I understand, I'm stuck, and I *know* this is beyond my ability. Why are you helping me?"

"More bloodshed will be spilled the longer you hide. You are crucial to the coming conflict. If you step out from the shadows, many lives could be saved."

"How do *you* know all of this? I thought I was the one with the *gift*." The young man spat out the last word with obvious loathing.

A low chuckle emanated from the stranger. "If I told you, it would take the fun away."

"This is fun to you? People *dying* is amusing?"

"On the contrary, it is a necessity. The insurgent is starting a war; *I* am merely embracing the repercussions. You should as well."

"Embrace it! You're mad!"

"I don't mean to enjoy the coming storm; you must merely accept it. Work with it instead of against it. The longer you hide, the further you run, the more it will destroy before it finally bursts, taking you with it. Where does that leave everyone else? Blind and deaf, groping through a burning building with no escape. War is a fearsome beast that snatches up everyone in its jaws, whether they desire it or not—people such as you doubly so. You must allow yourself to be taken by its current, making the necessary adjustments to reach the other side."

Rom furrowed his brow. Who was this man? It sounded like he knew more about the future than he who could actually see it. An image of a spider weaving a web around many helpless flies popped into his head. He was right: This man was dangerous. Very, very dangerous.

"But there are two sides. Which is the right choice?"

"There is no right or wrong decision. Choose which cause rests easier on your conscience. You'll hear from both—I can almost guarantee it. The chancellor has the power and resources; hence, the insurgent... well, he's certainly desperate enough to try anything. In fact, you shouldn't need to lift a finger. Everything should fall right into your lap." The stranger laughed again.

When no response was uttered, Rom finally stepped back from the door. He heard enough. This was far too important for him, a simple innkeeper, to be wrapped up in. Tiptoeing back to the stairs, he descended as quietly as possible.

Returning to the counter, he grabbed the glass he left, his mind racing. There was a war brewing between Winston Servailles and Chancellor Tench, while a Soothsayer—a legitimate Soothsayer—walked the land in secret. If the stories about Soothsayers were true, then the coming conflict had the potential to consume not only Corynthia, but possibly the surrounding lands, too.

He felt torn. Should he stay quiet, or risk his hide to let the authorities know what was happening under their very noses?

The thought of the money he could make from this information helped the thundering of his heartbeat slow. According to the stranger, everything he just heard was very important to Chancellor Tench.

And to Servailles. What if—

Footsteps sounded on the stairs. Rom hurriedly acted busy again.

Pausing at the bottom of the stairwell, the stranger gave him a piercing look. Rom stared back, his hand holding the cleaning rag stationary. The man's gaze froze him, seeming to stab through his eyeballs, burrowing deep into his mind and reading his secrets.

The man reached into his cloak, and for a moment, Rom thought he was a dead man, but he just pulled out a coin and flipped it to him.

"Have yourself a drink. It seems like you could use one." The stranger disappeared into the blustery day outside.

Rom breathed a sigh of relief and reached for a clean glass. The man was right: He did need a drink. He would collect his scattered thoughts better after a tall mug of ale anyway.

Or a few.

When Tedric Gallow huddled into the Golden Keg an hour later, he found Rom lying on the floor behind the counter, staring at the ceiling with unseeing eyes. Foam flecked the green hue tainting his lips, while broken glass glittered next to him, alcohol soaking into the floorboards amidst the shards. The authorities were immediately called. However, when they arrived and searched the inn, the rooms upstairs were all empty. There was no sign any of them had been occupied.

2

AMBUSH

THE MORNING SUN'S RAYS sifted through gently waving green leaves, dappling the ground in yellow swathes. Water dripped, splashing into puddles in the ruts of the dirt road coiling through the forest. Mingled with the chirping of birds, the gentle sound of the droplets created a pleasant symphony to the band of men and women hidden along the road.

Andre inhaled deeply from the tree he sat in, bow over his shoulders and buckler balanced on his knees. The air smelled fresh and green, and the sky above was clear, bright, and blue. A breeze flicked the stray strands of his brown hair rebelling against his ponytail. He was tall and wore a brown sleeveless cloak over chainmail. Stubble shadowed his cheeks, softening a strong jawline, and he scanned the forest with keen gray eyes.

The recent storm gave his party a head start on the supply train due to pass through the area. While the wagon was stuck in the mud, Andre's rebels found an opportune location to set up an ambush.

The road they watched wound through Malaki Forest within bow-distance of the hilly slopes heralding the Argos Mountains, a range separating the western border of Corynthia from Kaval. Inside the hills, a well-hidden cave not far from where they lay in wait served as a base for the rebels. Below, the road continued through the forest until it reached an outpost—a spot of interest for the rebellion. Although small, it was well-fortified and held a strategic position that would provide the rebellion a strong upper hand for their planned siege of the loyalist city, Cappus.

Sitting at the head of Drago Valley in the Argos Mountains, Cappus served as a pass between Kaval and Corynthia. In addition to being the center of commerce between the two nations, it was the quickest route between Kaval and Seruvia, the capital of Corynthia. Only two highways led out from Cappus: One to Clamiera in the north, and one to Markalv in the east. Both were guarded by an outpost. The northern outpost was already captured. Because the road between Cappus and Clamiera was seldom used, the checkpoint fell easily. The capture of the second fort was crucial. Once it fell and the rebellion garrisoned it with troops of their own, Cappus would be cut off from the rest of Corynthia. With the city under the rebellion's control, Kaval would be unable to send any aid through the mountains.

That is, if Berling Tench called for aid. More likely, the tyrant would be content to hang rather than sully his pride.

Be that as it may, it was best to cover all fronts. Capturing Cappus would give the rebellion more time to tighten the noose around Chancellor Tench—a noose that would hopefully put an end to his cruel regime.

The sound of hooves striking the muddied path broke through the cacophony of birdsong and Andre's thoughts. Sitting up, he gave a high, carrying whistle, signaling the rebels to be ready. As he watched, a large covered wagon pulled by two oxen came into view. A single driver held the reins, accompanied by three guards on horseback.

Fingers playing with red dog's head brooch on his collar, Andre frowned. The previous supply runs were always protected by at least three squads. This was just disrespectful.

Unless it's a trap.

Scanning the bend again, he tried to catch something that would betray a second detachment of soldiers. He saw nothing.

Andre gave two more whistles, telling the others to wait. He strapped his buckler to his left arm and dropped from the tree. Pulling his bow free, he stepped into the middle of the road and drew back an arrow with calculated precision.

The driver pulled on the reins, bringing the oxen to a halt. The three guards drew their swords as they noticed Andre, but stopped as well.

Andre spoke, "This convoy is now under the control of Winston Servailles and the rebellion. Surrender and dismount from your steeds. There is no need for bloodshed."

The guard on the left sneered. In his mid-twenties, he looked to be the kind of man to brag about how many women he had bedded since joining the army. "Servailles sent you to do his dirty work, did he?" he said brashly. "Who are you, then?"

"Lieutenant Andre Cordon of the Crimson Hounds." Andre's tone was casual, as though conversing with a friend. The arrow swiveled towards the guard, rock steady.

He noticed the driver start slightly at his words and glance at the red dog's head pin on Andre's collar. He knew he had a reputation from the Border Conflict; the Crimson Hounds had been an elite group of enforcers under his command and now operated for the rebellion with the same deadly efficiency. He smiled grimly.

"Crimson Hounds?" one of the other guards jeered. "I only see one *welp*. Are you going to fight us alone?"

"Maybe. Show your hand, and I'll show mine."

The soldier ignored the statement. "In that case, this should be fun. Run him down!" He and his companions spurred their horses towards Andre.

The first rider swung his blade at Andre as he passed, forcing him to dive aside. Andre rolled to his feet, bow still drawn, and fired his arrow after the guard, skewering him in the neck. The loyalist slipped sideways off his horse, crashing to the ground, dead.

Trying to string another arrow, Andre was forced to bail as the second horseman bore down on him. He dodged the soldier's pass and threw aside his bow, pulling out his sword instead. He parried the blow of the third guard, rocking him in his saddle. As the latter circled around again, the second guard slid from his steed to rush him with a cry.

Andre blocked the first strike with his buckler, then drove his elbow into the side of the man's head, stunning him. He quickly dispatched the soldier and turned to face the other guard riding towards him at a gallop. As he stepped forward to land a blow on the rider, the horse reared and kicked, making him jump back.

Standing in the stirrups to strike, the rider wasn't prepared for his steed's sudden movement. He lost his grip on the reigns and fell backwards over the animal's rear. He scrambled to his feet, swinging wildly at Andre, who sidestepped and lunged with his own blade. He caught the man on the shoulder, then finished him off with an overhand blow to the head, denting the man's helmet and knocking him unconscious.

Andre turned to the driver, who stared at the scene with wide eyes. "How many more guards?"

The man threw his hands in the air. "I'm just the driver!"

"And you don't seem like a fool. Tell me how many more guards there are, or I'll kill you, too!"

The driver hesitated for a second, then lunged for the satchel lying on the seat next to him.

Andre briefly considered throwing his sword at him, then thought better of it and sprinted for his bow. As he scooped it up, the sound of a horn rang out, echoing through the trees, sending birds swarming into the air in droves. He turned, nocked an arrow, and let it fly at the driver with deadly accuracy, cutting off the horn's call.

The soldiers' horses, having moved off to the grass on the side of the road, retreated farther from the scene while the oxen lowed anxiously.

Straining his ears, Andre listened for the sound of approaching troops. A branch snapped, and he peered in the direction of the noise. Without warning, an arrow whistled out of the brush, skipping at his feet. At the same moment, five armed soldiers burst out of the trees with a cry and ran at him.

He turned and fled, letting out a high, drawn-out whistle. As he reached the boulders littering the base of the hills, two Crimson Hounds leaped out with swords and shields. Now that he had reinforcements, Andre skidded to a stop and turned back to face the oncoming soldiers with a grim sense of purpose.

The skirmish was short and brutal. Andre took on two loyalists at once, killing one with a quick thrust before spinning around and knocking away the other's slash. He followed the parry with a punch to the face, breaking the man's nose and sending him sprawling. Dodging a third soldier's strike, a quick slash sent the man to one knee, where he flattened him with a crashing blow.

The other two loyalist soldiers were also down; though, one of Andre's own men bled from a wide cut on his sword arm.

"Are you alright?" Andre checked.

The man nodded. "I've had worse, but I should—" His words were interrupted by another arrow snapping on a rock next to him.

They whirled around to see more soldiers emerging from the trees.

"There's the rest." Andre turned back to the wounded man. "Head back to the cave, and take care of your arm. We'll return when we finish here."

"Lieutenant!" The other man pointed in the direction of the wagon.

Even more soldiers were stepping out of the underbrush. Andre counted already thirteen swordsmen with another eight carrying bows behind them. One of the men clambered into the driver's seat of the wagon, shoving the dead man to the ground.

Andre's heart sank. The soldiers were streaming out of the trees faster than he could count to join the formation around the wagon. There was no way the Hounds could win this fight. He whistled again to those still hidden: Their signal to retreat.

"Fall back! Into the hills!"

If the loyalists followed them into the hills, their odds were significantly better. Even vastly outnumbered, the Crimson Hounds knew the rocky terrain by heart. They could separate and trap their enemy in small groups, dispatching them without much issue.

Unfortunately, that didn't solve the problem of stopping the wagon. While the Hounds were off playing hide-and-seek with the main force, the rest of the escort could saunter its way to the outpost, which would be a debilitating setback. With renewed strength and an influx of fresh soldiers, the outpost would be much more difficult to capture. The weeks they spent isolating it would be wasted.

Andre quickly snuffed the idea of sending a team to circle back and stop the convoy. With the size of its escort, they needed full strength to take the wagon—a luxury they couldn't afford at the moment.

Deftly scrambling through the maze of boulders and skeletal evergreen trees, Andre arrived shortly at the cave where the rest of his band already waited.

A lookout slid down from his perch further up the hill and gave him a quick salute. "Sir, they're sending men after us."

"How many?" asked his second-in-command, a man named Mattias Berg.

"At least two dozen warriors."

"Try fifty," Andre corrected grimly. More than half of the loyalists marched after him as he slipped into the hills.

"*Fifty*?" Mattias was a short, well-built man with defined muscles. In his thirties, his short rusty hair looked like copper dust above green eyes now filled with alarm. The insignia pin borne by each of the Crimson Hounds gleamed dully on his shoulder. "Andre, we barely number twenty."

Andre frowned, counting. "Less. Where are Tahlia and Wes?" Murmurs of confusion filled the cave as the others noticed the missing pair.

"They were on the far side of the road. Maybe they were trapped. Donroe, you were with them."

Andre looked at Donroe to confirm. The rebel shook his head. Andre swore.

"We'll find them later. Right now, loyalists are climbing through the hills searching for us. That's our main concern. I know we could avoid engagement, but a company of soldiers wandering around our home base is not something I want on my mind. Once we've dealt with them and the supplies, we'll find Wes and Tahlia."

The Hounds nodded their agreement.

"Now, Tench's men are trained for direct, hand-to-hand combat, which means we have an advantage. Stay above them; try and separate them. Let's work quickly, but do *not* take unnecessary risks. I want everyone alive at the end of this, understood?"

"Aye, sir!" came the unified response.

"You all know the game. Pick a companion; don't lose them. Donroe, you stay with me. Let's play cat and mouse."

They dispersed through the rough terrain, staying low and out of sight.

The familiar feeling of nerves made Andre's stomach squirm as he stepped back into the sunlight. Search-and-destroy was nothing new to him or the soldiers under his command—the Crimson Hounds perfected the art during the Border Conflict—still, he found himself just as nervous, even after all of these years.

Like a greennose every single time, he thought dourly.

The hunt among the trees and boulders took nearly three hours as the rebels combed the hills from top to bottom. The loyalists, entirely out of their element, quickly lost themselves in the rugged maze, doing most of the rebels' work for them. Andre and Donroe themselves only found two separate squads of three, falling upon them before they were even aware they were being hunted.

When Andre was satisfied no more enemy troops remained, he gathered the others back to the cave.

The afternoon shadows had grown long, stretching as though fleeing the sun's glare. The rebels were tired, sweaty, and bloody; thankfully, all were accounted for, excluding the two already missing. Nobody sustained any serious injuries, and, after a few moments of recuperation, Andre led them back down to the road.

The wagon was long gone, as he expected. Still, he felt a small twinge of disappointment. He had held a tiny hope that fate might have smiled upon them, and some misfortune would befall the wagon. Alas, she was not so kind.

He shook his head in frustration as he stared at the tracks. All of their hard work for the past month undone in a day. It would take them weeks to again reach a similar point.

Winston's going to be disappointed. He groaned a curse.

"We could still catch them," Mattias offered. "It's a large group—if we take a direct path—"

Andre patted his second-in-command's arm with a gloomy smile. "I've always appreciated your optimism, Mattias. They have a three hour head start on us, and the outpost is only a few miles further. Unless a tree fell on them, they've already arrived." He jerked his head at the tracks. "Let's assess the damage."

Jogging at an easy pace, they moved into the trees close enough to see the road, though deep enough in the brush to stay hidden. If there were any loyalists lagging behind, Andre didn't want them to raise the alarm. The outpost had fresh soldiers now. They could spare a few to try and hunt them down.

After only about five minutes of marching, Mattias tapped on Andre's shoulder and pointed up to the sky. "Andre, look!"

He followed his finger through the forest canopy to a column of smoke rising into the air. The top of the pillar drifted away like wisps of rain cloud as the wind caught it.

Frowning, he signaled the company to halt. The smoke wasn't coming from the outpost; its location wasn't right. *It could be from the wagon, but how—?* A realization dawned in his mind. There was only one explanation he could think of as to why the wagon would be on fire.

"Pick up the pace!"

They took the road to avoid tripping through the forest as they increased their speed. In another thirty minutes, the group arrived at the source of the smoke.

The wagon lay overturned near the edge of the road, engulfed in fire. The crates of provisions were smashed open, their contents scattered across the road, or disintegrating among hungry tongues of flame. The oxen were missing from their harnesses, and the bodies of the guards were strewn about, all dead. White feathered arrows sprouted from them, and many were charred from the flames. The smell of burning flesh hung in the air.

"What in the name of the All-Mother..." Mattias's wondering voice faltered. The others echoed his words as they stared at the scene.

Picking his way through the carnage, Andre examining the bodies. The arrows were unmarked, yet handmade in a style he knew well. He pulled one free of a corpse, twirling it gleefully between his fingers.

Those crazy bastards.

At an exclamation from the others, he looked up to see two figures emerging from the trees. He went to meet them a grin growing from ear to ear.

"Wes and Tahlia!" He embraced them both at the same time. "You mad dogs! Why didn't you retreat when I ordered?"

The rest of the Hounds surrounded them, laughing and whooping.

"Didn't hear you, sir," claimed Wes as hands slapped him on the back.

He was tall with mischievous blue eyes twinkling under tussled brown hair. His large ears, far from spoiling his appearance, only complimented his careless sort of handsomeness. He smiled, flashing perfect teeth.

"When you retreated, we shadowed the wagon. After all, someone need-ed to keep them from reaching the outpost. We waited until they were comfortable, then took the initiative to give them a lesson in vigilance."

"With fire," interjected Tahlia, wearing a grin reminiscent of a child.

She was also tall, her black hair contained under a purple handkerchief. Her olive complexion peeked out under mud smeared on her face. Her hands emoted as she spoke, matching the energy in her almond-shaped eyes.

"We fired burning arrows into the back of the wagon, and shot them while they ran around like chickens with their heads cut off."

"It was quite easy," added Wes as casually as discussing the weather. "It's hard to believe these men are actually trained."

Mattias snorted. "Tench believes in strength in numbers; effectiveness be damned."

Wes grinned. "Anyway, you might want to see this. Tahlia found it at the last moment." He handed a satchel to Andre. "I think you'll be glad we saved it."

Andre took it from him. It was the same one the driver had pulled the horn from. It smelled of smoke. Even though the leather was cracked and blackened from the fire, the official Corynthian crest was still visible: A golden rose with three gold stars on either side in front of a silver triangle. He removed a wad of papers from it, shuffling through them. They were mostly expense reports for supplies and troop movement orders—not entirely useful information. Certainly nothing they couldn't obtain with their spies.

He looked up at Wes, who indicated back to the purse.

Reaching his hand back inside, Andre found an envelope, its seal already broken. He pulled out the letter and unfolded it, his brow furrowing as he read. "Is this a trick?"

"No, sir, that's the official seal of Corynthia. Dear old Chancellor Tench penned it himself."

Andre read the note one more time. "Did you save any horses?" If the contents of the letter were indeed true, he needed to inform Winston Servailles immediately.

"Aye." Wes indicated back to the trees behind him. "We thought you would want to use them."

"Good." Andre turned to his second-in-command. "Mattias, lay low for now. It'll take some time for news of this failed delivery to reach Seruvia."

"Aye, sir." Mattias pointed at the letter. "What's that about, may I ask?"

Andre didn't answer at first. His mind spun with the implications of the letter. Knowing Winston how he did, the rebel leader would try to change the rebellion's entire trajectory for the war. Whether that would be a good or a bad thing...

Folding the parchment, he slipped it into his tunic. "It claims they've discovered a Soothsayer."

# 3

SERVAILLES'S PROPOSITION

S LUMPING IN HIS SADDLE, Andre let out a slow breath. This was the third straight day of riding, and he was exhausted. Nevertheless, his weariness could not prevent him from soaking in the scene of breathtaking beauty before him.

A lake stretched out in the terrain below like a sheet of polished sapphire. Dense woods of cedars and hemlocks bordered the glittering expanse, crawling up to the base of the Argos Mountains. A river flowed through rolling hills of golden grass and winked at him as it wound its way south towards the land of Salamoa. A few herds of deer meandered through the waving stalks, small brown spots on the flaxen canvas.

Andre stared after the silver snake of water for a moment, unpleasant memories stirring in the back of his mind, before returning his gaze to the lake. It was here at the edge of the foothills that the rebel camp sprawled.

Aptly named Liberá (derived from the word liberty), it was more akin to a city than a refugee camp. Thousands of cabins and tents were surrounded by a wall of stone with watchtowers at regular intervals. The encampment existed in a state of constant growth. Remnants of defenses from its younger stages peeked out between newer buildings, attesting also to the improvement in the builders' skill. The population of the refugee city numbered just over ten thousand, with more than half rebel soldiers.

Tench's unforgiving cruelty and inclination towards violence left people afraid for their welfare as they simply lived their lives. When rumors of Servailles's uprising started, many Corynthians left their homes in search of it. Word of the rebel base spread secretly throughout the land, somehow never reaching the wrong ears, even as it filtered through the loyalist armies marching towards the borders.

As a result, the rebellion grew quickly. Soldiers in the Corynthian army, unwilling to participate in a display of intimidation towards neutral countries, deserted and sneaked down to Liberá. Able-bodied men and even women with fire in their hearts left their families, trading tools and utensils for swords and shields. The latter were forbidden to join the Corynthian army; however, Servailles welcomed them gladly into his ranks. Many refugees gathered up their loved ones and brought them with, feeling they would be safer from Tench's prowling police. Still others used Liberá merely as an escape from the fear ripening in the cities. Regardless, whether willing to fight or not, all were welcome.

Andre straightened as he approached the gates of the city. A breeze blew across the plain, ruffling his long hair and refreshing him. He breathed in deeply, savoring the warm sun on his face and the smell of early spring air.

Spring was a wet time in Corynthia. Because of its position between two mountain ranges and the sea, rainfall was frequent. Clear, sunny days like this one were rare.

"H'o Andre!" a guard hailed him from the wall. "Welcome back!"

Andre reined in his horse and returned the greeting. "I have an urgent message for Winston. Is he here?" Servailles preferred to be personally involved with the rebellion's affairs. Hence, he was often away from Liberá on reconnaissance missions and the like.

"He's inside." The watchman waved below him to the people manning the gate. "How goes the blockade?"

"Well enough. It's nearly time we make our move. The men in the outpost are at their breaking point."

The guard grinned as the gate slowly groaned open. "Excellent. Good luck."

Liberá was bubbling with activity. People trotted to and fro with loads of supplies in their arms. The ring of hammer on metal from blacksmith forges permeated the air, along with shouts from soldiers drilling in fields. Livestock grazed in picketed yards nearby. Children darted through the camp, laughing and chasing each other, while their mothers called after them in reproachful voices as they hung laundry to dry. Cooking fires blazed throughout the camp, and the smell of roasting food teased Andre's nostrils, making his stomach growl regretfully.

He stopped in front a large stone building near the center of the camp, smoke rising from a red-brick chimney. Sliding from his horse, he handed the reins to a guard waiting outside and entered.

The interior was simply furnished. On one side of the room, a stone fireplace full of wavering flames threw dancing shadows on the walls. Two large tables filled the center of the room, chairs pushed under them. Woven quilts and wolf hides covered the walls while hanging lanterns glowed cozily from the rafters, swaying gently in the draft let in by Andre's entrance. There were no windows, and the room smelled of smoke.

A group of people were gathered around the tables. Andre approached them, the wooden floorboards groaning under his feet. "Winston," he cut through the voices.

They looked up at him with flickers of recognition. Smiles broke onto their faces as they saw who interrupted. Some murmured greetings to him, which he acknowledged with a nod.

He presented the papers from the satchel to one of the men, the letter on top. "I apologize for the interruption, but this can't wait."

The man took the stack from him, shuffling through them with a frown.

Winston Servailles was a tall, handsome man with messy dark hair that fell lazily into his eyes. His pale, angular face was clean-shaven and clear. A green tunic with a rose stitched on the breast hugged his lean frame. He scanned the reports with intelligent brown eyes and quirked an elegant eyebrow at Andre. He looked out of place in the primitive meeting room surrounded by rough men—a nobleman among soldiers.

"A little rudimentary for a full return journey."

"The letter." Andre pointed at the envelope. "Read the letter."

Setting aside the reports, Winston took out the note. His smile faded as he read it, and Andre saw his eyes dart over the words a second time. He flipped it over to check the back, then looked back up at Andre. "Is this true? Did they find him?"

"They claim to have."

Winston cursed quietly. "This may force our hand." He folded the letter up again, laying it on the table. A map was spread over its surface, and he bent over it to trace one of the roads with his finger.

"Find who? The Soothsayer?"

Andre wasn't surprised that the officer guessed correctly. Tales of a Soothsayer had spread throughout the land over the past few months, like a case of the flu. Rumors of a troubled young man visited by terrible visions—visions of fire. Rebel spies returned with reports of loyalist soldiers moving through the northern towns, asking questions and searching.

Andre wasn't convinced the rumors were true; likewise, many of the others thought it was a hoax—the peoples' desperate hope of a solution to Tench's tyranny. However, Winston was very keen on obtaining any information he could, almost to the point of an obsession. *What's important to Berling is important to me*, was his explanation.

Still examining the map, Winston grunted confirmation. "They're holding him in Clamiera. He's scheduled to move to Markalv the day after tomorrow. Seruvia from there."

In the ensuing pause, Andre saw some of the officers exchange looks. He knew what was on their minds. Most of them thought Winston was wasting his time chasing the rumors. Still, like Andre, they weren't sure what else to do besides humor him. His interest was odd, though inconsequential at this point.

"We have time, then," one offered, pointing at a location on the map. "It's at least a four-day journey to Markalv. We can send a messenger to Andre's company and have them set up an ambush to capture him before he arrives."

Another scoffed. "What, waste men and compromise a valuable location for a fairy-tale character? For all we know, it's a ruse to bring us out of the woodwork. We could have been meant to find the letter."

Andre shook his head. Even though he wasn't convinced that there really was a Soothsayer, they were certainly not meant to find the letter. "We fought through nearly a hundred loyalists and discovered it only by luck. If this is a plot, then Tench has improved his tactics considerably. I think he believes this to be true. And if it's important to him..." He trailed off with a glance at Winston.

He did agree, though: Wasting resources on someone seemingly right out of a children's book was not a good idea, especially if that meant abandoning the outpost he worked so hard to wear down. Still, he wanted to see what Winston thought.

The rest of the officers began to speak, each of their opinions lost in the others' as they tried to make themselves heard.

Winston finally took his eyes off the map. His quiet voice cut effortlessly through the tumult. "No, I agree with Pitt."

Everyone stopped at once.

The officer who scoffed, a bald man with fiery eyes by the name of Delvon Pitt, stared at him in surprise. The tattoo of a fist adorned the left side of his head above his ear, the mark of the Stone Legion from the Border Conflict, and the numerals XIV were inked on the back of his head. More tattoos covered his neck and swirled down his arms. Standing well over six feet with muscles to match, he was a terrifying man, made for battle. From the look on his face, it seemed he had expected one here.

Smiling, Winston continued, "Although not entirely for the same reasons. We've waited far too long to begin our campaign, and the outpost is the last piece to fall into place. If we abandon it now, relief could arrive in our absence, and we will have to begin again. Besides, the Soothsayer will be heavily guarded, and I would like to avoid unnecessary bloodshed. We shall find another way to take him."

"*You'll* have to," Pitt muttered.

"Andre!" Winston burst out suddenly, his smile broadening as he gave his full attention to his friend. "How are you? Everything running smoothly? You're not having too much fun?"

Andre couldn't keep a grimace from showing on his face. "They've increased the pressure. We fought off a small army with this last supply run. No casualties, though. Morale is fine." He would mention Wes and Tahlia's heroics later.

"Good. We should strike soon if Berling is sending more soldiers. Means he's realizing the threat."

"And what *is* your plan for the Soothsayer?" Pitt demanded. Andre could still detect a hint of derision in his tone.

"Leave that to me. For now, we proceed with the agenda—capture the outpost, then Cappus. I don't want to throw away everything we've accomplished thus far merely because they found the Soothsayer first."

Andre swayed and grabbed the table for support as a wave of fatigue hit him. He felt Winston's hand on his shoulder.

"Go rest. We can talk later."

With a grateful nod, Andre said goodbye. Leaving the building, he made his way towards the nearest barracks. Once inside, he staggered to a cot and collapsed into it, not bothering to undress first. He was asleep as soon as his eyes closed.

When he awoke, the sun was still in the sky. Its light crept under the closed door, leaving a soft yellow glow just inside the threshold. A mirror and shaving necessities sat on top of a bundle of clean clothes at the foot of his bed.

He sat up stiffly, regretting his decision to sleep in his tunic and chain-mail. He painfully pulled the stiff leather and clinking links over his head and tossed them aside, groaning in relief as he freed his torso. Using the bowl of water, he splashed his face, then picked up the mirror.

Gray eyes stared back atop of dark circles from lack of sleep. His beard had thickened considerably over the past few days, and he scratched it ruefully. He liked his facial hair, but it tended to become a nuisance during wartime.

After he shaved, dressed, and washed, Andre stepped outside into the bright sunlight. The sun sat just above the tips of the Argos Mountains, confirming his suspicion that he slept until the next day. The sky was bright blue, and the few clouds in it floated high and thin over the mountain range like downy feathers.

The smell of cooking food greeted him. His stomach grumbled in response. Stretching, he set out in the direction of the cooking fires.

He found some of the men from the previous day's meeting cooking breakfast. Winston Servailles sat closest to the fire, moving strips of sizzling bacon on a pan elevated over the flames. He gave Andre a wink as he sat down. Delvon Pitt was speaking with another officer named William Draytus, who Andre knew well.

William was Andre's commanding officer during the Border Conflict: A bloody and inhumane war from when Corynthia was still a part of Kaval. A well-built, somber-looking man, he wasn't much older than Andre, though his brown hair was streaked with gray, handsome, oak-tree face worn with lines—for good reason. The Border Conflict took years off of all of their lives. He smiled quietly at Andre before returning his attention to Pitt, who was describing some military tactic while drawing diagrams in the dirt.

William was the reason Andre met Winston Servailles. William, already friends with Winston, deserted the front lines of the war to join the latter in his campaign to secede Corynthia. Andre was ordered to pursue and arrest him for treason against Kaval. Being a young sergeant eager for glory, he proceeded without question. However, when he caught up to them, Winston opened his eyes to a future beyond war. To a future of life lived to fullness.

When the Border Conflict finally ended, Winston requested that Andre join him in solidifying Corynthia's new identity. They quickly became close friends, their drive and ambition a solid foundation for connection. When Winston was sentenced to exile, Andre and William were among the first to leave with him.

Keppen Bailer, the man on watch when Andre arrived at Liberá, reclined against a log, his hands clasped behind his head and eyes closed as he basked in the sunshine.

Sitting next to Keppen, Andre grabbed a loaf of bread. He ripped it into pieces, shoving one into his mouth with a contented sigh. "I haven't eaten properly in three days."

Keppen opened an eye. "Save some for the rest of us. We haven't eaten since last night." He was a round-faced, kind-looking man with messy straw-yellow hair. His appearance was deceiving; Keppen was rock-steady and a deadly fighter.

"And we're famished!" announced Winston, setting down his wooden spatula and sitting back on his heels. He grinned at Andre as he watched him wolf down the bread. "How did you sleep?"

"Like a dead man. You?"

"A full thirty minutes." His tone was cheery.

Pitt snorted. "He never left the building. I found him in the morning, snoring on the maps."

Snatching a chunk of bread from Andre, Winston rolled it between his hands. "Tench won't overthrow himself." He popped it into his mouth.

Andre looked closely at Winston. There were dark circles under his eyes that, despite his sunny demeanor, looked uneasy. "What were you doing?"

"Planning."

William interjected, "He won't tell us what about."

Winston returned to his pan. "Bacon's nearly finished." Andre knew he wasn't going to discuss the subject anymore. At least for now.

"Smells wonderful." Andre's stomach let out a pitiful whine, and the men burst out laughing.

The five of them sat around the fire eating their breakfast and exchanging reports.

On developments regarding the main rebellion force at Liberá, Tench's armies had finished deploying to the borders, except for occasional groups transporting supplies and orders, which meant the highways were now open for the rebels to use without much risk. Scouts returned from Cappus with slightly worrisome news. There was a standing army of around five thousand troops stationed in the city. However, the army was on guard for an attack from Kaval, not from inside Corynthia itself, especially since Tench didn't consider the rebellion a threat.

After being caught up, Andre summarized his own adventures from the last ambush. The others laughed appreciatively when he described how they came upon the burning wagon with its guards slain, and how Wes and Tahlia appeared to coolly explain what they did.

William shook his head. "Those two never cease to amaze me."

"I, for one, do not believe they didn't hear you call for a retreat," Keppen commented. "I've heard you shout; I'm sure you were heard in Markalv."

Andre laughed with the others.

Keppen stood up. "Well, gentlemen. Thank you for the warm meal and excellent story. I have a large, grassy area of nothingness to watch for a few hours. Good day." Bowing with a flourish, he departed.

Pitt and William followed, each leaving to tend to their duties. With the rebel army on the brink of departure, there was much to do.

As Andre also stood, Winston motioned for him to sit back down. "I was thinking last night," he began quietly, brushing his hair out of his eyes.

Here it comes. Apprehension made Andre's neck prickle.

He had been waiting all morning for Winston to inform him of his daring yet dangerous plan to capture the alleged Soothsayer. He felt it forming from the moment he presented the letter and knew it was forthcoming when Pitt announced he had found him asleep in the command building.

Winston was well known for his brilliant, though often high-risk plans that relied more on luck than much else. The idea to secede Corynthia from Kaval, thus bringing an end to the Border Conflict, was his to begin with—an idea written off by many due to concern for retaliation from the emperor, Lord Artreus. As it turned out, there had been no reason to fear.

"We need the Soothsayer badly. Even with how quickly our force grows, it's not enough. Tench's armies outnumber us vastly, and our path from Cappus to Seruvia passes through the rest of Corynthia. Because Tench controls the land, most people are too afraid to stand up to him. Once the Soothsayer arrives at the capital, Tench will declare his sponsorship; at which point, there will be naught we can do to win this fight. You know how superstitious people are. We'll lose what little support we have, which is a development we *cannot* afford."

Andre chewed on the inside of his cheek, trying to think of what to say. He didn't believe the credibility of the Soothsayer rumors. It was a legend—a fairy tale to be told around a fire for the entertainment of children—but Winston latched onto the rumors from the first time he heard them. And when Winston found an obsession, Andre found it best to just roll along with him.

He must have done a poor job of hiding his skepticism, because Winston let out an exasperated sigh.

"I know everyone thinks I've gone mad chasing after dragons, but consider it! In every tale with a Soothsayer, their insight is vital to the conflict. If there is the faintest possibility these rumors are at all true, then Tench can manipulate the war while we stay blind. If we don't know what we're walking into, he will drag the rebellion down to its knees before we can even begin. We *need* the Soothsayer," Winston repeated forcefully when Andre stayed silent.

"Then we can take him before he reaches Seruvia. We have the men and the resources. I can arrange for—"

"And therein lies the problem," Winston interrupted. "Like Pitt pointed out yesterday, we cannot move our soldiers from the outpost in an effort to retrieve him. That will compromise the entirety of our progress thus far. Besides, no offense to you or your Crimson Hounds, the Soothsayer will be heavily guarded. Rose Soldiers, cavalry—not something you and a score of troops can simply ambush and slaughter."

Andre frowned. He did take a little offense to that. The Crimson Hounds toppled staggering odds time and time again during the Border Conflict without batting an eye. Then again, Winston never saw them in action, so he forgave the insult.

"We certainly won't have time to gather a large enough strike force," Winston went on, "Regardless, even if we took him by violence, there still lies the puzzle of securing his allegiance. He must be convinced our cause is the correct one to endorse. It doesn't make much sense to have him without his support; don't you think?" He continued before Andre could answer, smacking his fist into his palm. "No, there is a correct way to proceed—one Tench will never expect." His eyes glittering with excitement, a smile sliced across his face.

An uneasy feeling settled into the pit of Andre's stomach. "Winston...?" he cautioned, pleading for his friend to respond reasonably.

"I must speak with him face to face. Since he is already in Tench's clutches, there's only one way I can do that."

"No." Andre knew exactly what Winston was leading into.

The smile on Winston's face took on a slightly crazed hue. "It's the perfect plan! No, listen!" he pleaded when Andre opened his mouth to argue. "If I can secure an audience with the Soothsayer—as a prisoner under the threat of death—and say my piece, can you see how strong of a gesture that is? Think about it!"

He was up on his feet now, face glowing with emotion. "The leader of the rebellion, desperate enough to face execution to speak with him! It will throw the plight of the people and our subsequent desperation to free them into sharp relief. Think how powerful that is! The lengths I'm resorting to for the salvation of Corynthia!"

Andre glanced around to see if anyone was in earshot. The surrounding fires were cold and empty; people were off fulfilling their duties. A lone man passed by, thankfully too absorbed in a muttered conversation with himself to pay them any attention.

He looked back at Winston, who was staring at him expectantly.

"Think about it!"

Andre shook his head in disbelief, hardly able to comprehend the debate he was having. He knew to expect the extreme from Winston, but this eclipsed all. "There are countless ways this madness can go wrong! For instance, what if they execute you on the spot?"

"They won't. Tench will never pass up an opportunity to display his power. Furthermore, he hates me. He'll draw it out, organize it into a spectacle."

"Alright. Say everything runs according to your..." he restrained the word *insane* with some difficulty, "plan, and you, somehow, by some miracle, speak with this Soothsayer—who may not even be real. Let's say you even manage to convince him to join the rebellion. You're still imprisoned in the most secure city in Corynthia, and have an appointment for a *very* public execution. What is your plan to escape?"

Winston grinned even broader. "You are! While I speak with the Soothsayer, you shall infiltrate the city with a squad of men, and break me free once I'm brought out before the public—saving the day!"

Andre immediately thought of a multitude of issues with Winston's solution, the forementioned Rose Soldiers among them. Nevertheless, he gritted his teeth and addressed his main concern. "What if I can't save you?"

"Then I die a martyr, and incite rebellion among the citizens from my sacrifice!"

"You're mad! If Tench executes you publicly, the rebellion is finished. The people will lose the little hope they held. You said it yourself—they're already gripped with too much fear. Besides, we need you to fight Tench. You know him better than anyone else, and you're the best military strategist we have."

"Then the fate of the rebellion will rest on your shoulders!" Winston laughed carelessly, though he stopped at the look on Andre's face. "I'm sorry. I trust you Andre. You won't fail."

Andre felt as if he were watching the conversation from outside his body. It didn't seem real. "I refuse to go through with this! There's far too much at stake here! This plan is suicide for you *and* the cause! I will not let you walk willingly to your death, no matter how much you justify it. Right now, our focus should be on Cappus, not *chasing dragons*."

"What about the Soothsayer and his involvement in the war? He shall very quickly become the face of this conflict. Once Tench has his hands on him—the knowledge he carries—Andre, we need him. He is *crucial*."

"Winston, you *need* to forget about the Soothsayer," responded Andre, almost scathingly. "There are far more important matters that must be addressed. As we've already decided, we can't afford to waste resources on the Soothsayer. That includes you. We're fighting a real war here, not a fairy-tale one!"

Winston glared at him.

A couple of minutes passed, during which neither man moved nor spoke. The fire crackled, orange coals sparking and popping callously. Finally, Winston put his head in his hands.

Andre broke the silence. "Winston?"

No response.

He sighed. "You don't need to carry the entire cause on your back. I know you feel responsible, but it's going to take all of us together to achieve victory. You understand that, don't you?"

Winston sat up and rubbed his eyes. "I'm sorry. I'm tired, and I'm not thinking straight." He stood and stretched. "I'm going to get some sleep, then we'll make a plan for the outpost when I'm coherent. Agreed?"

"Agreed."

Brow creased, Andre watched him depart. He understood Winston well enough to know he wasn't about to just forget this conversation. His mind never stopped scheming, not when there was a problem that needed solving.

I just hope he doesn't do anything foolish.

In hindsight, Andre should have expected nothing less.

A SHADOW AND A SKIRMISH

The officers bent over a map of the outpost while Andre outlined terrain and defenses. Winston plied him with questions and offered suggestions as the others looked on silently, not wanting to interrupt the young rebel leader. They all knew Winston had a brilliant mind—he was widely regarded as a political and military genius—and nobody wanted to interrupt his processing. Even Pitt, ever quick to insert his own opinion, stayed quiet.

Finally, Winston rapped his knuckles on the table. "What do you think?"

Andre shrugged. "We've been through harder battles. I would like more soldiers, though. I'll take the Hounds any day for hide and seek, but I would prefer more than twenty soldiers for a full assault."

"Take your pick, then. Start the assault at your discretion. Just don't wait too long."

The meeting turned to the capture of Cappus. While Andre traveled to the outpost, the rebellion's army would march to besiege the city, though a few hundred troops would stay behind in Liberá to protect those who lived there. Once the outpost was captured, Andre would leave his soldiers under Mattias Berg's command and join the rest of the army at Cappus. He would rather stay with the Crimson Hounds, but he knew Winston wanted him near as they proceeded with their conquest.

After the meeting, Andre selected his additional forces from William's company. Despite the inexperience shared by much of the rebel army, he was confident they would be well-trained and resourceful. Assembling a squad of thirty soldiers, he briefed them on their assignment, then instructed them to prepare for departure as soon as possible.

Liberá was a tornado of movement and noise as thousands of soldiers prepared to leave. Men and women rushed back and forth carrying armor, weapons, and packs filled with food and supplies. Officers shouted orders that were lost in the chaos. Children became unintentional hazards as they scrambled excitedly around the camp, tripping soldiers, and knocking things over in their haste to help. Horses and livestock, excited by the commotion, added bleats, brays, and groans to the already deafening noise.

It was evening when Andre's squad assembled in front of him for further orders. He glanced at the sun hovering low and bloody on the horizon. It was too late to begin their journey now.

Turning to the expectant soldiers, he grinned apologetically. "Relax. Go have some dinner and a good night's rest. We'll leave at first light."

They dispersed, groaning at the change of plan.

Winston walked up behind Andre, chuckling. "Keeping them on their toes?"

"Someone has to. Let's find something to eat. I'm famished."

"It's as though you've just discovered food."

They went off, Andre protesting exuberantly. Though he would never admit to his friend's face, he enjoyed being back in Winston's company immensely.

The next morning dawned cold and wet. Dew clung to the grass like a sodden blanket, and the sky to the east was tinged orange, signaling the approach of the sun. Birds twittered sleepily from their roosts, while the sound of waves lapping gently against the shore added a calm melody to the stillness of the early morning.

Andre walked through the camp, waking his soldiers and enjoying the peace. Once they began their march, this would probably be the last time he would have an opportunity for such serenity in a long while. After instructing the soldiers to gather at the main gate, he waited there, watching the sunrise as they arrived, yawning and rubbing their eyes.

Once everyone was accounted for, they set off in formation. Most of the group walked; the rebellion needed as many horses as possible for the heavy lifting on the way to Cappus. Their path to the outpost skirted the edge of the foothills, and Andre estimated a five day journey to their destination.

The first three days passed without incident. The sky was clear; the sun shone during the day, while stars winked secrets at night. As dusk fell on the third day, they arrived at a small rebel checkpoint. Those stationed there were glad of the company, and the evening was spent singing and gambling.

On day four, near noon, one of the rear guards hailed Andre from her position.

"Lieutenant Cordon! Sir!"

Andre looked back to see the woman waving at him atop her horse from the rear of the column. The eight horses they did have were all assigned to the guards on duty.

He let her to catch up and plod beside him. "What is it..." He paused, looking up at the woman for her name. With so many people from every part of Corynthia in the rebellion, he wasn't familiar with everyone just yet.

"Leana Palmer, sir." Her short blond hair poked out rebelliously from her leather cap. Rosy cheeks matched lips currently pursed as she shot a glance behind her. She leaned down, azure eyes holding a hint of concern, and wrinkled her delicate nose. She was too fair to be so comfortable in a warrior's garb. "I think we're being tailed."

Andre involuntarily glanced at the trees. Of course, nothing was there. "What do you mean?"

"It began after we left the camp. I kept glimpsing movement in the trees out of the corner of my eye. At first, I just ignored it, figuring it was due to drowsiness or shadows, but there's definitely something there. Ben thought he saw something too." She nodded at the other rear guard. "I don't think it's an animal. It's very quick."

"Thank you for informing me, Palmer. Tell me if anything else happens. Alert the others on rotation."

"Yes, sir." Swinging her horse around, she trotted back to the rear, slight form rocking smoothly on her steed.

Andre took another sweeping glance at the trees, seeing nothing except underbrush. He gave his head a shake, trying to dispel his concern as he would a bothersome fly. If they were being followed, the lookouts would catch it. That was their job after all.

Despite that, he kept catching himself checking his surroundings for a flash of movement or a shadow flitting through the trees. The few times he thought he spotted something, it turned out to be a falling leaf or a fern waving in the wind. The more he dwelt on the thought, the more nervous he found himself growing; hence, he forced himself to put it out of his mind. He couldn't afford to be paranoid.

As the evening sky turned into an inferno painting the forest in vibrant color, they set up camp in a large clearing. In the gathering darkness, fires sprang up, throwing the flickering shadows of the rebels onto the ring of trees surrounding them.

Andre sat with others around a fire, eating an apple. While they chattered and laughed, he was silent, his mind elsewhere.

What if there *was* someone watching them from the darkness? What if they arrived to find an entire loyalist army waiting for them? He wasn't confident these soldiers could respond. Many of those present were inexperienced in combat outside of training drills, and nobody was expecting such a disastrous turn of events. After all, they were prepared for a fight against men weak and frightened from weeks of being blockaded.

Besides, if the loyalists somehow managed to break through the blockade and reinforce the outpost, Mattias would have sent a messenger to warn them.

Unless they've all been killed.

Finishing his apple, he tossed the core into the flames and stood up to find Leana Palmer.

The lookout sat near the fringe of the clearing by herself, staring into the darkness. Andre tapped her on the shoulder. "Still on watch?"

She nodded. Andre followed her gaze into the trees. "Did you see anything else?"

She was silent for a moment, a frown shadowing her pretty face. Finally, she spoke, "It's not an animal; that much is certain. It's too fast, too quiet. I don't believe it's a loyalist soldier either," she added as though hearing Andre's unspoken worry. "They sure as hell wouldn't be gliding through the woods like a dream. I lost track of it a couple of hours back. I think it realized I had noticed."

Andre cupped his chin in his hand. "Should we be worried?"

"I'm not sure, sir. We should stay alert, but I don't believe we need to frighten any of the greennoses."

He smiled at her use of the endearing term for fresh recruits; Leana was hardly older than many of her peers. "Keep an eye out for me. Good luck with the rest of your watch."

"Aye, sir. Thank you, sir."

Returning to his place by the fire, Andre unrolled his bedroll. It was a cool night, and the glowing embers provided a pleasant aura of warmth. He wriggled into the blankets and stared at the stars twinkling in the sky above.

Leana was right. Loyalist soldiers were not trained for sneaking through forests. They would bumble around like oxen, scaring birds out of trees and making their presence well-known. With that reassuring thought in mind, he drifted off to sleep.

Andre stirred before anyone else the next morning. He had not slept well. Phantoms flitted through his dreams, slitting throats in the darkness and waking him numerous times in a cold sweat. The dreams faded reluctantly during the company's quick breakfast before the final leg of their journey; Andre estimated they would join up with Mattias that evening.

Birds sang arpeggios as the perfect weather continued. Sunlight painted the road in mottled patterns like splashes of ichor. Leaves flashed their pale underbellies as a breeze danced through Malaki Forest. The sounds, smells, and sights of spring enticed Andre's senses, lulling him into a near-stupor. Even though their potential stalker still lurked in the recesses of his mind, he felt happy and content.

All of a sudden, the calm was shattered by a shout from one of the lookouts.

A rider had burst through the trees further down the road, clad in a blue tunic Andre immediately recognized as a Corynthian uniform. The rider skidded to a halt, his horse rearing at the sudden yank on its bit. A horrified look was plastered on his face at the sight of the rebels, and he wheeled his steed around, galloping into the woods instead of back down the path.

"After him!" The rebel riders spurred into action, lurching after the scout.

Andre grabbed the reins from the man next to him before he could pursue. The rebel understood immediately and slid off.

Heaving himself onto the horse, Andre called to the rest on foot, "Stay the path! We'll catch up with you! Hyah!" He snapped the reins, bolting after the others.

Branches whipped and clawed at him as he tore through the forest, scratching his face and hands. He could see the blue tunic of his quarry flashing between the trees ahead of him. The shouts of his own soldiers floated back to him, mingling with his heavy breathing.

Suddenly, he charged out from the forest into a blast of blinding sunlight.

A horn rang out ahead of Andre, a shout answering from somewhere to his right. Squinting through the sunspots imprinted on his vision, he tried to locate the noise. As his eyes adjusted, he saw seven more blue-clad horsemen bearing down on him with intent all too clear on their faces. Yanking on the reins, he swung his horse around to face the new threat, drawing his sword and pulling his buckler from the saddle.

Andre's horse fought its bit as he shouted after his own soldiers. They were oblivious to the ambush, still chasing the first rider.

"Rally! *Rally!* To me!"

They obediently rode back to him, drawing together as the loyalists surrounded them. Another four horsemen appeared, bringing the enemy's total to twelve. They formed a ring around the rebels and slowed to a standstill, facing them.

"Steady," Andre cautioned when one of the rebels moved his horse in expectation. "On my command, we charge and break the ring." He turned his head to look at them. Many were white as a sheet with anticipation.

The circle of loyalists sat silent and unmoving, as though the sky itself opposed them. Their weapons glinted in the sunlight. Most of them held swords and shields, though a couple leveled spears at the rebels. It seemed like they were waiting for Andre to make the first move.

Then I'll oblige.

"Hyah!" Andre dug his heels into his horse's sides.

His steed leaped into motion, charging the nearest spear-wielding loyalist as the rest of the rebels split off to attack different points of the ring. He swung his sword, knocking the spearhead aside before redirecting his blade at the soldier's neck. The man jerked his horse to avoid him, and the ring broke.

The sound of battle behind him sounded distant and muted as he pursued his target. The loyalist turned in a wide arc to rejoin the fray, but Andre adjusted his angle of approach to cut him off. The man, seeing him coming, threw aside his spear and drew his sword in haste to defend himself. It was too late. Andre's blade crashed down on his shoulder with a powerful blow, shearing through his spaulder and toppling him from his horse.

His target dispatched, Andre wheeled around to assess the battle.

He had chosen his men well, for the rebels made quick work of the enemy. Nine bodies lay unmoving in the grass, though three of them were Andre's own, to his dismay. Two riderless horses cantered around a pair of fallen soldiers, snapping at anyone who came close. The rest had vanished, presumably frightened off by the fighting. There were still five loyalist soldiers, three of them on foot, defending themselves.

As he watched, a horseman broke away from the fight, trying to escape into the trees.

"Don't let him get away!" Andre reached for his bow.

Before he even touched it, an arrow whistled through the air, burying into the man's back. He slumped over in the saddle, and the horse disappeared into the forest.

Leana sat astride her steed, bow at the ready with another arrow already on the string.

"Good shot," Andre called.

"Thank you, sir." She gestured, businesslike, to the remaining loyalists who had thrown down their weapons. "Shall we?"

Together, they rode over to the surrender.

"Remove your armor, and leave it with your weapons," Andre commanded as he slid from his saddle. "Then, you can round up the horses, and don't even consider running. There will be consequences if you try."

The prisoners looked forlornly around at the clearing without moving.

Glancing over his shoulder, Andre saw that the loyalist's horses had all vanished. They must have all galloped into the forest. He sighed. "Or you'll walk."

He ordered his soldiers to gather up the loyalists' gear and secure the prisoners while he walked around the clearing to check the bodies. Apart from the six he already counted, Andre discovered a seventh blue-clad body in a swath of tall grass near the clearing's edge. Three of his own were killed during the fight. Two he didn't know; the last he recognized, yet couldn't recall his name. He felt a pang for the missed opportunity to connect with them. He couldn't remember if he ever spoke directly with them. The realization sent him into a foul mood.

The captives were being bound by the wrists, but Andre stepped in before they could finish.

"They'll stay with me. And you, Palmer. We're burying the bodies. Or"—he jerked his thumb at the prisoners—"they are. The rest of you catch up with the others. If they're not with Sergeant Berg yet, inform them not to wait for us."

After the rebels departed into the forest, carrying the extra gear with them, Andre untied the loyalists' wrists and pointed out the bodies. "You made this carnage; now start digging."

"We have nothing to dig with," protested one of the captives.

"Then use your bloody hands! MOVE!"

The men jolted as though burned and began to dig.

Leana leaned over to Andre. "What about the horses? They'll return to familiar territory; won't that alert the outpost of our coming?"

Watching the prisoners scoop dirt and throw it aside, Andre tapped the crimson dog head on his collar. "You're forgetting about the Hounds. In any case, that first scout looked startled when he saw us, which means he wasn't expecting rebel activity in the area. They were probably a survey team gathering a report to bring back to Cappus."

"But the ambush. Do you think whoever is following us brought them here?"

"I don't know. You said it yourself: You don't think our shadow is loyalist. They would have come in force if they had been tipped information." Andre scratched his chin. "More likely it was just foolish luck they happened to pass through at the same time as us."

Leana subsided, looking satisfied with his answer.

Andre, however, considered her point. A survey team riding this close to the outpost without Mattias knowing about it was a stretch. It seemed a likely connection that a spy could have tipped them off. *Then why not come with more men or lay a better trap?*

The ambush was weak and certainly did not account for a large force, which would correlate with his theory of a scouting team. He recalled the reports of the armies now deployed on the borders and wrinkled his nose. Tench was aware of their efforts to starve out the outpost—the last supply run testified to that. Maybe this was just a half-hearted attempt to soften them up without access to his expansive strength.

The day dragged on. Andre and Leana grew tired of watching the captives struggle under the warm sun and pitched in, working alongside their enemies. It may have been Andre's imagination, but he sensed a change in the loyalists' attitudes as they labored together. It seemed almost as though their fear melded into an apprehensive sort of respect, especially towards Leana—a woman doing man's work.

When the graves were dug, the bodies were lowered carefully into the holes, and the mounds of dirt piled back on top. Andre marked the earth with little cairns from stones he found throughout the clearing. Then, after sharing some water, Andre tied the prisoners' hands again. Finally, he and Leana mounted their horses, and they set off; the captives in front, riders behind.

Picking through the forest, they soon arrived at the road. It wasn't much longer until the terrain began to grow rougher. The maples and alders of the lowlands grew sparser, trading places with tall, thin hemlocks that stood like roadside sentinels. Boulders glowered stubbornly on chossy slopes that marched away to higher elevations.

Calling for a halt, Andre let out a piercing whistle that hung in the air for a moment before fading away into the ambiance. They stood in the road waiting for a response. There was none except for the robins singing happily in the forest.

Andre frowned. He felt Leana shift next to him and glanced over.

She looked back nervously. "Do you think—"

Waving her off, Andre whistled again. He listened, head tilted to one side, ears straining to penetrate the cheery sound of birdsong. Just as he was coming to the conclusion that everything had gone horribly wrong and the Crimson Hounds were captured or dead, an answering whistle rang out in the distance.

"Thank the All-Mother. Carry on."

Soon, they were joined by a familiar face. Wes trotted down the road wearing his incorrigible grin.

"Lieutenant! Your greennoses told us what happened! You're later than we thought."

"There were bodies to bury." Andre nodded at the captives, who looked convincingly remorseful.

Wes's smile faded. "They mentioned that." He glared at the loyalists. "How many did we lose?"

"Three."

"Such a waste." Wes spat on the ground at the feet of the prisoners. He turned to greet Leana while they shuffled uncomfortably.

They set off again. Wes, walking beside Andre, filled him in on the developments in his absence.

"We're no longer hiding in the hills. There hasn't been another supply run since the last, and the men inside the outpost are so terrified of sticking even a toe from the safety of their walls, we can do just about anything we want. We're careful not to venture too close, though. They still have plenty of ammunition."

"Then the squad we encountered wasn't from the outpost?" *What the hell were they doing down south?*

"No, sir. Everything is locked down tighter than Donroe's drawers. The way I see it, we merely have to knock on the door and politely ask them to remove themselves. After that, we should be able to move in."

Andre grinned wolfishly. "Then let's oblige."

5

UP IN SMOKE

A NDRE SCRUTINIZED THE FORT from a large maple tree, noting the positions of the guards.

It was a simple structure. A wall made of stone and mortar surrounded a cluster of log cabins inside. Two watch towers rose on opposite corners. Mattias estimated that the fort previously housed about sixty men. Due to the rebels' blockade, their numbers had thinned some. However, the remaining men were cornered and scared, much like a wounded animal. Andre knew what happened in such instances: They could be more dangerous, as weak and frightened as they were. If pushed, they might fight viciously and recklessly.

They decided to forgo an assault on the gate; for it would place them in an extremely vulnerable position as they tried to force entry. Instead, the rebels fashioned ladders from saplings they cut down in the woods. Using the ladders, they would climb directly over the wall and bring the fight right to the defenders. They split into two groups. Andre's squad would advance first; then, when they gained the attention of the soldiers, Mattias's group would rush out from behind. A classic pincer movement: Simple, yet effective.

They were waiting until the middle of the day when the sun was at its highest and the glare its warmest. The guards, tired from standing in the bright heat for hours, would be looking forward to the changing of the watch where they could relax in the shade. Right before the guards were replaced, the rebels would rush out from the trees carrying the ladders, while archers supplied covering fire from behind.

The land around the outpost was cleared of cover for a good hundred meters. Andre hoped the element of surprise, along with a healthy volley of arrows, would provide enough confusion to close in and scale the walls.

Once they were over, it was a matter of who fought the hardest. He had full faith in his fresh, well-rested soldiers.

Climbing back down, he looked around at them. They were quiet; most of them were pale. Some even looked like they were going to be sick. He reminded himself that few of these soldiers had real experience in combat. Some of them could barely be considered more than children. The skirmish had posed no issue because they weren't given time to think. However, this was an entirely different beast. Assaulting a reinforced position took preparation and planning, which meant time to consider all of the possible ways things could go wrong—Andre knew from experience. Nerves were to be expected. Fear was unavoidable.

"It's almost time. Are you ready?"

There were a few nods and murmurs of assent. A couple of them closed their eyes, lips moving in prayer, while others merely stared ahead silently, white as ghosts. Andre missed Wes and Tahlia with their careless, cheery attitudes. They were professionals at easing tension. Unfortunately, they were in Mattias's group.

Leana Palmer met his gaze and gave him a nod. Her cheeks were flushed, azure eyes intense. He knew she wouldn't falter.

Andre returned the gesture before speaking to the whole group, "Stay under the wall when you reach it. It'll be more difficult for their archers to target you. Once we're on top of the wall, keep together. Always have your back to someone else. They're weak and frightened, and it may not take much to subdue them, but they may also fight harder because they're cornered; so *be vigilant*. Look out for each other, and this will be over shortly. Then we're one step closer to taking back Corynthia."

It wasn't a great speech. Andre wasn't one for rousing perorations—Winston would have made them sprout wings and fly over the wall. Still, it would have to do. All in all, they did appear a little less pale when he looked around at them all.

He glanced from the shadows pooling under the trees to the outpost wall. Since no guards were visible, he guessed they were in the process of being relieved. *Time to move.*

"Let's go."

He picked up one end of a ladder, hoisting it onto his shoulder. The weight distribution changed as Leana lifted the other side. They were awkward enough that they had to be carried by two people, yet light enough that the bearers could still move quickly. Andre began to move, breaking into a jog once he and Leana established a rhythm. Together, the rebels emerged from the shelter of the trees, dashing towards the outpost.

They made it halfway across the clearing before they were spotted.

A cry hailed from the ramparts. Andre could see men scrambling on the wall, rushing to their positions and shouting down to those inside. He sped up, calling out to his men to do the same. By the time the defenders had some semblance of order, the rebels were at the wall, scaling the ladders.

A healthy flow of arrows from the rebel archers darted towards the battlements, keeping the enemy archers from firing back. One of them connected with its target, and a loyalist fell screaming from the wall.

First up the ladder, Andre was attacked at once. Arms wrapped around him, trying to wrestle him back over the edge. He smashed his forehead into the man's nose, staggering him. He threw him off, ignoring his wail as he tumbled from the ramparts, and turned to face another loyalist.

The inside of the outpost was swarming with enemies. There seemed to be more than Andre had accounted for, and he wondered briefly if he had erred in his preparations. He brushed away his misgivings as a sword flew towards his face. Blocking the blow with his buckler, he kicked the man in the chest, knocking him into another soldier.

Someone let out a cry right behind him, and he whirled around in time to see a loyalist collapse to the ground.

Leana stood over the man, sword glistening red, a slightly maniacal smile on her face. "Vigilance, lieutenant!" she sang.

Mattias's squad was on top of the wall now, throwing the loyalists into further confusion by their appearance. Soon, the ramparts were cleared, and the defenders were in full retreat. It wasn't long until the remaining loyalists surrendered or barricaded themselves into one of the barracks, providing a reprieve from battle.

Andre ordered one squad to surround the building and another to count the fallen. As the bodies were collected and prisoners rounded up, he went to find his second-in-command.

Mattias sat on a barrel, wiping his sword clean. He looked up as Andre approached, face shining with sweat. "That went surprisingly well, I'd say. There were more than I previously estimated."

"It's not over yet," replied Andre with a nod at the barracks. "Did you see how many made it inside?"

"Around fifteen, I think. I didn't have much time to count them as they fled." He chuckled and sheathed his sword. "There are no windows and only one door. Ideal for keeping people out temporarily, but a poor holding position, ultimately."

"Think they'll be willing to talk?"

"I guess you could find out."

Andre sauntered to the barracks and rapped thrice on the door. "You're trapped in there. Why don't you send someone out, and we can have a civil discussion about the terms of your surrender?"

There was no response.

He knocked again, then glanced around at Mattias, who shrugged. Stepping back from the door, he looked the building up and down with a frown. Either they were keeping quiet in the childish hope that he would grow bored and leave, or there was a secret hatch they were in the process of escaping through. If the latter was the case, he wasn't sure why they hadn't done so sooner.

Tahlia caught his attention. "We could always burn it down. That would have them out in a hurry."

A couple of the others laughed. Andre, however, gave her a stern look. "They're our prisoners, and we will treat them as such. We're not savages."

She flushed and dropped her gaze, looking contrite. "Sorry, sir."

Andre turned back to the door and banged on it forcefully. "If there is no response in the next thirty seconds, I will burn this building to the ground!" He winked at Tahlia, who grinned back.

There was a moment of silence, then Andre heard the sound of footsteps. A muffled voice spoke, "We will discuss terms."

"A wonderful idea! How about you come out of the barracks so we may speak face to face?"

"No."

It was worth a shot. "How many are in there?"

"There's thirty armed men ready to fight to the death!"

Andre chuckled amiably. "It must be a tight fit. We have about two hundred soldiers out here, also armed and *hungry* for blood." He looked around at the fifty-or-so rebels gathered. "So why don't you set aside your weapons and come out?" He reiterated his words to Tahlia, "You'll be protected and taken care of. We aren't savages."

"What makes you trustworthy?"

"We already have some of your men held captive." Andre looked around for the loyalists they had captured during the skirmish. They sat with the other prisoners under the watchful eyes of a couple guards. "They can vouch for me. I have not mistreated them in any way."

"Let me speak with them."

"Of course." He waved over for one of them to join him, jerking his head at the door as the man approached. "Speak some sense into him."

The man swallowed and nodded.

Andre stood by while the prisoner told those inside about the skirmish and his capture, describing how Andre and Leana joined in with burying the bodies, and assuring them that they were being treated well enough. When the prisoner finished, Andre sent him back and asked the man inside if he was willing to consider surrendering now.

"I will discuss it with others. Needless to say, *I* am willing to surrender myself rather than starve in here."

Andre nodded, forgetting the other man couldn't see him, and returned to Mattias.

"Finished already?" Mattias asked him as he sat down.

"I don't believe they'll need much convincing. You'll still fine with keeping them here? I can send an escort for them when I arrive at Cappus." They discussed what to do with any prisoners before they attacked; still, Andre wanted to make doubly sure Mattias was comfortable guarding them.

The sergeant scratched his ear. There was still a small smear of blood on it. "That's not an issue. The extra hands may be helpful, and who knows? Perhaps we might convince them to join our cause."

Andre snorted as he watched Donroe lug a crate out of a storeroom.

The rebels were exploring the fort and consolidating any supplies they found outside. Andre had given them orders to take inventory of the fort's stores once they secured it. He wanted to know how much food to request from Liberá. After all, those staying behind would need supplies of their own.

After a few minutes, Andre rose and stretched before walking back to the barracks, knocking on the door with his knuckles. A latch clicked, and he stepped back, placing his hand on the pommel of his sword as the door swung open.

A man with a thick black beard stepped out, hands in the air. "We surrender. Let's discuss terms."

"Weapons?"

The man jerked his head back through the doorway. "Inside." He walked into the ring of rebels followed by the rest of the loyalists.

Andre counted them: Sixteen. He motioned for a couple of his men to gather the gear from inside and search the building. He lingered for a moment, watching them enter the barracks, then walked over to the huddle of loyalist prisoners.

Clearing his throat, he waited until everyone's attention was on him before speaking, feeling rather like a rabbit being stared at by a pack of dogs from behind a fence.

"Good afternoon, gentlemen. I'm the officer in charge here." He waved his hand vaguely around him, indicating the fort's new ownership. "Since you are now prisoners of the rebellion, I am in charge of you as well."

He omitted his name on purpose. While many people were horrified by how Tench was abusing Corynthia, there were plenty of others who believed that the chancellor's work was exactly what the nation needed, and that any resistance was a blight that must be stamped out. Andre was well aware of his reputation from the Border Conflict; hence, he was reluctant for the enemy to be aware of his involvement. He knew his name was high on the list of "enemies of Corynthia."

"You will treat the men you see around you as your superiors. You will not go anywhere or do anything without the express permission of an officer. If you are given orders by someone, you will carry them out to their entirety. You are prisoners. Thus, until the terms of your surrender are finalized, you are without the right to act on your own power." Andre paused and surveyed them. "Am I clear?"

There was a smattering of acknowledgments.

He crossed his arms, glowering. "Am I *clear*?" he barked. The prisoners responded again, this time clearly and in unison. "Good. Now, which of you will be your spokesman?"

The bearded man raised his hand. He was shorter and stockier than Andre with ragged hair as thick and black as his beard.

"What's your name?"

"Gerrit."

"Very well, Gerrit. I must confer with my associate. Afterwards, I will have you join us. Come when I call you." Andre motioned for Mattias to follow him.

He noticed Wes staring at the loyalists, his face contorted into a mask of disgust. He made note of it to himself. He would address it if issues arose.

When they were out of earshot, he faced Mattias. "There's a fair amount of them. It wouldn't be too much trouble to escort them to a more secure place."

"No, the additional hands will be welcome," Mattias reaffirmed. "If Tench marches on Cappus, we must hold him off. To do that, we need to reinforce this outpost, because currently, it wouldn't hold off a herd of deer."

"You're confident you can keep them in line, then? What if they start a fight?"

"We outnumber them, and I trust the Crimson Hounds. They took this outpost—they sure as hell can hold it."

Hearing footsteps approach, Andre looked around to see Wes walking towards them. "H'o, Wes."

"H'o, lieutenant." Wes's face was set in a dusky grimace. "What's the verdict?"

"They'll stay here at the outpost," Mattias explained. "We'll put them to work making this place impenetrable."

"You cannot be serious."

Andre narrowed his eyes. "Yes, we are, Wes."

He knew exactly what was on the young soldier's mind. At the beginning of Tench's reign of tyranny, Wes's home was raided by the chancellor's soldiers. His father put up a fight and was killed in the struggle. His mother and two sisters were dragged off to some dark hole where they were undoubtedly subjected to some form of horrifying treatment. Wes, who was among the original Crimson Hounds, had already followed Andre into exile and received the news by letter from a relative. His devastation was awful to witness: Grief and rage like a winter storm. Ever since, the rebellion became a personal vendetta against Tench and his loyalists. Andre needed to remind him often of their true agenda. Thankfully, Wes's counterpart Tahlia, kept a close eye on him and held him accountable most of the time.

"They're Corynthians, like you," Andre reminded him. "Merely doing what they believe is right. Whatever the case, they're our prisoners, unarmed and helpless."

Wes scoffed. "They're not helpless. You don't need a sword to fight, and you don't need a weapon to kill. And *whatever the case*"—Andre caught the resentment in his voice—"they don't consider us Corynthians. To them, we're insurgents—enemies of the nation, to be captured or killed. Tench won't extend this same kindness to us."

"Wes, stand down," Mattias growled, for Wes's hand had drifted to the pommel of his sword.

Andre held up his hand to silence the sergeant. "That's precisely what sets us apart. Tench is willing to abandon his humanity and rend everyone else's just to wield power. We have a responsibility to Corynthia to keep ours..." he smiled sadly. "We already lost it once, remember?"

Wes's jaw tightened at Andre's words, but he shook his head, unwilling to relent. "What happens if they resist? You're letting a pack of wild dogs walk free among our people. It's the same as keeping an ember smoldering under a pile of brush—it *will* ignite at some point and could take us all with it."

Andre huffed, irritated at the young rebel's persistence. "Free? They aren't free. We have them outnumbered and surrounded. If they attempt anything, they'll be swept away. There's no need to worry."

"In my opinion, as long as they can walk and speak, they're free," Wes countered belligerently. "Even a small scuffle can lead to casualties or a death."

Before Andre could retort, shouts broke out from where the prisoners huddled. He looked over to see the rebel guards wrestling with the loyalists. Everyone in the fort dropped what they were doing and rushed to help curtail the struggle.

Andre cursed.

"My point, sir," Wes jabbed.

Whirling back towards him, Andre snapped, "Shut your mouth!" then ran towards the commotion. By the time he arrived, it was over.

Almost.

A man stood on top of a pile of crates holding something up in his fist. Andre's Hounds surrounded the pile, hackles raised and weapons trained at him. The rest of the prisoners knelt in a cluster, hands on their heads. Tahlia, dark hair wild, held her naked blade against Gerrit's neck. The spokesman looked aghast at what was unfolding.

Andre approached the man on the crates. "What are you hoping to accomplish, here?"

The loyalist stared at him, recognition flickering in his eyes. "I know who you are. You're Andre Cordon. You served with honor in the Border Conflict. You were a hero, and now you're fighting alongside the rebellion? You've abandoned your nation for *these* vagrants?" The man laughed loudly. "Just another lapdog for Servailles. Look how the great have fallen!"

Brushing aside the insult, Andre inclined his head to the man. "And who might you be?"

"I'm the man who will become a hero—by killing you. By killing all of you!" A crazy look was flooding his face.

Andre felt his stomach twist into a knot. He knew people like this: Radicals willing to do anything for their cause, including perish in a blaze of what they considered glory. This was exactly what he had wanted to avoid. If this madman were not stopped, he could put a serious blight on their fresh victory.

"And how will you do that?" Andre inquired politely, insides screaming.

"With this." The man brandished what he was holding: It was a match. He gestured at the buildings around him. "These buildings are coated in pine resin to protect the wood from rain. It's also a contingency plan to keep the outpost from falling into enemy hands. One flame and the whole fort will ignite with all of you inside!"

"And yourself." Andre was unable to keep a desperate edge out of his voice. He was playing with fire now—literally. "And your companions. Do you think that's what they want?"

"If they aren't willing to die for Corynthia, then they're traitors, just like you! You've brought shame to our land! Weakness like you must be stamped out!"

"How... loyal of you. You're aware Tench doesn't actually care about you, right?"

The man crowed, a high-pitched mad sound. "How will the rebellion continue without its greatest commander? You'll be crushed." He struck the match on his bracer, holding the flame out dramatically in front of him.

There was a sharp inhale from Mattias, and Andre felt his own heart jump into his throat. *Now or never.*

"I'm sure Winston will manage. Shoot him!"

Arrows converged on the man, sticking into him like quills from a porcupine. Teetering on his perch, he dropped the lit match. The brief feeling of relief immediately vanished as a small flame sprung up among the wooden crates, bone dry from sitting in storage. Andre watched in horror as the man fell, and the containers toppled into the side of the barracks.

The effect was instantaneous. Flames raced up the side of the building, spreading until the entire structure was ablaze. At the same time, the other loyalists sprang into action, tackling the closest rebels and grabbing their weapons.

Andre drew his sword. "Contain that!" he yelled, pointing at the fire.

An enemy swung at him, nicking him in the side as he twisted away. He thrust the blade of his weapon through his assailant's throat, killing him instantly.

The inside of the outpost was in chaos. The flames jumped to nearby buildings with frightening speed, and smoke billowed into the sky. Shouts and the clashing of swords joined the sound of rushing flames as the rebels tried to organize. More than a dozen of them were already on the ground—injured, or worse.

Before Andre could call his remaining soldiers to rally around him, two loyalists charged him with cries. He blocked an overhand swing from one of them and threw an elbow into the stomach of the other. As the latter stumbled back, Andre focused his efforts on the first soldier, disarming him with a deft strike of his sword, then cutting him down.

Without warning, a searing pain ripped through the back of his leg as the second attacker recovered and sliced his hamstring. Adrenaline flooding through him, he managed to turn without falling. With a deadly strike, he separated the loyalist's head from his shoulders.

Andre began to cough, wiping his stinging eyes with the back of his hand to no avail. The smoke was thick—a black, oily curtain obscuring his surroundings. From what he could tell, the majority of man-on-man combat seemed to be over.

However, the battle with the fire was not. Flames licked the outer walls of the fort. Roofs caved in with horrible squeals as the structural integrity of buildings failed. The sound was terrifying.

Spotting Wes, Andre limped towards him. "Out!" he cried, voice cracking from the smoke. "Get everyone out!"

Wes dashed towards those still fighting the fire. Vague shapes of people, looking like spirits from another realm, rushed around, grabbing the wounded and dragging them towards the gate.

Andre stumbled in that direction. A building crumbled in front of him, burning logs spilling into his path and showering him in sparks. He fell backwards, coughing. Covering his mouth with his hand, he struggled back to his feet.

The way in front of him—the quickest route to safety—was completely blocked. He spun in a circle, looking for a path through the burning wreckage on all sides of him. Something in the smoke cracked next to him, spilling more sparks into his path. He lost his balance again and collapsed, vision blurring as he gasped for breath. The sound of his heartbeat crescendoed in his ears, mingling with the roar and crackle of the flames. Then, darkness.

6

ILL NEWS

ANDRE AWOKE FROM DREAMS of racing through dark, twisting corridors full of shadowy figures that tried to trip him and drag him into their black lairs. Screams echoed in his ears, and flames chased him as he ran through the passageways. Smoke filled his lungs, and he emerged from his dream coughing and hacking.

While he convulsed trying to regain control of his breath, he was dimly aware of someone helping him roll onto his side. Gradually, the fit subsided, and he lay there, chest heaving. After a moment, he pushed himself up into a sitting position.

He was inside a large tent. A lantern flickered on the ground, illuminating a bare interior.

The man who helped him stared down at him. Wes's eyes peered concerned through the soot smears on his face. "How do you feel?"

Andre swallowed with difficulty; his throat felt swollen. "I've felt better." The words came out like gravel. "May I have some water?"

Wes removed a water skin from his belt, handing it to him.

Tilting his head back, Andre let the water trickle down his sore throat in increments. When he finished, he went to hand it back, but Wes gestured for him to keep it.

Andre stifled a cough. "What happened?"

"You lost consciousness. You were lucky. The wreckage missed you, but if I hadn't found you..."

"Did everyone escape?"

"Most. Some didn't." Wes's shoulders slumped, and he ran his hand through his hair, dislodging flecks of ash. "They're in bad shape."

"How long—"

"You've been in and out of consciousness for two days," Wes answered before he finished. "We've been doing the best we can, but we don't have enough supplies to tend to everyone. Everything in the fort is now ash, and we're close to dipping into the reserves of what we do have."

Andre took another swig of water, licking his lips. They were blistered and felt warm to the touch. "How many were lost?"

"Well," Wes began hesitantly, "there's thirteen of us on our feet. Another eighteen wounded, a few seriously. There are some loyalist casualties as well." The venom in his voice was palpable.

Andre let his head drop into his hands as the brutal reality slammed into him. Almost half of his forces were gone—dead. He cursed quietly. "This is my fault!" he cried, pounding his fist into his injured leg. He immediately regretted it as pain struck back.

"It's not your fault."

"It *is*, Wes! I assumed they would comply! I thought they were intimidated! I should have listened to you and tied them up! We're at war, not playing guards and goblins in the woods! Now there's over twenty soldiers dead because of my—" he stopped as dry sobs racked him.

He felt his throat tear, fresh pain searing through it. He didn't care. This pain was nothing compared to the lives lost. Those men and women were gone because he failed to lead—because he failed to control a group of unarmed soldiers half their numbers. Even though there wasn't enough moisture in him for tears to flow, his eyes still stung and smarted. His lips cracked, and the taste of blood filled his mouth. He doubled over as coughs overtook his sobs.

Regaining control of himself, he sat up, throat smarting.

Wes seemed reluctant to look at him.

"I'm sorry," Andre told him in a raspy voice.

"Don't worry about it, sir." Wes hesitated for a moment, then gestured to the tent flap. "When you're ready, they will want to know you're awake."

"Of course."

What was he supposed to tell them? A wave of guilt washed over him. Their comrades, friends that they trained with and shared meals together, were gone, yet he was still alive—a walking testimony to his own failure. *How am I supposed to look them in the eye?*

He tried to stand up, nearly collapsing again as his leg protested. Wes caught him and hoisted him to his feet. Andre clung to him, teeth gritted against the burn.

"You suffered a large cut on your hamstring. It's wide, but nothing was severed. We cleaned and bandaged it. You'll be sore for a while, but it'll heal. Come on. I'll help you walk."

With Wes supporting him, Andre limped out of the tent. The bright sunlight made him squint as he emerged. The perfect weather had a mocking quality to it now. Smoke still rose from the destroyed outpost in the distance, highlighted against the clear backdrop of blue sky—a pillar erected to his negligence.

The Crimson Hounds were already gathered in front of the tent, newcomers mingled with the veterans. Their soft voices fell silent, and they watched Andre with grim faces. Many of them sported bandages and angry red blisters from burns. He could see Leana among the crowd, her arm in a sling. Tahlia sat next to Donroe, both with matching abrasions on their cheeks.

Andre took a deep breath. "I'm... sorry. I failed you. Victory sat in our hands, and I allowed it to slip away. Even more importantly, we lost lives because of my neglect. Friends, brothers, sisters—people who had families—gone because of my failure to ensure those prisoners were properly contained. It's my fault."

They watched him silently.

A wave of weariness washed over him, and he sat down on a moss-covered log. "Where's Mattias?"

The sergeant stepped forward through the crowd. "Here."

"What shape is the fort in?"

"Bad," Mattias replied with a grimace. "The buildings are completely gone, and the foundation is in shambles. The fire did a thorough job."

"No chance of rebuilding?"

"It would have to be from scratch."

Andre's heart thumped resignedly. The bad news just kept piling on. "Then we'll go to Cappus. All of us."

"What about this position?"

Andre surveyed the Hounds silently watching the exchange. They were dead tired; he could see it in their faces and posture. Blood and soot from the battle still covered some of them. He recalled how nervous they were before they attacked. *They're no longer greennoses, that's for sure.*

"If Tench decides to send soldiers this way, you won't stand a chance here, not in this state. It's better that we abandon this position and join the main army. I won't leave you to another slaughter." He stared absent-mindedly into space, the faces of the young soldiers who lost their lives swimming in front of his eyes. His mind felt numb.

Mattias put his hand on Andre's shoulder. "We don't blame you, you know. We didn't expect anyone to be a hero."

"It doesn't change—"

"Punishing yourself won't change anything, and it sure as hell won't help their morale," Wes interrupted in a low voice. "I'm sorry, but there's no room to wallow. These people are looking to you, waiting for you to lead them. So lead them. The battle's over—it's finished. Right now, you're failing them by sitting here aimlessly. You're Andre Cordon; you've been through worse than this. You can sulk when you're dead." He walked away, disappearing into the tent.

Andre looked after him. Wes was right: He was being foolish. Losing soldiers was not a new ordeal for him. He recalled his own words to Wes from earlier: *We have a responsibility to Corynthia to keep our humanity.* There was a delicate balance between being ruled by his emotions and being a stone-cold killer. He needed to find that line again.

He reached up to Mattias, who grasped him by the forearm, pulling him to his feet. He wobbled for a moment, then turned to address the Hounds again, his hand on his sergeant's shoulder for support.

They stared at him, their gaze feeling like it was burning into his skin. Despite Mattias's reassurance that they didn't blame him, the eyes felt accusatory.

"We can't stay here. As you know, the plan was to garrison the outpost to protect the army's back while they besieged Cappus. Unfortunately, now that is no longer practical. If we stay here and loyalists do come, we'll be destroyed. Instead, we shall march to Cappus and join the rest of the army. I'll inform General Servailles about what happened, and we'll have to hope Tench doesn't suddenly become worried about what's happening out west.

"Again, I take full responsibility for this disaster. I thought our presence was enough to subdue them, but I underestimated what some men will resort to for what they believe in. Needless to say, what's done is done. You can hold this against me if you'd prefer, though in the end, we must move forward. All of us," Andre added more for himself than the others. "Rest up. We'll leave tomorrow."

Wes emerged from the tent holding a crutch. He held it out to Andre, who was painfully aware of the gash on the back of his leg.

Mattias jerked his head to the tent. "Go rest. I'll watch this lot."

Nodding gratefully, Andre hobbled back into the tent.

Frustration and despair still lurked in the back of his mind, waiting for an opportunity to strike again. Mercifully, he found a remnant of the cold shield again to keep them at bay. He lay for a long time inside the tent, staring at the ceiling, wondering how much more blood would be spilled before the war ended.

The first part of the journey to Cappus was horribly uncomfortable. Mattias insisted that Andre ride a horse on account of his injury; however, every bump jostled his leg, sending fresh pain shooting through it. His lungs, still recovering from the smoke he inhaled, were assailed regularly by coughing fits until his voice sounded more like a frog than his own. On top of that, Wes and Tahlia reported that they saw something unusual in the woods the night before they embarked, which did not put Andre's mind at ease. Even though Tahlia was very vague with her description, stating it was more of a feeling than anything, he could put two and two together: They were still being followed. From an officer's standpoint, that was a harrowing thought.

The rebels moved very slowly indeed and were painfully vulnerable. The march to Cappus lasted much longer than it should have because of their wounded. A few of the injured required constant attention at the behest of their already meager medical supplies. Andre refused anything other than an occasional change in his bandages to conserve supplies. With all of their afflictions, he couldn't help but look over his shoulder the entire journey. Any form of attack—if any loyalist party somehow caught wind of them—and they were done for.

Thankfully, there was no sign of any pursuers, and Andre began to relax as they drew closer to their destination. His throat finally recovered, while the pain in his leg subsided to a dull, aching throb. The sun continued to shine, and he felt his spirits rise despite his misgivings. Now that the outpost was no longer an issue (albeit not how Andre preferred) and they were poised to besiege Cappus, the rebellion was beginning to make some significant progress.

Finally, the city of Cappus came into view before them. At a break in the trees, Andre paused to savor the sight from a ridge.

Built right into the crags of the Argos Mountains, in the shadow of Landour Mountain, Cappus lorded over Drago Valley like the valley's namesake over its gold. The city had two levels. The lower section was the working-class district where the poorer inhabitants of the city lived and where the merchants pinched money with overpriced wares. Most days, it was filled with people of all sorts, selling and buying or laboring at their trade. An imposing skirt wall surrounded the shops and houses, rising well above the roofs. A large, paved road climbed from the main gate until it reached the dividing wall separating the lower level from the upper.

While the bottom half of the city curved out into the valley, the top section was shaped like the bottom half of a capital **H**. The forefront spurs held towering estates (impressive complexes with soaring towers and gilded roofs), luxurious inns, and restaurants, where the upper class enjoyed most of their leisure. In the center, separated from the wings by a large courtyard, was the governing hall, a lavish building of buttresses and windows. It was here that Governor Tullin and his administration dithered over political matters.

The city was an impressive structure, even in relation with the mountain towering above it. It was also considerably ancient; Andre knew its construction dated back to before Kaval. It had survived many a siege.

The rebellion's army sprawled out in the valley below them, thousands of tents disrupting the fields about a mile from the city walls. Even from the group's vantage point, they could hear the racket of soldiers preparing for the siege.

The Crimson Hounds went unnoticed at first as they entered the camp. There was a great deal of activity, and the arrival of another group of soldiers was not a novel occurrence. A few recognized them and called out greetings, which led to more heads turning. Soon, a crowd of soldiers formed behind them as they moved deeper into the encampment; the state of Andre and his companions was quite clearly worse-for-wear.

Someone had run ahead to alert the officers because Delvon Pitt and William Draytus appeared, hurrying toward them from the center of the camp.

"Andre!"

The crowd parted to let the commanders through. Dismounting gingerly from his horse to meet them, Andre grasped Pitt's hand.

William stepped back to survey the soldiers with a frown on his weary face. "What happened? I was under the impression they were to stay at the outpost."

"There were... complications. The outpost is gone," Andre explained reluctantly.

"Gone?" Pitt asked. "What do you mean gone?"

"We lost a lot of soldiers, and the rest are weary and injured. Can we speak after they're settled?" Andre gave them a pointed look; those around them were watching curiously.

William shouted at the crowd to help the Hounds unload, then motioned for Andre and Mattias to follow.

"We have a problem of our own," he announced as they walked, "but I want to hear your story first."

They entered a large, yellow and blue colored tent, where three other officers were gathered around a table covered with maps and documents. They uttered candid greetings, though Andre noticed they seemed tense.

Looking around at those present, he realized someone was very conspicuously missing. "Where's Winston?"

Pitt and William exchanged looks. "After you," insisted Pitt.

Apprehension crawled into Andre's chest as he remembered the plan Winston confided to him at Liberá. He berated himself for not telling someone else to keep an eye on him. If his friend *had* decided to proceed with his suicide mission, he would have taken action after he sent away the only person who knew of the plan. *How have I not learned?*

The others watched him expectantly.

"Fine." With help from Mattias, Andre relayed the events at the outpost. He saw the looks of worry deepen as he talked, but he ignored them until he was finished.

"So we have no one to protect our backside," remarked Pitt after a moment of silence.

Andre, his mind still on Winston, didn't respond.

"It doesn't matter, anyway," someone else interjected. He was an older, grizzled man named Corence with gray hair and a permanent scowl on his face, reminiscent of a granite cliff. He crossed his arms, corded forearms flexing. "If Tench wanted to send an army to Cappus, he'd tear through a rear guard in no time."

"You forget that Tench doesn't have any men to send," corrected William. "Save from the five thousand soldiers here, they're all at the border. It would take weeks to relocate a sizable force. Regardless, he doesn't seem concerned about us, as long as he's protected in Seruvia."

"He probably doesn't think we'll have any success sacking Cappus," Pitt added. "It would be nice to have someone at our back, nonetheless."

Andre nodded. "Agreed. Sadly, that isn't the case."

"We can apply a garrison of soldiers anyway," Mattias offered. "We don't really need the physical outpost. I can return with the Crimson Hounds once we've recovered; we know the area. I'll spare Wes and Tahlia. They'll be useful with Cappus."

Grunts of agreements poked the air before silent tension descended over the tent, dripping until it inevitably overflowed.

The question screaming inside Andre's head finally leaped out of his mouth. "Where's Winston?"

William scratched his head in obvious discomfort. "Gone. We don't know where."

"What do you mean gone?" He wasn't sure why he asked when he already knew the answer.

"He just vanished," clarified one of the other officers. "Shortly after we arrived. He gave no warning, not even a note."

"He was quiet the whole journey over. Brooding," said Pitt. "We thought he left on a reconnaissance missions and just forgot to tell us—you know how he is. I certainly hope his disappearance has nothing to do with his blasted Soothsayer."

"He didn't tell you anything before you left?" William shrewdly met Andre's eyes.

Sighing, Andre relented, "Actually, he did. I'm just reluctant to actually acknowledge his foolishness. I thought I convinced him otherwise. Obviously I should have known better."

"Where has he gone?" William's face was fraught with alarm, the lines tracing it deepening.

Andre realized his jaw was clenched and relaxed it. "Have you informed the men?" he asked, ignoring William's question for the moment.

"No. We thought it best to keep it quiet until we knew more."

Andre leaned on the table, frustration surging inside of him. Clenching his hands into fists to stop their shaking, he closed his eyes and exhaled slowly.

He knew exactly the game Winston was orchestrating. Andre was the only one who understood just how deeply he had sunk into this obsession; furthermore, he was the only one (besides William) who knew how far he was willing to throw himself, risk be damned. Ultimately, William was too important as a strategist to afford embarking on a rescue mission, which left Andre the only option. Winston was forcing him to respond or to let his friend perish.

The damn fool.

"Andre?"

Someone touched his shoulder. He straightened up, opening his eyes to find Mattias, concern etched into his face.

"I'm alright," Andre assured. "It's been a hellish week. Proceed with the siege. You all know the procedure, and we certainly can't wait for Winston to begin. The sooner Cappus falls, the sooner we advance our agenda.

Besides, we can't afford to stall in the event Tench finally decides to move against us."

"What about you?" demanded Pitt, hard face darker than the mountain's shadow.

"I'm going to bring back Winston."

"And where did he go?"

"Unfortunately, Delvon, he went after the Soothsayer."

7

THE CHANCELLOR AND THE SOOTHSAYER

W INSTON LAY ON HIS cot, counting the tiles on the ceiling for dozenth time. As it was his third day locked in the room, he was understandably restless.

The room was far from extravagant, though it was more comfortable than he had expected. Situated in one of the towers of Audax Keep—the impressive fortress at the center of the capital city, Seruvia—Winston could stare out over the rooftops through the single window cut out of the wall. The afternoon sun slanted through the window's slats, bathing the room's furnishings in warm yellow stripes. A simple cot pressed flush with the wall, the mattress covered in linen sheets. A small wooden table topped with an empty vase sat on a woven rug in the middle of the room. A painting depicting the sun setting behind Seruvia hung on the wall opposite the bed, breaking up the cream-colored walls with a pleasant splash of color.

Bored, Winston swung his legs over the edge of the bed and pushed himself to his feet in one fluid motion. He walked over to the window, pursing his lips at the hustle and bustle of the city.

Seruvia had changed drastically since Tench gained power. Previously the crown jewel of Southern Kaval, it used to be full of beautiful buildings topped with elegant spires, each unique to itself. Now those swooping, airy towers were torn down, replaced by drab, boxy apartments. The streets, once open and winding—almost organic—were constricted to a criss-cross of dark, dirty alleys that served as shelter for homeless vagrants.

Seeing how such a beautiful diamond was sullied made Winston sad and angry every time he looked out at it.

A few days after arriving at Cappus, he slipped away from the rebel army. Despite Andre's condemnation of his plan, Winston still knew it was the only way he could convince the Soothsayer to join the rebellion. He didn't mind being in danger. He made peace with the thought of dying many years ago, having survived a few assassination attempts while working to separate Corynthia from Kaval. Although assurance of rescue would be comforting knowledge to have, he knew that sharing his plan with anyone else would elicit the same response as Andre. Secrecy was, unfortunately, the only option.

Besides, he reasoned to himself, *Andre has likely arrived at Cappus by now. He'll realize where I am.* He felt better knowing he confided in Andre. His friend wouldn't let him rot here to die.

After leaving Cappus, Winston rode straight for the capital. Around a week-and-a-half ride generally, fair weather brought him to the city of Markalv in five days. He booked a single night at an inn without trouble, but when he woke up the next morning, soldiers waited for him. He gave himself up willingly. They confiscated his horse and effects, tossing him in the back of a prisoner cart where he collected bruises the remainder of the way to Seruvia.

Upon arrival, Winston was placed in a holding cell in Audax Keep's dungeon. He expected Chancellor Tench himself to come and gloat in his face, but after a couple of hours in the pungent, dimly-lit room, more guards appeared instead to escort him to the room in the tower. Thereafter, the door was shut and locked behind him.

Except for the delivery of meals, precious little happened since.

The sounds of city life drifted up to Winston as he observed. Carts pulled by horses rattled woodenly; conversations too far away to hear details sounded like the buzz of insects. Nothing seemed out of the ordinary. No crowds gathered; he sensed no excitement that could be linked to his capture.

He frowned, sweeping his hair out of his eyes. This didn't seem like Berling Tench.

Back when Winston ran against him for the presidency, Tench took every opportunity to gloat and show off. Emphasizing every mistake Winston made, he reveled in his failures. With the lack of spectacle, Winston couldn't help but wonder if he had made a mistake.

If Berling doesn't come to me... No, he would never miss an opportunity to laugh in my face. It felt odd hoping to see his enemy when he had spent so much time striving to do just the opposite.

No sooner had he finished his thought than a knock sounded on the door.

A muffled voice barked gruffly. "Alright, prisoner, stand against the opposite wall and raise your hands above your head. Give acknowledgment when you have complied."

Obeying the instructions, Winston replied calmly, "You can enter." Heart thundering in his chest, he clenched his jaw involuntarily as he watched the door.

A jingle of keys preceded the sound of the latch clicking. Then, the door swung open, revealing an armed guard.

Winston immediately noticed the man's attire. He wore the sky blue of Corynthia, except instead of a blank tunic, a golden rose splashed across his chest. Four gold stars on the collar indicated his rank. This wasn't a regular soldier. The golden rose represented the chancellor's office—this was a personal guard for Tench himself.

Speak of the devil.

The guard stepped aside, and a man entered the room.

Berling Tench did not seem like a cruel man. He was of average height and rather stout. His brown hair was streaked with gray, while a carefully groomed mustache adorned his upper lip like a large, fluffy caterpillar. His hazel eyes were surrounded by wrinkles from countless empty smiles. They were the only indicators of Tench's true nature: Cold and empty, devoid of kindness as he looked Winston up and down.

"Winston, my friend!" Tench's voice was jovial, for good reason. "It's been too long!"

Winston forced a laugh. "We were never friends, Berling. You've always hated me, and I've never liked you. Why don't we move past the pleasantries?"

Tench affected a surprised appearance. "Since when have you become so blunt with your words? Have you finally revealed your agenda and stopped *lying* to your people?" He spat out the question like spoiled milk. "Is that why you're here? Because they sent you to receive your due punishment?"

"I haven't lied to them. I—"

"Never spoke the full truth," interrupted Tench, "but by all means, keep denying it." He waved the guard out of the room. "Leave us."

The Rose Soldier saluted and left, closing the door behind him.

There was silence as the two men glared daggers at each other.

Finally, Winston went to the chair and dragged it out. "Where are my manners? Please, sit."

Tench, giving him a panther grin, sat.

Perching himself on the edge of his cot, Winston leaned forward with his elbows on his knees. He forced his jaw to relax, returning the smile. "I wondered if you would visit. I must admit, I grew a little worried when you didn't parade me through the streets in chains. I nearly fell under the assumption I was to be executed quietly with no ceremony."

Tench chuckled. "Not at all, Winston. You're the face of insurgency; your death shall be public. The people will watch your head separate from your shoulders and realize there is no rebelling against me. To that matter, invite your friends! They can watch, too. Afterwards, I'll do the same to them."

He paused, looking thoughtful. "However, your appearance caught me by surprise. I expected a trap—another desperate design to assassinate me. Yet you are truly alone, aren't you?"

"I am."

"Arrogant to the very end." Tench clicked his tongue and sneered. "Why have you come, then? What is there to gain from strutting to your own demise?"

"It's not about what there is to gain, Berling. I have everything to gain from this. More to the point, I have nothing to lose."

"Nothing to lose? You're delusional! You have everything to lose! You're the very heart of your senseless rebellion. Who will lead when you're gone? Draytus is too soft; he lacks the gall to do what's necessary. Without you, it will tear itself apart! Who will be the champion of all the little people then?"

A wave of hatred washed over Winston at Tench's smug, gleeful expression. This man was destroying everything he had accomplished and reveling in the misery left behind. *I'm going to kill him,* he decided. *If it's the very last thing I do, he will pay.*

"There are others capable of leading if I die, because unlike you, I trust people. Do you remember Andre Cordon? And Delvon Pitt?"

Tench's lip curled at the mention of the second name.

Delvon Pitt, once a celebrated officer from the Kavalan army, played an important role in Tench's victory over Winston. However, despite his fiery, brutish personality, he was a man for the people. He renounced Tench when he realized how much damage the chancellor was causing. A botched attempt at a staged murder saw him fleeing for his life directly to the rebellion. Needless to say, Winston could see Tench was still sore over the matter.

"Many people are willing to stand and fight against your tyranny. Not least of all is William. He has more courage than all of your spineless supporters combined. My death will do nothing but fuel the fire of rebellion—I can't think of a finer reason to die."

"Is that why you've come? Is your band of miscreants losing its heart? If that's the case, I can certainly execute you in private and tell them how you *ran* like the coward you are."

"I'm not the coward here, Berling. You sit barricaded in your fortress, preying on the very people you govern, growing fat on their emaciated lives. *That's* cowardice." Winston raised his finger when Tench opened his mouth to retort. "I'm not finished. Those people who have summoned the courage to stand up to your cruelty are far from weary. The fire is hardly smoldering."

Tench leaned toward him. "Then why are you here?"

"I think you know."

"Humor me."

Winston brushed his hair to the side and crossed his arms. "The Soothsayer. He should have arrived a few days ago. I want to speak with him."

The chancellor's shock didn't last long before it was replaced with another vicious grin. His shoulders started to shake as he was consumed with laughter. Soon, he was braying like a donkey, his knuckles turning white on the table as he held himself upright.

For a moment, Winston felt panic rise inside of him. Had he misjudged his timing, or had the letter indeed been a trap meant to lure him out? Had his obsession played him the fool?

"I'd forgotten how audacious you are," Tench gasped. "What in the name of the All-Mother has driven you to such madness? Why should I grant you an audience with the Soothsayer?"

Winston stared at him, a detached look on his face despite the relief flooding through him. "I traveled here alone, without speaking to anyone of my plan. I've walked into the welcoming arms of death—my own execution—willingly, to convince him to join the rebellion. Do what you wish with me afterwards; in this, I will not be denied."

Tench crossed his arms, mustache propped up on top of a lopsided smile. Winston tried to kill him with a glare.

Finally, the chancellor stood and strode to the door, giving it a rap. As the door opened, he turned and bowed with a flourish, his eyes glittering mockingly. "By all means, be my guest."

He left the room, and the door closed again behind him.

Exhaling the tension from his body, Winston flopped backwards onto the mattress. He had played his hand right into Tench's arrogance, just as he planned. *Now I must make it count, whether Andre is coming for me or not.*

The next day, a pair of Rose Soldiers opened the door and entered the room, one of them pulling out wrist bindings.

"Are these necessary?" Winston nodded at the bindings.

"Chancellor's orders," replied the guard, holding them out.

With a sigh, Winston presented his wrists. The bindings were applied quite loosely to his relief.

After the cuffs were secure, the guard led him out into the passage. Descending the stairs at the end, they proceeded through the fortress, passing plenty of the Keep's occupants. Guards, officials, and cleaning staff stared as Winston walked past, whispers breaking out like dried grass blowing in the wind behind him. Some of the officials (many he had worked with before his exile) looked straight ahead, not even acknowledging his presence.

Winston found this oddly amusing. *Interesting to see where people's true loyalties lie.* The thought made him chuckle as he walked, a mongoose in a nest of snakes.

Marching through a hall with vaulted ceilings, they arrived at a door that Winston knew led to the Royal Wing, where the more lavish quarters could be found. These rooms were typically reserved for high-ranking officials and ambassadors.

Don't want to keep your delegate of fate uncomfortable.

He wondered what sort of person the Soothsayer was, and if he relished the comforts of the rich.

The wing consisted of a spacious corridor with doors lining the right wall. A rich, crimson carpet ran down the length of the hall. A stairway ascended to the left, turning out of sight at the landing.

At the third door down, they stopped.

Knocking twice, one of the guards unlocked the door with a key from the collection on his belt. Without waiting for a response, he opened the door and gestured Winston inside. "We'll be in the hall. You have half an hour."

Winston raised his bound wrists. "May I have these removed? I promise I won't strangle him."

"The bindings stay on."

Winston made a face, then stepped inside the room. The guards locked him in.

He studied the apartment. Despite living in Audax Keep during the early years of Corynthia, he had never actually been in one of these rooms; he preferred simpler arrangements instead.

The chamber was split into two sections. The front was a lounge of some sort. Sofas and low tables were strewn about, giving an air of leisure that made Winston's stomach churn. Oddly shaped decorations and golden candles perched on the tables in a way he assumed was supposed to be tactful; in reality, they made the room seem even more cluttered. A single step raised what appeared to be a dining area with a large oak table and several chairs above the entryway. Four floor-to-ceiling windows stared out into the eastern sky, letting in a flood of sunlight. There was a door to the right that Winston assumed led to the bedroom and lavatory.

"Hello?" He stepped deeper into the room, voice echoing slightly on the cathedral ceilings.

Skipping the step between the sections, he walked to the windows facing the distant Estarus Mountains sequestering the Wilderness beyond Corynthia's eastern border. Significantly larger than the Argos range to the west, few knew what lay behind them. Even fewer had attempted the perilous journey to the other side. An ominous cloud front shrouded the peaks.

He frowned at it.

His thoughts wandered to the rebellion army at Cappus, and he wondered if the siege was underway yet. The other officers knew the importance of speed in their conquest. At some point, Chancellor Tench would have to acknowledge the rebellion as a true threat; thus, it would be best if they made as much progress as possible before he did.

Tench could only ignore them for so long. Especially after the coup Winston was about to pull off.

The sound of the side door opening interrupted his thoughts. He turned to see a young man watching him with a book in his hand.

The Soothsayer was younger than he expected, maybe around nineteen or twenty years of age. Tall and lean with short, sandy hair, his posture was relaxed, though cautious withal, like a cat assessing a threat. He wore handsome clothes: A gold-trimmed crimson tunic and blue trousers, likely from the wardrobe Tench provided. His feet were bare.

What struck Winston the most about his appearance, however, was his face. It appeared somehow both young and old simultaneously. It was smooth, yet lined with an odd, hollow look that was almost inhuman. His hazel eyes were ringed with dark circles and appeared both frantic and calm at the same time, filled with fierce apprehension while also conveying a hopeless resignation. They were alien, those eyes. Winston found himself unable to meet the Soothsayer's gaze for long.

"Hello." The Soothsayer's voice was mild. "You're Winston Servailles, aren't you?"

"I am."

"I'm Caito Lazar." He motioned around the room. "You can sit if you'd like."

Winston took one of the many couches and smiled invitingly at the young man. Lazar sat across from him, placing his book, dog-eared, on the closest table.

Winston pointed at it. "You can read?" He winced at the pretentious sound of the words. Reading was not a very common skill; poorer families generally had few opportunities or time to learn. "I'm sorry. I didn't mean—"

"That's alright." Lazar gave him the shadow of a smile. "My mother taught me. It helps keep my mind occupied from... other things."

"I can imagine."

Silence lapsed between the two as they continued to study each other. Winston opened his mouth to break the hush, but Lazar was quicker.

"The chancellor told me that you walked into the capital alone. Do you have a plan to escape?"

Winston laughed. "None."

Lazar's eyebrow twitched. "That's... admirable." Winston could tell that wasn't the word he wanted to use. The boy was already savvy to the game of politics. "Aren't you afraid of death?"

"I'll live on through the others," Winston brushed off the question easily.

"So, martyrdom. Why?"

"I have my reasons."

"Please"—Lazar gestured for him to continue—"elaborate."

Winston drew himself up as he began his pitch. "You are a very important piece in this conflict, Caito. Your name carries weight and power. Moreover, people are superstitious; they shall see your endorsement as a sure sign of victory. After all, you've seen the future. Whichever side controls you has a significant advantage over the other. If the people know you support the rebellion, they'll rise up against Tench's tyranny. If there is hope, they will have courage to fight back."

"So you want to use me."

Winston pondered for a moment how best to explain his thoughts. "Yes. I need the influence of your name to rally the nation to my side. However, I have more to offer than Berling."

Lazar cocked his head questioningly.

"Berling desires *only* the influence of your gift. He will place you in a cage like an exotic animal on display to the people. You'll sit in Audax Keep until your master orders you onto the balcony to wave at the masses and make an impressive speech riddled with half-baked predictions of the future. You'll waste away, growing fat on food and drink, becoming lazy and dull, until you're nothing more than another senseless, selfish bureaucrat trading the happiness of the common people for wine and whores.

"What I have to offer you is the opposite. The benefits of your support are crucial, it's true; however, there is more to making a difference than just a name. With the rebellion, you will have a purpose—something to *fight* for. You can be more than just the Soothsayer. You can be a hero—someone for people to stand behind."

Winston stood up and started pacing around the room. "The smell of blood and sweat filling your nostrils, and the rush of combat as death stalks you on the battlefield—it's invigorating! Your blood coursing while your body shakes as you fight for your life! There's nothing like it." He turned to Lazar, who watched him impassively. "Especially when you have a worthy cause to fight for. What say you?"

"What *is* your cause?"

Winston frowned, confused by the simple question. "To free Corynthia from Berling's oppression."

"Oppression?" Lazar remarked shrewdly. "It's my understanding that the people delegate their fate. They chose this. It's a democracy, is it not? You made it so, yet you're now fighting against your own creation."

"Far from it." Winston was enjoying himself. It had been a while since he had stretched his debating wings outside of a military setting. "I'm fighting for it. Berling has destroyed democracy. Under his law, it's become a fascist regime in which he is sovereign in all but name. Corynthia is being oppressed, beaten, and tyrannized. They don't hold a voice in Tench's rule; he's stifled their cries. Do you remember what came of their protests to his new reforms?"

Lazar nodded, his jaw tightening almost imperceptibly.

"He attacked them, struck them down." Winston knew he didn't need to elaborate; however, it was important to drive his point home. Emotion was easier to play than reason. "Now, he bleeds them dry as they cower in their homes, too afraid to step into the streets or even look out through the shutters of their windows. They're afraid to open their mouths, to think their *thoughts* for fear they'll be overheard. One mistake—one wrong word—will bring soldiers to rip them from their homes. Thereafter, their families will be forced into the streets to scrounge through garbage for scraps.

"*This* is not democracy. Tench has turned Corynthia into a breeding ground for tears.

"This will be your legacy, Caito. Fear, oppression, suffering, *pain*. Your name will be associated with darkness for as long as you remain in the history books. Do you really wish to be remembered in such a way?" He searched the Soothsayer's face.

Lazar's expression remained a mask. "You have a compelling argument."

Winston tried to spread his hands, forgetting they were bound. "What say you?"

"I'll have to think about it."

"Think ab—" Winston blurted out before he could stop himself. "Considering my position, there's no time for you to think about it."

"I thought you weren't afraid of death?" shot back Lazar, raising his eyebrows. "You told me you would live on through the others. If that is the case, I will certainly tell them if I decide to join your cause."

Winston realized his mouth was hanging open and closed it. *I like this boy.* There was fire inside of him, which he supposed was necessary for his survival. Winston couldn't imagine how difficult his burden was.

Lacing his fingers together in front of him, the Soothsayer continued, "We don't have much time left together, and I have some questions for you. Firstly, if you wanted to speak with me so badly, why didn't you take me as I traveled? I assume you were tracking my movements."

"My colleagues wanted to stage an ambush, and capture you before you arrived at Markalv."

"Why didn't you?"

"Violence is never the right way to sway someone. Intimidation can work wonders, but it instills fear and distrust, leading to a fragile relationship. However, if one walks willingly into the jaws of death, they will reap respect—maybe even awe. It builds an image of confidence and considerably more trustworthiness."

Lazar tilted his head, piercing Winston with his haunting eyes. "You're a manipulator."

Winston laughed softly. "Of course. I'm a politician, Caito."

"There's some irony." Lazar's lips quirked in a small smile. "A politician who admits he's a snake. So, to prove your worthiness of my support, you walked into your enemy's open arms."

"Actions speak louder than words. I went to great lengths to pull Corynthia from Artreus's idle hands; I'm willing to lay my life down for her. Now she is bleeding. What wouldn't I do to help?"

There was a knock on the door. With a glance at it, Lazar stood. "Last question."

"Ask."

He spoke hesitantly, as though sharing a secret, "You haven't asked about my... gift. About what I've seen."

Winston shrugged. "I hadn't thought of it, truly. My focus was on convincing you to join the rebellion. You're more important to me as a person, I suppose."

It was true. He had been so preoccupied with forming his speech and accounting for any questions the Soothsayer might ask that he hadn't even considered addressing Lazar's visions.

The door opened, and a guard poked his head in. "Time to go, Servailles."

Winston weaved through the couches, turning back when he reached the door. "That must count for something," he added with a small smile.

As the guard led him out of the room, he glanced over his shoulder. Caito Lazar was sitting back on the sofa with his head in his hands. It was the first time Winston had seen him show any weakness.

The door slammed shut. The sound echoed through the hall, mingling with Winston's thoughts of the young man who bore the weight of the world on his shoulders.

8

THE TRIAL OF WINSTON SERVAILLES

WINSTON AWOKE SUDDENLY TO the rising sun playing across his pillow. He sat up, immediately energized. He felt curiously calm considering what the day held in store. A wry smile touched his lips as he savored the thought of the trial. Laughing to himself, he swung his legs out of bed, feeling a little delusional. He made his habitual trip to the window and looked down at the streets with a stretch and a yawn.

Dominus Square was out of sight from his vantage point, though a steady stream of tiny people were making their way in its direction.

They were gathering to watch him fall.

A knock sounded at the door. He automatically turned, placing his hands on his head. The latch clicked, and the door creaked open, revealing two guards with wrist bindings.

Smiling lazily at them, Winston held out his hands.

As they marched him through the Keep, he noticed that it seemed strangely deserted. The only people they passed were cleaning staff, and even less than usual. He assumed everyone was off preparing for the trial.

He was taken to a small study off of the front entrance hall where a desk was laden with breakfast. His hands were untied, and he sat down to eat. He did so slowly, savoring his food. The eggs on rye bread and orange slices were quite a lavish meal compared to the bland oatmeal he had grown accustomed to.

Once finished, he looked around the sparse room. Besides the desk and chair, a single bookshelf filled with books and a painting were all that decorated the room.

Grabbing a book from the shelf at random, he opened it to find it completely blank. He flipped through the pages before scoffing and throwing it aside. Only Tench would fill a bookshelf with empty tomes. *What a vain dolt*.

As he reached for another, a jingle of keys at the door announced visitors. The door was thrown open, and Tench strode into the room, mustache fluttering jovially.

"Good morning, Winston!"

Winston narrowed his eyes. "I fail to see the good in it."

He already knew it would be difficult to keep his poise, yet he refused to lose control. He would not allow Tench that victory. He snatched the book he had been reaching for. It, too, was blank. He tossed it onto the floor to join the other.

"I see your sense of humor hasn't been quenched!" Tench chuckled. "That's good; that's good. It won't be much help, however."

"I thought the trial was scheduled for midday," Winston commented, ignoring him.

"It is, but I wanted to..." he trailed off with a flourish.

"Show off?"

Tench smiled nastily. "Precisely."

Winston imagined squeezing the man until he popped, running his tongue over his teeth as he entertained the idea. His hands were untied; what was stopping him? A guard's head appeared around the door, deflating his vision.

"Everything ready, sir?"

"Yes, of course," Tench said. "Bring him out."

Out in the hall, a small entourage of people waited. Most of them were Rose Soldiers, though Winston recognized the other two.

The first was a thin, balding politician wearing an extravagant tunic slightly too large for his frame. He watched them approach with a delighted expression on his hairless, rat face. Named Pilkley, he was one of Tench's closest supporters. Winston despised him; hence, he made no effort to hide the curling of his lip as his eyes passed over him.

The other was Caito Lazar.

The Soothsayer inclined his head as they joined.

Winston returned the gesture and looked at Tench. "What's this?"

Pilkley answered before Tench could open his mouth. "Berling informed me he was gathering you for the trial," he explained in a wheezy voice as weak as his appearance. "Naturally, I wanted to come along and wish you luck, my dear old colleague."

"Go polish your head, Prickly," shot Winston scathingly. "The men with brains are speaking."

"It's Pilkley," sniffed the other stiffly.

"What is?" Winston did not even grace him with a glance.

Tench chortled. "Winston, you must be more courteous. After all, you are a guest in our house."

"I generally try not to speak to vermin at all," Winston replied in a casual voice, "however, it's difficult when they insert themselves into conversations they have no part in."

"Vermin?!" Pilkley squawked. "You little–"

"Alright, enough!" shouted Tench. "Pilkley, just... be silent."

Pilkley deflated a little.

"Down, *dog*," Winston hissed at him with a vicious smile.

Pilkley lunged at him with a strangled cry. A guard grabbed him firmly by the shoulder, halting him. It was good he did, for Winston would have been more than happy to murder the peacock of a man even with his hands tied. Then there really would be legitimate charges against him.

Tench whirled back, annoyed. "*And* you." He motioned to the guards. "Carry on."

Winston winked at Lazar as one of the Rose Soldiers grabbed him by the elbow, leading him past the fuming Pilkley.

They halted in front of the towering main doors. Made of heavy oak wood with iron bands securing them to the walls, they were massive, standing three-and-a-half times Winston's height. A huge metal ring was fixed to each of the doors at chest height, and it was to these that another pair of guards hung, ready to open them at Tench's command.

Winston could hear the muffled buzz of the crowd on the outside and swallowed. He suddenly felt lightheaded.

Tench motioned to the guards. They strained against the rings, hauling the heavy doors apart with bone-shaking groans. The chatter of the crowd filled the hall, brought in by a draft from outside.

Winston turned to Lazar. "Well?"

"Well, what?"

The guard began to move, but Winston held back, just for a moment. "What's the verdict, Soothsayer? Do I live or die?"

Lazar gave him a small smile. "Good luck, Winston Servailles."

Steeling himself, Winston emerged from Audax Keep into the spring air charged with excitement.

The chatter of voices faltered. The people stared silently at the group making their way down the steps. Winston looked out at the sea of faces before him. The weight of every single eye on him was like a tidal wave slamming into him through a thousand accusing gazes. It made him feel small.

The silence persisted as he and his guard gained the stage constructed in front of the steps. A podium commanded the front, while a row of chairs lined one side. Winston was led to a lone seat on the opposite end. He sat, studying the square while another guard joined the first, posting themselves on either side of him.

A line of Rose Soldiers stood before the stage to keep back the crowd, while regular guards were posted at various points around the square. A flash of movement from the roof revealed archers with crossbows.

Winston scanned the crowd, hoping to pick out a familiar face; sadly, there were none. Only strangers.

Tench began to speak from the podium, "Welcome! Welcome all, to this significant and momentous day! This day marks the end of anarchy, the end of unrest, and the beginning of unity! Today shall be the start of a new era! One of peace and prosperity; of happiness and goodwill!"

"Whose happiness, Berling?" Winston allowed his voice to carry over the heads of the spectators. They muttered to each other, some of them nodding at his words.

Tench continued, spewing lies into the tense atmosphere, "Today shall usher in Corynthia's golden age, signified by the condemnation of our greatest enemy!" He pointed at Winston. "This man has caused too much grief for you, people of Corynthia! He took this nation from Kaval's clutches, promising democracy—a land where *you* could decide your fate!

Yet when you exercised your rights, removing him from power, he attempted to take it back!"

Holding up his arm, Tench tore back the sleeve, revealing a large white scar on his forearm. "Now, he answers for his crimes against Corynthia. Today... he *pays*!"

More grumblings came from the crowd, and a hiss cut the air. The guards shifted menacingly.

Tench acted as though he did not notice. "His trial shall be conducted by the highest esteemed judges in Corynthia!"

He spread his arms as the front doors opened once more, and a file of important-looking men and women traipsed down the steps. Ascending the stage, they took their seats opposite Winston.

Winston snorted as he surveyed them. He recognized many of them, including Pilkley, who he knew was only there because he was buttering up to Tench. *Esteemed,* he thought savagely. *How little integrity must be left for* these *people to be* esteemed?

"These men and women, who work day and night forging Corynthia into the great nation it is, shall evaluate this man's crimes, and thereupon decide his punishment. The trial shall commence in an hour's time. Tell your friends and family! The market stalls are open! Enjoy yourselves, for today is a glorious day!"

Cheers, catcalls, and complaints about the delay jumbled together as the crowd began to dissipate.

A voice cut through the noise, making everyone stop where they were.

"What about the Soothsayer?"

Tench, who had turned to talk to the judges, slowly faced the woman who uttered the question. "I'm sorry?"

"What about the Soothsayer? He's here isn't he? Will he come out?"

The crowd erupted into shouts for the Soothsayer.

Holding up his hands, Tench laughed, though Winston could see his irritation behind the curled ends of his mustache. "Nothing escapes you people. Yes, the Soothsayer is here. I was planning to save him as a surprise, though I suppose that's been ruined now. Nevertheless, have no fear. You shall have your Soothsayer." He turned away again, but more calls assailed him to bring out the Soothsayer.

Winston saw Tench's jaw clenching as he stomped back to the podium. The chancellor stood there, glowering at everyone until their clamor ceased.

"Now that you've finished, kindly disperse. You *will* have your Soothsayer when *I* say so."

The guards clanked threateningly again.

Still grumbling, the crowd obeyed. Many left to indulge themselves in the market, though plenty stayed, eyeing the stage whilst talking excitedly amongst themselves.

Winston continued to scan the square for something, anything, indicating the presence of a rescue party. Now that there were less people in the square, it would be easier to notice any stragglers trying to catch his attention. Unfortunately, all he saw were strangers, and not very sympathetic ones.

Desperation clawed its way through him. What if he *had* misjudged his decisions, and Andre wasn't coming for him? What if his friend abandoned him, deciding the rebellion's progress was more important? The thought frightened him, because he knew it was something he himself might do. He didn't want to die like this: At Tench's mercy.

He cursed under his breath. *Whatever happens, I will not lose my head. If I die, then...* He didn't finish the thought.

A few people stood close to the stage, watching him. They looked innocently curious, except one winked at him, then vanished back into the crowd.

Winston frowned. He didn't recognize the man. Nevertheless, he felt a glimmer of hope. It had to mean something—some sign he wasn't abandoned.

As time wore on, clouds slowly crept across the sky. The light dimmed, and a chilly breeze swept through the square. A canopy was erected over the other half of the stage where Tench and the judges gathered. Winston, of course, was neglected, and the wind's bite stung him through his tunic. Still, he refused to complain, not while there was breath in his lungs.

The hour drew to a close, and Dominus Square filled again, even more than previously. The air was as laden with excited voices as the clouds were with the promise of rain.

Returning to the podium, Tench raised his hands for silence, a smile on his face.

"Good people!" he cried when the noise died down. "It is time! Before we begin, it is my privilege to present to you—as promised..." He turned, pointing at the doors of Audax Keep, which opened for a third time. "The Soothsayer!"

Lazar, flanked by two soldiers, emerged.

The crowd, as when Winston walked out, fell silent. People stood on tiptoe, necks craning to see the young man. Those in the back attempted to climb on market stalls, much to the annoyance of the peddlers.

Lazar joined Tench, who put his arm around his shoulders. Winston noticed the Soothsayer's jaw tighten as his eyes darted from face to face. He looked like a cornered animal.

"This young man," Tench pontificated, "has an incredible gift. However, the ability to perceive what the future holds does not come without a price. He has suffered much hardship in his short life; much more than any of *you*. His journey has been difficult; nonetheless, he has blessed us by agreeing to share his gift for the purpose of stamping out the idealistic anarchy threatening our great nation. His visions will guide us to a grand and prosperous future!"

All at once, the crowd erupted, cries for advice and pleas for help bombarding the stage. People reached out to Lazar, pushing against the guards. They grasped at the stage, as though they could be saved by just a touch.

Winston studied Lazar's face as he looked out over the crowd. The Soothsayer didn't move, unlike Tench, who leaped back from the onrush. Instead, he stared at the desperate masses with a look of such sadness that Winston averted his gaze.

He feels their pain, he realized.

He found himself more and more in awe of the young man. The way he held himself under such pressure—quietly, calmly, as people groped at his ankles, pleading for him to help them—was extraordinary and, quite frankly, terrifying to see from someone who was little more than a boy.

Lazar glanced at Winston, who met his eyes and gave him a small, sad smile.

Tench recovered, once again calling for silence from the podium.

Lazar turned and walked to the second-to-last chair on the stage, wiping his eyes as he sat down. The noise subsided, yet the crowd seemed anything but subdued. The air felt charged.

"I know you have many questions. Now is not the appropriate time." Tench smirked. "He is merely here to greet you today. His journey was long, and he is quite weary."

"Why don't you let him speak for himself?" someone shouted.

Cries for Lazar to come up again were hurled from the crowd. They pushed forward determinedly.

"Guards," Tench ordered quietly.

The Rose Soldiers jumped into action, no longer trying to hold the mob back. They lashed out, striking people down with their fists and shields. The crowd fought back, but they were no match for the chancellor's armored brawn. The beating was brutal to watch.

Tench stood over the chaos like some pompous gargoyle before bellowing into the disorder, "SILENCE!"

Immediately, the crowd was chastened. As the guards waited, they picked themselves up and drew back from the stage. Many needed help gaining their feet. The crowd seemed significantly smaller after the soldiers returned to their positions.

"Now that you're finished," declared Tench, reasserting himself. "Let us proceed with why we're here. Please turn your attention to these venerated officials."

For the next couple of hours, the assortment of "judges" (in reality, lecherous bureaucrats personally selected by Tench) took turns at the podium pressing accusations and presenting evidence against Winston. They shot him questions intended to trap him into a confession while making exaggerated claims of negligence about his time as leader of the nation.

Completely aware of their intentions, Winston put little effort into his answers. He knew the trial was merely for show; his fate was already sealed, and nothing he said or did would change the outcome.

He was pleased to see that the crowd was losing interest. He knew they were expecting excitement: A heated debate, along with a possible rescue attempt. They were certainly not enjoying watching pompous politicians gloat over him while he sat lethargically on the side.

It was a small victory over Tench to rob him of the spectacle he planned, yet one he accepted readily.

People trickled out of the square as the hearing went on, bored and disappointed.

Feeling a drop of rain, Winston sighed. One more person stood to say his piece. Afterwards, the judges would convene and "decide his fate." He almost wished to be executed now, if only to spare him from this torture.

Finally, Tench retook the podium. "Thank you, your honors." He bowed to the men and women behind him. "Now," he continued, this time addressing Winston, "any words from the accused?"

Standing up, Winston opened his mouth, sarcastic remark at the ready.

Before he could say anything, a shout rang out from the crowd. There was a shriek, and an arrow sprouted from the pulpit.

9

GRUDGINGLY INTO THE MAW

S ERUVIA LOOMED FORBIDDINGLY ON the horizon. A cloud front advancing from the east cast its shadow upon the capital city, making it seem even more sinister compared with the surrounding land still embraced by sunlight.

Unease washed over Andre as he gazed at the city. He remembered how it looked before Tench rose to power, at Corynthia's birth. Seruvia had been bright and open; elegant buildings reached twisting into the sky with sensational detail like so many exotic flowers. He recalled how unique the buildings had been, each with a design unto itself—almost like a personality. Standing amidst the ancient framework caused chills to run through him every time he visited.

Now, as he stared at it, the capital looked dead and gray like a prison. Or a graveyard.

Where there used to be miles of farmland surrounding the city, the tilled earth and flourishing crops were now mud and weeds as farmers could no longer afford to sustain their land. In many cases, Tench bled them from their very homes, leaving the houses to fall into disarray. The lush orchards that once filled the surrounding countryside were decrepit and overgrown, clawing at the wall now surrounding the city with gnarled fingers. The beautiful towers were torn down, replaced with ugly apartments that peeked bitterly over the top of the wall. Smoke rose from behind Seruvia where mills and metal-working foundries provided most of the jobs for its citizens.

The city reflected the plight of Corynthia—a filter of baleful strength hiding the disparaging truth of the land.

Andre turned from the sight to look at his men. Hunched over cold rations, they sat quietly, staring at their food, dark circles pooling under their eyes. He could feel resentment radiating from them.

In preparation to follow after Winston, he selected a team of five men led by a fresh-faced sergeant named Markus Thomilson. Andre didn't know any of them, but with his own soldiers still recovering, he needed reliable people who were up to the challenge. William recommended Thomilson as such a man, and so far, he had delivered on the praise. They made the journey at a blistering pace with hardly any rest, and Thomilson did an admirable job of keeping his rather sullen men in line.

Be that as it may, they were all exhausted; consequentially, their tolerance was fraying quickly.

Andre was not exempt. His leg hurt like hell, and he was so sore he could barely stand up straight. But none of that mattered, not with the dire nature of their mission. It was a necessary sacrifice to save Winston.

We have to adapt, he thought. *Either that or we die.*

Andre joined them, barely receiving an acknowledgment. He forced an encouraging tone into his voice as he addressed them, "Final stage. We'll find somewhere to stow the horses, then travel into the city on foot."

"How are we going to sneak in?" The man's tone was underlined with frustration. "There are guards everywhere."

"The road is busy enough. We can find something to carry inside to stay inconspicuous. Something we can hide our weapons in."

"And once we're inside?"

"One step at a time. Let's move." Grabbing his pack, Andre mounted his horse, gritting his teeth against the pain in his legs.

The men did not hide their discomfort. They grumbled and groaned as they donned their packs and climbed on their horses. Even Thomilson made little effort to quiet them.

When they were ready, Andre led them out of the grove, looking for a suitable hiding place. It wasn't long until they discovered an abandoned farmhouse a half-mile from the main road. Picketing their horses in the barn, they explored the property for anything useful.

One of the men found an intact wagon on the side of the house, and the investigation of the storehouse yielded some large covered crates. They stashed their weapons in the crates, filling the rest with odds and ends they found around the property: Mostly hay, firewood, and apples. A quick search inside the farmhouse provided a few weather-stained cloaks.

Andre donned one of the cloaks, adding a floppy-brimmed hat to complete his disguise, as he was more likely to be recognized than the others. He hooked a knife to his belt, then, after a brief moment of consideration, slung his bow over his shoulder and hung his quiver from his belt. He wanted access to something a little deadlier than a dagger in case they ran into trouble. A bow wouldn't raise questions that he couldn't think of an answer for.

Once they finished preparing for entry, they hitched a couple of the horses to the wagon (much to the animals' displeasure) and set off towards the city. Thomilson sat up front with Andre, driving the horses while the rest of the rebels rode in the back of the wagon.

The road grew more crowded as they neared Seruvia's gate. Merchants, travelers, and workers made a steady stream of moving bodies. Beggars shuffled through the crowd, shaking tins, or sat in the shadow of the gate, eyeing the uncaring travelers miserably. Soldiers watched impetuously over all.

Andre could feel his men growing more tense as they drew near the city's open maw and forced himself to relax. The presence of soldiers set him on edge as well, but he hoped his calm example would ease his men's agitation. Taking a deep breath, he bowed his head as they passed through the gates into Seruvia.

"Halt!"

Andre's stomach flipped, but he ignored the call, hoping it was directed to someone else.

"You there, in the wagon! Halt!" A guard appeared in front of them, palm held outward.

No such luck. He nudged Thomilson, who pulled on the reigns, stopping the horses.

Two more guards approached them on either side, pushing through the crowd to reach them. One of the rebels in back made a movement towards the hidden weapons, but Andre gave him a look. Such a careless blunder would be suicide.

He turned his attention back to the guard in front. "Is there a problem?"

"What's your business here?" barked the guard in return.

"Just passing through." Andre kept his voice light. "We're traveling to Larathal."

Larathal was a small town near the coast, inhabited mostly by crabbers and junk collectors. Though he had never been, he was confident that the guards hadn't either.

"Passing through, huh?" The guard on the left pointed at the rest of the group. "All six of you? What's your business in Larathal?"

"Land," replied Andre, thinking quickly. He cursed at his foolishness in not preparing a cover story.

There was a pause. The guard looked at him expectantly. He peered back, feigning ignorance. By playing a fool, he hoped the guards would be annoyed enough to let them by. The flow of people passing through the gates parted around the wagon like a river current, completely ignoring the interaction taking place.

With a sigh, the guard made a "continue" motion with his hand.

Andre obliged with a shrug. "More specifically, we're looking at some land. Thinking about buying a piece of property out by the sea. They say the sea air is good for the soul, and I've always wanted to set my eyes on it. They say it's bigger than you can imagine. Travelin' has always tickled my fancy, so I says to myself, what better way than a trip to the coast?"

He took a breath, mentally kicking himself for stepping more into character as he rambled. Fatigue was making him sloppy. Fortunately, the guards didn't notice his voice and manner change.

"So anyway, me and these lads decided to go to Larathal and take a look at some land out there. And we all wanted to see for ourselves that it was satisfactory, see? Wouldn't do any good to buy a plot, and then someone who hasn't been hates it, eh?"

"That's a long journey," stated the third guard. "There aren't many supplies back here." He stood at the back of the wagon, trying to peer around those seated in the rear.

"Well, see, that's why we're stoppin' here." Andre exaggerated an eye roll, as if the guard was stupid. "We have to replenish and rest up a little. Sleepin' in the open countryside is hard on your rear, even in this beautiful weather we're havin'. Stay out here long enough, and you start developin' sores in spots I didn't even—"

"Alright, alright," interrupted the lead guard hurriedly. He pointed at the bow across Andre's back. "That's quite a handsome weapon you have there. Where'd you find it?"

Andre feigned offense. "What are you suggestin'? That a... a... *common folk* like me can't afford a nice bow?"

Looking slightly uncomfortable, the guard opened his mouth to say something, but Andre plowed ahead before he could speak. "For your information, I couldn't. My da passed it down to me. Some noble gifted it to him when he was young. Anyway, he gave it to me when I came of age, probably expectin' me to pass it to my own son when *he* comes of age, except I haven't found my a lady to settle down with."

The guard rolled his eyes at his companion, who wore a bemused look. "I can't imagine why," Andre heard him mutter under his breath.

Forcing down a chuckle, he continued his ramble. The guards were in the palm of his hand now. "Anyways, I use it for huntin' and defense. None of these lads can shoot worth an ox's yoke." He grinned broadly as he caught a glare from one of his men, like it was a private joke. "Wild animals and thieves and such, or bandits rather, seein' as we're travelin' on a road, can be—"

"OKAY! You're harmless. Move along!"

Andre tipped his hat. "Thank you kindly." He elbowed Thomilson.

The sergeant hurriedly twitched the reins, and the horses plodded forward through the gates. Glancing over his shoulder, Andre saw the soldiers returning to their posts. One of them was still shaking his head.

Thomilson whispered to Andre, "Did you plan that?"

"Nope," Andre said, unable to keep the grin from his face. "Fabricated it on the spot. We were lucky they were lazy. If they actually searched the wagon, we would have been in trouble."

They crawled through the streets. The markets were open. Large crowds milled about stalls full of food, stones, and other wares. People of all sorts flowed from vendor to vendor, lingering when something piqued their fancy, rather like the pigeons that hopped and fluttered in droves. Noise was master here: People, livestock, dogs—everything clamoring to be heard by something.

Craning his neck, Andre scanned the chaos for any clue about Winston. A flier on a nearby building caught his eye, and he pointed it out to one of the men, asking him to retrieve it. The man hopped out of the wagon, pushed his way through the throng, and tugged it from its nail. He made his way back, handing it to Andre.

It was a picture of Winston with a noose around his neck—a clear message for those who couldn't read the words that followed:

Trial of a Traitor
The Trial of Winston Servailles will occur at midday on the 16th of April.
The hearing will be held publicly in Dominus Square.
All are welcome to bear witness.

Andre read the second-to-last line again and grimaced. Dominus Square was in the heart of Seruvia, right in the shadow of Audax Keep. It would be packed with citizens, in addition to a healthy number of guards. It was going to be difficult to find a way close, much less break Winston out.

Thomilson frowned at the words. "What does it say?"

Andre read it to the rest of the group, raising his voice to be heard even in this proximity. "What day is it?"

Thomilson thought for a moment, his brow furrowed. "The fifteenth, isn't it?"

Just in time. Andre handed the flier to the sergeant. "How do you feel about a warm meal and bed tonight?"

Finding an available inn with enough space for the six of them turned out to be more difficult a task than they had bartered. Upon speaking to a few of the innkeepers who turned them away, Andre learned that Winston's trial was announced almost a week ago, and Seruvia had seen a large influx of visitors since. There was also excitement about another supposed event. Rumors that a Soothsayer would make an appearance were as numerous and flighty as the pigeons in the streets. As a result, most of the inns were full.

The band finally found a small hostel a few blocks from Dominus Square with rooms available and space for the wagon. As the men settled in, two to a room, Andre stepped outside to see if he could gather information.

The streets were very busy. Taking advantage of the increase in visitors, many businesses were open late into the afternoon. The festive garments of the shoppers and the colorful advertisements helped break up the otherwise drab, brick-red that seemed to be uniform for the new buildings. Posters for the trial were everywhere, fluttering in the evening breeze. With so much motion and life, Andre could almost ignore the air of unease accompanied by furtive looks of many people who waltzed by. One could pretend it was a normal market day in the city until one noticed the glowering soldiers posted on every corner.

Propped against a raised flower bed, Andre watched people pass, listening to their conversations. The snippets he caught were, as he suspected, almost entirely about Winston.

"They say he just walked right in. All alone."

"It's a plot to kill the chancellor. Servailles is a genius, you know. Something will happen tomorrow, mark my words."

"I've heard he's given up. His rebellion is finished before it even started."

"Well I heard—"

"In my opinion—"

"He's mad. I've always said—"

After a while, he stood. There was nothing useful here. *Might as well rest and plan for tomorrow.*

"Nothing catching your eye?"

Andre stopped and glanced around for the source of the voice, noticing a man leaning casually against a gutter less than ten yards away. The stranger wore a cloak with the hood pulled up, shadowing his face. His mouth was visible, an odd smile hovering on his lips.

Andre's hand crept to the knife hidden under his cloak. "I'm not one for markets."

Stepping closer, the man pushed his hood back, revealing a thin face. The smile no longer seemed threatening.

Andre relaxed. *I'm too wound up,* he realized. It was a sign of how exhausted he was that he saw enemies everywhere.

"Neither am I." The man had an odd accent, more prim than a typical Corynthian, although there were people from numerous foreign countries who called this land home. "I prefer watching. It gives me a fresh perspective."

"Hmm." Andre wondered why he was telling him this.

"Although, an odd trinket occasionally catches my fancy," the man continued, unaware of his disinterest. "You traveled here for the trial, then?" he inquired suddenly.

Andre stopped his slow retreat to the door. "Yes. It's quite an event." He stared at the stranger, who watched him benignly.

"Indeed. Was it a long journey? You look weary."

"A little." Did the stranger know something, or was his paranoia taking advantage of him again?

"I would rest well tonight, if I were you." The man turned away, though not before Andre caught a sparkle in his eye. "Tomorrow should be an eventful day." Disappearing into the crowd, he left Andre staring after him in confusion.

Still trying to make sense of his interaction, Andre stepped back inside the inn. As he climbed the stairs to their floor, the sound of voices shook him out of his thoughts about the curious conversation. He paused on the landing to listen. It sounded like Markus Thomilson and one of his men.

"Where's the trouble? We're in the heart of Corynthia."

Andre couldn't remember the man's name. He hadn't engaged much with Thomilson's squad on the ride to Seruvia—another thing he regretted. It was important for an officer to build relationships with his soldiers. It allowed for a closer, more trusting bond. However, his worry about Winston left him far too preoccupied to form any connection with them.

"Kent, we have no insurance for ourselves," Thomilson replied. "If we move forward with what you suggest and make it out alive, there's no guarantee we'll be safe. And we wouldn't be able to return because, well, hell..."

"This is a suicide mission, Markus," snapped Kent. "I didn't sign up for this—none of us did. Even if we somehow survive, we're still fighting a war against the entirety of loyalist Corynthia. I would rather act now than die for a pointless cause."

"Pointless? What happened to your resolve?"

"My desire to live is stronger. If fighting for the rebellion means facing impossible odds over and over, I want no part in it."

"You knew it wouldn't all be victory and glory, Kent. This is war."

"But I thought I would have a chance!"

Andre shifted his weight, and the floor creaked. The voices went silent.

He swore silently. He needed to move now or be found eavesdropping. Deliberately slamming the door, he advanced down the corridor at an even pace. Since his room was beyond Thomilson's, he paused in the doorway, acting as though he were merely passing by.

The sergeant sat on his bed, while Kent stood against the wall. Both men were staring at the open door.

"I thought I heard your voice, Markus," Andre remarked lightly, leaning against the frame.

A look of distress flashed across Thomilson's face for a moment. Just as quickly, it was replaced with one of polite interest.

"I would like to speak with you about tomorrow. Have you had dinner yet?"

"No, sir. Not yet."

"May I join you?"

"Of course, sir."

Kent excused himself from the room.

"Close the door, please," requested Andre as he left. His men were the only lodgers on the floor. Still, one could never be too careful of eavesdroppers.

Sitting across from the sergeant, he briefly mulled over what he heard in the hallway. Kent's frustration was understandable; their odds were certainly not favorable. However, he couldn't afford his men to abandon him now, not when so much depended on tomorrow.

Blast it, Winston. If they made it out alive, he was going to give him the beating of his life.

He fixed Thomilson in a serious stare. "Is everything alright, Markus?"

Thomilson grimaced, then released a tired chuckle. In his mid-twenties, he was an unassuming man with a patchy beard and a strong nose. Half of his right eyebrow was missing. "Yes, sir. I have everything under control."

Andre watched his face for a moment, then nodded. He had to trust the man. Thomilson hadn't let him down yet, and he had no other choice.

After nearly an hour of swapping ideas for the next day, a rough plan was formulated. Obviously, there was a high possibility that something would run awry. For that reason, they kept it simple. The wagon would stay behind. It was too bulky for the packed streets and would only draw attention. Instead, they would mingle with the multitudes, hiding their swords under their cloaks as best they could. The tightly packed bodies would render them nearly invisible against the guards on lookout, keeping them safe from discovery until, of course, they made their move.

Plan in mind and now with ravenous appetites, Andre and Thomilson migrated to the dining area, where the others were eating dinner. After Andre instructed them to meet him in his room later that evening, he sat down to eat a plate of roast squash and baked chicken.

About thirty minutes later, everyone was packed in Andre's room while he relayed the plan with Thomilson. The men were quiet as they listened, yet Andre still felt a hint of resentment in their manner. Kent, especially, seemed unable to wipe the scowl off his face.

DOMINUS SQUARE

ANDRE WALKED INTO THE dining area to find his men already awake and eating breakfast. Thomilson gave him a nod as he pulled up a chair next to the sergeant. The others remained absorbed in their food.

"How did you sleep?" Andre inquired.

"Fine, sir, thanks. You?"

"Alright." He omitted his misgivings that kept him awake most of the night. "Are your men ready?"

"As ready as they'll ever be." Thomilson was silent for a moment. He opened his mouth as if to say something, then closed it again.

"Something you want to add, sergeant?"

"No sir. Just wondering if we'll make it out alive."

Andre clapped him on the back. "Don't worry. We will. Just keep your head, along with the plan, and we'll be fine. Now, where can I find some breakfast?"

Thomilson pointed to where servers were passing in and out of the kitchen with platters of fresh food, setting them on a long table against the wall. It appeared breakfast was included with their stay.

Andre grabbed a plate and heaped it with roasted potatoes and sausage, smiling at a young serving girl who passed by with a stack of dirty dishes. Blushing, she awkwardly curtsied before hurriedly ducking into the kitchen.

As Andre ate, the door to the inn opened, and a man moseyed inside, weaving his way to the bar where the innkeeper lazily surveyed the room.

Andre half-listened in on the pair.

"What'll it be, Denner?" the owner asked.

"I'm not staying," Denner stated. "The trial is happening in an hour. They've already brought out Servailles."

Andre looked up, paying full attention, as Denner continued.

"It sounds like we'll see the Soothsayer, too. Can you tell Sam when he drags his lazy shanks out of bed? I'd tell him meself, but I want to save us a good spot."

"An hour? That I can."

"Thanks, Harry. Are you going to come watch?"

"I'll try to get away."

The men bid each other farewell, and Denner turned to leave.

Andre looked over at Thomilson, who stared back. *You heard?* he mouthed. Thomilson nodded.

Standing up and rushed over to Denner, Andre grabbed him by the arm before he could leave the building. "I'm sorry. You said the trial is in an hour?"

Alarmed by his sudden appearance, Denner nodded apprehensively.

Andre released the man. He could feel Harry the innkeeper's eyes on him. "And they've already brought out Winst—er, Servailles? How many people are attending?" *How many guards are there?* was what he wanted to ask, but refrained.

"Um—didn't count," Denner replied with a shrug. "May I go?" he added sarcastically, raising an eyebrow at the innkeeper.

"Yes." Andre patted the man on the arm. "Sorry for my intensity, friend."

Denner gave him a tight smile and excused himself.

Turning back to the men at the table, Andre saw them watching him, their faces a mixture of alarm and displeasure.

"Ready and outside in fifteen minutes."

They grumbled to each other until Thomilson caught Andre's look and barked at them to move.

Andre noticed Harry the innkeeper watching them. He walked over and slid a coin across the counter-top. "Best forget about this if you would like to keep your business." He turned away, adding, "And your life."

He was the first outside, his sword and bow, which was stored in a birch wood tube, hidden under his cloak. The others joined him shortly, all clad in cloaks that hid their armor and weapons. When everyone was gathered, they set out for Dominus Square.

The streets grew busier the closer they drew to Audax Keep. Excited conversation about the upcoming event filled the air like the chatter of birds. Vendors advertised their wares at the top of their lungs. Nobody seemed to care about the cloud front rolling in or the chill wind.

Andre looked up at the sky, pregnant with the promise of foul weather. *Seems like it might rain. Lovely.*

It took nearly an hour to reach Dominus Square. The streets were tightly packed with people all jostling each other as they advanced towards the same destination. The rebels repeatedly stopped to move aside for wagons and carts clattering down the road, their drivers shouting mercilessly at anyone in the way. Troops of soldiers also tramped through the streets; people needed no encouragement to step out of their way. Every time soldiers appeared, Andre and his men ducked into a side alley to avoid even a brief moment of contact, drawing stares from the dirty vagrants who had made their homes there. As a result of all of the delays, Andre was quite frustrated by the time they finally arrived at Dominus Square.

They stepped into the crowd as Tench was finishing up his address at the podium.

Craning his neck at the stage, Andre sensed tension in the atmosphere. The air tasted sour. Whispers and mutterings from the people swirled like a second breeze through the square.

We missed something, he realized. Some people were nursing injuries or supporting others out of the square. Andre noticed that Tench's darkened brow as he sat down at the back of the stage.

Filling the remainder of the seats was an assortment of men and women he knew to be part of Corynthia's senate. There was also a young man he didn't recognize sitting right next to the chancellor. He looked ill at ease, eyes flitting constantly over the crowd. He appeared unlikely to be a threat, so Andre dismissed him and found Winston sitting alone on the other side of the stage.

Looking bored, his friend was staring vaguely into the crowd.

Andre next turned his attention to the guards. A formidable line of them stood at attention in front of the stage, all wearing a gold rose on their tunic. Rose Soldiers—a whole company of them.

He groaned quietly. While he expected them, they were still an unpleasant sight.

Well-trained and merciless, Rose Soldiers were the best of the best, selected specifically to protect the chancellor. Under Tench's rule, they had become downright ruthless with nearly free rein to do as they pleased when it came to matters of enforcement. Andre preferred to avoid engaging them when at all possible. It seemed it might be difficult to avoid them here.

Regular guards were posted at each of the square's entrances, while archers on neighboring roofs watched over the crowd. The square was well guarded.

Andre grimly decided that using the crowd as a buffer would be to no avail, especially since Tench's soldiers had no restraints. There would be too many casualties. *I need to think of an alternative...* His eye found Tench again, and he smiled.

While the string of judges began their work naming the plethora of Winston's crimes against Corynthia, Andre whispered to Thomilson and his men to spread out through the crowd. "Wait for my signal."

They began to disperse. One of them stopped and turned back. "What *is* your signal?"

"You'll know it when you see it."

He stared at him a moment, then nodded, vanishing after the others.

The hearing dragged on. The judges sent accusations Winston's way, peppering him with questions designed to trap him into a confession. Winston answered listlessly. It began to drizzle. Andre could feel the mood of the people change, their excitement fizzling into disappointment. The crowd began to thin, which lifted some of the weight off of his chest. He would feel better with more elbow-room to operate.

After what felt like hours of judges droning allegations. a short man in a violet robe stepped up to the podium, and Andre heard a man next to him grumble, "Finally. He's the last one, I think. What a waste of my damn time."

Smirking at his words, Andre slipped the tube containing his bow out from his cloak. He would give the crowd something to remember. He carefully slid the weapon out and strung it. Nobody noticed his movement, and he looked around for one of his squad. Finding one, he caught his eye and signaled him to alert the others. Then, he nocked an arrow to wait.

Finally, the last judge stepped away from the podium.

As Tench stood up, Andre sidled closer to the stage. He kept his bow down, moving quickly, but smoothly, so as not to draw the attention of the soldiers too soon. He kept his eye on his target, visualizing his mark.

A couple moved in front of Andre as Tench began his closing statement, right as he began to draw the arrow back on its string.

He growled and shouted at them, raising his bow. "Out of the way! MOVE!"

Heads swiveled towards him. The couple screamed, diving out of the way at the sight of the weapon. Shouts of surprise escorted the arrow to its target as Andre released the string. It flew true, burying itself in the soft wood of the pulpit, inches from Tench's hand.

Tripping backwards, the chancellor fell as the crowd scrambled away from Andre, creating a clearing around him.

Andre pulled another arrow from the quiver at his hip, fitting it to the string. "TENCH!" he bellowed. He moved forward slowly, his bow trained on the chancellor.

There was complete silence as Tench picked himself back up and straightened his garments. "Halt!" he shouted, throwing a hand out in protest. "Guards!"

The Rose Soldiers advanced, drawing their weapons as they went.

"I wouldn't," warned Andre calmly, still approaching the stage. "Arrows fly a lot faster than men can run, and I *don't* miss." He thought he saw a touch of panic in the chancellor's tomato-red face.

"Stop moving! Don't take another step!"

"Or what?" Andre challenged savagely. He glanced at Winston, who sat in his chair with a big smile on his face, as though it were his birthday. "Are you alright?"

Winston laced his fingers behind his head. "Never better! I was curious if you were waiting until the actual execution to rescue me."

"Be silent!" Tench growled at him. "Where are the rest of your men?" he demanded to Andre. "I know *you* aren't foolish enough to come alone."

"They're around. Six dozen men ready to spring into action at my signal."

Or they've melted into the crowd and left me for dead.

Nobody else had made a move since he fired the arrow. The conversation he overheard between Kent and Thomilson resurfaced unpleasantly, like sewage in a reservoir.

"Six dozen?" Tench sneered. "I don't believe you, Cordon. Guards!"

Andre let loose the second arrow. Several people screamed, but it skipped off the boards at Tench's feet, ricocheting back into the enthralled crowd. The chancellor hopped in place with a strangled yelp, his face darkening to puce. If the situation wasn't so delicate, Andre would have laughed.

"Here's what will happen, Tench," announced Andre, another arrow already drawn. "Winston is going to come down, then we shall walk back through the crowd. You will not send men after us. We will be on our merry way, and you can be on yours."

"Why shall I not stop you, pray tell?"

"Because"—he leveled his weapon at Tench's face—"this next arrow will be buried in your throat if you do. Winston, it's time to leave."

Standing, Winston stretched dramatically. "Excellent. The weather's turned quite unpleasant." He hopped off of the stage and casually walked through the guards, who looked at Tench for orders.

Tench said nothing, though a look of intense hatred burned on his face. He was a coward at heart, and Andre knew he valued his own life above even revenge.

Joining Andre, Winston turned to address the chancellor. "Well, this has certainly been an enjoyable reunion, Berling; however, I'm afraid you'll have to reschedule that execution. At least I'm assuming that was the final verdict—it's not like anyone has much of a say over what you want."

Tench curled his lip. "You can run, Servailles, but you *cannot* hide from me. I will hunt you down like the *cur* you are, then you shall see what my final verdict is."

"How original," Winston quipped lightly. "In any case, I have a tyrant to overthrow. Goodbye, Berling!" He saluted mockingly and began to strut away.

Andre backed up with him, still aiming his arrow at the fuming chancellor.

Winston suddenly stopped.

"*What?*" hissed Andre. His arm was growing tired, yet he refused to relax it until they were out of the square.

Winston wheeled to address the young man Andre noticed at the beginning of the trial. Unlike the others on the stage, he was still seated, a look of quiet interest on his face.

"If you decide to join the rebellion..." Winston shrugged. "Well, I'm sure you'll be able to find us."

"He won't be going anywhere!" Tench cried with a laugh. "He's mine!"

"There you have it!" Winston turned to the people gathered in Dominus Square and spread his arms. "Your chancellor! The man you put in charge! Arrogant, selfish, despotic, and furthermore, a damn enslaver!

"I told him." He pointed to the young man Andre now realized must be the Soothsayer. "I warned him you would take the only thing he has left—his freedom!" His finger swiveled towards Tench. "You are not in their good graces, *chancellor*! You may have beaten them, robbed them, imprisoned them—*killed their families*—but such actions will only return as consequences far more grievous upon your own head!"

"Winston," Andre warned: Tench's face was growing more and more purple under his mustache. Guards were pushing their way through the crowd on both sides of them. Worryingly, there was still no sign of Thomilson.

Winston didn't hear him. "We were making something good, Berling! Corynthia was supposed to become a garden, yet you turned it into a graveyard!"

"Winston!" Andre shouted. "We need to leave, now!"

Winston spun around. "I'm not finished."

"GUARDS!" screamed Tench, his eyes blazing with rage. The soldiers scrambled towards them.

"Oh," remarked Winston. "You're right."

"*Go!*" Andre shouted, firing his arrow at the nearest soldier. It skewered him in the thigh, and he went down with a cry.

The pair turned heel and broke into a run. The crowd parted around them and closed back together as they passed, hindering Tench's men.

As they fled, Andre threw his bow across his shoulders and shouted for Thomilson, more in desperation than with any real conviction. To his surprise, the sergeant and his men appeared next to them.

"Where the *hell* were you?!" cried Andre as they ran through the streets, shoving aside astonished onlookers. Neither Thomilson nor any of his men answered.

"After them!"

Andre risked a glance behind him. The guards had forced their way out of Dominus Square and were now struggling through the chaos that the rebels left behind.

Winston pointed to a side street. "Go there!"

The others followed him. It was a narrow alley with crates stacked against the wall, and side doors to the shops on the main road. An opening beckoned at the other end. Quickly, the group sprinted towards it.

Before they advanced far into the alley, a door opened, and a figure ran in front of them. They all skidded to a halt. Andre pushed Winston behind him and raised his weapon.

"No," the newcomer uttered, in a vaguely familiar accent. "Inside."

They looked at each other for a second before Andre whispered, "Go."

They crowded through the door without question.

Sprinting further down the alleyway, Andre kicked over some crates to make it appear they had passed all the way through, then rushed back. The stranger stepped in behind him, closing the door and throwing them into darkness.

II

THE BOOKKEEPER

THE DARKNESS WAS BROKEN by a match. In the brief moment of illumination, Andre saw the stranger put a finger to his lips. The light fizzled out again.

Nobody moved. As far as Andre could tell, nobody breathed.

He heard the sound of rushing footsteps and raised voices through the door as what sounded like an entire army careened through the alley. They waited until the crash of weapons and armor faded before letting out a collective breath.

"They're gone."

"How about another light?" That was Winston.

With the sound of some rummaging, another match was lit. The stranger held it to a lantern he acquired in the darkness.

A mild glow breathed the room into being. They stood in some sort of storeroom. There were barrels stacked in the corners in addition to shelves laden with boxes and scrolls lining the walls, which were made of pockmarked stucco. More boxes sat at the base of the shelves, filled to the brim with parchment and other materials.

Andre turned his attention to their rescuer and started. It was the man who approached him back at the inn.

He wore a simple cloth shirt and trousers that hung loosely around his tall, lean frame. A faint white scar crossed his cheek, tracing its way down his thin face. Dirty-blond hair, longer on top than the sides, limply covered his scalp. He looked back with soft, slightly mournful, green eyes. There was a different air about him this time. He was reserved and analytical, rather than the chatty, grating person Andre met earlier.

Winston broke the silence, "I recognize you. You were there in the square."

The man merely looked at him. "Let's talk inside. The soldiers might come back." He led the way through a door on the other side of the room into another dark chamber.

They stood in the doorway as the stranger moved around the room, lighting more lanterns. The space was slowly illuminated to reveal a circular room with tall bookshelves set in concentric circles and stuffed with books. Dusty, honey-colored curtains covered the windows, blocking the gloomy glow from outside. A ladder for reaching the top of the bookshelves leaned in the corner like a sulking child.

The stranger told them to make themselves at home. They did so, drawing chairs at the two round tables in the middle of the room, and stared silently at their surroundings.

Andre was astonished by how many books there were. He opened his mouth to ask the stranger about them, but was interrupted by a rap on the outer door from which they entered.

"I'll handle them." Their host's voice cut through the sudden scrape of swords being drawn. "Excuse me." He left, closing the door behind him.

As they listened to the muffled voices on the other side, Thomilson leaned forward to whisper to Andre, "What do you think? Can we trust him?"

"He was there," murmured Winston.

"What?" Andre looked at him.

He appeared thoughtful. "He was at the trial, watching me before it started. He winked at me and left."

"So..." Andre spoke slowly, "we can trust him because he... winked at you."

"Well, I was thinking more because he saved our lives. I just remembered."

The door opened again, and they fell silent. The stranger reentered, looking entirely unconcerned about the soldiers. "Are you hungry?" he addressed the entire group.

"Yes, please!" Winston exclaimed enthusiastically.

The others made grunts of approval. Andre's stomach growled in agreement. The trial had dallied much longer than he anticipated. Breakfast seemed like forever ago.

"I'll return in a moment, then. Feel free to explore." The stranger disappeared through a second door in the chamber.

Looking around the room again, Andre felt more relaxed now. The thought of food in his stomach made him trust the stranger a little more.

Winston stood up and began to browse the shelves. Andre joined him, tilting his head sideways to read the titles. Some of them were in languages that he didn't recognize. Most of the books looked quite new; their colors were full, material unblemished.

"They don't seem to be put to much use." Reaching out, he ran a finger down the spine of a handsome red and blue volume with the title *Trade Trails of the North*. It came away with a thin film of dust.

"Yeah, well, who has any use for reading?" grunted Thomilson from the table. He was picking at his nails with a knife, flicking dirt across the table. "Waste of time."

"You'd be surprised." The quiet voice made them jump.

The stranger had returned, entering the room without making a noise. Andre supposed that when one lived alone with only books for company, one became quite adept at sneaking up on people. He carried a platter arranged with loaves of bread and slices of cured ham, as well as a rucksack over one shoulder. He placed the platter on the table.

Andre, his stomach growling, dug in alongside his men.

After he inhaled a quarter of a loaf of bread and three slices of ham, he looked up at the man. "Thank you. Not just for the food. I don't think we would have made it far without your intervention."

The others made hearty noises of agreement through their chewing. One of them stood up and clapped the stranger on the back.

He bowed. "It's my pleasure. I'm Declan, by the way. Declan Row."

They introduced themselves in turn. Winston, still immersed in his book, was silent; though, Andre figured Declan knew who he was.

"You're a bookkeeper?"

"Yes. Though there isn't much business to be had. People underestimate the potential found in literature."

Thomilson snorted, spewing crumbs across the table, and hurriedly tried to cover it up with a cough.

Andre cringed, but Declan merely glanced at him before continuing with a small smile.

"There is no greater advantage over the general public than being able to read and write. No weapon is more powerful than a keen and educated mind. Your friend over there knows what I speak of." Declan nodded at Winston. "Literacy is the absolute tool for control. Alas," he sighed, "it is too often overlooked. People would rather be practical than ambitious, and sharpen their swords instead of their minds. They'd rather stay *ordinary*." He spat out the last word with an odd vehemence.

Andre studied Declan. He seemed quiet and mellow, which, combined with his slim figure, painted quite a nonthreatening character. However, he sensed a very clever and zealous mind behind his soft green eyes and decided he would make a very dangerous enemy.

He let out a slightly nervous laugh. "You feel strongly about this, then?"

"I just wish I had more business."

Andre laughed again, this time genuinely, and looked over at Winston. "Whatever this man says, books can't fill your stomach," he called. "Unless you would like to try."

Winston seemed to remember that he hadn't eaten in hours. Replacing the book carefully on the shelf, he sat down and grabbed a piece of bread. Taking a bite, he brandished the rest at Declan. "You have quite the collection of history," he stated thickly, his mouth full. "Dago Roark, Arche Kallius, *Age of the Ivory Crowns*. Quite a collection, indeed. I'm Winston Servailles, by the way."

"I know." Declan nodded at the bookshelves. "It's a highly interesting subject."

"What's so interesting about history?" Kent uttered. Kicking his feet onto the table, he rocked back in his chair. "Isn't it just muddling through dusty maps and pages of gibberish? What king married what princess, and who lost which meaningless war? I don't see much of a point."

A couple of the other men snickered. Thankfully, Declan didn't seem to take offense at Kent's insolence.

"History is full of important lessons. It helps us understand change and learn from past mistakes. It builds critical thinking, while broadening the mind when addressing new political and moral occurrences. It also helps predict future events. History is our greatest teacher."

Kent frowned and looked around at his peers, who appeared equally lost.

"*If* you're willing to learn," Declan added.

Thomilson cleared his throat. "I hate to break up this scholarly discussion, but we need to talk about our predicament here. We're trapped in the middle of Seruvia, which is definitely crawling with loyalist soldiers, and we're sitting in a dimly lit library. Now, this is all fine with me, until they start searching buildings. We barely escaped Dominus Square—how are we going to survive this?" He looked around at the group, raising his one-and-a-half eyebrows as though expecting an answer.

Andre suddenly remembered that he was upset at the sergeant. "Speaking of Dominus Square—where the bloody *hell* were you? I ordered you to wait for my signal. I was under the impression you had my back!"

The men had the decency to look sheepish.

Thomilson scratched his neck. "Well, sir, to be honest, we weren't sure what your signal was. You didn't exactly tell us."

"*You weren't—*" Andre stopped in disbelief. "I FIRED AN ARROW AT THE CHANCELLOR OF CORYNTHIA! WHAT MORE OF A SIGNAL DO YOU NEED?!"

"We were ready if things got ugly," Thomilson backpedaled quickly.

"They *did* get ugly sergeant!"

Andre saw Winston open his mouth out of the corner of his eye, but continued before he could interject. Maybe this wasn't the right time to chew the men out. It didn't matter; he was too angry to care.

Even though he tried to ignore it, the confrontation with Tench left him shaken. Standing in the middle of a silent crowd, bow drawn on the most powerful man in Corynthia while a hundred blood-thirsty soldiers glowered at him from all sides, had been no easy task. Doing it alone had been even more harrowing.

"I was standing there, *alone!* If I didn't have an arrow on Tench, I would have been torn apart! Was that your plan?"

Winston hissed at him to lower his voice. Andre waved him off, though he continued in a slightly quieter tone.

"Let me try to rescue Winston while you blend safely into the crowd? Bloody brilliant idea! After all, if I failed, you could slip out of Seruvia, and none would be the wiser!"

"No, sir. That's not what happened, I swear. We just—"

"Sergeant, I heard your conversation with Kent. You told me everything was under control. Did you lie to me?"

The men looked very uncomfortable at that. Winston raised his eyebrows, now more interested than chagrined.

Thomilson sighed. "I guess I just froze," he said slowly with a glance at Kent. "It won't happen again."

"It better not! Because next time, the deaths of these men will be on *your* head."

Kent suddenly brandished a finger at Andre. "This isn't our fault! You led us into this suicide mission! We're under pressure because of you!"

Andre turned his glare towards Kent, who swallowed and flushed, but held his gaze. "General Draytus gave me a glowing report that you could handle this mission. I would expect nothing less from someone he recommends."

Winston put his arm around Andre's shoulders. "They're also human, and they have far less experience than you in dire situations. The odds are stacked against us; thus, mistakes are to be expected. Your frustration is valid; however, this is not an appropriate time. We'll report them to General Draytus for disciplinary action when we return. Right now we need to trust each other."

Thomilson and the others hung their heads at Winston's words, except for Kent, who merely glared.

Andre huffed before remembering the reason they were there in the first place.

"Now wait a damn minute." He whirled around to Winston, slapping his hand away. "None of this would have happened if you hadn't decided to embark on the *sorriest* excuse of a mission I've *ever* witnessed! I cannot *believe* the audacity—after you *agreed*—tried to get yourself *killed*—"

Andre lapsed into spluttering, too angry to form full words. All of the frustration from the past month flooded out of him at once. His own failure at the outpost, combined with the subconscious dread plaguing him since Winston revealed his plan at Liberá, erupted all together, flooding out of him in incoherent outrage.

Winston waited patiently for Andre to subside before giving him a small smile that only made him scowl more. "Andre, you know this mission was vital. I needed to speak with him."

"You could've been killed!"

"Victory begets risk," Winston rejoined firmly. "It's the peril of war—you, of all people, should know that. I took a risk, and by the grace of the All-Mother, it paid off."

"Did it? Where's your Soothsayer now?"

"Enough." Visibly frustrated, Winston's tone made it perfectly clear he was finished with the conversation.

Andre wasn't going to be dismissed so easily.

"That *boy* looked perfectly happy to sit behind Tench's protection! Face it, Winston, you were tricked! You're chasing a hoax! You and some good men were almost killed because of it!"

"*Enough!* I don't expect you to read the signs, but I did! Do not condemn me for acting! You didn't have to follow me—that was *your* decision."

"You didn't give me a choice!"

"There's always a choice, Andre. Sometimes it requires sacrifice." Winston turned to Declan before Andre could retaliate, killing any retort.

The bookkeeper was leaning against a shelf, his face partially covered in the shadows lingering around the flickering light from the lanterns.

"Is there a way out of Seruvia that doesn't involve fighting hundreds of guards through a maze of buildings?" Winston inquired.

"Actually," Declan announced, moving back into the light, "there is. Follow me."

The men trailed after the bookkeeper to the first room.

Still seething, Andre hung back for a moment to take a deep breath before following. As a result, their escape route was already open when he joined the others.

It was a small hole in the wall that had been hidden behind one of the crates. The passage beyond, too dark to make out details, looked tight and damp. Andre wrinkled his nose as he looked at it; he hated enclosed spaces.

"Here," Declan announced.

There was silence as the men stared at the hole.

Andre felt a strange pull as he peered into the darkness. It was as though his soul was being drawn from his body into the abyss before him. Barely discernible whispers seemed to seep out of the shadows, attempting to seduce him with promises beyond his comprehension. He didn't believe in magic, yet something about the tunnel unsettled him in a way that wasn't natural, almost as though there was a hole in reality.

Shaking himself, he glanced at the others. All of them, except for Declan, stared blankly at the hole.

"What is this?" Andre demanded, shattering the stillness.

"Our way out."

I would rather fight the soldiers. "I gathered, but where does it lead?"

"Into the catacombs," Declan stated forbiddingly. "It passes under the city." The words carried an unmistakable hint of menace, causing a chill to run down Andre's spine.

There was a look in Declan's eyes he didn't like—a covetous, almost perverted expression. As soon as Andre noticed it, however, it was gone.

The bookkeeper gestured to the group. "Follow me." Crouching down, he crawled into the passage.

Andre glanced at Winston, his anger forgotten. Winston gave him a smile of forced cheerfulness and ducked into the hole after Declan. Swallowing back the revulsion forming in his throat, Andre reluctantly followed.

12

TUNNELS OF THE PAST

T HE TUNNEL WAS, IF possible, even more unpleasant than Winston imagined. The walls were cold and clammy to the touch, making him shudder every time he brushed them, which was often since the passage wasn't very large. He swore he could hear voices whispering to him from the darkness, accompanied by the feeling of miniature hands tugging at his clothes. It was as though the darkness desired to hold him down and trap him there. He kept unconsciously swatting the air around him.

"Declan?" He forced himself to speak above a whisper.

"Yes?" the bookkeeper's voice came back from in front of Winston, calm and unconcerned.

"I don't like this." He felt like a child. "How much longer?"

"Nearly there."

Winston returned to crawling in silence. The tunnel slanted down now, forcing him to shift his weight so as not to fall into the bookkeeper. It felt as though they had been in the tunnel forever.

Suddenly, his face was smothered by the backside of Declan in front of him. "What in—"

Declan spoke, "There's a ladder at the end of the tunnel. I'm going to climb down and strike a light. Don't move until you see it." His voice remained quiet, although it carried a tone of authoritative warning that made Winston suck in his breath.

He heard a whisper behind him as Declan's words were passed along to the end of the line.

With the sound of squeaking metal, Declan descended the ladder. The noise faded, and they sat in the dreadful darkness as whispers swirled around them. The voices seemed to grow more agitated in the bookkeeper's absence. After a few moments, a faint light came to life at the end of the tunnel. Its glow seemed to chase away the whispers, and Winston let out a breath.

"Let's go."

He crawled towards the opening, trying to not seem too eager. In the closeness of the tunnel, the darkness felt alive and hungry. He was anxious to be out of it. Climbing through a metal grate and down a rusty ladder, Winston skipped the last two rungs, landing heavily on the ground. He straightened himself with slight difficulty (his legs were stiff from crawling) and looked around, wiping his sweaty hands on his trousers.

He stood in what appeared to be a huge sewer. The tunnel was tube-shaped, the walls curving up and over their heads. Winston estimated the space to be about forty feet wide and a little over half as tall. The floor was a smooth, gray path, while the walls were made from yellow stone brick. No other colors popped out in the light, just the uniform pattern of brick and mortar.

Despite the monotonous design, something struck Winston as odd. He peered closer at the wall, unable to place what was bothering him. He reached out to run his hand on the surface, almost mechanically. The whispers were back, egging him on. His fingers were inches away—

"Stop! Don't touch the walls!"

Winston's hand fell to his side.

Declan stood arm outstretched, finger pointing at him almost accusingly. There was a fierce look on his face, somewhere between hunger and jealousy.

Winston stepped back. "I won't." He raised an eyebrow carefully, unsure from the bookkeeper's ferocity.

Those present looked between the two men uncomfortably. Water dripped from somewhere further down the tunnel, echoing menacingly in the silence.

The last man climbed down the ladder and collapsed at the bottom, providing a welcome distraction. It was Kent. He was white and shaking as he climbed clumsily to his feet. "Never..." he panted, "never again... am I going... last." He bent over, retching.

Andre helped him straighten up. "We should go," he told Declan. Even he looked a little green.

The bookkeeper held out another lantern to him, lifting his own. "Follow me, then. Stay together. Don't touch anything."

Moving through them, he advanced down the yawning tunnel. The group huddled closer to each other and followed after him.

Winston walked a little apart from the others, still wary of Andre. His friend's anger was justified: He *had* lied to him, although it had been necessary. The Soothsayer was a crucial key to winning this war—Winston had never been so sure of something in his life. Besides, the adventure was exhilarating. Exile didn't agree with him. It was boring laying low and biding his time, as well as very mundane building an army. He didn't *mind* doing it; however, a death-defying escapade into enemy territory had been very much needed.

The tunnels seemed to stretch on forever, endless possibilities branching out in every direction. Even so, Declan walked confidently, taking turns without hesitation. There was no change in their surroundings. The walls stayed yellow, curved, and intriguing.

Winston studied them as they went, finally realizing what was wrong. They were too smooth—no sign of aging, chipping, or crumbling; not even a pockmark. It was unnatural.

With questions burning on his tongue, he sped up to walk beside Declan. "What *is* this place?"

Declan didn't answer for a moment, an unreadable expression on his face. Finally: "It was a transit network built ages ago for people to move quickly about the city."

"Ages?" Winston was surprised by the word. He knew that Seruvia was one of the oldest cities in Corynthia, but ages gave the impression it was far older than he thought.

"This city is far older than you think," Declan explained, as though he read Winston's mind. "It's one of the oldest cities on the continent. Once, it had a different name before it became Seruvia. It also used to be much larger."

Winston, under the impression he was about to be given a history lesson, obliged gladly. On top of his own interest in history, it would keep his mind off of the unnaturalness of their surroundings. "Do tell."

"These foundations were built long before the idea of Kaval was even nurtured. Back when the world was ruled by another race."

"Another race?" He had never heard of such a thing.

"The Athere. They were an ancient, powerful people, gifted with ingenuity and creativity far beyond your comprehension. They didn't just build, you see; they breathed life into their creations. These catacombs are *alive*, imbued with ancient magic. This is a dangerous place." He glanced sidelong at Winston.

With a nervous chuckle, Winston glanced at the shadows flitting at the edge of the lantern light. He thought about the whispers again. "Don't touch the walls—I remember. That's why they're so smooth, then?"

"They were designed to withstand aging; thus, their very existence opposes the passage of time. They look the same now as they did thousands of years ago. The past is brought to the present, here."

"Intriguing." Winston felt a jolt of excitement at Declan's words.

Magic. It was such a touchy subject. While he took a keen interest in it, he found himself never able to discuss the topic. Most people didn't believe magic was real; that it was made up for children's fairy tales, much like Soothsayers. However, Winston could never bring himself to dismiss it like everyone else. This, of course, led to much scoffing among his colleagues; nevertheless, he was unperturbed by their criticism. Especially now, after meeting Caito Lazar...

Even though he hungered to hear more, the thought of the Soothsayer brought his mind back to their current predicament.

"Does Tench know about these catacombs?" He expected a "no." After all, he never discovered this giant maze under the city, and Tench was certainly lazier than he.

"Of course. He uncovered every nook and cranny in this city."

Winston stared at him. Declan spoke so calmly he almost thought it was a joke. However, he wasn't sure the bookkeeper was capable of joking.

"Don't worry. No one ventures down here. The chancellor is well aware of the power of this place, even if he doesn't understand it, and is far too terrified to lose his men in these tunnels. The exit will be guarded, I'm sure."

Winston shrugged, feigning indifference even as his chest tightened. "I suppose it would be remiss if we escaped without a fight. You're sure we're safe here?"

"Most likely."

Sighing, Winston tried not to strangle the man. "What is *that* supposed to mean?"

"Hopefully you won't find out."

"What do you me—" he stopped and glared at the bookkeeper. "Are you always this frustrating?"

Declan seemed to understand that it was a rhetorical question and didn't answer.

Winston glanced back at the rest of the group. They looked miserable, and he didn't blame them. It was cold and dark; moreover, when he wasn't occupied with talking to Declan, the whispers came to the forefront of his senses. The darkness definitely seemed alive. It writhed, grasping at the edge of the lantern light—a gaping, hungry maw, ready to consume them as soon as the glow faded. There was no doubt about it: This place was filled with magic. Ancient, dangerous magic.

Andre caught his eye, giving him a thumbs down. He looked sick.

Winston returned the gesture with a shrug, then turned back to Declan. "What are the whispers saying?"

Declan gave him a wary look. "Whispers?"

"The ones *swirling* around us?" He made a circling motion with his finger. "Can you hear them?"

Continuing his stride, Declan stared straight ahead. "I know of no whispers. We've almost arrived. You should alert your men, but do so quietly."

It seemed to Winston he was avoiding the question. He couldn't fathom why Declan would want to withhold such information, though he certainly had proved himself eccentric. He probably had his own reasons.

Even so, he couldn't figure the man out. Winston prided himself on his ability to understand how people worked after just a few minutes of interaction with them, like a window opened up into their mind. Except with Declan, it was as though a cloud surrounded him. Winston could glean nothing besides an enormously clever mind. It was quite frustrating.

Still, the bookkeeper had yet to lead them astray, which meant Winston had no reason to stop trusting the man over a mere brush-off.

He passed Declan's words to the rest of the group. Immediately, they became more alert and began checking their weapons.

Andre quickened his pace to catch up to Winston. "What's the situation?"

He seemed to have forgotten his anger, which Winston was grateful for.

"Apparently, these secret tunnels aren't secret. Also, they're magical. What an eventful day we're having."

Andre raised an eyebrow dubiously, but Winston continued before he could comment. "Declan claims the exit will be under guard." Struck by a question, he peered at the bookkeeper. "Where *do* we come out?"

"A farmhouse a few miles beyond the city gates. There is a cellar that connects to the catacombs."

"Will we have to crawl through another tunnel?" Kent called from the back.

"No," Declan's voice carried even though there was no fluctuation in volume. "The people who built the house attempted to install an underground well, completely unaware of what lay below them. I believe they lost themselves wandering through the tunnels and went mad. I have many theories; unfortunately, I have yet to find the bodies." He sounded almost delighted by this tidbit.

Winston exchanged a concerned look with Andre.

"You know your way, right?" Andre confirmed uneasily. He glanced around him, and Winston knew he was hearing the whispers as well.

I'm not mad, then, he thought gratefully.

Declan suddenly stopped. "Yes, I know my way. We're here." He nodded to a ladder chiseled into the wall.

It stood out from the rest of the tunnel like a stain on a white garment. Instead of a metal ladder, the rungs were carved directly into the wall, interrupting the curve with an flat vertical surface. It was still made of the same yellow stone brick, which seemed to be layered quite deeply behind the outer surface. However, what really drew Winston's interest was that it looked old. The stone was rough and pockmarked, and the rock ledges forming the rungs were crumbling. Some were missing all together.

"It's falling apart," he stated blandly, pointing.

"It's solid," Declan assured.

"Is it safe?" asked Thomilson. "Back there, you said to not touch the walls."

"It's safe to touch. The aging means that the magic is absent—a single pocket of normalcy in an entire network of beautiful mystery." There was a subtle trace of distaste in his voice.

"Well," Winston declared, "if you say so." He reached for the first ledge, but Thomilson stopped him.

"Wait, sir. One of us should go first."

Winston smiled at the young sergeant. "Very kind of you to volunteer. I'll be fine."

Thomilson pulled out his knife, handing it handle-first to him. "At least take a weapon."

"Quite right."

Winston took it from him, testing its weight in his hand. It was a simple steel dagger with a leather wrapped handle. It wasn't much, though it would do should they run into trouble. He slipped the weapon into his belt. "Thank you."

Reaching again for the ladder, he grabbed a ledge with some slight consternation. Nothing happened when he touched it. In fact, it was quite solid. He figured it only seemed so fragile because the rest of the tunnel was pristine in comparison.

Looking up to the top, he saw that the exit hole was covered. "I'll have a look."

To hold the ledges, he had to pinch with his fingers. Fortunately, the stone was large and rough, making it easy to grab. Even so, he was relieved by the time he reached the top and propped his back up against the wall while he examined the cover.

Constructed with a criss-cross of light, wooden boards, it lifted easily when Winston pushed on it. Using his head, he raised the cover just enough to peek through the crack.

The well opened up into a small, unimpressive cellar—unlit, though enough natural light purveyed through a small window near the ceiling that Winston could make out the room. The walls were made of rough stone, and the floor was nothing more than dirt. There were no furnishings and, more importantly, no soldiers. He spotted the narrow stairs leading out of the basement and ducked back down into the hole.

"The cellar's clear," he called down softly. "It's dim, but no soldiers."

He pulled himself out of the hole, carefully setting the lid in the dirt beside it. Then, he helped up the rest of the group as they climbed through. Andre was the last one to ascend, and Winston replaced the lid after him.

Thomilson had gone to the door at the top of the stairs and was attempting to listen through the keyhole.

"I don't hear anything," he relayed. He tried to look through it. "I can't tell if anyone is there."

Declan advanced up the stairs. Thomilson flattened himself hurriedly against the wall and sidled out of his way as one would avoid a spider.

"They're here." The bookkeeper pressed his ear against the door. "Hiding," he breathed, seemingly to himself.

Andre and Winston exchanged looks again.

"I'm not sure about him," Andre murmured so only Winston could hear. "He makes me uneasy."

"Right now, he's our only way out," Winston whispered back. Andre grimaced in response.

"Well?" Kent demanded after a couple moments. "Can you hear them? How many are there?"

Holding his finger to his lips, Declan tried the door. It was locked from the outside. Then, to everybody's astonishment, he stepped back and kicked it with tremendous force. The handle snapped, and the door crashed open, bouncing against the wall and shuddering like a frightened dog.

Declan strode out of the room, leaving the group speechless.

"I suppose we're clear, then." Winston bounded up the steps after him.

The others followed, spreading out to search the house. There were only four rooms in the building: A parlor with a crumbling fireplace, and three smaller chambers likely to have been bedrooms. The house was bare of furniture besides a couple of moldering cabinets. The scent of mildew hung heavy around them, and the shuttered windows looked lonely on the blank walls.

After clearing the rooms, the group gathered by the front door.

Andre peeked through one of the boarded windows. "There's nobody out there. I don't like this." He turned to Declan. "You said this place would be guarded."

"It appears we made it here first."

"In that case," started Thomilson, "we're fr—"

"Shhh," Winston shushed. He thought he heard a creak from the side of the house, like someone creeping across a porch. "Declan. Is there another entrance besides the front door?"

"Yes." The bookkeeper gave him a sharp look. "In one of the back rooms. It's blocked."

Winston recalled a door in one of the bedrooms reinforced with rotting planks. His heart sank. *Not well enough*. He drew his knife. "Move away from the door and windows. Form up. We have company."

Immediately, Andre drew his weapon and moved with Winston, facing the room with the back entrance. The others were a little slower, exchanging worried looks before they pulled their swords from their sheaths. They huddled into the middle of the room, circling Declan, who was weaponless. Ears pricked, eyes darting from window to door, they held motionless. Muscles tense, breath quick—the calm before the storm.

Another creak whined, this time from the front of the house, then nothing. They waited as the hateful silence stretched longer.

All of a sudden, there was a huge splintering sound, and the front door was smashed to pieces. Soldiers in blue uniforms streamed into the room with cries, led by two gilded Rose Soldiers. Thomilson and one of his men met them immediately.

Winston turned to face the first assault, but the door behind him slammed open, the rotting boards across it exploding. He spun back around as more loyalists rushed in through the back. He leaped forward with Andre to engage them.

Thanking the All-Mother for the close quarters, Winston was able to step inside one of the soldiers' guard and grapple with him. It would be more difficult for the man to utilize his longer blade in the enclosed space than for Winston with his smaller knife. The soldier seemed to realize this and dropped his sword, apparently understanding that it would do nothing more than render one of his hands useless.

They struggled desperately for the knife in Winston's hands. The loyalist was strong, and Winston's fingers were growing slick. His other wrist was caught by the soldier. He tried unsuccessfully to wrench it out of his grip. He was going to lose this fight. Desperately, he spat in the other man's face.

As the soldier involuntarily released him to wipe off the saliva, Winston took advantage of the momentary lapse, throwing his fist into the man's jaw. The soldier reeled back, head smacking into the wall with a sickening thud. He slid to the floor, where he lay motionless.

Winston stood over his incapacitated adversary, breathing heavily. It had been a low move to spit at his enemy. Even so, he didn't feel guilty, not at the cost of his life.

Andre was fighting a third, axe-wielding Rose Soldier in the back room. The loyalist was swinging his weapon wildly, and Winston saw Andre administer a sweeping gash in his side. Confident his friend had the situation under control, he went to locate the others.

They were in the front yard where more loyalists had come to join the fight. Thomilson had acquired a shield, which he used to ram an enemy. Declan, sword in hand, was deftly matching strikes with a burly fighter. He disarmed the man, kicked his knee in sideways, then pierced him through the torso with deadly speed.

Rushing out to join the fray, Winston slipped his knife back into his belt, scooping up a sword and shield as he exited the house. In his hurry, he failed to hear the shattering of a door as Andre was thrown through it.

13

BLOOD AND BROKEN BONES

Cursing, Andre rolled in the mud to avoid the axe strike aimed at his head. He finally managed to climb to his feet while the Rose Soldier pulled back. Blood trickled down his face from a cut on his forehead, threatening to blind him. He wiped it with the back of his hand, gasping as he did so. He was pretty sure at least two of his ribs were bruised, and the old wound on his leg felt like it was being split open all over again.

The Rose Soldier bared his teeth in a vicious smile. The brute, a half-head taller than Andre with broad shoulders and meaty arms, was bleeding from large cuts on his shoulder and side, yet he seemed not to notice.

Andre's gaze moved past him to where his sword lay half-buried under the wreckage of the door. He needed it if he wanted to survive this fight. The dagger in his belt would only keep him alive for so long against a blood-thirsty killer like this one.

Drawing his knife, his twirled it between his fingers, fixing his enemy in a death-glare.

The man laughed. "Is that supposed to scare me?"

Andre answered by whipped the dagger at him, breaking into a sprint as he released it. The dagger flew true, slamming point-first into a crease between the soldier's armor at the armpit. The man howled in pain, grabbing at his shoulder.

Andre barreled into him, knocking him over and bouncing off of him to where the hilt of his blade peeked out from under the remains of the door. He snatched it up and straightened, whirling around to face his adversary.

Now to end this.

He wiped his face, flicking rain off of his fingers. His whole body protested against him and every breath came with effort, but he gritted his teeth, pushing aside the pain.

The Rose Soldier didn't even bother pulling out the dagger in his shoulder as he regained his feet. With a grunt, he swung at Andre's head, leaving his side completely exposed.

Andre knocked the axe head aside, then thrust his blade into the golden rose on his chest, piercing his mail at the sternum. The soldier roared and spun away from him, his weapon dragging in the dirt.

Andre stared at him in disbelief. *How is he still standing?*

The man had been far too aggressive, and Andre had dealt him numerous what-should-have-been-mortal blows. He was far past the point where anyone else would have passed out from blood loss, but the soldier just didn't seem to care.

"You tired yet, dog?" the loyalist jeered. He raised his axe again, his wrist glinting as a piece of jewelry caught the afternoon light.

"Go to hell," growled Andre, striking at him again.

The soldier deflected his blade and retaliated. Andre mistimed his parry and felt something crack in his elbow. Shards of pain exploded through his arm, quickly robbing all feeling from his shoulder to his fingers. Before he lost his grip on his sword, he funneled every ounce of strength he had left into a broad, sweeping upstroke, severing his enemy's arm at the elbow. The man screamed in agony until Andre buried his blade into his side, driving him into the ground.

The Rose Soldier lay still, blood streaming from the many wounds in his body. His glassy eyes stared blindly at his executioner. He was dead—finally and mercifully dead.

Vision darkening, Andre's knees buckled. He hit the ground numbly, only vaguely registering his surroundings. Forcing his eyes to open, he found himself staring at the severed forearm of the loyalist, a leather strap with a silver pendant still wrapped around the wrist.

The red jewel in the center seemed to beckon to him.

Without thinking, he reached out and took the amulet with his good hand. The leather thong was long enough that the man had wrapped it three times around his wrist. His vision cleared as he held it, and the pain retreated until he was able to sit up. Unconsciously pulling the loop over his head, he struggled to his feet.

Pain flared anew, and his vision dropped out of focus. Then, just as quickly, the pain faded, and his eyesight returned to normal. Leaning on his sword, he held himself upright for a moment, taking deep breaths, surprised and grateful that they came with minimal effort. Finally, he straightened, holding his injured arm to his stomach.

He needed to make sure the others were alright. He was confident in the skill of his men, and he had seen Declan pick up a sword to kill two loyalists suspiciously quickly for a bookkeeper. Even so, there had been a lot of soldiers, and he wasn't sure of fate's intentions.

It became a little easier to walk as he sheathed his sword and limped his way through the obliterated door frame. The pain in his elbow turned from knives stabbing him with each step to a throbbing ache.

Reaching the front door, he looked out to see carnage. Bodies littered the yard, all of them wearing blue.

A man was running to the house from the road, and Andre felt relief wash over him when he recognized Winston.

"Andre! Thank the All-Mother, you're alive!"

"You sound surprised." He could barely force the words out. "Where are the others?"

"Retreating. We need to follow. Can you run? Foolish question," he said before Andre could answer. He grabbed him around the waist. "Wrap your arm around me. I'll help you walk."

"I'm alright." It was strange: He *did* feel alright. His energy seemed to be replenishing, his pain diminishing. "I can walk."

"Are you sure?"

Andre nodded. "We'll move faster."

Winston released him, and they set off towards the tree line.

Despite how he was somehow recovering from the punishment dealt by the Rose Soldier, moving was still uncomfortable. The wound on the back of his leg ached, and his elbow and side both throbbed. However, he wasn't in nearly as much pain as he expected, considering the extent of his injuries. He continued to hold his injured limb to his chest, afraid that if he loosened his grip, it would fall off. Not a preferred outcome. He hugged his arm tightly, trying not to think about it.

They were in the woods now. Through the thin haze clouding his vision, Andre saw cut marks on the trees as they went. Since Winston was following them, he assumed they were left by the group as they fled.

"How much longer?" he asked, stepping over a fallen log with some difficulty.

"Not entirely sure. We hadn't gone far when I turned back to find you."

Andre's vision brightened unnaturally for a moment. He groaned, grabbing a tree to keep from keeling over.

"You don't look well," announced Winston.

Andre wanted to roll his eyes at him, but since the trees were still pulsing, he squeezed them shut instead. "Why do you say that?"

"You're a very pale shade of green," Winston remarked as though commenting on a shirt Andre was wearing. He grabbed him around the waist again. "Come on. The sooner we arrive; the sooner you can pass out."

Andre stumbled forward. Now, there were a number of black spots scattered across his vision. He could feel himself losing touch with his surroundings. His head began to loll, and he nearly fell a few times as his knees buckled. Soon, Winston was the only thing keeping him up; ergo, he held onto him probably tighter than necessary.

Suddenly, he was startled out of his stupor by a shout. He jerked his head up, believing they had been caught by pursuing loyalists. After a brief moment of panic, he realized the man waving at them up ahead was one of the rebels.

They had set up camp next to a wide creek bubbling through the woods. Andre collapsed next to it with a groan. Dipping his head into the flowing water, he scrubbed off the blood on his forehead, rinsed his hands, then splashed his face. The water was cold and helped rejuvenate him a little. When he finished, he didn't even bother climbing to his feet and instead crawled over to join the others.

He heard Winston ask if anyone was a medic and was only mildly surprised when Delcan crouched down next to him.

"You are an enigma aren't you," he rasped weakly. "I saw you wielding that sword. What can't you do?"

Declan smiled, rather grimly it seemed. "Plenty."

He began to feel Andre's side, pressing lightly around his ribs. The pain made him suck in air through his teeth. Declan grunted, then switched his attention to Andre's elbow. He gently prodded it, and Andre yelped, grabbing the bookkeeper's wrist with a growl.

Glancing down involuntarily, the bookkeeper's eyes widened for a fraction of a second when he noticed the amulet on Andre's chest. The moment passed so quickly that Andre wasn't sure if he actually saw it.

Sitting back on his heels, Declan pointed at Andre's head. "How bad is your head wound?"

"Not bad, I think." He felt for the wound with his good hand. There was a small cut on the top of his head, likely from a sliver of the door, and his fingers came away with more blood. "Just a flesh wound."

"It will keep bleeding. I'll wrap it for you." He pointed at Andre's arm. "Your elbow is broken, although I don't know how badly. I'll set your arm in a sling; it's the best we can do for now. You have a couple of bruised ribs. That will be painful for a while, but they'll heal. You need rest. How much pain are you in?"

"Not much, surprisingly."

The bookkeeper glanced at the amulet again, and a look of triumph flashed across his face.

Andre looked down at it, then back up at Declan. "What is it?"

"Rest," was all Declan said.

Retrieving his rucksack, he produced various medical supplies from it. He wrapped a bandage around Andre's head, then made a sling for his elbow. When he finished tending to his wounds, he gave him another admonishment to rest before rising and moving to the creek.

Winston jerked his thumb at Declan's turned back. "What can't he do? You should have seen that man with a sword. I'd hate to see what he can do with a pen."

Andre studied the back of the bookkeeper's head. Something about Declan deeply unsettled him, yet he wasn't able to place what it was. He had seen something behind his eyes similar to the look he caught before they ventured into the catacombs—something almost sinister, like a mask had been removed for just a moment.

He would have to keep an eye on the man.

As the others quietly discussed their circumstances, Andre lay back and closed his eyes to relax. However, after a few minutes of listening to the rain pattering gently on the trees and the murmurs of his companions, he decided he wasn't going to be successful. His weariness had all but vanished, and he now felt wide awake.

Prompted to examine the amulet again, he propped himself up with his back to the others.

The pendant was beautifully wrought: Silver and oval-shaped with a perfectly smooth red jewel nestled in the center of the ornament. Filaments of twisting silver wound across it like miniature snakes holding it in place. Unfamiliar markings and grooves were carved into the casing around the jewel—intricate shapes and symbols etched into the metal with incredible detail. The leather loop Andre wore around his neck was fed through a hole in the top of the amulet.

He flipped the amulet over to look at the back, and his eyes widened in surprise.

An entire picture was inlaid on the smooth silver of the opposite side: A scene depicting a noble-looking man holding a heart-shaped object above his head that appeared to be emanating rays of light. Garbed in an elegant suit of armor with a cape flowing behind him, a crown adorned his head, and his face held a look of amazement as he stared up at the object in his hands. At his feet, people with swords in their hands and ugly looks on their faces fought and killed each other. Other, more pitiful characters crowded on the edges of the scene, cowering and weeping.

The entire picture was set into a space not four centimeters wide and only about six centimeters high, yet it was so intricately crafted that it seemed like actual minuscule people were trapped in the silver of the amulet. They almost seemed to breathe.

Andre flipped it back over and stared at the red jewel in the center. It almost glowed in the gloom of the forest. He held his hand over it and swore he could feel a very slight warmth emanating from it.

On a hunch, he pulled the amulet over his head, setting it on the blanket.

The effect was instantaneous. A wave of fatigue slammed into him with such force that he almost passed out. Suddenly he became acutely aware of every cut, scrape, and bruise on his body; his ribs seemed to be burning his insides. He groaned through gritted teeth, hastily picking the silver piece up again.

"Are you alright, sir?" Thomilson looked over.

Andre nodded, still staring at the pendant. He was relaxed now, aching and sore, but alert and somewhat comfortable.

What is this witchcraft?

He felt afraid. He didn't believe in magic, but whatever effect this amulet had on him wasn't natural.

He thought back to the Rose Soldier he fought at the farmhouse. Already tougher than a normal fighter, the man had refused to succumb to the wounds he sustained. In fact, he had hardly seemed aware of them. Only when Andre sliced off his arm, removing the amulet from him, did he respond to the damage dealt.

Andre glanced over to Declan. He knew something about the amulet—the fleeting slip in his expression confirmed that much.

And he better tell me.

With that resolved in his mind, he donned the amulet again, tucking it beneath his collar. He carefully picked himself up and, ignoring Winston's demand for him to, "lie back down immediately, idiot," made his way over to the bookkeeper.

14

THE LEGEND OF THE VIDA IMRALTA

"VIDA IMRALTA," DECLAN UTTERED as Andre thumped down next to him with a groan.

"What?"

"Vida Imralta," he repeated as if Andre would understand the second time. He looked up from the little book he was writing in. "Everlasting life."

The book snapped shut, though not before Andre stole a glance at the contents. It looked like a journal. The pages were full of sketches accompanied by notes scribbled in loose, flowing cursive. He thought he glimpsed an outline of the very amulet he wore around his neck.

"You lost me."

Declan folded his hands over the journal. "There's a legend of an amulet that grants immortality... to a point. The Vida Imralta." He glanced pointedly at the leather thong around Andre's neck. "Care to hear a story?"

Hearing Declan, Winston called over to them. "A story? Nothing like a tale to dispel the chill! Come join us, you two."

Declan cocked an eyebrow at Andre and helped him to his feet.

Once everyone shifted to make room for them, Declan began with the air of a teacher speaking to children.

"Long ago, this land was part of a greater nation that bore the name Atheralyn. The people of Atheralyn, the Athere, were accomplished in the customs and practices of ancient mystical arts—what is commonly called magic."

"This is a fairytale," interrupted Kent. "Magic?" He looked around at the others with a smirk.

Andre glared at him. He didn't like Kent, even if he did share the same opinions about magic. The man was disrespectful, crude, and tactless. Not to mention untrustworthy.

"Kent, don't be an ass."

"What? I'm only asking a question."

"No, you're disturbing the story. Be quiet and listen."

Kent gave him a look of intense dislike before glancing at Thomilson. The sergeant shook his head ever so slightly.

"Fine. I'll *be quiet.*"

Winston lay back, propping a foot on his other knee. "Go on, Declan."

Declan continued, "According to legend, the Athere were descendants of an ancient celestial being that had a hand in the very creation of our world." He paused, looking around at each of them. "The All-Mother, Iyala herself. Traces of her magic flowed through the Athere's veins, granting them their power. They imbued this magic into wood, stone, and metal, creating marvelous structures meant to stand until the end of time. Although the Athere were powerful—their bloodline running strong for many centuries—alas, they eventually died out. Thereafter, most of their secrets were lost.

"In the period this story occurs, the land of Atheralyn was ruled by a wise and powerful man named Helio. He had a daughter, a beautiful young woman named Evyelna. Evyelna's features were compared with star and moonlight, and it was said there was nobody more gracious or kind. Naturally, many suitors sought her hand.

"Now, a smaller nation, Esheria, bordered Atheralyn. The Esherian monarch had a son who became obsessed with the tales of Evyelna's beauty. Resolving to see this angel with his own eyes, Idus traveled to the capital of Atheralyn under the ruse of a diplomatic mission, where he successfully secured an audience with the princess. Upon their correspondence, he grew even more smitten by her compassion and character. She was the perfect woman; he decided she would be his wife.

"Evyelna, in turn, had fallen for the handsome young man from Esheria. His charm and kindness were exactly what she desired in a husband. On the other hand, the suiters sent her way by her father were considerably less enjoyable. The two young lovers promised each other their undying love and parted ways."

"It's a damn love story," Kent muttered under his breath.

"Yes," Declan agreed tranquilly over Andre's subsequent growl. "Many of the best stories are. There's so much emotion, so much more at stake when hearts are on the line. You've never been in love, have you?"

The other men snickered.

Kent flushed. "Just... whatever."

Smiling, Declan went on with his story. "Both rulers elicited very different reactions to the news from their children. Idus's father, extremely pleased by such a development, encouraged his son to continue courting Evyelna. Marrying into the Atheralyn nobility would provide him access to power and riches previously unobtainable. A union between the two nations would catapult Esheria into a position of incredible prominence.

"Helio, however, thought quite the opposite. You see, he was a jealous man. After all, he ruled the most powerful nation on the continent and was loath to share its treasures with such an ambitious rival. He warned Idus and his father to halt their advances, or he would declare war on the smaller country.

"Although his father was cowed and relented, Idus refused to give up. Secretly traveling back to the Athere capital, he presented a plan to Evyelna to elope back to Esheria. She agreed, and the two lovers slipped away in the middle of the night.

"When he discovered what happened, Helio was furious and threatened Esheria with an invasion unless his daughter was returned to him. However, now that the Esherian ruler held Evyelna in his possession, he regained his courage and refused. The two countries clashed—Esheria determined to keep its prize; Atheralyn set on returning its property.

"A fierce and bloody war broke out. Esheria gained many allies as other countries saw an opportunity to topple the Athere juggernaut. The alliances were effective, and, as powerful as it was, Atheralyn was unable to gain ground towards the Esherian capital.

"However, Helio, determined to prevent the union from happening, disguised himself and infiltrated the capital. Once he found his daughter, he revealed himself, commanding the girl to come with him or suffer the consequences. Though Evyelna pleaded for him to see the extent of her love for Idus, her father remained opposed. In the end, she declared she would rather die than return. Enraged, Helio granted her request, stabbing his daughter through the stomach and leaving her to bleed to death on the floor.

"Using an ancient power to send a vision to Idus, Evyelna cried out for her betrothed, who led the Esherian troops on the front lines. Then, using the final trace of magic she could muster, she channeled her life-force into the garnet necklace around her neck. As she released her final breath, she folded her hands over the amulet on her chest and died.

"The moment he received the vision, Idus rushed back to the capital, bursting into Evyelna's chambers. His heart broke when he found his beloved lying in a pool of her own blood. He knew immediately who committed the act and vowed through his grief and fury to destroy Helio if it was with his last breath. He gathered up the necklace as a final token of Evyelna's love and rode without break towards the Athere capital, cutting down all who stood in his way. Neither magic nor steel seemed to pierce the red cloud that surrounded him; neither pain nor weariness could quiet the rage in his mind. He was invincible.

"When Idus arrived at the gates of Helio's castle, the Atheralyn monarch emerged to meet him. He warned the boy to turn back, promising he would destroy him if he didn't. Idus, too blinded by revenge, never stopped to consider the power of Helio and threw himself at his enemy. Yet, despite Helio's superiority in combat and his influence over the magical arts, Idus refused to succumb. The boy flung himself over and over at Helio, long past the point where other men would have died from sheer exhaustion, until even the Athere ruler faltered.

"Alas, Helio overcame Idus at last.

"Broken and bloody, kneeling at the king's feet, Idus begged to die, for he longed to see his love again. The young man removed the necklace from his neck and put it to his lips, kissing his beloved one final time before Helio separated his head from his shoulders.

"He ordered Idus's head to be sent to the front lines, and the body back to his father. Heartbroken, the Esherian ruler recalled his armies." Declan's eyes glittered as he spoke, "From that point, the man was useless, doing nothing but wallow in his misery over the loss of his son."

"What about the amulet?" asked Thomilson through a splinter of wood he was using as a toothpick.

Andre absently tugged on the leather loop around his neck as Declan explained.

"When Helio picked up the necklace, he could feel its power and knew immediately what his daughter had done. Using an incredibly powerful form of magic, Evyelna's life-force would abide forever in the garnet. What's more, the strength of the love she died for gave the gem a potent aura. The bearer would live indefinitely as long as the pendant was on their person; neither weariness nor wounds would hold sway over them. Until Idus removed the necklace, he was nearly immortal.

"Helio sent the amulet to his best craftsman, instructing him to fashion a worthy case for the garnet—one that would neither age, nor break, nor tarnish. The craftsman did as Helio asked. However, upon feeling the power of the Vida Imralta, he kept it and stole away in secret.

"When he discovered this betrayal, Helio sent his most dangerous assassins after him. The king's men found the thief next to a river and managed to kill him. Unfortunately, the amulet was lost in the process, vanishing into the current never to be seen again."

Declan suddenly looked around at Andre. "May I?"

Surprised, Andre stared at the hand Declan held out to him. He knew what Declan suspected; even so, he was taken aback that the bookkeeper would so blatantly reveal his secret. He didn't know what he believed; his mind was still searching for a logical explanation. Nevertheless, he knew he didn't want his discovery shared with the others.

Winston, he trusted, but Kent...

An artifact that could grant immortality would be tempting for anyone to get their hands on. Even if they didn't believe in magic, it might be worth the risk. Who knew the lengths someone might resort to in order to attain it?

Besides, when Andre released the pendant for that one moment, his body felt every injury from his recent adventures, and he was reluctant to feel them again. However, he knew how it would appear if he refused—now that Declan had already revealed his secret. With that in mind, he steeled himself and removed the amulet from around his neck, dropping it into the bookkeeper's hand.

Once again, his body was overwhelmed with pain and fatigue. He couldn't stop himself from reacting, letting out a strained breath. Fortunately, the others were watching Declan examine the piece.

"Of course, many imitation amulets have surfaced. None of them have been anything more than an ordinary stone encased in ordinary silver. While some have been quite convincing, this..." He tilted his head. "This is the best replica I've ever seen. Such amazing detail..."

That distorted look had returned to his eyes, the soft green color replaced by an emerald fire longing to possess—to *consume*. It was a look that made Andre think of the fabled dragons hoarding gold and jewels—another fairy tale.

He glanced at the other men all still fixated on the amulet hanging by the end of the strap. Kent wore a nearly identical expression to Declan's. Winston's mouth was slightly open.

"Alas," Declan announced suddenly, making everyone start. "It is a fake, like all the rest."

He held it out to Andre, who took it from him with a feeling of relief he found himself unable to place.

Glancing at Declan's face again, he saw his eyes were the same soft color as always.

Did I imagine it? Maybe he was delirious. His stomach squirmed uncomfortably as he looked away from the bookkeeper.

The already poor lighting was growing dimmer by the minute, and the air colder as night fell. Since there was too much risk in lighting a fire, the rest of the group huddled closer together, discussing the story. Andre lay back, squirming to find a comfortable position. He stared up at the darkening canopy, listening to the soft patter of rain while turning the pendant over in his hands.

The possibility that the stories of magic he had been told as a child could actually be true was an uncomfortable thought. However, as he considered Declan's tale, he began to wonder. He was long past the point where his adrenaline was the only thing keeping him together. And yet...

Pulling the loop back over his head, he tucked the amulet under his collar. He could feel himself nodding off. Whether the pendant was magical or not, he was exhausted. Declan said that the wearer wasn't affected by weariness; maybe it was all his imagination, and his wounds weren't as bad as he thought.

Lulled by the tapping of rain on the leaves and the quiet murmur of voices, he passed into a fitful sleep.

Andre awoke to the insistent croak of a crow in the tree above him. He opened his eyes to a dreary, overcast sky visible through the leaves of the forest canopy. It was morning. The muscles in his back ached uncomfortably. It appeared the amulet's alleged magical powers did not extend to soreness from sleeping on a root.

Trying to sit up, his groan turned into a sharp inhale as his broken elbow crackled with pain in its sling, and his ribs stole his breath. He reached for the amulet only to find it absent from around his neck. Forcing his breathing under control, he sat up slowly, looking over see the others awake and watching him around a smoldering fire.

Alarm shot through him at the sight. Tench likely had soldiers searching for them; a fire would lead them right to their location. He was about to shout at them for their foolishness when he noticed Winston was missing.

Something felt wrong. The men were staring at him with displeased faces. Thomilson looked uncomfortable.

"Good morning," he greeted them cautiously. "Where's Winston?"

Nobody answered.

Kent sauntered over to Andre, crouching next him with a smirk. "How do you feel, Cordon?"

Andre straightened himself as best he could, a horrible feeling washing over him. "You will address me as sir, Kent."

Kent slapped him on the side with the back of his hand and laughed at his subsequent growl of pain. "Of course, *sir*." Andre did not miss the mocking tone in his voice. "You're not feeling too great, are you?"

Kent held something up in his fist. It was the amulet. "That freak thinks he's clever. I'm not a fool—I saw his face. I saw *your* face. This"—he dangled the amulet enticingly—"is as real as your bruised ribs. I feel like a new man."

"I thought you didn't believe in magic," Andre stated, eyes flicking carefully to the others. They still appeared mutinous. He had no friends here. And he was in no state to fight them all off.

What happened to Winston?

"True, but I just had to see for myself. Immortality is such a tempting offer! Once I felt the Imralta's power..." Kent laughed again.

"Where's Winston?" Andre demanded again. He was stalling now, trying to buy more time to come up with a plan. At the moment, he could think of nothing.

"Not here."

Andre raised himself on his good arm until he was face to face with Kent. He wrinkled his nose at the man's breath. "Where is he?"

His fragile attempt at intimidation only made Kent curl his lip at him. "Does it matter? They won't be back in time to save you."

Confused, Andre frowned before realizing Declan was gone, too. His concern deepened, and he almost missed the rest of Kent's words.

"By the time they return, you'll be dead, and we'll be long gone with the Vida Imralta."

"You're going to share? How considerate of you." Andre tried to push himself up, but Kent kicked his arm out from under him, causing him to sprawl back on the ground with a cry.

The traitor leaned over him as he lay gasping for breath, immobilized by pain. Hot breath tickled his ear as Kent whispered, "They can try to take it."

Andre heard him stand up, then the slithering sound of his sword being drawn from its scabbard. He tried to move, but quickly realized he was helpless. He squeezed his eyes shut, waiting for the end. However, instead of the *swish* of a blade cutting the air and the sharp pain of a fatal blow, he heard Kent straighten with a curse.

"Well, this is awkward."

Andre's eyes snapped open, and he jerked his head around so quickly that his neck popped.

Winston was leaning against a tree, arms crossed. Despite his lighthearted tone, his face was dangerously serious with no trace of mirth in his brown eyes. "You weren't intending to kill him in that state? He can barely muster enough energy to move his head."

He stepped forward, voice dripping with contempt "You're disgusting. A rat amongst filth. And *you*"—his eyes snapped onto Thomilson—"an accomplice to this? You're an officer. You've built up trust. I even advocated for you in Seruvia. What is your excuse?"

"I pledged my loyalty to my men," retorted Thomilson, hands curled into fists. "And I'm keeping it."

"No, you pledged your loyalty to the *rebellion*. That's the oath you took when you joined. This is treason, not loyalty!"

Andre caught a sudden movement from the other side of the creek. Declan stood in the shadow of a maple tree with a crossbow in hand.

Where did he find that?

Seeing him look, Declan held a finger to his lips. Andre quickly turned his attention back to where Winston was berating Thomilson. He tried to calculate how much effort it would take to reach his sword and came to the conclusion that his aching body would probably crumble if he attempted to fight, much less move at all.

"You're failing everyone!" Winston shouted. "Not only your fellow soldiers and friends, but the people of Corynthia as well! The very people you *swore* to fight for and protect! Yet, you still stand there with a clean conscience, saying this is a worthy act, *coward?*"

Thomilson was sneering now. Any of his conflicting feelings seemed to have been driven out by Winston's indignation. "I don't need to listen to this. Kent is right: Following the rebellion is suicide."

"It's better than slavery," Winston retorted with a dry laugh. "Nevertheless, I won't preach to you the ideals you've abandoned." He drew his sword. "The penalty for treason is death; I might as well carry it out myself."

"Then *your* sentence is long overdue!" Kent stepped forward, swinging his sword up to strike.

As they converged on Winston, Declan made his move. The bookkeeper smoothly pulled the crossbow to his shoulder and fired a bolt at the tight knot of traitors. It pierced straight through one's neck, burying into a rotting stump upon its exit. The man flopped to the ground and flailed there, gurgling. The others whirled around with cries of surprise as Declan tossed aside the crossbow and bounded across the creek, drawing a sword as he went.

What happened next was so quick Andre almost missed it.

The other three traitors, forgetting Winston in the face of the new assailant, charged Declan. The latter met them deftly, parrying the attacks of Kent and another man in the same motion. He immediately dispatched the latter, and, before the traitor even readied his sword again, separated Kent's head from his neck with a lightning fast swipe.

The third man stumbled backwards as Kent's head bounced to halt in front of him. He was given no reprieve and dropped dead in a matter of seconds.

Thomilson, who stood frozen as he watched Declan butcher his men, turned to run.

"Don't you dare."

Tearing his eyes away from the carnage Declan caused in mere seconds, Andre found Winston.

The rebel leader moved through the campsite to stand in front of Thomilson. He pointed his blade at the treacherous sergeant. "Though you may be a disgrace to Corynthia, you will *not* run like the coward you are. Stand and fight as if you have some shred of honor left!"

Thomilson stared back and forth between him and Declan, licking his lips nervously. Finally, he straightened his back and unsheathed his own weapon.

The sound of metal striking metal rang through the forest as Winston and Thomilson started to fight, cutting through the quiet that had fallen following Declan's massacre. The two spectators watched silently. Not wanting to distract Winston, Andre refrained from shouting any words of encouragement. He grew more and more tense as the fight dragged on, his heart leaping into his mouth on multiple occasions as Thomilson nearly landed blow.

Finally, Winston was given an opportunity to end the duel.

Thomilson's foot landed on one of the swords that lay in the grass. The sergeant slipped, dropping his guard as he tried to regain his balance. Winston lunged forward, piercing him in the stomach. Clutching his wound, Thomilson staggered backwards towards the creek, dropping his sword as he did so. Winston yelled and stabbed him again, pushing him backwards into the water.

Thomilson landed with a splash and lay unmoving. The sword quivered slightly from its resting place in the traitor's chest.

Breathing heavily, Winston turned to face Andre and Declan. He was soaked in sweat, but he broke into a smile and let out a tired chuckle. "I don't believe I've *ever* lasted that long. On the battlefield or in the bedroom."

Andre let out a sigh of relief and laughed, which he stopped quickly because it hurt. *He's fine,* he thought, feeling slightly giddy. Only Winston would fight a battle to the death and say such a thing immediately afterwards.

Declan began walking through the dead bodies, peering back and forth as if searching for something. Andre deduced the bookkeeper's intentions and shot Winston a warning look. Winston's face turned serious again, and he shadowed Declan cautiously.

The bookkeeper bent down to rummage through Kent's headless corpse. When he straightened up, the Vida Imralta dangled from his fist. He held it up in the gloomy daylight, examining it.

Winston stopped a few feet from him. "I'll take that."

Declan looked at him, then to Andre raising his eyebrows. "I was thinking Lieutenant Cordon would benefit more from it."

"It *is* real?" Winston asked with a surprised look. "I was under the impression—" He stopped as Declan dropped the amulet into Winston's hand.

Immediately, Winston straightened his back, staring at the Imralta in wonder. "Amazing..." he breathed. He looked back up at Declan. "Then why—"

"I was trying to prevent what just occurred. An unsuccessful attempt, although I'm glad we forced their hand before they found a moment when we were all vulnerable."

Andre frowned. *They left me on purpose, then.*

"I had a feeling," Declan explained, as though hearing Andre's mental disapproval. "From what you said happened in Seruvia, as well as their manner, I guessed their foul intentions and decided to test my theory. Obviously I was right. I apologize that my plan placed you in harm's way."

Andre merely nodded. He didn't like how the bookkeeper seemed to know what he was thinking.

Winston handed him the Imralta, which he took semi-dubiously. His body relaxed as the amulet's mysterious power flowed through him again, rejuvenating and healing him. The unease that accompanied it persisted.

"You hold onto it until we return to Cappus. Once we arrive, we shall decide what to do with it. No one else must know about this. It's too dangerous. Does that sound reasonable?"

"That's fine by me," Andre agreed. Declan merely nodded.

Winston rubbed his hands together. "Good. Now, we must move. Tench is still searching for us, and this blasted fire might as well be a blaring trumpet."

Now reinvigorated, Andre pushed himself to a sitting position and was helped up by Declan. "We left horses laid up in a farmhouse. It'll make travel much easier."

"Do you remember where?" Winston queried as he kicked mud on the the fire.

"Yes, but we'll have to return to the road."

"It's risky. Declan, what do you think?"

Declan finished tying his rucksack closed before answering. "I think we need to leave as quickly as possible. As you said, Chancellor Tench will have soldiers combing the countryside who will certainly have noticed the fire. Still, Andre is in no shape to travel on foot. The horses, but we must be careful."

Winston walked to where Declan had thrown aside his crossbow and swung the weapon onto his shoulder. "Then there is no time to waste."

PART TWO: HOPE

15

COUNSEL FROM THE SHADOWS

(A burning city. A figure limping down a ruined street. The air is clogged with smoke, screams, and the pouring rain. A silver amulet lies on a pile of rubble next to a pair of broken bodies. Flames quaver around a distorted figure in the polished reflection)

Caito lay on the floor in his room as he did every night. He tried sleeping in the four-poster bed dominating the room, but the soft down mattress and pillows were far too fluffy to be comfortable. It felt like sinking into a pile of mulch. Hailing from a poor, farming family, he found himself unable to acclimate to the extravagances of the higher class.

Besides, lying on the floor helped some with the nightmares.

(Bloody water swirls around rocks. A body lies face up in the creek, a sword protruding from its chest like a steel sapling)

The curtains were drawn back from the window, allowing the moonlight to stream through the glass, illuminating the floor in a long silver rectangle. Caito lay in the middle of it. He was soaked in sweat, and his bedclothes clung to his body like a second skin. He ignored the unpleasant feeling as he stared at the shadowed ceiling. While lower than the one in the main room, it was still taller than that of his childhood home, with space to spare.

The vision that pulled him rudely from sleep loomed intrusively in his mind. It was the same one plaguing him for weeks, robbing his rest at night while haunting his waking hours with flashes of violent images.

It first came after his parents died, and he had gone to live with his Aunt Gertie. At first, he hid it from her, growing moody and sullen from its influence. Since she was ignorant of his gift of premonition, he was reluctant to give her another reason to worry about him. However, as the visions began to take a physical toll on him as well, he finally indulged his aunt's concern and explained what was troubling him to avoid seeing a physician.

She sent for one anyway, taking his visions as a sign of madness from losing his parents. Everything fell apart from there.

(Lightning flashes, revealing two figures locked together in combat high on a bridge)

The images swam stubbornly behind his eyelids no matter how hard he squeezed them shut. Moaning, Caito pressed the heels of his hands into his eyes, trying to squash the vision from his mind. After a few moments, his headache lessened, and he opened his eyes again, panting slightly.

In an effort to distract himself from his misery, he thought about Winston Servailles. He had heard stories about the man who almost single-handedly secured Corynthia's independence from Kaval, including rumors that at least eight attempts were made on his life—all of which he single-handedly foiled. Caito seriously doubted the validity of some of the stories. Nevertheless, he truly believed Servailles was a greatly resourceful man. He was certainly intriguing.

And brash, thought Caito as he recalled Servailles's predicament.

Ever since he was visited by the hooded man over a month ago and made the decision to finally become involved in the brewing war, he had been looking forward to meeting the rebel leader. When Chancellor Tench told him he was being given an audience with the man, he was equally incredulous and impressed.

Winston Servailles—sworn enemy of Berling Tench, the man with a bounty worth half of the entire nation—has come to speak to me. He was either a sorcerer or a madman. After yesterday's interview, Caito still wasn't sure which to believe.

When he finally laid eyes on him, three days prior, Caito was surprised by how young Servailles truly was. Despite the posters and pictures of him hanging all over Corynthia, it never actually occurred to him that the rebel was still in his twenties. The stories surrounding him all projected the image of a weary, downtrodden soldier. Yet Servailles's face was young and fresh with a wry smile on his lips and mischief in his eye. Even with death's maw closing around him, he spoke like a man with the rest of his life to live.

The intensity and emotion in Servailles's speech stirred Caito enough that he had to force himself to appear indifferent during their conversation. Seeing just how important the rebellion was to him—how important the freedom of the people was—made Caito want to act instead of just hoping that Chancellor Tench would drop dead of his own accord.

A shadow fell across him as a voice spoke, "He's an intriguing man isn't he?"

Caito bolted upright. A dark figure stood in front the window.

"How did you...?" he trailed off. He recognized the sly voice: It was the man who came to see him in Baggot. He changed his question, curious as to the stranger's presence, although not displeased. "Why are you here?"

"To offer advice."

"Advice? Isn't it my decision to make, now?"

"Have you made one?"

"I'm still afraid of choosing wrong." Caito passed his hand over his eyes. "I don't want to be involved," he added, feeling a little childish.

"A word of caution, then. I won't persuade you to one side or the other, but you have no choice."

Caito stayed silent.

Shifting his weight, the man continued, "The insurgent is an intelligent man and a powerful speaker—adept at manipulating and controlling conversations, situations..." He paused. "And people."

"He was very honest with me. He said he *wants* to use me for the influence of my name and reputation, but he told me he can offer me more than Chancellor Tench."

"What is more?"

"Control over my own legacy. By fighting for the rebellion, I can actually help elicit change through actions of my own. Servailles is right: Tench will only lock me away and place me on display."

"Very astute. Do you want to fight?"

"No." Caito heaved a sigh. "Though, I would prefer it to the alternative. The people are suffering; I *must* respond. I've seen Chancellor Tench's work firsthand," he continued bitterly. "I couldn't truly support him after what he's done to Corynthia, and I certainly couldn't live with myself if I stepped into agreement with him. I want to help Servailles free the people. Only... supporting the rebellion would mean promoting war, which doesn't sit right with me either."

A soft chuckle emanated from the man, like oil slipping over water. "The insurgent wants to free the *nation*."

"What do you mean?" Caito asked, narrowing his eyes at his inflection.

"Have you considered how the current chancellor came to power? What measures were taken, or lack thereof, that allowed him to take advantage of his position? It wasn't merely poor luck that a man such as Berling Tench rose to power with virtually no opposition," the man uttered slyly. "I digress. You'll have a much easier time here than out there fighting."

Rubbing his eyes, Caito shook his head. He was too tired to work out what the cryptic statement about the presidency meant. He was too tired for any of this.

"I won't live in comfort while people suffer and die. I've experienced the cruelty of the chancellor's laws. Meeting him and seeing how little he actually cares about others... I want his tyranny to end."

Caito grimaced as he recalled the suffering of his family and friends at the hands of Tench's men. The thought gave him resolve. He had known deep down what his decision was from the start, and the memories resurfacing were enough for him to be sure. Besides, there would be consequences no matter the path he took.

The silhouetted head inclined. "Then I have nothing more to say. You've made your choice."

He opened the window, then turned back to Caito. "One last piece of advice: Be careful who you trust. The devil disguises himself with honeyed words." He stepped onto the ledge.

"Wait!"

The figure turned once more.

"Who are you?" Caito implored. "Or at least, what do I call you?"

The man was silent for a moment. "Silarius," he said and dropped from the window.

Dashing to the window, Caito leaned out and scanned the dark rooftops below. There was no sign of Silarius.

Wind ruffled his hair as he stared out into the night. The army of clouds gathering to the east marched closer, reaching their ragged arms across the moon as though trying to steal it from its place in the sky.

Caito's head spun with questions. His mind was made up, yet the man's cautionary advice kept him unsure.

Servailles seems sincere, but what did Silarius mean about freeing the nation? Who can I trust? He closed his eyes, putting his head in his hands. He was in too deep already, though he never really had a chance to wade in to these murky waters. *I can only follow my heart and hope I'm choosing the correct path. Between war and continued suffering...*

He wanted to put an end to Tench's tyranny, to alleviate the yoke around Corynthia's neck; however, he hated the necessity of war to succeed. As he wished there was another way, Silarius's words from their meeting at the Golden Keg returned to him: *You must decide which cause rests easier on your conscience.*

Caito only hoped that he would still have one in the end.

16

THE STREETS OF SERUVIA

A KNOCK SOUNDED ON Caito's bedroom door. He sighed back, assuming Chancellor Tench was summoning him for yet another audience.

He was left to himself for a day after the excitement of Servailles's trial. That was his last taste of peace. Ever since, Tench had badgered him endlessly about his visions. Caito provided only what he viewed as unimportant snippets, saying he couldn't figure them out himself. While partly true, the reality was that he simply wanted no part in helping the tyrant continue to lobotomize Corynthia, something Silarius's visit had helped him realize.

Tench didn't believe him, of course. After discovering how distrustful the man was, Caito was surprised more of his advisers weren't already rotting in a dungeon. It was obvious Tench was growing frustrated with his lack of cooperation, and he figured it was only a matter of time before the chancellor also tossed him behind bars. He had decided he didn't want to find out how far he could push his luck.

This brought him to the issue of fleeing Audax Keep.

In between appointments with Tench, he sat in his room and kept a close eye on activity in the city, which dissolved into chaos after Servailles's escape. With all of the riots sweeping through the streets, Caito was heartened to think he might find help if he managed to escape the fortress. Unfortunately, his spirits always dampened when he considered the latter subject: Soldiers patrolled the halls constantly, and the interior itself was a maze. Not to mention the personal guards that Tench had assigned to him, likely to prevent the very thing Caito intended to do.

The fortress was, well... a fortress. And Caito felt little more than a woodpecker in a forest of stone.

Opening the door to a heavyset man in uniform waiting to escort him to Tench's office, Caito marched through the outer chamber into the hall, ignoring the guard's greeting. He had traveled the route to the chancellor's office so often it was ingrained into his head. He forged through the halls without slowing. His patience was low today, and he wanted to be finished with Tench's interrogation as soon as possible. As a result, the out-of-shape guard was sweaty and breathless by the time they arrived at the office.

Before the man could open the door and announce their arrival, Caito pushed past him, bursting into the room. "You asked for me?"

Tench glanced up from an unfurled scroll with an alarmed look. He stared at the red-faced guard, then at Caito, seeming flustered by their sudden appearance. "Um, yes. Please sit down."

Caito did so in the high-backed wooden chair before the desk.

The office was an expensively studious space. Bookshelves stuffed with tomes and elegant trinkets stood at attention along the walls. The dark, grainy desk squatted reminiscent of a sleeping bear in the center of the room, ink bottles and various gold and silver measuring instruments cluttering the margins; a significant stack of reports dominated much of its surface. A large window gleamed behind Tench's seat, deep purple curtains bunched on the edges of a gilded rod fixed above it.

The room reflected the chancellor himself: Rich, pompous, and boastful.

Tench waved away the guard, who saluted and closed the door behind him. He gestured at the stack of papers on his desk. "I was reading through some reports here. Fiscal matters, state of the troops, and such." He wiped his shining forehead with a handkerchief from his lapel.

Caito stared at him. He had never seen Tench rattled before. Even when threatened at arrow-point at Dominus Square, he had been relatively composed—offended and enraged, though confidently so. As Tench clasped his hands in front of him, Caito noticed that they were shaking slightly.

The chancellor adopted a strained smile. "How may I help you?"

"You requested me."

Chancellor Tench's face cleared. "Ah, yes, of course. I apologize; I'm stretched a little thin at the moment. How fares your interpretation?"

Caito withheld a sigh. At least he was right to the point. Tench usually led off with small talk, probably to give the appearance that his visions weren't the only reason Caito was here.

"Nothing has changed," reported Caito in a flat voice. "Still."

With a chuckle barely concealing a scoff, Tench affected what he obviously thought was a warming smile. To Caito it looked more like a leer.

"I don't think you realize the importance of your job here. A group of anarchists threatens the peace and integrity of my country, while you hold the key to their destruction. I've given you all the privacy and quiet in the world"—Caito bit his tongue to hold back a retort—"there is no reason you shouldn't have had a breakthrough by now. My sources reported you saw this vision months ago! Unless you're stalling on purpose, which would be incredibly unfortunate..." Tench trailed off, but Caito understood the words left unsaid: *For you.*

He felt a hot stab of anger. Not only at the silent threat, but also at the implications behind how long Tench had been searching for him. Knowing the tyrant's tendency for inflicting hurt, he could only imagine what happened to poor Aunt Gertie at home. He silently cursed the loud-mouthed physician who began this whole mess.

I can't control what's already come to pass, he reminded himself. He could only keep pressing forward with the hope that he could right the wrongs in his wake.

"If you're so concerned about these anarchists, why aren't you doing something about it? You have armies don't you?"

Tench examined his manicured cuticles. "The money and resources it takes to move thousands of men makes it incredibly tedious to migrate armies back and forth. At this point, national security takes precedence over this nest of aggravated ants that is Servailles's insurgence. Cappus will hold. However, even a small colony of ants can destroy a house, given enough time. Which is why your visions are paramount to exterminate them before any lasting damage. A quick strike at the heart of the issue will end this foolishness from the rebels."

The laziness of Tench's reasoning made Caito stare. From what he could glean, the chancellor had enough men to pose a significant threat to the rebellion should he decide to mobilize against them. One order, and

Servailles would be forced to retreat from Cappus or risk being crushed between the Corynthian army and the mountain. Any sensible strategist would have fallen upon the rebels as soon as possible. Tench's conceited arrogance was actually helping the freedom fighters gain a foothold.

Caito didn't share any of this with him. Instead, he focused on why he was there, rather than point out Tench's negligence. "I don't have the answers. The visions are scrambled, blurry, confusing; I can't control them. And it's not like there's someone who can teach me."

Tench tilted his head, still wearing that hateful smile that said *I understand what you're going through, and I want to help.* "All I hear are excuses. You've had this gift your entire life. If you desire a reward for your trouble, then name it. I'm growing weary of your pretenses." He heaved a dramatic sigh. "I'm beginning to suspect fraudulent behavior, Caito."

All of Caito's efforts to stay calm vanished at those words. He stood up violently, knocking over his chair, indignant fury poising like a snake.

"*Fraudulent behavior?!* You think I'm lying? That I want to be dragged to your office every day to be interrogated and accused by *you*? You think I enjoy being stared at, poked, and prodded like an animal in a cage? The sleepless nights and endless nightmares that bleed into my head even when I'm awake—you have absolutely *no* idea about my suffering or the toll it takes on me!"

Tench's smile turned mocking, and his eyes glinted cruelly. He looked to be enjoying Caito's outrage. "Tell me something, Caito," he gloated smugly. "What is a Soothsayer who cannot decipher the future? After all, it's your purpose. Failing that, you're of no use to me."

Caito glared at him, the urge to strike the man making his fists shake. "Tell *me* something, *Berling*. What is a leader who doesn't help their people? After all," he remarked, fury coloring his voice, "it's your purpose."

Tench worked his jaw, face slowly turning red. Recognizing the danger sign, Caito suddenly realized there was a good chance he would have to flee. Still, he stood his ground.

Finally, the chancellor stood up and straightened his tunic. "Get out." He pointed at the door, finger shaking with suppressed rage.

Caito curtsied scornfully. "As you wish, *my lord*."

As Caito went to the door, Tench bellowed after him, "I gave you an opportunity to be something great, Lazar!"

Caito laughed. "No thanks, I won't become a tool in your conquest of tyranny. I would rather die." He wrenched open the door, stepping out to where the guard waited to escort him back to his room.

"Be careful what you wish for! I can make all of your dreams come to pass—*especially* the nightmares!"

"Go to hell," Caito shot back, slamming the door shut on the chancellor.

Thirty minutes later, as he pushed the wardrobe in front of the door to his sleeping quarters, Caito considered that maybe *go to hell* hadn't been the best retort. If Tench didn't want him dead before, he definitely did now.

Hindsight I guess, he thought with a twinge of regret. *At least I found a use for all of those couches.*

After his disastrous meeting with Tench, Caito stormed back to his room escorted by the same guard. Figuring he didn't have much time until Tench sent soldiers to arrest him, he began barricading the door with furniture as soon as it closed. However, when the door shook unceremoniously from what sounded like a battering ram only ten minutes later, Caito suspected he might have misjudged the chancellor's ability to act.

Hurriedly stacking another table on top of the small mountain accumulated in front of the door, he bounded to the large ceiling-high windows on the other side of the room, only to find that they did not open. A splintering sound from behind stimulated him to retreat into the bedroom, where he began to panic.

Now, stepping back from the wardrobe, his eyes fell on the window where Silarius had vanished in the middle of the night. Running to investigate, he threw it open and looked down. It was a sheer drop. Unless the man could fly...

No, wait.

Leaning out farther, Caito noticed a thin ledge in the outer wall. He hadn't seen it at first because of how the window extended from the side of the Keep. He groaned, cursing to himself. The times he had stared through that window at the ground below, wondering how Silarius managed to vanish without a trace, when all he had to do was look a little closer.

Caito studied the ledge for a moment before hopping onto the windowsill.

Protruding a few feet below the window, the outcrop ran along the side of the fortress until a shingled roof presented itself as a reasonable landing spot. He would have to lower himself backwards out the window, drop, and catch the ledge. If he missed or slipped... well, he wouldn't have to worry about Tench anymore. From there, it was a matter of hanging by his fingers and traversing over to where he could fall onto the roof.

Easy enough.

The shaking in his legs disagreed as he took a deep breath and went over the edge.

Hanging from the windowsill over a hundred feet from the ground was easily the scariest thing that Caito had ever done. His palms grew slick at once as he tried to locate the ledge with his feet. The wind whistled around him like vengeful spirits while rain stung his face, making it even harder to focus. He took another breath as he visualized the maneuver that would save his life. He wished he could wipe his hands.

Then, he released the windowsill.

Even though the outcrop was only a few feet down the wall, the brief moment of free fall felt endless. Caito scrabbled for the ledge, managing to catch it with one hand. As his body swung into the wall, his fingers started to slip, pulled down by his momentum—his pointer finger, then pinky. Frantically, he swung his arm up and caught the ledge with his other hand. After a few moments of panicked adjusting, Caito hung securely, heart beating out of his chest. Then, he let out the air trapped in his lungs and began to shift towards the roof.

He did his best to avoid the wet spots left by the drizzle, almost missing the ledge more than once as he moved his hand. The wind blew angrily around him, lashing the falling rain into his face and shaking his concentration. He wondered if the soldiers had broken into his room yet, and if they would look out the window in time to watch him fall to his death. Thankfully, he found plenty of footholds to help take some of the strain off his fingers.

Finally, after what felt like hours of inching his cold, aching fingers over his stone lifeline, he was above the roof and let go.

Although he bent his knees to absorb some of the shock as he landed, Caito still went sprawling. He slid down the wet roof, splaying out his limbs and digging his tired fingers into the shingles, knocking a couple loose in his scramble to stop his momentum. He skidded to a halt mere inches from the roof's edge and lay there, letting the rain fall on the side of his face.

A feeling of elation filled Caito, lifting him like a cloud onto his feet. He had made it out of Audax Keep—alive!

Using his hands to steady himself, he crawled along the roof, dropping onto a second, lower one at the end of the first, then sliding down a gutter into a clump of bushes at the bottom. Peeking out from between them, he found himself in the backyard of a house in the shadow of the fortress. Caito scanned the property, checking the windows. They were shuttered and dark, though a dog was barking somewhere nearby. He rolled cautiously out of the bushes, darting across the lawn to the gate on the other side. Mantling over it, he loped away from the Keep, making sure to keep close to the houses lining the road.

Very few people were in the open. The couple figures Caito did pass looked frightened and hurried to the other side of the street when he approached. As he passed by dark alleys, lackluster eyes followed him from the shadows—the homeless and neglected in their shelters of plywood and garbage, kept warm by their own waste.

He was inexplicably reminded of his own home when the soldiers came, which made him sad. He recalled the crowd at Dominus Square during Servailles's trial—their faces, their pleas; the overwhelming feeling of despair, fear, and frustration he had felt from them—and hot anger surged through him.

This is all Tench's doing. He's torn apart these people's lives.

After a few minutes of darting through the streets, Caito heard shouts in the distance. His curiosity peaked, and, against his better judgment, he turned towards the cries.

As he drew closer, he heard the sound of breaking glass and a crash. Cutting through an unoccupied alley, he peered out of the shadows at the commotion.

A scuffle between a few soldiers and a group of angry looking young men was playing out before him. The soldiers, all in Corynthian blue, seemed to be trying to detain the rioters; one of thugs was on the ground, struggling against a guard on top of him. However, as Caito watched, the guards abandoned all of their attempts to constrain them, drawing their weapons instead. The thugs broke away and retreated back down the street, yelling obscenities. The soldiers gave chase, except for two who stayed behind to bind their new prisoner.

Caito turned and went back the way he came. As he reached the end of the alley, he heard the sound of footsteps and dived back behind a stack of boxes. Peeking around his hiding spot, he saw a lone man walking down the street with his head bowed against the rain. He sat back, waiting for the person to pass.

Without warning, a massive explosion rattled the nearby windows and threw him into the wall.

Caito lay stunned for a minute, ears ringing, then he pulled himself up with a groan, flinging water from his hair with a shake of his head. He staggered to the edge of the alley to investigate.

One of the apartments had been blown to pieces, chunks of wood and brick cratering the cobblestone street. Some of the debris was flung into nearby buildings, splintering doors and smashing through walls. Screams sounded, tinny and weak to his battered ear drums. The poor soul in the street was still struggling to his feet.

As the person looked around dazedly, Caito registered running footsteps accompanied by cries from the end of the street. Any soldiers nearby would have heard the explosion and would be sprinting towards the source like moths to a flame.

Without thinking, he dashed into the road, grabbing the bystander's arm and pulling him back into cover.

"What—who—" the man cried, trying to struggle out of his grip. He slipped, almost dragging Caito down with him.

"Stay down, and be quite," Caito commanded urgently.

The man obeyed and looked at him with trepidation for a moment. "What in the blazes?" he exclaimed, starting as though to stand up.

"For the love of the All-Mother. *Be quiet.*"

"But you're—"

"*Yes,*" Caito shot back with a jab of his thumb back towards the street. The footsteps were growing louder.

The man shrank down beside him. He was a large bear of a man with a ferocious black beard streaked with gray and thundering eyebrows. However, the way he cowered against the wall made Caito almost want to laugh. Apparently, his mettle did not match his appearance.

Sounds of combat floated over the blockade of rubble, and Caito realized with a jolt that the fastest way around the wreckage was through the very alley they hid in. Abruptly, he grabbed the stranger's elbow, pulling him roughly to his feet.

"Wha—"

"Trust me."

Dragging him to the other end of the alley, he paused to make sure the coast was clear, then ran into the street, still towing the man behind him. The guards were gone with their prisoner; the street was deserted. The two of them ran up the road a ways before slowing next to a dark shop.

As they huddled under its dripping eaves, Caito stole a glance behind them. Six soldiers emerged from the alley, trotting down the street away from them. A plume of smoke from the exploded building struggled to rise against the rain.

Caito breathed a sigh of relief and slid down the wall onto his haunches. He looked at the man doubled over next to him. "I'm sorry about that."

"Sorry...?" the man gasped. "What—why—" he spluttered for a moment before finally bursting out, "*What the hell is happening?*"

"Sorry," Caito repeated. "I'm—"

"The Soothsayer. I know that; I was at the trial. But why in the blazes are you out here running from guards? Why am *I* running from guards?" He paused and frowned, wringing water from his beard. "Why did you grab me?"

"The soldiers would have seen you."

"So?"

Puzzled, Caito cocked his head at the man. "Do you realize how that would've looked to them? You were standing in front of a building that had just been destroyed."

"I didn't do anything," stated the man obstinately.

Caito bit his lip with some consternation at what he might have walked himself into. "What's your name?"

"Martin Runlow."

"Well, Martin," began Caito, peeking down the street again to make sure the coast was still clear. He didn't know why he was taking the time to explain to the man why he saved his life when soldiers were actively searching for him. "Imagine this. You're a soldier ordered to patrol the streets and arrest any rebels or rioters. To summarize, you're essentially fighting a war against the city's inhabitants."

Runlow frowned again. Caito ignored his confusion.

"You don't know who's complicit and who isn't, which means you must act under reasonable suspicion. With that in mind, if you saw someone standing in front of a recently exploded building, wouldn't you think that's reasonably suspicious?"

"I was just in the wrong place at the wrong time! I had nothing to do with it!"

Caito pinched the bridge of his nose. *Why am I bothering?* he groaned to himself. *I'm risking too much for this.*

"They won't care, Martin. You were in the wrong place at the wrong time; that's enough for them. I was doing you a favor and saving you. Do you know what Tench does to rebels?"

"I'm not a rebel and didn't want saving, boy! I *want* to go to the damn butcher!"

"Fine!" snapped Caito, wondering why he was so worked up. "Go to the damn butcher! See how that works out for you!"

"I will!" Runlow bellowed and marched out into the rain.

Caito watched him leave for a moment before swearing and striking out in the opposite direction. Runlow's obstinance would heap trouble on his head if he wasn't careful. No matter, he couldn't help someone who refused to accept it.

"Stop there!"

Caito spun around, ready to run, but the cry wasn't directed at him.

Three soldiers in blue uniforms had just appeared in the street about thirty yards in front of Runlow, who froze and gawked stupidly at them. They advanced menacingly.

"Bad time to be out," the lead soldier warned. "On your knees!"

"I didn't do it!" Runlow cried, backing away from them.

"I said *on your knees!*"

Caito looked back up the street for a desperate moment. The soldiers, focused on Runlow, hadn't noticed him yet; he could escape. Then, he remembered Tench's smug face as he spoke of the sources that had revealed Caito to him—the hell he must have brought on those back home, just because they knew him. He couldn't leave another innocent man to suffer punishment because of him.

Gritting his teeth, he turned back to the panicking Runlow. "Martin, come on!"

This time, Runlow moved on his own volition, scrambling up the street towards Caito, who broke into a run himself.

He could hear the guards clanking and crashing behind them as Runlow wheezed by his side. He abruptly cut into a side street shouting, "This way!" He had no idea where he was going, nor did it matter—they just needed to lose the soldiers.

A pair of women dove aside as the two rushed past, their baskets of ointments spilling over the cobblestones. Caito gasped out a hurried apology and made another turn, skidding to a stop when he found himself face-to-face with a pair of guards. The soldiers quickly recovered from their surprise and drew swords as the pursuing guards rounded the corner behind the pair, trapping them.

Runlow threw his hands in the air crying, "I'm not involved!" Caito withheld the urge to hit him.

One of the soldiers behind them cleared his throat. Caito and Runlow turned to face him.

"So," the man drawled, "Caito Lazar, the Soothsayer."

Caito said nothing.

"You know, I couldn't believe it when Chancellor Tench issued a warrant for your arrest. Wanted for treason against the nation, fleeing arrest... fraud."

That was fast. Caito caught sidelong glance from Runlow, which he ignored.

"Wanted dead or alive," the soldier added ominously. He grinned, revealing a few missing teeth.

"Are you sure you want to do this?" Caito stalled while he assessed the situation.

There was an opening past the two soldiers they ran into, but even if he managed to break away, he couldn't just leave Martin at their mercy. Tench would likely execute him. If Caito abandoned him, he was ensuring his death. Guilt for dragging the man along filled him. *I should have let him be.*

"I am an important person, you know."

"Oh, we know. After all, the chancellor wants you dead." Meaty chuckles accompanied the statement.

"Or alive," Caito contradicted desperately. His heart sank. There was no mercy in these mens' eyes. There was no way out.

The soldier laughed evilly. "We'll tell him you struggled."

Caito raised his fists in what he knew would be a futile last stand. "I'm so sorry," he murmured to Runlow.

As the soldiers tightened their circle around the pair, a tinkling crash rent the air, and a table flew through an upper window, smashing into a couple of the soldiers. Caito cowered, covering his head with his arms to shield himself from flying glass and wood splinters, while Runlow yelped and dropped like a frightened goat.

As the guards reeled away with cries of shock and pain, Caito used the confusion to pull Runlow to his feet and drag him towards freedom. Once again, he ran without direction, making turns and jumping into different streets at random. After a few blocks, when he could no longer hear the soldiers shouting, he ducked into another alley, leaning against the wall to catch his breath. Runlow collapsed to the ground again.

Wiping sweat and rain from his face, Caito heard the sound of running footsteps approaching them. Assuming that one of the soldiers broke loose, he braced himself to leap out at their pursuer.

The footsteps grew steadily louder, slapping against the wet stones, until a figure crossed in front of the opening.

Stepping out with a yell, Caito swung his arm, catching the person in the neck. They let out a grunt as their feet went into the air, and they landed on their back.

Caito stood over their pursuer as he lay on the ground, wheezing for air. He was a boy younger than Caito wearing a red shirt and trousers soaked from the rain. A gray band circled his bicep.

"Are you a loyalist?"

The boy coughed and tried to sit up. Caito placed his foot on his chest and pushed him back down. Wincing, the boy tried to move his foot. "Do I look like a soldier?"

Kicking his hand away, Caito applied even more pressure, causing the other to inhale sharply. "I didn't ask if you were a soldier. Not all who are loyal to Chancellor Tench carry swords."

"No, I'm not a loyalist. I'm an Acolyte of the Seer, and I'm here to save you."

17

THE ACOLYTES OF THE SEER

"**A**COLYTE OF—WHAT?"

It was Martin Runlow who answered, his voice taking on a churlish tone as he wrinkled his nose. "Acolytes of the Seer. They're an activist group trying to overthrow Chancellor Tench through extreme measures. A bunch of violent anarchists is what they are." He spat on the cobblestones. "They support that cursed rebellion in the west."

The boy slid himself out from under Caito and climbed to his feet. "We are *not* anarchists," he told Martin hotly. "We are simply fighting fire with fire. Please, we need to leave the streets. Come on. We have a hideout this way."

"I'm not going with you, *boy*," Martin snorted.

"Then don't," the boy snapped back. "This way, Seer." He began to walk away with an expectant look at Caito.

Caito turned to Runlow. "Martin, don't be a fool. Come with us. If you're seen by a guard you'll be arrested. I don't know who these people are, but anything seems safer than Tench's soldiers."

"Safer?" cried Martin indignantly. "The Acolytes of the Seer are enemies of the nation! They're also operating under your name! You of all people should beware, especially after the chancellor took you in. Speaking of which"—he looked curiously at Caito—"why—"

Caito interrupted him. "It went sour. I can explain, but you'll have to come with us," he gestured to the rebel peering anxiously down the street. "I'll take my chances with them; you should too. You can't keep lying to yourself about Chancellor Tench. He doesn't care about you, and neither do his soldiers."

Martin stood there for a moment, jaw moving as though chewing on the idea. "Fine."

"Good. Lead the way," Caito told the boy.

He grunted and jogged up the street, Caito and Runlow trotting behind. It wasn't far when the boy turned down a set of stairs leading to the basement of a building, unlocking the door with a brass key from his belt.

Before following, Caito glanced around once more through the rain. He could hear fighting in the distance and wondered briefly who was winning.

Inside, they passed down a dimly lit corridor to another door, through which the sounds of muffled voices could be heard.

Caito paused, looking back at the rebel, who nodded at him encouragingly. He swallowed and turned the handle.

His first impression was of a dingy, ill-lit pub. The walls were made of red stucco, and the ceiling was low enough that Caito felt the urge to duck his head. Lanterns flickered from a number of circular tables throughout the room, giving it a cozy feeling. Peeling wooden boards creaked under feet, a discordant tune beneath the murmured conversations. There was a bar at the opposite end with another door behind it. A woman stood behind the bar chatting with a man occupying one of the stools. A large number of others were present (Caito estimated around thirty), all of them wearing a gray band around their bicep. Many of them, Caito was surprised to see, were women.

The room fell silent as everyone turned to look at him standing in the doorway. Martin lingered just off to the side, looking frightened and uncomfortable. Caito briefly commiserated with him; he had always hated crowds and attention.

The boy stepped around him and strode to the center of the room. Everyone's attention shifted to him as he spoke in a loud voice, "Attention, Acolytes!" He pointed at Caito, who felt the sudden urge to back out of the room again. "May I introduce to you, Caito Lazar! The Seer!"

Every single eye turned to Caito, even Martin's.

He stood there unsure of how to respond. They all seemed to be waiting for one, so he gave them a half-hearted wave.

All at once, the room exploded into noise and movement. People crowded around Caito, introducing themselves, bombarding him with questions, and trying to shake his hand or clap him on the shoulder. Others swarmed the young rebel, patting him on the back and congratulating him. Through the cacophony of noise, Caito managed to catch the boy's name as he shook hand after hand and was pulled into more embraces than he could count.

Finally, he extracted himself and advanced on the boy, who was grinning from ear to ear. "Gregor, is it?"

"Yessir. Allen Gregor."

"Right, I'm leaving. Don't follow me."

"What?" Gregor's beam was evicted by panic. "You can't leave! We're here to help you!"

"Help me?" Caito narrowed his eyes at the boy now bright red in the face. Silence fell around them as the room realized what was happening. "You don't know anything about me, yet you have the presumption to call yourselves my Acolytes? As though I endorse your violence? What I see, Gregor, is someone eager to make a name for himself, through which I'm merely a means to an end. If this is what the Acolytes of the Seer are, then I don't want any part of it."

"B-but—" Gregor stammered.

Caito cut him off. Hot anger coursed through him, and he felt a savage pleasure at Gregor's distress. All these people, even the children, thought they could use him as their tool. *Everyone's a damn opportunist*, he thought, feeling bitter regret that his so-called allies had so quickly revealed their intentions. He had hoped these Acolytes could help him escape Seruvia. No such luck.

"Goodbye, Gregor." He turned to the door. "Martin, are you coming with?"

Martin hurried to join him, harrumphing as though to say *I told you so*. "Seer, wait!"

The woman from behind the bar made her way over to them. Tall and thin, her hunched shoulders and protruding neck gave her the appearance of a shorebird. Her black hair was pulled back in a ponytail so tight it seemed as though she was trying to remove any wrinkles on her face. Her brown eyes, with irises so dark her pupils looked to be trying to swallow up the whites, measured him almost sardonically. A painful-looking smile fractured her pout as she approached.

"Alice Jryer," she introduced herself, extending a hand. "I lead these soldiers."

"You lead these... soldiers?" Her words took him by surprise. He had never heard of a woman as a soldier, much less as an officer. He always considered war a man's job.

Jryer's hand dropped to her side, her smile following. "Of course I do." There was now a touch of frost in her voice.

Caito immediately realized his error and tried to apologize, "I'm sorry. That's not what I meant. It's just—"

"Would you expect me to sit back and leave the liberation of my home to the men when I am able to fight?"

"No, I—"

"I took charge when nobody else would. These people need hope. Something more than a distant rebellion led by a disgraced politician. That's why we fight with you as our figurehead, Seer. You represent hope. The people believe you to be their savior, and I do too. I'm willing to lay my life down for that idea if it means Corynthia can be free again."

Her eyes flicked to Gregor standing ashamedly in the middle of the room. "I apologize for my scout's behavior. He may be overeager, but he means well. I can assure you we truly want to help you, just as I know you want to help us."

Words failed him, and he found himself suddenly unable to meet her eyes. Jryer's speech held a ring of confidence that made him feel horrible for his earlier attitude.

"I'm sorry," he apologized quietly. "It's just odd to see a woman leading soldiers. Not that I have experience with war."

Jryer's smile returned, more gently. "Most have the same reaction. It took a long time to gain the trust of these people. However, I think they would agree I've led them well."

Murmurs of agreement swept the room, and a few of the Acolytes even broke into applause.

Caito gave her a warm smile. "I'm sure you have. May we talk?"

"Of course. This way, please, Seer." Jryer turned and walked towards the back room behind the bar.

Caito jerked his head at Martin to follow. As he moved through the crowd, he felt everyone's eyes on him; some wondering, some hopeful, some predatory. He ignored their stares despite fighting the temptation to dash into the room and close the door.

At the bar, he looked back. Martin hadn't moved.

"Martin," Caito said. "Come on. I owe you this."

He took one step into the room before everything turned blindingly bright.

(A figure stands in a barn, speaking to someone astride a large, tan horse. A body is crumpled next to them. Rain pours down outside. An arrow flies through the air, and there is a cry. A flash of crimson slashes through the air like a blade, and the vision gives way to a familiar image of a burning city. Two figures fight high above on a bridge. A silver amulet shines ember-orange. Eyes glint behind a black compass mark—)

"Seer?"

Opening his eyes, Caito found himself prostrate on the floor. The floorboards swam dizzily in and out of focus before his face. A pair of boots stepped into his line of vision, and he slowly followed them up to the concerned face of Alice Jryer. He saw her mouth move, faintly hearing her ask if he was all right. He stared at her blankly, still processing what he had seen. The black ponytail had been unmistakable, and the cry of pain as the arrow pierced still echoed in his ears: It was Jryer he saw in his vision.

"Seer," Jryer repeated, "are you alright?"

Caito finally nodded. Grasping her extended hand, he pulled himself up, painfully aware of the room watching him. "Sorry," he mumbled to nobody in particular, then jerked his head at the doorway. "Can we...?"

Jryer waved him inside.

Still shaken from his vision, Caito took a moment to study the room. Heavy shelves of rough wood stood abutting the walls; parcels of food wrapped in cloth on some, rolled up papers and bottles on others. Barrels of mead were stacked in the corners, weapons piled against them. A table sat in the middle of the room with a map of the city laid flat upon it.

Closing the door behind her, Jryer walked around to the other side of the table, peering at him. "What happened? Did you have a vision? What did you see?"

Caito held up a hand to stem the flow of questions. Jryer shut her mouth immediately, and he felt a flash of gratitude towards her. He studied her face, feeling much older than he was. Her body buckling to the ground played through his head again, and he made a split-second decision.

"That is my business."

Disappointment ran across Jryer's tight-set face, though she quickly covered it up.

"I'm sorry," Caito amended. "The visions are difficult to decipher." He felt a surge of guilt at the lie. "I have some questions if you're willing to answer them," he added quickly before his conscious could eat at him too much.

"That depends on what they are." Jryer glanced at Martin. "What do you want to know?"

"Who exactly are the Acolytes of the Seer?"

"In an ideal world, we're here to bring down Tench from the inside, but the truth is we don't have the numbers or strength to fight him for long. Instead, we're trying to give the people hope and courage for as long as we can. We want to show others that Tench *can* be opposed. Unfortunately, if we wait long enough, he will root us out and overpower us. We wanted to help you escape before he can. Afterwards, we'll go into hiding."

"What about the rebellion? Couldn't you ask for aid?"

Jryer smiled bitterly. "They don't have the resources to help us at this time. Their agenda takes precedence."

"Their agenda? Isn't it the same as yours? To remove Tench from power?"

"They're taking a more... methodical approach. Instead of striking at the heart of the problem, Winston Servailles prefers to cut him off from the rest of Corynthia. It's understandable—he's fighting a war. The problem is, *we* are fighting for our survival, and we're taking the brunt of Tench's vexation."

Martin scoffed quietly. His eyebrows formed a dark storm front above his eyes, and his face was flushed under his twitching beard.

"What?" Jryer snapped.

Given permission to do so, the man exploded at once. "*You're* taking the brunt of it? You've turned this city into a blasted battlefield! You say you're doing this for the people, yet they seem to be the last thing you've considered! Are you under the impression we're content to cower in our homes while you fight your righteous battle? You're not giving us hope; you're giving us another reason to live in fear! If Chancellor Tench wants to raise taxes, *fine*. I couldn't care less! Just as long as soldiers aren't waylaying me in the streets or knocking down my door!"

Jryer opened her mouth to retaliate, but Martin brandished a finger, cutting her off.

"One of your little anarchist skirmishes nearly *killed* me this morning! Don't you sit there and tell me you give a *damn* about us! If it wasn't for this boy"—he jerked his thumb at Caito—"I'd be locked up or bloody dead!"

Caito smiled. He couldn't help it. The blatant, angry honesty was a breath of fresh air after weeks with politicians. Even Jryer was picking her words carefully—sculpting a story of righteousness, where the Acolytes were victims merely trying to survive, rather than picking the fight them-selves. Martin was doing what Caito wanted to do but couldn't: Saying exactly what he thought.

If only more people were like Martin Runlow, he wished wistfully.

Jryer gaped like a suffocating trout.

Leaning against the table, Caito raised his eyebrows at her. "You've heard from the Corynthian."

Her lips turned white as she pressed them together. Although she didn't seem particularly pleased with Caito's nonchalance, she chose to address Martin instead.

"Firstly, we are not *anarchists*. We fight for those who understand what's truly at stake. More than your money is in danger. Tench has already begun to take your basic freedoms; next, it's total subservience. He doesn't just care about your wallets when there's more he can have. That's what we're fighting against."

"And *yet*," retorted Martin, "all was fine until you started your revolt! By the All-Mother, the market was open right before you began burning everything down! If you don't poke the bear, it'll continue to sleep!"

"And sometimes it wakes up and mauls you regardless!" Jryer screamed back, red in the face.

Fairly sure everyone in the other room could hear what was transpiring, Caito held up his hands. "That's enough, both of you. Shouting at each other won't accomplish anything. What's done is done. Alice, I have a favor to ask of you."

"And it is...?" Jryer asked stiffly, as though trying to hold back the words.

"I've, uhh"—Caito chose his words carefully—"fallen out with the chancellor. While he was kind enough to take me in, I did not live up to his expectations. He tried to have me killed. I managed to flee the Keep, though I could use your help escaping Seruvia and finding Winston Servailles."

"Of course, Seer. That's precisely why we're here. However, I am curious; what happened between you and Tench?"

Martin mumbled something from the door.

"What was that?" Jryer demanded scathingly. There was a look of extreme distaste on her face that gave Caito the feeling any of the Acolytes who crossed her did not end up with favorable jobs.

Martin set his jaw. "The soldiers spoke of fraudulence." He nodded at Caito even though there was no reason to specify.

"Fraudulence?" Jryer turned her gaze back to Caito, who smiled quietly at her.

"My business is my business. I am entitled to my privacy—even from the chancellor of Corynthia."

"Well, *I* believe I'm entitled to an explanation. After all..." She indicated to the gray band on her arm. Caito noticed for the first time a red eye stitched into it: The mark of the Acolytes.

Realizing Jryer was right, he sighed. She had just given him a speech about how he was the hope of the people, then heard he had been accused of being a liar. Caito had a sinking feeling he would never escape the politics of his circumstances.

"I *am* the Soothsayer, and I've received visions I believe are connected to the civil war. I do, however, choose who I share them with. I withheld my knowledge from Chancellor Tench, for I have many reasons to distrust him. He grew frustrated and, deciding I was lying, threatened to execute me for fraud and treachery. Needless to say, I do not desire to be murdered. I fled, which leads us here. Unfortunately, Alice, I am not going to tell you either. The knowledge could be too dangerous in the wrong hands, and I don't believe it is pertinent to your work here."

Besides, he didn't know if he *could* tell her about the vision that he just had, in which he saw her die—at least he assumed she would die. Everyone seemed to. Having the knowledge of one's own demise—it would destroy him if he knew.

Jryer studied him for a moment. She opened her mouth, but before she could speak, someone barged through the door, brandishing a sword.

18

HEAVY IS THE MANTLE

T HE WOMAN CRASHED INTO Martin, knocking him into a shelf. Regaining her balance, she found Jryer with wild eyes. "Alice, we've been compromised! Soldiers!" she shouted before dashing back into the main room from which Caito could hear a great ruckus.

He caught a glimpse of blue, and his heart skipped a beat.

Jryer swore and threw herself at one of the shelves. "Help me!" she yelled at Caito.

He rushed over without a word to heave alongside her. The shelf slowly moved aside, revealing a door painted the same color as the walls. Caito pushed even harder at the sight.

As soon as the shelf was out of the way, Jryer threw the door open, beckoning earnestly for Caito to follow. He dashed over to Martin, who was spitting out curse words and bits of his beard as he struggled to extract himself from the sea of cheese, bread, and paper. Pulling him to his feet, he cried, "Come on!" for what felt like the hundredth time that day.

They rushed through the doorway up the stairs beyond to another door waiting stoically at the top. The rain drummed determinedly outside; it sounded like it had picked up during their time indoors.

Jryer addressed Caito, "We need to make for the stables quick as we can before the soldiers finish here."

"But—" (*A body on the hay-strewn floor. An arrow flies through the air.*)

"We have to. You need a horse if you want to reach Servailles's army before Tench catches you. Just follow me, do what I say, and we'll be fine."

"Alice," Caito started, gritting his teeth against what he longed to say.

He couldn't let his vision happen—he couldn't let someone take an arrow for him—yet the words were trapped behind the lump in his throat. *Just tell her!* He railed against himself to no avail.

She smiled sadly, as if she knew of the fate waiting for her. "I'm willing to take this risk, Seer. After all, what can we do without hope?"

"What about your people?" Caito glanced down the stairs. The Acolytes were still putting up a fight; the sound of clashing weapons harmonized strangely with the rain.

"They'll be fine. They're warriors, all of them. What matters is you. Now are you ready?"

Caito nodded. After a brief pause, Martin did as well, pulling his hood over his head.

Jryer slowly opened the door. Rain poured from the sky in earnest, rattling on the cobblestones like money falling to the floor. Motioning for them to follow, she slid through the doorway into the street.

They only encountered a few guards as they ran through the city. Jryer dealt with them easily, leaving them incapacitated rather than dead to Caito's relief. He found his spirits rising the closer they drew to Seruvia's wall. However, when they turned the next corner, his heart immediately plummeted.

Half-a-dozen soldiers sat under a shop awning. They jumped to their feet as the trio screeched to a halt in front of them.

"RUN!" yelled Jryer, bolting in the opposite direction.

Caito promptly slipped, falling hard. His kneecap cracked against the cobbles, and he yelped a curse. Hands lifted him to his feet, shoving him after Jryer. As he scrambled away, he glanced over his shoulder, skidding to a stop and almost falling again.

Martin stood in the middle of the street between them and the soldiers, a grizzled sheepdog defying a pack of wolves. His hood had fallen off, and he held his fists up in front of him. "Come on, you bastards!" he roared.

"Martin! What are you doing?!"

He glanced back, angry and obstinate. "I'll have no peace if I go with you, and I'll not spend the rest of my life running and hiding! I know who I am, and I'll go proudly! Go put an end to this ridiculous war!"

The loyalists were laughing at soaked, graying man standing defiantly before them.

"I'll have it out with you!"

"Seer! Come on!" Jryer reappeared at Caito's shoulder. "He's made his choice!"

No, no, no! He tried to limp back towards Martin, but felt arms grab him around the waist and pull him back. *I dragged him into this! It's my fault! He can't die!* He desperately tore at the hands holding him back. "NO!" he bellowed as Martin threw a punch at the blue-clad soldiers. "Martin!"

They turned the corner. "We can't leave him!"

"We have to."

They turned another corner and another. Caito was following Jryer again, though his resolve had been left behind with Martin. *I'm sorry Martin. I'm so sorry.*

The wind blew in aggressive spurts, sending the rain nearly sideways into them and soaking Caito to what felt like his very bones. He didn't care—he was already numb inside.

They stopped encountering soldiers, and the streets seemed terribly empty as they raced through them. The only sign of life was the occasional light shining through the crack of a curtain in the windows of the silent houses—glimpses into a world of warmth Caito couldn't share. The beating of the rain echoed in the alleys, making it difficult for him to hear his own thoughts, which he was glad for.

They stopped in the shelter of a doorway, and Caito finally noticed his surroundings. They stood next to the wall. While not nearly as tall as the walls of Audax Keep, it still stood at least three meters higher than the slanted shingles of the closest roofs.

Jryer wiped water uselessly from her face. "The stables are right around the corner. There's a barracks beside it, though, knowing Seruvia's guards, they'll be indoors rather than out in the rain watching the horses. They'll leave that to the stable attendants, who won't be an issue."

"You don't have to come with me," Caito stated. The vision of Jryer flashed through his head along with other disjointed, foggy images. Wincing, he pressed a hand to his forehead.

"I'm not letting you walk in there alone."

Looking up towards the wall, Caito blinked away rain or tears; he wasn't sure. He didn't think he could handle another person sacrificing themselves for his sake.

Then why can't I warn her? It was as though something was physically preventing him from forming the words. Besides, even if he did tell her, she would probably insist on accompanying him regardless. She wasn't the kind of person who feared death.

He thought back to her statement about hope, then to her Acolytes. They were most likely all dead or captured. What's more, she knew it—he could tell from her body language. Helping Caito was probably the one thing holding her together.

"Fine," he relented. "But let's be careful."

They crept back out into the rain. The stables lay ahead of them, silent and still as the rest of the city. No guards were visible, but that did little to hearten him. He noticed the barracks a little further away Besides the lights flickering in the windows, it was peaceful and unassuming.

"We'll have to be fast." Jryer was also studying the barracks, her brow furrowed. "But not too fast. We don't want to seem overly suspicious should they happen to glance out the window. Are you ready, Seer?"

Caito smiled grimly. A cloud of anxiety had settled into the pit of his stomach, making it squirm uncomfortably. "As ready as I'll ever be."

Heads down, they ventured out, walking quickly as though they had no motive other than to escape the downpour. Nobody exited the barracks to apprehend them, and Caito was able to breathe freely when he stepped inside the barn.

Shaking water from his hair, he looked around.

There were twenty stalls for the horses, nine of which were occupied, along with a door to the barn attendant's quarters. The floor was hard packed dirt and littered with straw. The smell of the place (wet horse combined with straw and feces) assaulted Caito's nostrils, forcing him to breath through his mouth. Pigeons fluttered back and forth between the rafters, their wings whistling hurriedly through the air.

Jryer gestured to the horses. "Take your pick."

Caito strode down the aisle of pens, examining the animals. It had been a while since he rode a horse; hence, he wanted one that didn't seem too spirited.

A large tan mare with a black mane and white muzzle caught his eye. Quietly observing him in turn, she nickered, shaking her head when he looked at her.

Caito walked over to her and reached out to pat her nose. "What's your name?" The horse snorted, and he smiled. "I'll take this one."

Jryer joined him at the pen. "That's a beautiful animal," she commented, reaching out to pet her as well.

Someone cleared their throat behind them. They started and spun around to see a heavy man with sideburns in grimy clothes standing in the doorway, hands on his hips.

"Do you have papers?" the man grunted.

Caito and Jryer looked at each other, alarmed at how easily he had sneaked up on them.

The man sighed, mistaking their alarm for confusion. "You need authorization to leave the city," he droned with repetitive familiarity. "The leasing of any steed must be accompanied by a form stating your name, business, and the duration and distance of your journey; along with your destination as per decree of Chancellor Berling Tench. Do you have papers?"

"Um," Caito stuttered. "No. I was hoping to purchase a horse?" He raised his eyebrows hopefully at the man.

"Purchase a horse?" the stable attendant scoffed. "This isn't a shop; this is a city stable. I can *lend* you a horse *if* you have the correct papers."

Caito opened his mouth then closed it again, unsure of how to respond.

The man scoffed again and pointed back out into the rain. "Then leave. I've already notified the guards of your arrival"—Jryer swore—"so don't even think about—" He stopped, frowning as though trying to remember something. "Wait..."

He stepped closer, peering into Caito's face. "You're—" His eyes widening, he turned to dash back to the safety of his quarters.

Jryer was quicker. Tackling him before he could take more than a few steps in retreat, she wrapped her arms around his neck in a choke hold. She was a lot stronger than Caito figured, because despite the man's advantage in weight and size, he slowly stopped struggling and went limp.

"You killed him!" Caito exclaimed.

She stood up, panting. "Don't worry; he's only unconscious. The horse!"

Agitated by the brief struggle, the animal trotted in a circle around her pen, blowing worriedly. She slowed when Caito approached and allowed him to rub her cheek. He spoke softly to her, thanking the All-Mother that Aunt Gertie taught him how to handle horses.

Grabbing a lead hanging on a hook next to the stall, he slipped it over the horse's head. Then, he opened the pen and led the animal out, tying the lead to a post. A quick search for tack yielded only a brush accompanied by a set of reins on a bench nearby.

"Alice!" he called to Jryer standing watch at the entrance. "I need a saddle and a blanket!"

She stepped into the attendant's office while Caito readied the horse.

With the straps fitted and the bit in place, He began brushing the animal, speaking soothingly to her as he did so. The mare appeared to enjoy the treatment; she lazily closed her eyes as he murmured to her.

"You're being awful thorough," Jryer noted, reappearing with a saddle and blanket in her arms.

"My aunt taught me not to skip steps." He scratched the mare's neck. "If you take care of them, they'll take care of you. Besides, they can ride further and faster if they're not uncomfortable."

"Your aunt was wise. Unfortunately, we're out of time," Jryer reminded him. "Soldiers are on their way." She dropped the saddle and held out the blanket.

Tossing the brush aside, he took it from her and threw it over the horse's back before placing the saddle on top. After tightening the buckles so it wouldn't slide, he heaved himself up into the saddle with a grunt.

"Well," Jryer remarked, stepping back and looking up at Caito, "this is it, Seer. You should find Servailles out west. Last I heard, they were still besieging Cappus."

"Thank you, Alice."

"You're our best hope. Good luck, Caito Lazar."

That's when the arrow buried itself into Jryer's leg.

19

WESTBOUND

"**A**LICE!"

Jryer buckled with a cry of pain.

Caito's horse jumped sideways, nearly throwing him off her back. As he steadied the horse, a voice shouted through the rain, "Come out of there! You're surrounded!"

A dozen blue-clad soldiers had appeared outside, some carrying loaded crossbows. One of them was reloading, tongue poking out in concentration.

Staggering to her feet, Jryer drew her sword and faced the soldiers.

"What are you doing?" Caito demanded.

"Buying you time."

"You can't! They'll kill you!"

"I'm already a dead woman, Caito," Jryer countered dryly. "The main gates will be shut, and it'll be hell to ride through the streets. You'll have to make for the pasture."

"The pasture?"

"Dismount from that horse, and put your weapons down!" the soldier called again. "Come out, or we're coming in!"

"Behind the stables," Jryer explained. "It leads to a field beyond the wall. There's a portcullis, but it's being repaired. If you ride hard, the guards there can't stop you." She limped forward, holding her sword above her head as if to surrender. "Go on my signal."

The loyalist soldiers slowly advanced as Jryer stepped out into the rain. Wincing from the bolt still protruding from her leg, the rebel leader slowly went to her knees.

The mare fidgeted nervously, but Caito brought her steady with a calming hush.

The captain approached Jryer, still with her sword above her head, and gestured for her to hand it to him. In one fluid motion Jryer swung the weapon around her head and into the loyalist's chest. Using the soldier as a counterweight, she pulled herself to her feet, shouting, "GO!" to Caito.

Digging his heels into the horse's side, Caito spurred her into motion. She belted out a bray before charged forward, scattering the soldiers. One of them fired a bolt wildly; it whizzed harmlessly into the air.

Even with steel buried in her leg, Jryer danced through the rain like a demon, keeping the soldiers scrambling in confusion.

Scanning the area for the pasture, Caito noticed a field behind the stable and urged his steed towards it. The mare jumped the fence with ease, Caito bouncing on its back as another missile flew past his ear.

The pasture was surrounded by fencing on two sides while buildings lined the perimeter to his right; the city wall loomed ahead of him. A half-constructed portcullis leaned to the side of a large arch cut from the stone. A canopy erected next to the portcullis sheltered seven soldiers underneath it. They started to their feet as Caito rode towards them; however, they were too slow to do more than shout as he tore through. Their cries sounded tinny and small.

Elation bloomed inside of him: He was out of Seruvia—he was *free*. Then a shadow blotted his joy as he remembered Jryer still inside the city at the mercy of the loyalists and Martin abandoned to guards.

Leaving the dismal farmland surrounding Seruvia, he rode through rolling hills of tall grass dotted with small clusters of trees. His adrenaline since dissipated, the riptide of fear and despair built up over the last few hours flooded in. He slumped over in his saddle, tears flowing as he mourned Martin Runlow, Alice Jryer, and the rest of the Acolytes. All of them would be dead for helping him—because of him.

Before long, he managed to take control of himself again. He straightened, wiping his eyes and taking a deep breath. *What's done is done*, he reminded himself. *Martin is right. I need to end this ridiculous war.*

Jryer told him he would find Servailles's army at Cappus; however, the city, as far as he knew, sat on the other side of Corynthia with plenty of wilderness in between. He was already exhausted; moreover, he had no supplies, and he wouldn't make it far without food or water.

He spent the night in the shelter of a thicket of trees off of the road. Thankfully, the rain lessened from a steady pour to a light drizzle, and the copse offered fair protection from the elements. As a result, he was only a little damp when he awoke. However, the cold morning air chilled him to the bone. With no fire to warm himself, he resorted to tromping around in a circle, smacking and rubbing his limbs until he was loose enough to ride.

The next day was miserable. There was no sign of pursuing loyalists, but he was cold, wet, and hungry. The only indications of civilization were far on the horizon—small oases of trees and windmills in the yawning sea of hummocks. Besides a few wild berries he found, his stomach was painfully empty.

Luck finally smiled upon him near midday when the road passed through a small town with a wayside inn.

Taking pity on Caito, the owner gave him a bowl of warm stew, which he sat down to eat a little regretfully. He disliked begging. It felt dirty and dishonest, as well as awakened painful memories of his home.

He listened in on a few of the locals while he ate, but their talk consisted mostly of the harvest season along with the drenching rain passing through—nothing about Tench nor the rebellion.

When he finished, Caito wandered back over to the innkeeper.

"Thank you for the meal and your kindness," he said with a bow of his head. "I'm sorry I have nothing to pay you with."

The gray-bearded man smiled kindly at him. "I would've felt I was assistin' a murder if I hadn't. Besides, I can afford to feed a wet dog from time to time." Caito understood the statement was meant to be endearing rather than insulting and smiled back.

"What else can I do for you, son?" the innkeeper added when he lingered for a moment.

"I'm traveling west, except I heard of a rebellion out that way," Caito tried to speak innocently.

The innkeeper raised an eyebrow. "You been livin' on an island? The rebellion's leaked into every part of Corynthia, not just out west. The capital's been riotin' for over a week now. Say, didn't you come from that way?"

"No, no, Therule," Caito lied hurriedly. Therule was further South than Seruvia.

The man nodded knowledgeably. "Anyway, Servailles's army is out west still besiegin' Cappus. 'Parently it's turnin' pretty bad. A few soldiers came ridin' through and had a bit too much to drink. The rebels are bleedin' them dry out there, and the chancellor won't send relief."

He leaned in, dropping his voice as if spies might be listening in. "There's talk what Tench is losin' his grip on the nation, that his days are limited. Astonishin', how quick Servailles turned things 'round."

"How far away is Cappus?"

"About thirty leagues west of Markalv."

"And how does one get to Markalv?"

"Oh, just keep on this road for..." the innkeeper thought for a moment before giving up and waving a hand. "It's a bit of a journey. You'll arrive at a crossroad after a while. Take the left one and Markalv's only a little further." He peered curiously at Caito. "Where're you from? You've got an interestin' look about you."

"Up north," Catio answered vaguely, forgetting he was supposed to have traveled from Therule.

"Alright. I won't ask questions. I suppose it's safer that way, anyway. Good luck with your endeavors, son."

"Thank you. And thank you again for your generosity today."

"Don't mention it," the man chuckled. "You looked like you needed it."

Caito wished him well. He was still exhausted, though he felt asking for a room would be overstepping. Besides, he had a long way to ride, and he was sure Tench's men were on his heels. No rest; that was his penance for the allies he was leaving behind—their hopes, his ghosts.

He entered the small stable adjacent to the inn. His horse was the only one there. Looking up from her meal of hay as he entered, she snorted a greeting. Caito leaned against the wall to watch her. He felt bad for how hard he was pushing her and figured the horse must be even more tired than he.

"How are you doing?" She snorted softly without looking up from her food. "We're leaving soon. Not much longer, okay?"

I hope.

When the horse finished eating, Caito readied her for travel. Then, swinging his aching body onto the saddle with a groan, he directed the mare back to the road. At the edge of the town, a weathered marker pointing west faintly displayed the word *Markalv*. With a tired sigh the horse seemed to echo, he flicked the reins, and they clopped away.

It took another four days of steady riding until Markalv came into sight. As the plains gave way to farmlands and vineyards gathered like children around creaking windmills, Caito faintly remembered he was a fugitive. He didn't know how quickly Tench could send word throughout Corynthia; regardless, he realized he should be careful not to draw attention anyway. He wouldn't be able to protect himself if he ran into soldiers, which meant traveling close to the city would bring more risk. Since the safest option was avoiding contact with people altogether, he left the road and entered a small cluster of trees.

He tethered the horse to a branch and, sliding off of her, collapsed at the base of the trunk. His exhaustion took over, and he drifted off to sleep.

Caito woke abruptly to the sound of hushed voices. Adrenaline surged through him, his eyes almost snapping open when he remembered his circumstances. The urge to jump up and flee filled him, fueled by the staccato beat of his heart. However, he forced himself to breath evenly and lie still as he listened.

"You think he's dead?" inquired the first voice, a man's.

"No," a woman responded. "His eyes are moving, look. Besides, his horse looks fine, if a little tired."

"You never know. People die in their sleep all the time." There was a pause. "It's a little wet out. Also, it's not like the inns are closed. He matches the description. Do you think...?"

"What are the odds?" the woman remarked a little sarcastically.

"I say we take him in. If it's not him, no harm no foul, right?"

"You say that now. For all you know, he could be a raging madman and murder us both."

"I'll say it was your idea," the man quipped with a laugh.

Caito heard the jingle of harnesses followed by two squishy thumps. As footsteps approached him, he opened his eyes and sat up with a suddenness that startled the two strangers. They both jumped back hastily with exclamations of surprise.

The woman was gripping the pommel of the sword on her hip. She was tall, with clear olive skin, and black shoulder-length hair peeking out from under a dark green cowl. Her elegant features were reserved, almond-shaped eyes flicking warily across Caito's face. A red hound snarled on the breast of her jerkin.

"Easy there. We mean you no harm."

The man had his own cowl pulled back, revealing brown hair and large ears. His face was young, though slightly roughened by stubble. An easy smirk lightened his face as he watched Caito. He, too, was tall, taller than his companion, and wore a matching pin.

They looked at him as though he were a wounded animal that could lash out at any moment. Caito assumed that in his current condition, it was a fair assessment. He certainly felt the part.

Silently, he climbed to his feet, head swimming. The overcast daylight was somehow uncomfortably bright. His horse nickered in concern as he swayed, and he placed a hand on the tree to steady himself, wishing the two people in front of him would stay in focus.

"Are you alright?" the man asked with sincere concern.

"What are you doing out here?" questioned the woman at the same time.

"That's my business." Caito cleared his throat, forcing back bile attempting to erupt from him. "What are *you* doing out here?" he shot back rather childishly.

The man opened his mouth, receiving a nudge from his companion. He shot her a look before speaking anyway. "We're looking for someone, actually."

If they're from Tench, I'm finished. Caito swallowed, gripping the tree harder to ensure he stayed upright. "Are you?"

He felt very lightheaded now. One of the strangers said something else, but Caito didn't hear him. He pitched forward, and his vision snapped to black.

20

THE MESSENGERS

(THE SOUND OF HUNDREDS of hooves fills the air as an army marches across a plain. A figure stands alone on a hill watching smoke rise behind a distant city. A dagger gleams in the darkness, and eyes glint behind a mask covered in shadow. The mask starts to fall away, until he suddenly realizes he is the one falling, falling into fire—)

Caito woke to his stomach growling so ferociously that he sat upright with a jolt, afraid a wild animal was attacking him. After a moment of thrashing in his blankets, he realized he was in a bed indoors, and there was no beast mid-pounce. As his breathing slowed, he looked around the room.

It was a small bedroom, cozy instead of confining. An oil lantern flickered on top of a dresser across from the bed next to a bookshelf filled with various odds and ends: Bones and wooden carvings, but no books. A woven green rug covered the middle of the floor, and an armchair hunched under the window, which was covered with dark green curtains. Soft, blue-white light glowing around the edges indicated it was day.

Catching his reflection in a small mirror on the bedside table, Caito cringed.

He was very pale, lips cracked and red—a bloody slash on his ghostly face—and eyes ringed with grim circles. They looked wild. Running his hand through his dirty, scraggly hair, he averted his gaze.

Kicking the covers off of his legs, he attempted to stand. His head protested, and he fell back onto the mattress. As he blinked away the stars on the ceiling, he heard the door open.

The woman from earlier entered, setting a mug on the bedside table. "Drink. You're dehydrated."

Caito propped himself up and took a sip. It was some kind of tea: Cold, yet sweet and refreshing. He took a second, longer draught. "Where am I?"

"Outside of Markalv. We have a safe-house."

"We?"

"My name is Tahlia. My companion, Wes, and I were sent by Winston Servailles to find a young man named Caito Lazar." She looked carefully at Caito.

"What does that have to do with me?" He took another sip of the tea, moistening his chapped lips.

"Well"—Tahlia spoke slowly, choosing each word with care—"we figured you might... know something, considering your predicament. You look like you might be on the run."

"You think I'm the Soothsayer."

Seeming taken aback by his directness, Tahlia faltered. Before she could respond, her companion stepped into the room, still wearing a friendly smile.

"Yes, we do. I'm Wes." He held out his hand.

Caito shook it. Wes's hands were rough, and his grip was strong. He gave Caito a wink.

Caito smiled back in spite of himself. There was something in Wes's eyes that he felt inexplicably drawn to: A mischievous glitter that seemed alien in the face of a soldier. Caito had the odd feeling he could trust this man with his life.

"Winston told us what you looked like. Also, you do seem like you just escaped from a certain angry dictator." Wes shrugged. "It's not difficult to add those together." He sat down in the armchair, crossing one leg over the other. "We're not loyalists—if that's what you're concerned about."

"I'm supposed to just believe you?" Caito glanced at Tahlia, who was scowling at Wes.

"Do you have other options?"

Caito studied the two of them. He didn't think they were sent by Tench to capture him; they had the perfect opportunity to do so earlier. Even so, Silarius's words from his late night visit wormed their way to the forefront of his mind: *Be careful who you trust.* In his weakened state, it seemed an important sentiment to have.

"How do I trust you're speaking the truth?" he asked again. Keeping his eyes on Wes's, he caught a flash of apprehension as the latter dropped his gaze, unable to hold eye-contact.

"Give it to him," Wes told Tahlia.

Tahlia's glower darkened even more. "We don't know—"

"Tahlia!"

She reached into her pocket and pulled out an envelope with an unbroken wax seal. She held it out to Caito without a word, still glaring at her friend.

Taking it from her, he broke the seal. The note inside had words written in neat, sprawling cursive.

Caito,

I am sending this letter with two of my most trusted friends in the hopes they find you free from the grip of Seruvia. My spies gave word that a splinter group inside the city had plans to free you from your prison and escort you to safety. Hopefully, they have succeeded; thereafter, Wes and Tahlia have located you in good health. I am aware you may not trust them at first, which is the reason for these words.

I have given some thought to your question about our cause. Not only do we want to free Corynthia from oppression, we also want to declare to the rest of the world that this is a free land. We shall not be oppressed by tyrants; we shall not let anyone wrest our freedom from us. This land belongs to those who wish to control their own life... provided it does not come to harm others.

The wind begins to turn in our favor, Caito—even as I write this, Cappus is all but ours—yet I would still have your support. I hope you will join me at Cappus to take part in our battle against the oppressor, though I will not force you.

My best regards,

Winston Servailles

Caito slowly refolded the note. The words felt unmistakably like Servailles: The eloquent, yet frank, wording—the choice given, rather than forced upon him. He tucked it into the pocket of his own tunic before looking back up at Wes and Tahlia.

"How far to Cappus?"

"A few days' ride," responded Wes immediately. "If we travel fast. Can you?"

"I'm as ready as I'll ever be. Tench's men are on my tail, I'm sure. I don't have time to recover fully."

"Then you are Caito Lazar?" queried Tahlia.

"Yes, I am."

They nodded simultaneously, Wes chuckling.

"Then rest as much as you can," Tahlia said with another glare at Wes. "We'll leave at first light tomorrow."

Caito nodded, and the two left the room. As the door closed, he heard Wes say something in a low voice, followed by a smacking sound and a yelp.

A smile come to his face again as he nestled back into the bed.

Through the next few hours, he drifted in and out of sleep. Exhaustion kept his mind in a dull, sedated state, but nightmares drove him repeatedly from sleep. His visions were now accompanied by images of Martin Runlow lying beaten and bloody in the street, and Alice Jryer being cut down by soldiers. Other faces, Allen Gregor prominent among them, paraded through his head, only to meet an equally horrible demise.

There was a brief reprieve from his tossing and turning when Wes reentered the room with warm stew and more tea. Accepting the meal gratefully, Caito was careful to pace himself to avoid his gut rebelling. His sleeping improved after that, and he felt much better when he woke next.

It was either early morning or late in the evening. The glow at the edges of the curtains had dimmed to a weak blue, and the lantern on the dresser was burning low. Muffled voices seeped through the door, the reedy chirp of crickets from outside masking individual words.

Caito sat up slowly, relieved when his head didn't perform another somersault. Noticing a glass of water beside the bed, he took a deep swig, savoring the cool drink.

A clean shirt, trousers, and vest were folded neatly on the armchair. He rose and gingerly dressed before walking unsteadily to the door. His entire lower body felt like kneaded dough from the constant riding; his legs shook slightly while he pressed his ear to the door to listen.

Caito heard Wes and Tahlia on the other side, along with a third voice, a woman's.

"—close to being compromised," the new voice was saying. "I've seen at least three units arrive today. They're locking down the city and setting up patrols. I've already warned Ollander. He's delaying until things are a little quieter."

"We'll travel through the wilderness, then," Wes declared.

"Do you think he'll be able to?" Tahlia asked. "He looks half-dead."

"He must. It's either that or be captured."

"Everything will be closed down by the morning," said the third person. "The roads will likely be blockaded for miles. It's your only option."

"This is a lot of trouble for one boy," Tahlia stated suddenly.

Catio frowned. The two rebels were not much older than he.

"Why are we risking so much for him? The Soothsayer is a fairy-tale. It's only been brought to life because of hysteria. I can understand if he and Winston had a personal connection, but they've met once, and now we're stepping into the fire for this boy? How does this make sense?"

"Winston is quite convinced. Besides there hasn't been a Soothsayer in—"

"There's *never* been a Soothsayer, Wes. You know as well as I do that Winston hears what he wants to hear and sees what he wants to see. That still doesn't make myths reality."

"Tahlia, he's not asking for you to believe, he's asking you to trust him. Regardless, Soothsayer or not, isn't it worth saving a life that Tench is determined to destroy? *He's* the enemy, in case you've forgotten. I trust Winston. He claims this boy is important, and I believe him."

There was the banging sound of a fist against a table. "He's *one*—"

Wes interrupted her. "One person? Do you remember how many *one* persons we wished we could have saved? That's a poor excuse to abandon a life, *Tyron*." There was silence for a moment before he spoke again. "Besides, we owe Winston everything. Without him, we'd likely still be participating in a genocide."

"You don't have to remind me." Tahlia's voice sounded muffled. "You're right. You're absolutely right. I suppose I'm just stuck on his belief in children's stories." She sniffed.

"I know, but *he's* real. And he's been through hell to get here. Let's help him the rest of the way. Come on. We should get some sleep."

"Go on," the other woman said. "I'll wake you when its time."

"Thanks, Bea," Caito heard Tahlia say in a subdued voice.

Chairs scraped against the floor and floorboards creaked as they retired to their rooms.

His mind buzzing, Caito returned to his bed.

Tahlia's adamant denial of his power gave him pause. It was one thing to be accused of fraud by Berling Tench; hearing a similar sentiment from an ally opened a whole new perspective. Alienation was not new, only his experience was from others his age who knew him personally before his secret was revealed. When he fled from home and rumors began to fuel his celebrity, he hadn't considered that not everyone might believe them. The threat of discovery from authorities had loomed much larger in his mind.

Servailles believes in me, he reassured himself as he pulled the sheets to his chin. *I don't need the entire world to support me if I can still do my part to end this war.*

A crash from the other room woke Caito next. His room was pitch black when he opened his eyes, except for a dim flicker of light under the door. He lay still, trying to listen until the door slammed open, startling him upright.

Tahlia stood in the doorway, breathing hard. There was blood on her shirt, a sword in her hand, and intensity blazing upon her face. "We need to leave. *Now.*"

Caito leaped out of bed without a second thought. Following Tahlia out into the main room, he froze at the scene in the next.

Two men wearing the light blue colors of Corynthia over chainmail lay in pools of their own blood. The room was in shambles. Furniture was overturned and destroyed. Deep gouges in the walls revealed where weapons had struck them. The front door lay rent on the floor from where it had been kicked in. Glass shards sparkled frostily on the floorboards, and one of the lanterns lay on its side, miraculously still burning.

Acquiring a cloak, Tahlia tossed it to Caito, who swung it over his shoulders before following her out into the chilly night air, where Wes and the other woman already waited for them. Wes sat astride a large stallion while the latter held the reins to two other horses, one of them Caito's. The mare carried two new saddlebags.

Caito pulled himself onto his horse, then took the reins from the woman.

"It's a pleasure to meet you, Soothsayer. My name's Beatrice," she said as she stepped back.

"Caito."

Beatrice grinned. A broad-shouldered woman with long, dark hair in a single braid over her shoulder, her garments were typical of a farmhand: A simple tunic and trousers stuffed into a pair of heavy boots. Her face was ruddy in the torchlight; wide, though not unpleasant.

"I want you to know, I have faith in you, Caito," she stated, handing the other set of reins to Tahlia.

Tahlia took them and thrust an object up to Caito before he could reply to Beatrice. "Take it."

Caito did so, discovering it was a short sword from one of the loyalist soldiers. "I don't—"

Wes cut him off. "None of that. You're going to need it."

Caito groaned. He didn't like weapons despite never having used one—the thought of taking a life, or even wounding someone intentionally, made him squirm. Nevertheless, he recalled the two dead men in the house and relented. He was a fugitive after all. He attached the sheath to his belt and hoped Wes's prediction wouldn't come true.

Tahlia, now mounted on her horse, looked down at Beatrice, who was already backing away towards the house. "Thanks, Bea." She touched her forehead in a salute.

Beatrice returned the salute. "The pleasure was mine. I'll keep them off your back as long as I can."

"Good luck to you," Wes said, with a hint of finality.

"And you. Now, go!" Beatrice turned and jogged back to the house, her braid bouncing on her back.

As Wes and Tahlia started to trot away, Caito took another look at the house. It looked small and lonely, all the more so when he thought of Beatrice fending of soldiers by herself.

The night air whipped against him, helping clear his mind of sleep as he caught up with the others. "What's happening?"

"They found us!" Wes shouted into the wind. "Beatrice noticed squads riding into Markalv yesterday, but I didn't think they'd send out patrols so soon!"

"Didn't you deal with them?"

"There'll be more," Tahlia said. "They typically operate in groups of four. They must have spread out to cover more ground. Those two will be missed, which means we have to put as much distance between us and Markalv as possible before they're found."

Caito felt sick. Tench's soldiers had moved fast, which meant Tench wanted him gone very badly. Shame filled him as he thought of what would happen to Beatrice once the loyalists found her. *Another sacrifice for my sake.*

Tears welled in his eyes. How could he be worth all of this suffering? He was just a lost, scared boy whose shadow was too large for him.

The dark mouth of Malaki Forest opened wide to swallow them. A few lights in the distance glimmered just inside the trees.

His heart sinking, Caito pointed. "Look there! What's that?"

Wes cursed. They reined in their horses and stood studying the distant specks.

"Roadblock," Wes growled, confirming Caito's suspicion. "We'll have to ride around."

All of a sudden, shouts came out of the darkness behind them. The trio looked around to see riders galloping up the road, torches leaving tattered trails in the wind. The farmhouse was ablaze in the distance; the sight was like a knife to Caito's gut.

"Into the fields," Wes ordered, anger coloring his voice; he had noticed as well. "They have more gear. That should weigh them down."

Leaving the road, they galloped into the soggy fields. The farmland, over-saturated from the heavy rainfall, clung to the horses' hooves, hindering them even as their riders urged them on. Glancing over his shoulder, Caito saw that the soldiers trailing them had split into two groups: One continuing down the road to the blockade, the other following them into the muddy farmland.

Fortunately, Wes's hunch was correct. The loyalists's horses seemed to be faring even worse with their heavy armor, and the trio began to draw away from their pursuers.

They slogged through the fields for nearly twenty minutes before turning towards the tree-line again. The loyalists chasing them were nothing more than small flickering specks of light behind them. As they gained solid ground again and rode into the forest, the lights disappeared entirely, allowing Caito to breathe a little easier.

They slowed their pace as they picked through the trees. It was very dark, and the underbrush was dense. Still, they didn't dare make a light to help guide them. Instead, they relied on the vague shapes of the forest, hoping they weren't straying too far off-course, though they paused often for Tahlia to light a match and check her compass. They didn't speak for fear of their voices carrying to the ears of their pursuers.

At long last, they stumbled from the thorny clutches of the forest onto the road. As there were no signs of loyalists, they brought their horses to a halt.

"The hordes of hell will be after us. It's unlikely we'll have time to rest." Wes checked the straps on his saddlebags to make sure none had been loosened by the clawing brambles. "I estimate about three days to reach Cappus, if we don't stop. Two and a half, if we're lucky."

Caito nodded despite the darkness hiding him.

Although he was physically exhausted, he was even more tired of being pursued. He thought of Alice Jryer, Martin Runlow, and Beatrice, who had all sacrificed themselves so he could escape. The sooner he made it to Cappus, the better he could avoid anyone else doing so for his sake.

"Then we won't stop."

"And won't look back," Tahlia added. Her voice was sad, and Caito knew she was thinking of Beatrice. She reached over, laying a hand on his shoulder. "We'll get you to safety. Don't worry."

"Come on, then," Wes said.

They had been riding at a steady pace for about ten minutes when the sound of pursuing hooves made Caito's breath catch in terror. Snapping his head around, his blood ran cold at what he saw.

Torches flickered through the trees back where the path twisted towards Markalv. The red light reflected wildly off of armor, making it seem as though chaotic spirits flew through the trees. Shouts and whinnies added to the rumble of hooves, creating a truly terrifying cacophony.

The loyalists had found them. The chase was on.

21

FLIGHT

G ROANING, CAITO SHIFTED IN his saddle. Dawn had broke, calm and unconcerned, yet they were still being pursued.

Their hunters were relentless. Though the trio managed to put a few miles between them in the night, they didn't feel comfortable enough to stop for a rest. The soldiers were slower than they were, however they knew they couldn't allow them to catch up, or they would be right back at square one. What was more, despite alternating riding and walking, their horses were exhausted to the point where Wes worried they would ride them into the ground. If that happened, they would be in real trouble.

The only bright side of their current predicament was that Caito's visions seemed unable to penetrate the fog of exhaustion occupying his mind. He was thankful for that at least.

The terrain grew rougher as the road wound into the foothills. Despite the ground they covered, it was still at least another two days (by Wes's estimate) until they were in sight of Cappus. For Caito, whose entire body ached in a way that he hadn't thought possible, that seemed like an eternity away.

All of a sudden, Wes called a halt. Leading his horse over to the side of the road, he slid off, wincing.

"Why are we stopping?" Tahlia demanded. Her hand sat on the pommel of her sword, her eyes searching the trail behind them as she brought her own steed to a stop.

Caito took the opportunity to collapse off of his horse into a fern. Taking off his shoes, he began massaging his feet. Beatrice had packed him a pair of traveling boots, though they no longer seemed to be helping.

"The outpost," Wes said simply. A smile sprang onto Tahlia's face at his words.

"Outpost?" Caito repeated curiously.

"Our company, the Crimson Hounds, is stationed in the area," Tahlia explained with a tap on her dog's head pin. "We captured a loyalist fort. It—uh—burned down, but the Hounds remained in the area as a rear guard while the main force besieged Cappus."

"As far as we know, they haven't been recalled yet," Wes added.

"Which means we could set up an ambush. We just need to reach them first," Tahlia finished.

"Then why have we stopped?" Caito forced his boots back on and stood up. His horse had wandered a little ways away to graze. He limped after her, calling back over his shoulder, "How much further?"

"Shouldn't be far. We had a base in the hills. We'll check there first."

They all remounted and set off again. Rain began to drip from the sky, so Caito was now wet as well as sore and tired. However, the hope of help down the road boosted his mood significantly.

They hadn't traveled for much longer when they heard the sound they had been dreading the entire morning: Hooves rumbling in the distance behind them. To Caito's fatigued mind it sounded like an entire army.

Nobody wasted any time in urging their weary horses into a begrudging canter. Caito didn't dare look behind him. Instead, he leaned low over the mare's neck, focusing down the road as far as he could. He had learned during the night that looking over his shoulder only made the fear worse. He knew they were there. There was no point in tormenting himself.

Foam lathered the sides of the mare, and she huffed and heaved as she went.

The road before them suddenly dipped down and away from the hills, the rocky slope they skirted turning into a cliff face in front of them. Speckled granite rose over a hundred meters high, ferns and moss spilling out of cracks and hollows in the ragged rock.

"We're almost there! This bend wraps around the cliff about half-a-league before the terrain becomes a little less—"

"Impossible?" Caito offered.

Wes grinned. "Nothing's impossible, my friend. Not if you have grit."

No sooner had the words left his mouth when disaster struck.

Wes's horse buckled and fell, throwing him into the dirt. Caito and Tahlia immediately pulled on their reins. Sliding from her saddle, Tahlia ran to help him up.

Wes sprang to his feet. His horse lay unmoving next to him. "Caito keep riding! Tahlia and I will hold them here!"

After a moment of hesitation, Caito also drew his sword, surprised at how light and comfortable it felt in his hand. "Not a chance."

"Caito, don't be a hero."

"I could say the same to you."

Wes growled at him, a guttural sound that made Caito flinch. "Don't be ridi—"

Tahlia put her fingers to her mouth and let out a piercing whistle, killing the rest of his words. It echoed for a moment before she spoke.

"Wes, Caito, don't be idiots. We don't have to fight them. We can hide."

"What about this huge lump on the road?" Wes challenged, waving at the dead horse. "They'll know we're short a ride."

"They'll probably assume you're with one of us. There are far too many for us to fight."

"If they search the area—"

"Are you really worried about those blundering oafs finding us?" Tahlia asked with a laugh.

Shaking his head, Wes pointed at the other two horses. "I'm more worried about them finding those."

"Good point." Hurriedly untying her pack, Tahlia smacked her horse's rear. "Hyah! Get!" Letting out an offended bray, the stallion lurched into a clumsy gallop down the road.

"How are—" Caito faltered, for Tahlia had already done the same to his mare, sending it after the first horse.

Taking his pack from Tahlia, he slung gloomily it over his shoulder. *I suppose we're walking.*

Wes pointed to the weapon in Caito's hand. "As a precaution, do you know how to use that?"

"No, though I'll have to learn now, won't I?"

Wes beckoned for him to hand the sword over.

Caito hesitated. The sound of hooves grew steadily louder like thunder rolling over the hills, heralding a wave of steel. As much as he knew he must, making the leap of learning to fight prickled every bone in his body. He wasn't sure he was capable of causing bloodshed, and he loathed the idea of doing so.

Wes beckoned again, more urgently. Reluctantly, Caito passed the blade to him, hilt first.

With a brief demonstration, Wes explained how to use the weapon.

"This is a shortsword. It's quicker than a typical longsword, and best used in close-quarters combat. Don't worry about technique, just attack the stomach and chest if you can." He handed the weapon back to Caito.

It wasn't much information—in fact, it was as little as he imagined he needed—nevertheless, Caito began to panic as he processed. The concept of fighting against trained soldiers made his knees shake even more than from fatigue. He felt he might collapse again.

"Hey." Tahlia was watching him. "You'll be alright. Wes and I are with you."

Caito could only nod.

The approaching horses sounded like they were right on top of them, and the ground was beginning to vibrate. Hastily, the three of them dashed into the forest to conceal themselves. Wes climbed a tree to watch the bend while Caito and Tahlia found some dense brush to hide in. Together, they waited with bated breath for their pursuers to pass.

They had vacated the road in the nick of time. No sooner were they settled in their hiding places than Wes waved at them to lie flat.

Ducking his head, Caito heard the rumble of horses mixed with the jingle of harnesses and rattle of armor. Although it was impossible to tell how many soldiers by the noise alone, there were clearly more than the small group that had been chasing them since Markalv. He glanced at Tahlia with wide eyes.

All of a sudden, a shout rang out, and the sounds of marching stopped. They had found the dead horse. Caito heard an unintelligible voice, speak followed by a few laughs. Then, another shout ordered the company to begin marching again.

After the sound faded, Caito made to stand up.

Tahlia grabbed him and shook her head. "Not yet," she whispered. "There could be a rear guard trailing behind."

A few more minutes passed until finally, Wes whistled once and dropped from the tree. "There's a whole platoon after us. I counted thirty-five soldiers, at least. They're not moving fast; we could definitely reach the Hounds and warn them in time to set up an ambush. We'll have to cut across the hills instead of following the road." He pointed up towards the cliff.

They jogged across the road and began ascending. Soon, despite the gloomy weather, Caito was sweating profusely from scrambling up the rough slope, where he used his hands as much as his legs. They kept the road in sight until they arrived at the cliff. From there, they turned parallel to the wall, now climbing in earnest.

"The hills plateau several hundred feet up," Wes puffed as they went. "It's a little easier from there."

The terrain grew steeper and more dangerous the higher they went. The earth was softened from rain, and loose scree threatened to send them back down to the road. The stunted, yet resilient shrubbery saved them more than once as a precarious hand or foothold failed. At least, as the burn in Caito's limbs began to peak, the ground leveled out.

All of a sudden, Wes skidded to a halt.

"What is it?" Tahlia whispered.

"Shhh. Hold still. There's a lion."

Caito scanned the terrain for the beast. "Where?"

Wes, ever so slowly, stretched out his arm and pointed. Following his finger, Caito finally saw it.

There, crouching between two trees, was a large mountain cat holding so still that Caito was amazed Wes noticed the animal at all. They must have startled it while it was on the prowl. The animal stared back at them with large yellow eyes, the tip of its tail twitching. Caito was awestruck by its powerful form. Huge daggers of claws gleamed on the ends of its paws while muscular shoulders bunched behind its head, as thick as boulders. There was no doubt in Caito's mind that it could easily take one of them down with little effort.

"What do we do?"

"Just walk. Because there's three of us, it probably won't attack, though I'd rather not scare it if we can help it. They're bloody quick."

Together, they edged around the lion, keeping their eyes glued to it the entire time. Eventually, the lion lost interest in them and slunk away in the other direction. Caito breathed a sigh of relief as the animal disappeared into the brush.

Soon after their brief delay, Wes led them downhill once more. All pretense of stealth was lost as they plunged their way down the chossy slope, weaving back and forth, sometimes sliding as the ground crumbled below their feet.

"There's a cave hidden in the rocks somewhere around here that we used as a base," Wes explained as he clambered down a boulder. "I don't remember exactly where, but they should have people on lookout. It's more likely they'll find us before we find them."

"I'd say the avalanche we're bringing with us is hard to miss," Tahlia joked, then promptly lost her footing. She skidded down the hill before anyone could catch her and disappeared over a ridge with a cry.

22

A TEST OF METTLE

SCRAMBLING DOWN AS QUICKLY as they could, they found Tahlia uninjured at the bottom of a short cliff. However, she was not alone. A woman in a mottled green tunic stood over her, holding a naked blade to her throat.

At the sight of her, Caito hurriedly tried to draw his weapon. Before he fully released it from the sheath, Wes let out a cry and tackled the woman. After a confused moment, Caito realized Wes was laughing while he wrestled the woman, who was trying to fight him off with muffled cries.

Caito helped Tahlia to her feet. "Are you alright?"

"A little bruised." Tahlia was grinning exuberantly despite being covered in dirty scrapes from her fall. Grabbing Wes by the back of his collar, she hauled him off of the other woman. "Let her breathe, Wes."

"Damn, it is good to see you two!" the woman exclaimed, taking the hand Tahlia offered. "It's been mighty quiet out here without you."

"Mattias isn't keeping you busy?" Wes asked.

"Oh, he has," assured the woman as she brushed herself off. "You should see what we've done to the old fort." Her blue eyes sparkling, she looked at Caito. She was very pretty, with full lips and rosy cheeks. Her short, blond hair was spiked from rain, giving her a fierce air that belied her slim form. "Who's this?"

Tahlia introduced him, "Leana, this is Caito Lazar. Caito, Leana Palmer."

Caito, still feeling the adrenaline rushing through his veins, hoped Leana wouldn't notice his hand trembling as he held it out to her. His tongue felt too large for his mouth and only allowed a grunt to escape.

Giving his hand a grasp, Leana gave Caito a nod. "Pleasure to meet you." She turned back to Wes with a frown. "As glad as I am to see you two, it is odd you're here. You were reassigned to Cappus, weren't you? What are you doing falling off mountains out here?"

Wes's grin faded as he seemed to remember their situation. "Can you take us to Mattias?"

Looking alarmed at the sudden change in attitude, Leana jerked her head for them to follow.

Descending the hill was much easier with Leana leading. It was apparent she knew her way and guided them efficiently down the slope. The rain turned into a light mist as a dense fog rolled in above them, obscuring the upper reaches of the hill. They stopped once for Leana to let out a shrill whistle, which Caito now realized was a signal.

"You didn't hear me, then?" Tahlia inquired.

"Nope," Leana quipped. "I don't think you're nearly as good at whistling as you think you are."

After a few more minutes of clambering, Leana stopped again. "Hold on. Hello boys!" she called to someone Caito couldn't see. "I've brought company!"

All of a sudden, seemingly straight from the ground, three men sprung into existence, letting out shouts of joy at the sight of Wes and Tahlia.

After some brief words and embraces Wes glanced at Leana again. "Mattias?"

She pointed in the direction of another ledge. "Just down there."

"You're still using the cave?"

One of the other rebels chuckled. "Cappus wasn't built in a day."

Following the others over the next ridge, Caito found himself at the mouth of a large cave. A camouflaged curtain of moss and branches hung across the opening, secured by pegs hammered into the bedrock above it. Leana held one corner of the curtain aside, revealing the interior. Blankets and furs hung on the walls to help insulate against the cold. Crates with cushioned lids were scattered around the cave, while a large campfire sat in the middle, currently cold and black. Numerous bedrolls rolled out on the floor testified to a larger group of people than were in the cave.

Wes marched toward one of the soldiers, a short, copper-haired man with toned muscles and the same dog's head pin as Wes and Tahlia on his chest. "Sergeant Berg." He snapped a quick salute. "I bring urgent news."

"Well, well," announced Sergeant Berg, returning the salute amid jubilant exclamations from the other rebels at their sudden appearance. "Look who we have here."

"There's a company of loyalists approaching this location, sir. We need to take preventative action."

The cave fell silent except for the steady dripping of water from the entrance.

"How many, and how much time do we have?" Berg's tone was now serious.

"Three dozen, maybe more. We let them pass us on the road, then cut across the hills. They weren't moving fast, but they won't be far off."

The other soldiers exchanged looks. Whirling around, Berg barked at them, jarring them into motion. "Enough standing around! We have an appointment with the devil! Let's move!"

The rebels started scrambling around. Many of them were already dressed for battle, while those who weren't geared up in a matter of minutes. As they streamed out of the cave, Caito counted fifteen soldiers excluding Berg and his own companions.

"Do we have enough?" Caito asked Tahlia worriedly. "They're twice our strength and on horses."

Hearing him, Sergeant Berg punched Caito in the shoulder before extending a hand to him. "Just you wait," he said as he shook Caito's arm out of the socket. "Those blasted loyalists will be running home with their tails between their legs before you know it. I'm Mattias. I don't believe I've seen you before."

"Caito Lazar. I'm new."

"I figured, worrying about the Crimson Hounds like that." Berg laughed and exited the cave, Wes trailing behind him.

Tahlia stepped in front of Caito. "You can stay here. I'll come back to find you when it's over."

He shook his head. He hadn't fled on the road, and he refused to back down here either. Even though it was barely over twenty-four hours since he met Wes and Tahlia, it was already apparent that they were prepared to fight and even die to protect him. Somehow, he was willing to do the same for these almost complete strangers. Odd as it was, he felt a strong connection to the two young rebels, as if they were long-lost siblings.

Besides, he couldn't cower in a cave while people fought and died once again for his sake. Enough was enough.

"I'll come with you. I want to fight."

"Are you sure?"

"Absolutely," he lied fiercely enough that he almost believed himself.

"Stay close to me, then. Bring your sword, leave your pack—we'll have to move fast."

Tahlia set off down the hill. After dropping his pack, Caito followed, tension twisting his stomach into knots.

Hiking down to the road, they ran along it a ways before coming upon a large clearing in which blackened, torn-down remains of a fort peeked out between newer construction. Men working with wood, stone, and mortar built walls and barricades while guards patrolled.

Berg and Wes had just arrived with the others from the cave. As they drew closer, more soldiers appeared from the ruins, gathering around the sergeant. Tahlia and Caito joined them just as Wes began briefing the men.

"A company of about three-dozen loyalists on horseback are coming this way. They weren't riding fast, but it won't be long until they're here. They've been pursuing us since Markalv. We managed to evade them and cut through the hills to reach you first. I'm not sure if they're aware of our setup here—Tench is quite occupied in Seruvia—and I was thinking we could prepare a nice little surprise."

Wes stepped back for Sergeant Berg to continue. It appeared they had formed a plan on the way down from the cave.

"We'll have two sentries watching for the enemy signal us when they're near. Levin and Ian, you'll be our scouts. I want you to post out a mile and a half from here and send a signal when they come in sight. Once you signal, we'll send out some bait to draw them in. Palmer and Donroe, you'll be our rabbits—"

Wes interjected, "I'll go with Donroe, sir. I was one of the ones they were chasing. That might help them take the bait a little better."

"Wes and Donroe, then. Your job is to bring them back here. We'll post archers in the trees to fire on them when they're in range. While they're disorganized, we'll send out more riders to lure them to the ruins, if they don't break for cover to begin with. Once they are close enough, the rest of us will finish them off. If they turn tail, I'll take that as a victory, too. Alright, positions everyone! Let's create some havoc!"

The rebels dispersed; a few of them rounded up the workers to take them away from the camp. Wes and the other rider departed to their horses while Caito and Tahlia sat down behind a barricade to wait.

Hands shaking, Caito forced himself to breathe normally. He was glad for the steady flow of combat advice from Tahlia because it gave him something to focus on, albeit another part of him wished she would leave him to his misery. The talk of battle made him nervous to the point of fainting.

Noticing how white his face was, Tahlia paused her lecture. "You don't have to do this, Caito. Combat is a terrifying experience. There's no shame in waiting in a safe place."

Caito tried to say that he would be fine, or really anything at all, but the words wouldn't leave his mouth. His hands, clenched into fists, shuddered worse than ever; his breath came in short, fast gasps. Fear gripped his heart and squeezed until it felt as if it would burst. He knew there was no way he could fight—he would freeze. Moreover, he was inexperienced and vulnerable against trained soldiers. He *would* be killed.

There is more to making a difference than just a name. With the rebellion, you will have a purpose—something to fight for. You can be more than just the Soothsayer. You can be a hero—someone for people to stand behind."

Winston's words from their conversation in Audax Keep came back to him along with all of the helplessness he had been feeling since he fled his home. None of this was fair. He never wanted to be involved. He certainly didn't ask for this curse.

All at once, his fear was washed away by a flood of anger.

Create your own legacy. No more running; no more hiding; no more sitting by letting others fight when he was capable of doing the same. How could he claim he wanted to help people if he couldn't fight for them?

Lifting his head, he met Tahlia's eyes. They quickly dropped from his—a common effect he had on people. He opened his mouth to utter some brave words, but he was cut off by the sound of distant shouts and a whistle.

He understood why they chose that as their signal rather than a horn or some other means. The sound cut through the air and carried over to them with no effort, sounding nearly as clear as if it came from the ruins. At the same time, it could easily be mistaken as the call of some bird of prey by the untrained ear.

The quiet voices around them faltered, and the rebel soldiers perked up. Some of them, Tahlia included, partially stood or peeked from their hiding places to see what was happening.

"They're coming," Tahlia murmured quietly, ducking back down. She glanced at Caito, her face flushed with anticipation. "Stay close to me."

Caito nodded. Words were impossible again. He could hear the distant thundering of hooves; it sounded like hundreds of riders. Partially drawing his sword with fingers slick from sweat, he briefly thought of praying to the All-Mother—something he had abandoned doing a long time ago.

Suddenly, the air was filled with screams from both men and horses. Caito looked out in time to see a small cloud of arrows descending onto a group of horsemen at the edge of the clearing. Two riders that he identified as Wes and Donroe were circling back to the loyalists who milled in confusion as several of their company fell from the deadly projectiles.

Sergeant Berg ordered his own riders out to engage the enemy. "Strike and fall back!" he shouted as they charged out of the ruins. "*Do not take risks!*"

Caito held his breath as the rebels met the loyalists, who were still trying to organize themselves. The rebel riders were vastly outnumbered: Ten against nearly forty. Even so, it was obvious the Crimson Hounds had plenty of experience fighting outnumbered. They circled and dipped, striking quickly, then retreating again before the loyalists could retaliate. Soon, the enemy was completely scattered, pursuing the rebels gradually drawing them closer and closer to the ruins.

As the enemy reached the barricades, Sergeant Berg gave the signal to spring their final trap. With a huge cry, the rest of the Hounds leaped out of hiding and converged on the riders.

Chaos ensued.

Although Caito did his best to stay close to Tahlia, he almost immediately lost her in the fray. He froze from fear, every fiber in his being screaming at him to run and hide as the deadly dance of battle whirled around him. Noise assaulted him from all sides: The crash of weapons on armor; the death screams of men and horses; swearing, shouting, and odd laughter overloaded his ears. The smell of blood, sweat, and metal congested his sinuses, making him nauseous.

A man was thrown to the ground in front of him, shaking Caito from his trance. He staggered backwards in shock, staring down at the lifeless body. It was an older man, maybe in his forties, clad in the sky blue of a Corynthian soldier. A trickle of blood ran down from his scalp as he stared at the cloudy sky with glassy eyes.

Another loyalist stepped in front of him, this one alive and murderous with a sword held in two hands. He swung at Caito, who faintly realized his weapon was still in its scabbard.

Caito managed to throw himself to the ground to avoid the blade, hearing the *woosh* as its sharpened edge sliced through the air above him. Instincts he didn't know he had took control of his limbs. He kicked at the man's knee and rolled away from his attacker. The loyalist stumbled, giving Caito time to regain his feet and draw his own weapon. His adversary struck at him again, except this time he raised his weapon to parry. The impact sent a shock through the sword and into his arm, causing pain to shoot from his wrist to his elbow, knocking the weapon out of his hand.

Yelping, he reflexively clutched at his elbow.

The loyalist seemed taken aback at how easily he disarmed him and paused. A horse thundered past, its rider flinging curses at the top of his voice.

Caito frantically tried to think of a way out of his predicament, completely disregarding his weapon lying in the dirt. The soldier advanced, kicking the weapon to the side. Caito tripped and fell as he retreated. He scrambled to find something to defend himself with, knowing full well it would be useless. His hand landed atop a stone, and he slung it at the loyalist. It bounced harmlessly off his armor.

The world around him seemed to slow as the soldier raised his sword. A hundred different thoughts and emotions tumbled through his head. He wondered what it would feel like to die. He had seen both of his parents pass from sickness, though that had been quietly in their sleep, not torn apart by another man as he was about to be. Would it be painful? There was probably no way around that.

Maybe I deserve it. The thought just entered his head, when someone barreled into the loyalist.

Tahlia made quick work of the soldier before helping Caito up. "I told you to stay close!"

"I tried!" Caito protested, his heart still hammering from the encounter. It didn't matter, for Tahlia was already rushing back into battle.

He picked up his sword, surprised to find that his hands were shaking no longer. Despite his mind still screaming at him to flee, he chased after his friend.

A rebel soldier cried out and fell next to him. He turned towards the sound to see another soldier in blue, sword red with blood, standing over him, about to finish him off.

Before he could freeze, Caito lunged. He inadvertently closed his eyes as his weapon made contact with the man and felt another jar run through his arm as the point of the weapon glanced off of the soldier's chainmail. The man grunted in surprise and turned his attention to Caito.

Caito felt a mixture of irritation that he hadn't managed to wound the man, confusion at how he was *supposed* to wound him, and panic that he now had the full attention of a very angry sword-wielding adversary.

Yet again, fate smiled upon him.

The rebel soldier wounded by Caito's opponent was still alive and functional. He kicked the loyalist's legs out from under him and tackled him, drawing a dagger from his hip as he did so.

Caito flinched at the brutality enfolding before him.

Rolling away from the lifeless body, the rebel sat up with a groan. Blood stained his tunic, and he held his side as he winced up at Caito. "Thank you, friend."

Caito merely nodded. He didn't know what to say in return.

The battle was finished. A small group of loyalist soldiers knelt with their hands on their head in the center of the ruins. Wes held a man against a wall with a spear, and many of the rebels were already gathering bodies and corralling horses.

Tahlia appeared at Caito's shoulder. "Are you okay?"

The concern on her face made Caito angry. "What happened to staying together?" he snapped.

His hands were shaking again, and his heart was trying to escape his chest. He felt stretched like tanned leather. Tears threatened to flow, and he desired nothing more than to hide somewhere and break down, except he knew he couldn't.

Catching the look on his face, Tahlia quickly apologized, "I'm sorry. My eye was on you the entire time. I wasn't going to let you get hurt."

Caito nearly retorted that he had almost been killed twice, but he held his tongue. It wasn't Tahlia's fault. Besides, she was right: She had been there to save him the first time. He had no right to be angry at her. He was just scared and shaken.

Maybe I deserve it. The words slunk through Caito's head again. "I'm sorry. I'm just..." He trailed off.

"Afraid," Tahlia finished with an understanding smile. "There's nothing wrong with that. *I* still am."

The confession surprised Caito. He never would have guessed that Tahlia was even nervous going into battle. She and Wes both conducted themselves with the utmost confidence and eagerness in everything they did thus far.

Wes joined them, dusting his hands, and Tahlia punched him in the shoulder. "I bet you Wes feels the same way."

"About what?" Wes asked.

"Feeling afraid."

"Of battle?" Wes grinned. "Never. Good fighting out there," he said to Caito. "Not bad for your first time picking up a weapon. That man would have had an ugly bruise." He mimed a jab with a sword, making Caito and Tahlia both laugh.

After the Hounds gathered around Berg for a casualty report and instructions after the battle, Wes led Tahlia and Caito to speak with the sergeant.

"Thanks for the warning," Berg told him. "That could have been disastrous."

Wes acknowledged him with a quick nod. "We have to leave now, sir. It's still a long way to Cappus, and we have no time to lose."

Berg glanced at Caito, who suddenly realized that the sergeant knew exactly who he was. The thought unnerved him for some reason.

"I can tell you're all exhausted. Are you sure you don't want to rest for a day?"

Caito thought the suggestion sounded like paradise; unfortunately, Wes shook his head. "We've already lost too much time here. We should return to Winston as soon as possible."

"Alright then, I won't press. We'll bring you fresh horses and supplies. Stay here and relax while you can."

While the three of them made themselves comfortable, Leana appeared next to them. "It's good to see you two again," she said to Wes and Tahlia. "I hope you'll be back with us soon."

"We're too useful as errand runners," Wes remarked sarcastically. "No offense, Caito."

"None taken."

Leana stretched and exhaled, running a hand through her short hair. "Well, back to work for me. No rest for the wicked." Her azure eyes looked tired, but she winked at Caito, who felt his face grow warm.

He watched her disappear into the fort, a flower in a gravel pit. He wasn't sure if he should be more attracted or afraid of her soldier's prowess.

He received an elbow from Wes. "Careful with that one. She'll bruise your jaw as soon as kiss you."

"Speaking from experience?" Tahlia drawled as she scrubbed her sword with a stained cloth.

Turning red, Wes mumbled something unintelligible, averting his gaze from Tahlia. Caito met Tahlia's eyes and they both burst into laughter.

All the tension in Caito's being began to dissipate as he laughed—a tightly bound rope of fear, loss, helplessness, and anger uncoiling and leaving his body. A strange feeling replaced it, one he had not felt in months: The contentment that came from the company of friends. After so much time spinning his words around politicians and other egocentric individuals, the unfettered happiness felt like spring of cool water in a desert.

Sergeant Berg returned and exchanged a few words with Caito's companions before turning to him. "It's nice to finally meet you. There's been a fair amount of speculation revolving around you; I wasn't sure myself what to expect. Wes told me about you on our way down here, and when my people have that much faith in someone, I know without a doubt I can do likewise."

Caito glanced at Wes, who was smiling widely at him. Tahlia, on the other hand, looked sheepish.

"You showed real courage today. You have some some work to do when it comes to combat"—Caito blushed—"but, I'm glad you're on our side. Welcome to the rebellion, Soothsayer."

PART THREE: LIBERTY OR RUIN

23

VISION OF FIRE

CAPPUS HAD FALLEN. THE sun broke through the clouds to shine upon a weary yet victorious rebel army. The siege lasted two weeks, culminating on the very day that Andre returned with Winston and Declan. Most of the time had been spent trying to take the walls; when they fell, it became a short battle of attrition. Governor Tullin was no king, and the Cappus soldiers refused to die for him.

The Soothsayer arrived shortly after, escorted by Wes and Tahlia.

Morale was high as the rebellion's wayward companies were summoned to Cappus. Word of the city's fall and that the Soothsayer escaped Tench, thereafter joining the rebellion, spread like wildfire (the latter part helped along by the rebellion's spies). As good consequence, the army's ranks increased to nearly twelve thousand as more people joined. Many of them were Cappus's own soldiers under the command of the city's captain of the guard, Captain Ubrik. Reports of splinter groups at work causing havoc in Corynthia's cities in the name of the Soothsayer flooded in with the new recruits.

On the other hand, the news of the rebellion's victory finally stimulated Tench to issue a massive recall of his armies at the borders. Curiously enough, instead of mobilizing them against the rebels, Tench summoned his soldiers back to the capital, Seruvia. It appeared the chancellor intended to wait for the rebellion to come to him.

This last piece of information was followed by the return of the Crimson Hounds from the ruined outpost.

Andre was occupied with a game of Pincher (played with cards and dice) shortly after the Soothsayer's arrival, when he was tackled from behind. After a healthy amount of shouting and swearing on Andre's part, he finally untangled himself to face his attacker. It was Mattias Berg, wearing a grin blazing as much as his hair. With a roar, Andre bear-hugged him as the others looked on, laughing. They stayed up late into the evening engaged in merriment.

Another full day passed before Winston finally summoned his officers for a meeting in the city.

Strolling through the city, Andre was pleased to see that the attitude of Cappus's residents towards the rebels had finally shifted.

Despite the peace following the siege in which the rebels worked to repair the city's damages, a layer of fear and distrust still hung in the air like mist in a graveyard. Protests and retaliation at the rebel occupation kept both Cappus guards and rebel volunteers busy, and forced Winston to spend most of his time with Governor Tullin, delegating and responding to indignation. At last, it seemed that the citizens realized the rebels did not intend to cause them any more grief, and they finally began to relax around their new neighbors, especially after Winston explained their agenda against Tench.

Although dirty looks were still thrown Andre's way as he walked through the streets, the majority of people nodded or raised a hand in greeting, to which he returned the gesture. A handful even broke into applause as he passed. Even here on the other side of Corynthia, Tench was far from favored.

Andre was the last to arrive at the tavern they were using as a meeting room. The owner, a rebel informant, had jumped at the opportunity to be of further service and had eagerly laden the tables with pies, vegetables, and a roasted lamb. Guards stood at the entrances to discourage any curious citizens.

Delvon Pitt and William Draytus sat on one side of the room, speaking with another officer and kept glancing at Winston at the center table. The topic of their conversation was engaged in discussion with a young man who looked vaguely familiar to Andre.

Andre took an open seat next to Keppen Bailer, who recently arrived from Liberá, and slid a meat pie over to himself.

Keppen clapped him on the shoulder. "It's been a while, my friend."

"No rest for freedom fighters," Andre replied dryly, cracking the pie's crust with a spoon. A tendril of steam curled out like a monster from the deep.

Keppen chuckled. "I've had an easy time of it keeping the children at Liberá out of trouble. Meanwhile, you've been chasing our leader around trying to keep his death wishes from coming true."

Andre was surprised to hear the disapproval in Keppen's voice. He understood the frustration from the likes of Pitt and William—many of them kept to strict ideals that Winston's latest antics completely contradicted. Keppen, however, had always been more tolerant of others' decisions, rashness withal. *As long as I'm not the one to clean up the mess*, had always been his philosophy.

Before Andre could ask Keppen what was on his mind, Winston rose and cleared his throat.

"My dear friends. May I have your attention, please?"

While the room quieted, Andre took a better look at the boy sitting beside Winston, convinced he had seen him before. In a crowd or—

On a stage.

Winston indicated for the young man to rise. He did so, smoothly pushing back his chair and standing in the same motion. His unsettling eyes scanned the faces of his audience, many of which dropped their gaze to the table.

"Many of you have discredited the rumors of a Soothsayer, claiming it's a hoax fabricated from hysteria over the current plight of Corynthia." Winston smirked. "Yet, he stands before you, flesh and blood. May I introduce, Caito Lazar." Indicating again to the Soothsayer, he took a seat.

Lazar gave no sign of apprehension in the room full of narrowed eyes and bated breath.

After a moment, he spoke in a quiet voice, "I do not condone this war. I do not wish to be involved in this violence. Sadly, it's become apparent to me that I cannot avoid it. I've seen Chancellor Tench's cruelty—I've experienced it firsthand—and it makes me sick to my stomach. While I feel there could have been a better opportunity to right his wrongs, what's done is done."

He took a deep breath. "I've had a vision. Many visions, actually. Some have come to pass; others I don't know. But one of them shadows the rest.

"It first came around a year ago, just before the rumors of a growing rebellion reached my village. I've always had my... gift. It manifests through feelings, hunches, and quick flashes of images—never separated by more than a day or two. Before this vision, I felt nothing for almost a week. It was like holding your breath before a plunge. Then, it struck me from nowhere: A chaotic mess of fire and noise—such a confusion of sounds and images that I couldn't piece together a single detail. The force with which it hit nearly knocked me unconscious.

"After the first vision, there was nothing again for over a week. It was unnerving. I felt normal, though at the same time, I was terrified of what would happen should I have another. The next was as violent as before. The pattern continued, except the time between the visions grew shorter, while they grew more vivid with each occurrence. Shapes appeared in the darkness. I saw the buildings of a city and the walls of a fortress, its towers stark against the black sky."

Lazar stared into the distance, his eyes focused on horrors only he could see. "I could make out figures running back and forth through blurred streets. Rain fell in sheets as thunder joined the chorus of screams.

"Soon, the visions attacked me daily, chasing away my dreams at night. I couldn't"—his voice broke slightly—"I can't sleep. I feel like a dead man walking. Even now, they sit at the edges of my eyelids, tormenting me. My powers aren't a gift—I'm locked in hell."

Everyone was fixated on the Soothsayer. Gone was Pitt's look of stoic disbelief. William was massaging his chin, and several of the other officers wore a blank, open-mouthed stares.

His voice taking on a dead monotone, Lazar continued, "There's a storm raging above a ruined city. Flames rise from a deteriorating fortress, and I can see a figure making his way down a cracked street filled with the dead and wounded. A flash of lightning illuminates two of the fortress's towers still standing, a bridge spanning between them. I can see two people locked in combat on the bridge. One of the towers starts to crumble, then the bridge breaks apart, sending one of the fighters to their doom. Then there is a great noise, and a flash, then it's over."

He blinked and seemed to return to the present.

Maybe it was Andre's imagination, but he thought Lazar looked a little livelier, a little less haunted. He sympathized with the young man. Keeping such terrible visions inside for as long as he did must have been torture.

Andre looked at Winston, who raised an eyebrow at him and leaned back in his chair. He recognized the description of the location, as vague as it was; apparently, Winston did too.

"The bell towers." Everyone looked at him. "Audax Keep. Seruvia."

"My thoughts precisely," Winston agreed. "Whatever happens in your vision, Caito, happens in Seruvia. Naturally," he added to himself.

Andre agreed with the sentiment. The rebellion was finding unprecedented success against all odds. Of course a wrinkle would be thrown in towards the end. *More of a mountain than a wrinkle,* he amended.

The silence was deafening.

"And you don't recognize anyone in your vision?" Pitt finally spoke. His bald head shone from the lanterns hanging from the ceiling.

Lazar shook his head. "They're just figures."

"If that's what awaits at Seruvia, do we really want to take such a risk?" William asked. "Besides, Tench will be waiting for us with his entire army. If that... *calamity* is what happens if we march on him, maybe we should focus on gaining control of the rest of Corynthia and force him to come to us.

"Tench is a mule of a man," Winston countered. "He'll be more than happy to hold Seruvia hostage as long as he needs."

"Then we gather forces and look for allies," Keppen suggested from next to Andre. "We can send for aide from other nations. Kaval has plenty of troops."

"No," stated Winston firmly. "Artreus may be a half-wit, but I do not want to be in his debt. No, Tench is right where I want him. He's cornered himself. We merely need to draw him out of his hole when we arrive."

"With fire?" Samuel Corence drawled from halfway down the table.

Winston gave him an exasperated look. "Caito, do your visions always come true?"

"More often than not, but not always."

"You see? If we keep Tench on the defensive, we'll avoid the outcome Caito has seen. Tench won't burn down the one thing preventing him from being hung."

"Who says Tench will burn it down?" Pitt challenged. "Samuel has a point. You don't always think your plans all the way through, Winston. While a scheme may seem innocent enough at first, it could turn drastically wrong in a heartbeat. By the All-Mother, you were nearly executed not a full month ago, and that plan was anything but sane!"

"For your information, Delvon," Winston replied calmly. "It worked perfectly. Moreover, it held the intended affect."

"Perfectly? You call the betrayal and subsequent deaths of the very men who came to rescue you perfect? Andre told William and me about Thomilson. It's plans like those that lead to disasters like that and worse, deserters."

Winston had the decency to look somber. "That was... unforeseen." He glanced at Andre, his face unreadable.

Andre held his gaze. "We don't do anything drastic, and we won't have to face the consequences."

"Look," William chimed in, voice as serene as his face, "only one of us here can see the future, and none of us can change the past. With that said, let's leave this discussion on the table for now while we wait for our scouts to return from Seruvia. Come, we have a delicious feast prepared for us by our generous host. Let us take this opportunity to celebrate our victory here in Cappus!"

Hearty agreements swept through the room.

As the officers moved to indulge in the spread before them, Winston held up a hand, his expression grave. "One last note. I don't want a word regarding the Soothsayer's vision to leave this room. Not yet. Tell of such destruction shall only tailor fear and doubt, two enemies we cannot afford to fight. So please, keep this meeting to yourselves." He smiled, breaking the tension. "Now, someone tell the innkeeper to bring out his best mead!"

24

TO TOPPLE A TYRANT

T HE SCOUTS' RETURN FROM Seruvia was delayed by another drenching rainstorm. The downpour forced many of the rebels into the city for refuge as it reduced the camp to a muddy mess. When the scouts did finally arrive, they brought mixed news.

The cities standing in the way of the rebellion's approach were all but cleared of loyalist presence, their officials and militia left at the mercy of the people. The road to the capital was open, yet Seruvia sat dark and foreboding, as menacing as the storm clouds above. A gigantic camp had sprung up outside the walls, and countless loyalist soldiers could be seen building up defenses. An estimated fifty thousand soldiers now occupied the capital.

"*Fifty thousand?*" Pitt cried at the briefing meeting. "Forget the Soothsayer's vision—we'll be slaughtered before we come within a hundred yards of the gates!"

Andre opened his mouth to point out there were now entire cities free from loyalist control, but William beat him to it.

"We'll send out messengers throughout the land. I'm sure many people will be willing to join us, especially now that Tench is on the defensive."

"Our cause has turned into a *death march*, William," Pitt countered. "They just regained their homes—do you really expect them to lay down their lives?"

"If that is how it ends, so be it!" Corence rumbled. "We'll go out in a blaze of glory! We *must* make an effort, or it's only a matter of time until Tench takes those cities back!"

Everyone began to speak at once, drowning out the drum of rain on the roof.

They were gathered once again in the tavern, *Galven's Oasis*. A fire roared merrily in the fireplace while rain and wind clawed at the windows, howling to be let into the warmth. Wes and Tahlia were present, inseparable as always, while Declan stood quietly on the fringe. The bookkeeper had been curiously absent after the capture of Cappus, though he turned up just before the storm breached. Pitt, William, and Corence were there, but there were a few other officers were missing. Preparations to leave Cappus were in full swing, and there was much to do.

The Soothsayer was off with some of the Hounds on a scouting mission. After he recovered from his flight from Seruvia, he dove into the numerous tasks of a rebel soldier earnestly, obviously determined to help make a difference. In this weather, such resolve was even more impressive.

Winston rose from his seat. There was a crooked smile on his face, and the firelight gleamed in his brown eyes. "A blaze of glory?"

Uh-oh, Andre thought. Winston wore the same look as when he divulged his plan to speak with the Soothsayer. The look that meant trouble.

Winston looked at him. "Do you remember the tunnels under Seruvia?"

Afraid of where his friend was leading the conversation, Andre nodded. He didn't have fond memories of the catacombs under the city, and he certainly wasn't enthusiastic about the idea of returning to them.

Winston turned to Declan now. "You said they were built to withstand the passage of time. Tell us more."

Declan folded his arms. "Seruvia was built by the Athere long ago. The Athere held special knowledge of a very old magic—magic that is extinct now. Very few of their relics still exist; the catacombs under Seruvia are one of them. They were imbued with magic preserving them against the weathering of time. In the centuries they've lain there, they haven't changed."

"Can they be damaged?"

Declan frowned. "What do you mean?" It was the first time that Andre had seen Declan uncertain.

"Can they be damaged or altered with force?"

"Of course. They are still subject to the same physical laws as everything else. The exit was proof of that." He narrowed his eyes. "Why?"

Andre's initial thought that Winston was proposing to bring soldiers through the tunnels died. While this unexpected question intrigued him, it also worried him.

"Well," began Winston. "Cappus is home to a network of mines and quarries throughout Landour Mountain. Since the miners don't have magic, they use a special powder made from a mixture of sulfur, charcoal, and some other ingredients. When lit with a flame it has a tremendous blasting power, capable of exploding sheer rock."

His words were like a stone sinking into a lake of silence.

"Wait," Wes finally said. "You're suggesting we blow these tunnels up?" He shared an excited look with Tahlia.

"No," Winston corrected. "We shall use them to hold the city hostage, specifically Tench's fortress. That's where your services are needed"—he pointed at Declan—"since you know these tunnels so well. We'll plant the blasting powder beneath Audax Keep to use as leverage against Tench. Under such a threat he must fold."

"A daring plan," Declan remarked, "but foolhardy. Those catacombs are incredibly old; they hold more secrets than just spells. Even I haven't discovered everything they have to offer. What I *have* found... well, it would be best to tamper with that entity as little as possible," he finished with an ominous tone.

Andre felt shudders crawl up his spine and thought briefly of the whispers.

"Not to mention Lazar's vision!" Pitt burst out. "He saw Seruvia in flames! This is inviting the damn disaster to happen! Did I not just say you don't think through your plans?"

"Suddenly you're a believer now?" Winston snapped back.

Pitt rose from his chair like an earthquake and loomed over him threateningly, his huge shoulder muscles bunching together in restrained anger.

Clearing his throat, William Draytus held up his hands as if warding off a blow. He looked more tired than usual. "Believer or not, Delvon is absolutely right. We cannot play with fate. If this plan were to run awry, the consequences will be devastating."

"Do you have a better alternative to fighting outnumbered five to one?" Winston retaliated. "This will give us an edge. Tench won't send people down there to remove the trap. Declan said it himself—he's too afraid of the place."

"For good reason," Declan agreed.

"Do we have to plant explosives if Tench is too scared to venture down there?" Andre offered. "We can bluff."

He didn't like the notion that they could be orchestrating the Soothsayer's vision. On the other hand, Winston had a point: There wasn't much of an alternative. Even if they were lucky with recruiting more warriors, they would still be nowhere close to the fifty-thousand-strong Tench had mustered.

"It must be convincing," Winston explained. "We have to control the stakes, which means the threat must have substance. Besides, how are we *supposed* to capture a city like Seruvia, especially now they're prepared? I've faced many odds in my life; these, I don't like. We won't be victorious in a head-on assault; furthermore, if we draw the battle out, there will come a point when we don't have enough soldiers to continue fighting. We have no room for error!"

"Why do we have to attack now?" Tahlia chimed in. "Why not bide our time and gather our strength?"

"Because time is something we don't have," Winston answered, voice tense. A vein throbbed in his forehead. "We have Tench right where we want him. We must strike now!"

"You mean *you* have Tench where you want him!" Pitt retorted. "To be honest, Winston, you don't seem to be fighting the same war as us."

"I'm trying to end this war, Delvon! We cannot drag this out! Corynthia can't sustain extended conflict! Drastic times call for drastic measures!"

William cut in again, his voice deadly serious. "Let me ask you this, Winston. What happens when Tench calls your bluff and refuses to surrender? You know it's unlikely he will believe you." Spreading his hands, he voiced the question Andre knew they were all hesitant to ask. "Will you light the fuse?"

"He *will* surrender." Winston's eyes were a flash of lightning in the dark thunderhead of his glare. "Besides, if he doesn't, only a small part of the city will be damaged. Thereafter, Tench's allies will turn on him. Why would they continue to support such a heartless leader? If he's willing to put innocents in harm's way like so to stay in power, what's stopping him from throwing his supporters to the wolves? A small sacrifice for victory."

"But you're the one putting the innocents in harm's way! You're the one snuffing out lives for the sake of your pride! Damn it, Winston, do you hear yourself? Think! This isn't about Tench, it's about Corynthia! Freedom from oppression!"

"My *pride*?" Winston seethed. "Tell me, William, have you ever tried to fell a tree with your words? No. You must chop it down with an axe or set fire to its trunk. There is risk involved. It's the same with Tench. He doesn't consider if his actions are moral, only if they benefit his coffers. The only way we can shake him is by endangering him. He sits in a fortress in a walled city, surrounded by tens of thousands of soldiers at his command. Right now, we are but ants to him; we pose no danger. The threat must be brought to him, and this is the only way to do so.

"No," declared William, every premature line on his face hardening. "I will not condone the destruction of Seruvia. If we must fight tooth and nail for the next year then so be it!"

"Bring me a better suggestion then! We won't win a battle against those numbers!"

Andre and the officers looked back and forth between the two men as their voices grew louder, none brave enough to interrupt.

Andre was surprised. It was usually quite difficult to work William up. Even frustrated, the man almost never raised his voice. He was always the calm, collected one between he and Delvon Pitt, who was fiery and quick to shout.

"Call for aide!" William cried. "Send a delegation to Kaval or Cedaline! Plead to them for troops!"

"I've said before; I refuse to put us in debt to someone else. This is our fight!"

"Then you're a fool!"

"I think it's a good idea," Wes commented in the brief pause as the two men glared at each other. "Obviously we wouldn't light the fuse. Maybe we can set off a warning blast, just to prove our point."

Pitt threw his hands in the air. "Or maybe—"

"Enough with the bickering!" Corence barked gruffly. "Let's vote on it."

"We're missing others," Pitt pointed out. "We can't until—"

"Blood of the All-Mother!" roared Corence. "We'll be here until spring turns to summer! We'll vote now!"

The rain drummed unsympathetically through the tense silence.

Looking around, Winston raised his hand. "All in favor?"

Wes, Tahlia, and Corence joined him. Winston looked at Andre expectantly.

"I can't agree to this," Andre announced, shaking his head. "William's right. There's far too much risk, too much room for a fatal mistake. Lazar's description—the *death* toll, Winston. We can find another way."

"All who are against?" Winston asked coldly.

Pitt, William, and Declan raised their hands. After a moment of hesitation, Andre followed suit.

"Then we sit at an impasse. I suppose we'll vote again tomorrow when everyone is present."

"And the outcome will be the same!" William returned sharply. "Over my dead body will I allow the reckless endangerment of the very people we're trying to help!"

"What happens when our forces are dashed against the sea of soldiers? We'll be slaughtered in the first assault! Everything we've worked for will be destroyed in the blink of an eye!"

Winston's shouting seemed to calm William down; his voice was even when he spoke again. "I do not wish to march everyone to their death."

"Yet you're afraid to do what is necessary to ensure victory?"

"It's not necessary! Not while we have people willing to fight!"

"We'll break like waves on a cliff!"

"Enough, Winston!" Pitt cried, buffeting the air with his hands. "You're not the one to be preaching about odds to us! We've been tolerating your mad schemes and suicide missions since you first heard rumors of the Soothsayer! It's time for you to stop being a *hero* and start being a leader! You have an army ready to fight and *die* for you—for *Corynthia*! So *lead* them!"

Andre nodded. "He's right, Winston. You've been carrying everything on your shoulders for too long. It's time for you to lighten that load now."

Reaching out, he gripped his friend's shoulder. "It's time to trust *us*. This fight must be finished together."

Winston's sharp face looked to be made of stone. Even so, Andre could see the cogs turning in his mind. He knew how proud Winston was, and how little he wanted to rely on others. It wasn't a desirable trait for a leader, especially one of his caliber and talent—he could sway entire nations to his side if he wanted to. Andre knew he felt that everything relied on him, and that he needed to take matters into his own hands. It was the curse of his brilliance.

Winston finally spoke, his face softening. "You're right." He looked each of them in the eye. "I'm sorry, I've been... carried away. You're all dismissed," he said abruptly and walked out of the room.

There was an astonished silence. Winston was prone to drastic mood swings that always left those around him reeling. He was as unpredictable as he was brilliant: Another unfortunate flaw.

"What in the blazes...?" Corence muttered, looking around for an explanation. Pitt grumbled something under his breath about Winston being a child.

Andre found Winston back at camp in his tent, poring over a book. "May I come in?"

"Of course."

Andre squatted next to him. "What are you reading?"

Winston snapped it closed and placed it on a pile of his belongings strewn beside his pack. "A tome on the Ivory Kings," he said conversationally, flipping his hair aside. "I borrowed it from Declan's place. Quite a cruel era of history. The Blood Reign, some call it. You don't need to check on my well-being, Andre. I'm just reflecting. You're right, all of you. I've been... absent as a leader." He laughed. "I'm sorry. I'm an unpredictable son of a bitch aren't I?"

Andre grinned apologetically.

"I suppose I have my parents to blame for that. Among other things."

Andre didn't know how to respond. Winston never spoke of his childhood.

Winston sprang seemingly from nowhere when he started his campaign for Corynthia. Even William, who had ties with him before his rise to fame, knew precious little about his origins. Nonetheless, he was charming, persuasive, and a had a way with words that outweighed his mystery.

"We're here to support you, Winston," Andre finally told him. "But we're also here for the rebellion, and most importantly, the people of Corynthia. You need to remember that."

"I know. Thank you for holding me accountable."

Pulling him into a hug, Andre clapped him on the back. "Someone must."

"Oh, I need a favor," Winston added as they separated. "Ensure nobody tells Caito. He's already a suspicious lad. I don't want him to think he's joined a madman and start having second-thoughts. He's done wonders for us merely by being here."

Andre gave him a reassuring smile, already resolving to waylay Wes and Tahlia. "Of course."

25

THE COST OF WAR

ANDRE WOKE TO WATER dripping on his forehead and mud in bedroll.

With the perspiring sky, many of the inns in Cappus offered rooms to the soggy rebels as a gesture of goodwill. Most of the officers took the opportunity gladly, but Andre and Winston elected to stay at the camp, the latter voicing his opinions about sleeping so close to "a treacherous worm like Tullin." Andre just felt bad about leaving him alone. He regretted it, of course, when the lining of his tent began to leak.

Extracting himself from the soaked mess, Andre heard a man's voice calling for Winston. He struggled his way to the tent opening and poked his head out alongside others to see what the fuss was.

A man was jogging between the rows of tents, looking frantic.

Andre stepped into his path. "What do you need, soldier?"

"Servailles, sir. It's General Draytus."

"What about him?"

The man seemed to struggle for words for a moment before bursting out. "He's dead!"

"What?" Andre wasn't sure he heard right. The words moved through his mind like molasses.

"He's dead!"

A jolt went through his body as if he had been stabbed. Without a word, he dashed to Winston's tent and threw open the flap.

Winston, one leg in his trousers, yelped in surprise and fell over. "Lovely," he quipped. "I haven't even finished putting my clothes on, and they're already soaked." He stopped at Andre's blank face.

"William's dead."

Winston pulled his other leg through and stood. "Explain."

Andre stepped aside. The messenger was just outside, looking very pale. A ring of people had quietly formed around the tent in the young light of the early morning.

The herald of the heavy news noticeably swallowed as Winston approached, tall and deadly in his seriousness.

"What happened?"

"I don't know, sir. We were staying in one of the inns. A maid found him. He was..." the man swallowed again, unable to say anymore.

"Take us."

The soldier led them up into the city to an inn on the first level. Already, a crowd of people waited outside. Questions began to pour heavier than the recent rain as the trio pushed their way to the door, which was guarded by two alarmed-looking rebel soldiers.

The main room was empty. Andre and Winston were led up the stairs and down the hall to where a door was cracked open. Voices murmured inside. Their guide pushed the door the rest of the way open and stepped back.

Pitt, Keppen Bailer, and a dark-skinned man were gathered inside the room. Keppen was speaking animatedly to the latter, who looked flustered and afraid. Pitt stared blankly at a corner of the room.

Like a moth to a flame, Andre's eyes were drawn to the bed, where a long, person-shaped object lay on top covered by a white sheet. He vaguely heard Winston speak as he stared at the object, his voice sounding muffled and far away. He reached out his hand to remove a corner of the cover, then hesitated. Did he really want to see what was underneath? His imagination was already forming horrible images in his mind's eye.

He suddenly became aware of everyone staring at him. Lowering his arm, he stepped back.

"I already saw." Pitt was pale, hands shaking. He looked small somehow. His red rimmed eyes found Winston watching impassively. "The son of a bitch who did this is going to pay."

"How did this happen, innkeeper?" Winston asked without looking at the dark man.

"I-I don't know, sir," the innkeeper stammered in the rich accent of Salamoa. His hands writhed together anxiously. "All of the exits are locked after hours, and there was no sign of a forced window. I couldn't hear anything over the rain. Things like this don't happen in Cappus, sir," he finished pitifully, looking to be on the verge of tears.

"Typically you're not keeping the nation's enemies under your roof, either. Keppen, Delvon, can you move William, please?"

"Where are you going?" Pitt demanded.

"To speak with Tullin."

"Then I'm coming with you."

Andre interjected before Winston could reply, "I'll help Keppen."

He knew there would be no stopping Pitt. William Draytus and Delvon Pitt had grown closer than brothers over the last couple of years. Andre knew Pitt was devastated and incredibly angry. He had no desire to stand in his way.

"We'll take care of him," he promised Pitt, who nodded and left the room after Keppen.

Winston began to follow, but Andre stopped him with a hand on his arm. "Don't do anything rash. Please. Delvon already won't be thinking straight. We don't need you making unnecessary decisions as well."

"I'll keep him in line. And myself." Winston gave him a small smile as he stepped out.

Andre stared at the empty doorway for a moment before realizing the tavern keeper was still standing there awkwardly. "Go wait downstairs. We'll speak with you later." It came out harsher than he meant it.

The man bowed timidly and left.

Andre tried very hard not to look at the body; still, his eyes kept being drawn to the sight.

Kind, level-headed William, his friend nigh on fifteen years—the man who had taught him war and brotherhood—would never share his quiet smile again. His gentle hand towards the lowly would extend no longer, nor would he stand defiant in the face of wickedness. The rain trickling down the window was only too appropriate.

Guilt filled Andre as the faceless form stared back. He and William had drifted apart after the Border Conflict. Separate duties drew them away in the aftermath, preventing regular contact with each other. Even in exile, they were far too busy with the rebellion to regain the steadiness they had. Andre and his Crimson Hounds spent much of their time out in the wilderness, striking at the loyalists, while William helped pave the path to their final victory.

Suddenly, the corpse's invisible gaze felt accusatory.

If Andre hadn't decided to stay with Winston, he could have prevented this from happening—William *had* asked him to join. He should have accepted, sought to resume their close friendship, rather than taking their time together for granted. Now he was gone, leaving Andre without a brother.

Tears spilled over his eyelids. He stepped out of the room and closed the door, sliding down the wall to the floor to wait.

It wasn't long until Keppen returned, bringing two men and a stretcher. He opened the door, revealing the shrouded figure once more. One of the men swore quietly under his breath. They entered, carefully moved William's body onto the stretcher, then awkwardly exited the room and descended the stairs.

The innkeeper sat at one of the dining tables in the lobby accompanied by another rebel soldier who opened the front door for them. A mixture of both Cappus and rebel personnel stood outside, keeping residents of the city away from the building. As the two carrying the stretcher emerged, a small entourage of guards converged around them to accompany them down to the camp.

Once they were out of sight, Andre and Keppen reentered the inn, dismissing the rebel soldier. They sat down on either side of the innkeeper, who looked frightened.

The innkeeper was a short, dark-skinned man with thick, wavy black hair and a gold earring in one ear. His eyes were bright blue, a striking detail among the rest of his swarthy features.

Keppen spoke, "We just want to ask you some questions. Nothing to worry about." The man did not look reassured.

"What's your name?"

"Rahin," the man responded, the *r* rolling along his tongue. His accent was thick and rich. "Rahin Collier."

"Can you tell us what happened last night, Rahin?"

"I closed an hour to midnight like always. Business was good with all of your people around. Everyone was in good spirits, even between them and my regulars. When everyone left, I cleaned, locked up, and went to bed. I heard nothing in the night."

"Were any suspicious people lurking about?"

"I watched your men as best I could. Not to offend you, sirs, but hosting strange soldiers, especially with all of the stories we've heard, kept me worried most of the evening." Rahin shrugged apologetically. "There was no trouble."

"William's door was locked last night? And the window?"

"Yes. The maid thought he was sleeping at first. Only when one of the other men asked her to fetch him did she actually enter."

"And it was locked from the inside?" Andre confirmed.

Rahin looked affronted. "I certainly don't hold guests hostage!"

"I'm sorry. I didn't mean anything by that."

Andre sighed. Rahin obviously knew nothing about the murder. Leaning back in his chair, he wondered how Winston and Pitt were fairing with Tullin. He hoped that neither of them had tried to burn down the governing hall yet.

After a few more questions, Keppen came to the same conclusion that Andre did. He excused himself to look around the inn some more, leaving Andre alone with the innkeeper.

In an effort to lighten the mood, he inquired about Rahin's story, quickly finding it to be more difficult to listen to than he thought it would be..

Rahin and his family were immigrants from the religious dynasty of Salamoa (Andre's heart immediately sank as he knew what was to come). They had been among those forced to leave their homes, persecuted because of their "unholy" attributes—as decreed by the Supreme Holy Voice, the religious ruler of the country. In Rahin's case, it was the blue eyes he inherited from his father, who was descended from a line of foreigners.

In the beginning of the Holy Purge—as the Voice named the genocide—Rahin tried to hide his family and continue about his business. "Eyes are hard to notice if they're pointed at the ground in humility," he explained somewhat bitterly.

Eventually, as the pressure from the Republic's intensive hunt to weed out foreign blood grew too great, he fled with his family to the border. However, they found no solace there (at this point in the story, Andre's lips became a thin, grim line) for Kaval was pushing the refugees back. In an effort to escape the bloody conflict, Rahin took his family north into the Argos Mountains to find a passage to safety.

Unfortunately, they fled just as fall was ending. Winter flew in swiftly on frozen wings and tormented them in the alpine terrain. Despite the piercing wind and the snow piling higher than their heads, Rahin persevered, leading his family through the treacherous pass to safety on the other side. Two of his little ones died during the journey, freezing to death during one of the long frigid nights. However, his wife and last child survived—frostbitten and weary, yet alive.

Eventually arriving at Cappus, he found work as busboy at one of the local inns. His employer was very kind to him and allowed his family to rent one of the rooms. Through hard work, Rahin quickly moved up the ranks until he reached a managerial position, eventually saving enough money to buy a house in the city and open an inn of his own.

Keppen returned as Rahin was finishing his story and sat down next to Andre.

Rahin had moved from the table and was scouring dishes as he talked. "Though I'm grateful for everything Corynthia has given me, this violence seems never ending. It was closer when we fled from our home, but this feels..." he paused looking for the right word. "Bigger. More dangerous. With what you call the Border Conflict and now this civil war... There's been so much pain in such a short time. It makes me feel as though this land is cursed."

He wiped his hands on a towel and leaned on the counter. "Now your army is here, and someone has died in my very inn..." He trailed off. "Why can't things be as they are supposed to?"

Rahin's words hung in the air for a moment, giving Andre pause. Being a military man, he was well acquainted with the consequences of war. He hated the destruction of home, land, the loss of friends and brothers; nevertheless, he accepted they were inevitable and, unfortunately, a little necessary—as a soldier, they were simply something he must suffer through. It had been so since he began his service in the Kavalan Army.

However, something about the simple sentiment echoed in his mind: *Why can't things be as they are supposed to?* Andre found himself commiserating with the words. Some previously sleeping part of him opened an eye and reached out a hand to grasp for an answer to the question, desperate for a reprieve from war.

War had been with him most of his life, so much so that he couldn't remember the last time he didn't have a sword strapped to his hip; Kaval had constantly been in conflict with other lands on its borders. Now, after Rahin's emotional story of family and loss, he wondered what it would be like for the fighting to end.

He could flee, like Rahin. He could abandon his duties to find a place of solace. After all, what would happen when they removed Tench from power? Would there really be peace, or would wickedness continue to claw at order, ripping apart what was good, like William's life being so unfairly taken?

He recalled the loyalist soldier back at the outpost who sacrificed himself to keep the fort out of rebel hands. He thought also of the dark looks from some of the citizens he passed on the streets here in Cappus. Discontent and greed always found a way to take hold of people's minds, festering like a sickness. Maybe things *were* as intended: War and misery rearing their ugly heads at every opportunity.

The door opened abruptly, expelling Andre's thoughts.

He shook his head. There was no benefit to such thoughts, especially if they were directed at the crooked nature of mankind—that was a very deep pit of despair to fall into. He had a job to do and a war to win. There was no redemption in running.

William wouldn't run.

They all looked around to see Winston and Pitt standing there. Pitt looked angry; Winston, thoughtful. Rahin tapped the counter, then disappeared into the room behind it as the pair joined them at the table.

"How did it go?" Andre looked between both men, trying to glean something from their expression.

Pitt clenched his jaw, the fist on the side of his head flexing. "It wasn't Tullin, apparently."

"What do you—?"

"Not here," Winston cut in. "Did you...?" He didn't finish, though Andre knew what it was he left unsaid.

Keppen answered for him. "Yes. William has been taken care of."

"Good. What did you learn?" Winston asked with a nod at the empty counter.

Keppen shared the lackluster results of his investigation, then Andre recounted what Rahin told them.

"I didn't look at the body. I couldn't..." he trailed off, his eyes burning.

"I understand," Winston uttered softly. He rose. "Come. We have much to discuss."

26

GOVERNOR TULLIN

AFTER THEY DISTANCED THEMSELVES from the crowd at the inn, Winston pulled Pitt aside. "Delvon, I need you to listen to me. I understand you're upset—"

"*Upset?* William is *dead*, Winston. He was *murdered*! The pig who is responsible needs to be drawn and quartered! I am going to make sure that judgment is dealt!"

"You will do nothing of the sort," Winston snapped back. "If you cannot conduct yourself and hold your temper, then I will send you back down to the camp. Do you understand?"

Pitt glared back, a giant full of black fury. Winston couldn't help but feel afraid. Nevertheless, he stood straight and mustered as much warning in his tone as he could. "Do. You. Understand. Me?"

"Yes," Pitt growled through clenched teeth.

"Good."

Winston began to climb the street again. He knew he wasn't being very sensitive, but Andre was right: It was times like these he needed to be calm and poised. William was his friend, too. Politics and war...

Damn it all.

"I know how close you two were, which is why I am allowing you to accompany me." Winston paused as a couple passed them staring at the two tall rebels. "However, this is a delicate situation. We have no proof that this is Tullin's doing; thus, we can't make rash decisions. Which means you need to follow my lead." He glanced over at Pitt, whose face appeared set in stone. "We will make it right."

Pitt's expression seemed to soften a little, although that may have been Winston's imagination.

At the top of the city, the street passed through a large arch, opening up into a huge boulevard easily a hundred yards across. Rows of flowering cherry trees ran down both sides of the road, their plots lined with polished quartz and jade. Walls enclosed the venue, and there were more arches to the left and right leading to neighborhoods of grandiose mansions. The cobbled stones upon which they stood bore swirling patterns of leaves dancing along a lively breeze to form a greater whole across the entire boulevard. The pink petals of cherry blossoms skipped and tumbled around their feet as they walked.

At the end, the governing hall sat in the shadow of the looming crags of Landour Mountain. It was a grand structure: Three stories tall, with many buttresses, arches, and pillars. The reflection of clouds above made the countless windows appear to be sheets of silver rather than panes of glass. The roof, trimmed with elegant spikes, curved upwards into a thin spire, a pennant bearing the black dragon of Cappus drifting limply from its point. There were two symmetrical wings on either side of the main section, a level smaller, though just as majestic.

The boulevard was sparsely populated, and the doors to the hall were locked with no guards in sight. Winston knocked commandingly, the sound echoing around the palisade. When no one came to answer, he peered at the windows, trying to see inside. The glare reflecting off of the glass made it impossible.

Pitt pounded on the door a few times, then kicked it. He glowered at Winston. "I'm going to break this damn door down and drag Tullin out by the ears!"

As soon as the words left his mouth, the door was opened by a porter in a black tunic. "Can I help you gentlemen?"

Whirling back around, Pitt opened his mouth to speak. Quickly, Winston stepped forward, placing a hand on his companion's shoulder.

"We are here to speak to Governor Tullin," he stated pleasantly.

"The governor is indisposed," the man replied shortly. The door began to close.

Winston stuck his hand out, stopping it. "I'm not asking." He locked eyes with the man, hardening his gaze. "This is a matter that cannot wait.

I highly suggest you warn him to make himself presentable." Pushing the door open, he stepped into the lobby. "We shall wait here until he is ready."

The orderly grimaced, then disappeared through a door. Winston and Pitt sat on one of the wooden benches lining the wall to wait.

After nearly an hour (in which Winston repeatedly threatened to send Pitt back to camp for demanding to assault Tullin's chambers), the servant reappeared and beckoned for them to follow. He led them down the length of a hall, following a violet carpet to a flight of stairs. Tapestries alternating between the Corynthian and Cappus crests hung between windows on the front-facing side. The opposite wall bores sconces holding torches at regular intervals, and there were several closed doors, each with a carving of some animal upon its face.

The orderly left them at the council room with a terse, "The governor is waiting inside."

Tullin sat in his usual spot at the head of the table, clad in a flowing gold and blue shirt. Three other men sat with him. Winston assumed they were there more for protection than anything else.

The more the merrier I suppose.

The governor was a large man, as tall as Winston and a good deal heavier. Despite the haughty expression on his round face, he looked a mess under his expensive tunic. His long black hair was tucked untidily into a bun, and there were purple bags under his watery, red-rimmed eyes, which squinted over a sharp nose that turned up at the end. He looked hungover, something Winston found highly amusing.

"Good morning, Tullin!" Winston called across the table. Tullin winced as his voice echoed around the chamber. "Or rather rough morning, I should say."

"What do you want?" grumbled Tullin.

Pitt growled like a dog and crossed his arms, his face clearly telling Winston to get to the point.

Pulling out a chair, Winston sat and waited for a moment to build anticipation. He couldn't help it—theatrics were an ingrained part of his game. Keep people nervous, keep them guessing, and he could keep them dancing on the tips of his fingers. Unpredictability was his trade.

Tullin watched impetuously.

Finally, Winston leaned forward, watching Tullin's face carefully as he spoke. "I received some very upsetting news this morning. A distressing discovery was made in an inn within your city walls. As I am sure you know, some of the innkeepers have been kind enough to let our officers sleep in the city rather than stay out in the rainstorm. Something I was initially grateful for."

He paused.

"I was... informed." Tullin spoke hesitantly, licking his lips.

Pitt scoffed.

"One of my officers was found dead in his room," Winston said bluntly.

Blatant shock lit up Tullin's face, as well as those of his advisers, who began to whisper among themselves.

The governor drew a shaky hand across his forehead. "I-I don't—I was told nothing of this," he stammered. His voice took on a frantic edge. "You're sure—?"

One of the other men sprang to his feet. "Are you accusing us of committing this act?"

Pitt's voice rang out harshly in response. The other shrank back at his ferocity. "Who else would have? You're not fond of us, Tullin—you've made that clear! It wouldn't be above you to murder one of ours and act surprised. You've already given us your word nobody will be harmed!"

Winston glanced back at Tullin to see how he would respond, his hand absentmindedly going to the chain around his neck at the end of which hung the Vida Imralta.

He and Andre had been unable to think of a practical place to hide the magical amulet. Since Andre adamantly refused to wear it any longer, Winston now wore it at all times, having swapped the leather strap for a silver chain.

Tullin shot to his feet, surprisingly quick for his size. Spittle sprayed from his mouth as he shouted back, "You threatened *my* position, fearmongering me and mine to ensure your safety, but I agreed nevertheless!"

He brandished his finger at Winston. "I know very well what you and your people think of me, Servailles! You call me a snake and a coward, but the last thing I am is a *fool*! You're right—I gave you my word! I showed you hospitality, yet you still come to accuse and dishonor me! If your only intention here is to discredit me, you can get the *hell* out of my city!"

Winston answered calmly before Pitt could boil over like a kettle. "Tullin, my friend, our accord was that I would allow you to remain in power so long as my men can shelter here without fear of harm. I'm afraid that agreement has been breached."

"By no fault of mine!"

"Who else, then?" Pitt rumbled again.

"Berling's agents, extremists!" Tullin waved his hand wildly. "A wayward soldier with dreams of glory! Take your pick! Not I! My end of the bargain is steadfast!"

Winston cupped his chin in a show of mock contemplation. "I seem to remember emphasizing that any outbursts from loyalists and subsequent damage to the rebellion's assets would be held accountable against you. My officers are certainly assets. And one of them has been killed under your so-called protection. Not much of steadfast bargain."

The man to Tullin's left laughed derisively. "You must be joking. You really expect us to control—"

"Really?" Winston interrupted. "You agreed to the terms. I can bring forth the documents signed by you and your lord." He turned his attention back to Tullin, who was suddenly quiet. "You expect me to leave you in power if you cannot control those under your jurisdiction? Maybe you didn't order it, Tullin, but William's blood is on *your* hands."

The governor's face blanched at the mention of who was killed. He had known William, had dealt with him during Winston's duration in office, and there had been no love there. This was no longer a matter of a simple accusation, but a cold-blooded strike against an opponent.

Panicking at the magnitude of his quandary, Tullin blustered, "I have done my utmost to keep the citizens in check! My guards are working hard to ensure peace! This is an isolated incident! An extremist! Certainly not with my benediction!"

"Yet it is the job of the government to predict and intercept such incidents, and *I* am not the government." Winston leaned forward and fixed Tullin in a stare a cat might give a mouse. "I am not your friend, Tullin. I have kept you in charge because it is in my best interest to do so. If didn't know how scared you are of losing your position and how desperately you will hang on to authority, I would have replaced you from the start. I truly believe that we can learn to work together, but that comes with the confidence that I do not have to fear my men being stabbed in the dark while I work to bring peace to Corynthia. Hear me when I say: You stand on perilous ground, governor."

Tullin puffed out his chest, summoning the pride of his pious position. "This is slander! *You* heap coals onto the fire *you* have kindled, and then demand that I contain the blaze! If this is to be the nature of our tenuous relationship, than I will be *damned* if I stand by while you try to relive your lost dreams of a failed monarch! Tench may be pig, but you... you are a *snake*!"

At his words, Winston saw red. He sprang to his feet, chair clattering onto its back behind him. The room immediately stilled before the waves of wrath rippling out from him. Even Pitt looked a little afraid.

Andre's cautionary advice whispered through thumping of blood in his ears. With difficulty, he restrained himself from flinging the dagger from his boot into Tullin's neck.

"Do not challenge me, Tullin," he hissed, his voice taking on the soft tone he spoke in when he was incensed. "Do not give me a reason to lay waste to you and your office. Insult me again, and I will drag you out by your hair, then *hang* you from your very roof."

Tullin shook his head, looking terrified. "You're insane!"

Insane. If only he knew the price Winston was slowly having to pay.

Winston's laugh echoed harshly. "We're done here. Come, Delvon." Throwing open the door, he stalked from the room.

"What was that?" Pitt exclaimed as they marched down the hall. "You tell me to keep my head, then you lose control like that? Now we'll be lucky if we can *force* him out of—"

"He didn't kill him," Winston interrupted. "Nor did he have a hand in it." They were at the door to the lobby. He opened it, standing aside for Pitt to walk through.

He stopped instead, staring at Winston incredulously. "What do you mean?"

"This isn't Tullin's doing. I don't think he actually had an idea anyone took rooms in the city."

"He said—"

"Tullin likes to keep up appearances."

He led Pitt through the lobby and out the front door. As they stepped outdoors, Winston shivered. A sharp breeze made the boulevard seem ten degrees colder.

"He needs to show people he's in control and knows what's happening. From the looks of it, he probably had no recollection of anything he did last night." Winston chuckled at the thought.

"This is amusing to you?" Pitt asked scathingly. "William is still dead."

"I'm sorry. Tullin is telling the truth. He's a lot of unpleasant things, but he's not a fool. He loves his power and won't do anything to jeopardize it. I was doubtful it was him to begin with."

"What?" Pitt's scowl deepened. "Then what was the purpose of our dithering? We wasted time that we could have used to find William's true killer!"

Winston held up his hands. "Peace, Delvon. It was not entirely wasted. Tullin will certainly redouble his efforts to snuff out any remaining loyalist groups in the city. It was to our benefit." He appraised the bald man with an affected look. "I am not wafting around like a wayward leaf on the wind. I'm leading the rebellion again, remember?"

Pitt did not soften. "Who did it then?"

"I have a theory."

The two fell silent as they walked.

Tullin reacted precisely how Winston suspected he would. By allowing him to keep his position, they also secured his protection of the rebellion. The governor would condemn anything that could destroy their tentative relationship and bring the rebel swords against him. The relationship was also important for the rebellion to maintain: With Tullin removed from power, who knew what could happen with the loyalist parties still in Cappus? Winston was well aware of extremists on both sides of the war.

Of course, someone needed to be blamed for William's death. Tullin had merely been the likeliest suspect.

Suspicion was malleable. Now that Tullin was cleared, the rebellion turning their ire towards Cappus would be highly detrimental to their momentum. They needed full support from as much of Corynthia as possible as they moved against Tench. Lashing out against the city would be far from beneficial for their cause.

And besides, if a loyalist was trying to strike a blow against the rebels, they would have attacked Winston, the one pulling the strings. He was Tench's prize after all.

No, they couldn't be distracted by their desire for justice, not with another layer added to the game. Winston would have to keep them focused.

Politics and war... damn it all indeed.

27

THE WOLF

Samuel Corence and Declan Row were waiting for them in their command tent. The former greeted them quietly. It was obvious the news of William's death left him shaken; his normally gruff tone and expression were considerably softer as he embraced Pitt.

"I'm sorry, brother."

Declan remained bent over a map of Corynthia decorated with little colored pins and wooden carvings to represent cities and troop placements. He gave no acknowledgment to their arrival.

"Where are the others?" Winston asked.

"I'll fetch them." Corence left the tent.

"Find Caito as well," Winston called after him. "I think it's time we could use his insight."

Corence ducked his head back into the tent with a confused look on his face.

"The Soothsayer," Winston clarified. "He should be with the Crimson Hounds."

Andre watched Declan, his mind running like a hunted rabbit. The bookkeeper had glanced up at the mention of the Soothsayer's name, a shadow on his thin face.

He joined Declan, also staring at the map without actually seeing it. *If it wasn't Tullin, then who was it?*

His mind ran back to the journey to the outpost all those weeks ago, where Leana Palmer reported a shadow. Someone had been following them, watching them. He recalled his interaction with Declan in Seruvia before Winston's trial. He had known why Andre was there. Furthermore, he always seemed to know what Andre was thinking. Then there were the times he saw Declan's eyes change—like someone else stepped out from behind them for just a moment.

He felt a strange coldness touch his insides.

Andre already didn't trust the bookkeeper. He had been wary of the man since they met him. Now, he realized just how little they knew about him; yet, they had accepted him into their inner circle without a second thought. Who was to say he wasn't a spy? Or something worse?

"I'm sorry to hear about your friend." Andre looked up to see Declan watching him. "The loss of such a talented strategist is unfortunate."

Andre stared hard into the bookkeeper's eyes. There was no sign of sympathy in them, just silent calculation. "Thank you. He will be sorely missed."

Declan laughed quietly. "You have something to say to me?" he surmised as if he again read Andre's thoughts.

Andre glanced around to see if anyone was listening to their conversation. Winston stood at the opening, waiting for the rest of his officers to arrive. Both Pitt and Keppen sat on the ground, absentmindedly fiddling with their tunics and staring into space.

Leaning closer to Declan, he asked in a low voice, "Why are you here?"

"I am here to help in any way I can." Declan tilted his head.

"Who are you?"

"A keeper of books and student of history. A vague question, Andre."

"You know damn well that's not what I'm asking. No historian wields a blade like you. Blast it, very few soldiers can. Who are you *really*, Declan?"

A dim fire glimmered deep inside Declan's green eyes, emerald and poisonous. "I have a long and complicated history, one I do not wish to disclose."

"Then how are we supposed to trust you?"

"You've done so without question up to this point. Do you have any reason to stop? I've led you through blood, steel, and stone without fail. If anything, I'd say you were in my debt, Andre." He dropped his voice to a serpentine hiss. "If you are accusing me of murdering your friend, I would consider that."

Giving up all pretense of studying the maps, Andre gripped Declan by the wrist. "Give me one good reason why I shouldn't."

"What's going on?" Winston asked from the tent entrance.

"Nothing." Andre stepped back from the table and averted his eyes.

Winston looked between the two of them curiously. "It didn't look like nothing."

"I'm just... frustrated."

Declan appraised him with an amused look and returned to the map.

Andre narrowed his eyes at him, insides writhing. The more he considered his suspicion, the more he believed it. He had seen how gracefully Declan moved through a battlefield; he was certain the bookkeeper was capable of moving through a forest like a ghost.

Reason gnawed at him. *If he was an enemy,* he debated with himself, *why didn't he kill both of us when we were weakest at the creek?* And why kill William? If Declan was an assassin sent from Tench, surely Winston would be the highest priority.

Andre hardened himself against his own mind's attempt to rationalize. He didn't have the full picture; there was something larger at work. Reason wasn't enough when dealing with an incomplete story.

Better to be cautious than regret it later.

Corence reentered the tent, followed by a troop of others: Caito Lazar, Wes, and Tahlia among them. Declan stepped back to his usual place at the fringe of the tent while everyone else crowded the table. Pitt and Keppen remained on the ground, where Wes and Tahlia joined them. The Soothsayer stood beside them.

Andre kept his eyes on the bookkeeper as Winston began to speak.

"I feel I must convey the context of this meeting, though it appears to be common news by now. William was found dead this morning in one of the inns in the city. I am not sure how—"

"He was stabbed through the eye." Pitt's hand disappeared into his tunic, and he pulled out a knife, tossing it on top of the maps.

It was a beautiful weapon. The handle was made from engraved ivory with a silver, blood-stained blade curving gracefully from a serrated base into a fine point. The silver pommel was nearly two inches long and as sharp as the blade's point, the crest of a bat head and the letter K carved into the thick base.

Andre had never seen anything like it. From the others' whispers, it seemed neither had they.

Winston held it up, the light glancing off of it. The mirrored finish of the blade seemed to flash red for a split-second.

Declan moved forward from the corner, a slight smile curving his lips. "May I?" He reached out a hand.

Winston gave it to him, handle first. Nobody spoke while Declan rubbed off the blood with his shirt.

"Do you know what it is?" Wes asked curiously. He was craning his neck from his seat for a better look at the weapon.

Twirling the dagger through his fingers, Declan stabbed it dramatically into the table.

"It's called Rödfang or Kellander's Dagger. It's an ancient weapon from before Kaval"—he glanced meaningfully at Andre and Winston—"when Atheralyn dominated the continent. It's said to be a cursed weapon once owned by a man named Ryska Kellander, who used it to murder his family, and in doing so, tainted the blade. A single cut drains the life-force of its victims, and with every life it takes, it grows more deadly. According to the story, the blade gleams red from the blood it has spilled."

"How do you know this?" Andre demanded.

"I study these stories, Andre."

"I mean, how do you know it *is* Kellander's Dagger? After all, I assume replicas would be made."

Declan inclined his head and indicated to the dagger's pommel. "The family crest is engraved into the pommel. What's more..."

He yanked it from the wood and held it under the lantern light. The reflection of the tent on the metal turned a deep crimson, their minuscule faces appearing as though drenched in blood.

The bookkeeper placed it back on the table. "We're growing quite a collection."

With a warning look at Declan, Winston took the dagger and tucked it into his belt. Andre saw him tug at the chain around his neck where he wore the Vida Imralta.

Andre had convinced him to keep it on his person once they arrived at Cappus. He didn't want to be under its effects, and they couldn't decide on a better place to hide it.

"Well, the weapon doesn't change the fact we have an assassin in our midst," Winston announced. "And it could be someone here."

The stunned silence was finally broken by Corence's incredulous, "*What?*"

Everyone spoke at once until Winston held up a hand. "Delvon and I spoke to Tullin this morning. He was very adamant that he had no hand in the murder."

"You believed him just like that?" This time it was Tahlia. She was leaning back against Wes's shoulder with her arms crossed, her lips were pursed dubiously, slim eyebrows drawn together on her olive complexion.

"There were a few other factors involved," Winston admitted. "I don't think he was even aware some of our officers were staying in the city. It also appeared that the lights were a little too bright for him this morning." A couple officers chuckled at the insinuation. "Tullin's not foolish enough to throw away his precarious standing with us. He has no love for us. Still, he cares about his authority more than he cares to try kill us off. Besides, Andre and Keppen couldn't find evidence of a struggle, and the innkeeper noted the door and window were locked from the inside."

His mouth drew a grim line. "Unless Tench has an assassin who can walk through walls, the other alternative is a wolf among our flock—someone able to move around without suspicion. Someone William would have known. Berling is certainly wealthy enough to buy someone off."

"A wolf with dangerous tools it seems," Lazar declared suddenly.

Everyone looked around at him in surprise. Andre had forgotten the Soothsayer was there.

"There's another image I've been seeing in connection with other events: A silver pendant with a red jewel. I have a feeling it's also magical"—he nodded at Rödfang on Winston's belt—"and very dangerous. It would make sense that this assassin could have possession of it as well."

Andre and Winston exchanged looks, the latter reaching for his neck again.

Declan noticed, and another smile touched his lips. "Indeed."

"Hold," Pitt interjected, still seated. "We don't know if this knife is magical. I know the story of Kellander. Only, it's just that—a story."

"Would you like me to test it on you?" Winston asked testily.

Andre interjected hurriedly before Pitt could snap back, "If it did have magical powers, especially those like Declan said, why would he just leave the dagger? A weapon like that would be invaluable to him."

Winston shrugged. "Maybe he didn't know what it was."

All of a sudden, Corence slammed his fist onto the table. "Why are we ignoring the fact that there might be a traitor in our midst? I think *that* is more important to address than fairy dust! Winston, if you're correct, then whom can we trust? How do we discuss plans? How do we *sleep* at night?" He spread his arms to indicate the tent. "Why are we talking about this *here?*"

"All very good questions," Winston agreed. "To start, nobody should be alone from this point on. Keep someone you can trust by your side at all times. We need constant vigilance, rotate watches. I'll work on assigning guard details for each of the officers. While there may be a few more sleepless nights, it will likely discourage any more assassination attempts. As for planning...

"We can't afford to be secretive. We're approaching the end—I can feel it. This war, Berling's reign, it's almost over. If we point fingers now, we'll fall apart before we can even attempt to take Seruvia. If we are to succeed, we must be unified. The fight of our lives lies before us, and I need every last one of you with me." He slammed his hand on the table dramatically. "All in agreement?"

After the meeting, Andre went straight to his tent, mind still spinning from the day's events.

It seemed surreal to him: William Draytus, his friend for many years, who led him during the Border Conflict—the man he loved as a brother—would never speak to him or fight beside him again. There seemed to be an emptiness in the busy camp, as though the hundreds of soldiers surrounding him were merely apparitions passing by.

Arriving at his tent, he began to unpack and repack his belongings. Because he always kept everything ready at a moment's notice, he knew his gear was all present and accounted for; however, he needed to keep his mind occupied.

After the third time securing his shield to his pack, Andre heard the flap to his tent open. He whirled around, drawing his dagger from his belt.

"Woah! Stand down! It's me!" Mattias yelped.

Andre sheathed the weapon. "Sorry, Mattias. I'm a little frayed."

"Understandable," Mattias sighed sadly. "I still can't believe it."

After a moment of comfortable silence between them, Mattias spoke again, "The Crimson Hounds are ready to leave. Even Wes and Tahlia have their things in order despite their new friend keeping them occupied."

Andre raised an eyebrow questioningly.

"It appears we've inducted the Soothsayer into our ranks. I don't know about all that talk of visions, but he seems to be a steady, reliable boy. He has plenty of heart, and when those two are done with him he'll be a damn fine swordsman. He's integrated himself nicely with the others in scouting and sentinel rotation."

Andre had yet to become acquainted with Lazar. Apart from the scant meetings he had attended, the boy had been out of sight, out of mind; though Andre had spent precious little time the Hounds himself. Still, a good report from his second-in-command was one he trusted.

His thoughts darkened again as he remembered Winston's revelation. Marching to the tent flap, he poked his head out to make sure nobody was loitering nearby. Once he was satisfied with their privacy, he turned to Mattias, a grim shadow on his face.

Winston had instructed the officers to keep the news of the Wolf within his inner circle, but Andre had known Mattias Berg for his whole life. They grew up together in the same town, shared the same childhood, and weathered the same battles together. He was a brother in all but blood to Andre. He was the one person Andre knew he could trust without fault.

"I have worrisome news."

"I'm listening."

"Winston doesn't believe that William was killed by Tullin."

Mattias shook his head. "Of course not. Why would Tullin place himself in that position?"

"He believes the killer is in our midst—a traitor."

"Not an assassin from Tench?"

Andre shrugged. "It's possible, but all of the entrances to the room were locked from the inside, and there were no signs of a struggle. It almost seems like William let the killer in."

"But why would they target William instead of Winston?"

"I don't know. It's inconsistent. It seems almost personal."

Mattias exhaled and sat down on Andre's bedroll. "Bloody hell."

"There's another thing," Andre added. "Declan Row."

"Who?"

Andre remembered that Mattias had only just returned from deployment. "You heard about Winston's mad plan to meet the Soothsayer?"

"Of course I did," Mattias laughed. "There's not a person in Corynthia who doesn't know about that insane gambit."

"Declan helped us escape. He led us out through some tunnels under the city. Then, when Thomislon and his men turned on us—"

"*What?*" Mattias roared. "That son of a bitch! I heard they didn't make it back! I didn't know they turned traitor!"

Realizing the sort of questions Mattias might ask, Andre spoke quickly to smother clarification. For some reason, he didn't want him to know about the Vida Imralta. The knowledge was too dangerous to share, especially since Kent and the others tried to kill him for it.

"Declan saved us. I was injured, and Winston certainly couldn't have taken everyone on at once. He fought like a demon. Even so, I don't trust him. There's something about him that makes me uneasy. He seems almost... rotten."

"Do you think he killed William?"

"I think he had a hand in it, at least. While I don't know if he's an agent of Tench, I don't trust him."

"What does he look like?"

As Andre described the bookkeeper to Berg, he found himself again remembering his eyes. Those snake-like green orbs put him most ill at ease.

Something coiled deep in their depths, biding its time, injecting fear into Andre's bones. He didn't know what would happen should it rise to the surface. He didn't want to find out.

Mattias nodded thoughtfully. "I've seen him around. Seems like a loner."

"Will you help me keep an eye on him?"

"Whenever I can spare one."

Andre felt some of the tension in his stomach ease and smiled gratefully. "And make sure he stays away from the Soothsayer. I've noticed his gaze lingering on the boy. I think he has an interest in him."

Still sitting, Mattias clapped him on the thigh, unable to reach any higher. "Of course."

"While you're at it, you might as well watch my back, too."

"Andre, I don't have two heads."

Mattias lingered as Andre resumed packing his bag. Sitting in easy companionship, they spoke for a while about small, unimportant matters until a soldier ducked her head in to inform them that a memorial was being held for William later that night. After Mattias left to finish his own preparations, Andre took out his armor and began to polish it. He wanted to look his best as he honored his fallen comrade for the last time.

28

ANDRE AND THE SOOTHSAYER

THE REBEL ARMY—THOUSANDS OF soldiers, horses, and wagons—slowly crawled away from Cappus. It was an awesome sight from the ridge. Despite being smaller than other musterings Andre had seen throughout his life, he still felt a sense of warm pride as he watched. There was more at stake for these warriors. They were fighting for something real: Freedom. And he had the privilege to help lead them.

The sight also helped take his mind off of William, if only temporarily.

The memorial the previous night had been the final straw. The shock finally melted away, and when he went to speak in front of his friends and cohorts, he found himself unable to do anything more than weep. His gloomy mood persisted through the night into the next morning, infecting his company, who mirrored his sullen manner. He didn't say a word while he tore his tent down and loaded his gear into a covered wagon. Mattias did most of the ordering for him as they moved their company into formation.

Now, as he singled out the Crimson Hounds in the mass of soldiers, Andre felt his spirits lift a little. William would have been proud to watch this final march to the capital, to see the final move against the tyranny holding Corynthia hostage.

At least Andre could witness it for him.

Coming down from the ridge to join the Hounds, he realized just how much he had missed them. He greeted them, addressing each by name and throwing out jokes and compliments as a maiden throws flowers at a wedding. His enthusiasm spread, and soon, they were all smiling and laughing. Some began to sing a jaunty tune about a blackbird that thought it was a fish as Andre drew even with Mattias.

"There's a pleasant sound," Mattias remarked. "I see you're feeling better."

"I never realized how much I missed these brutes." Andre whistled along with the lyrics.

"And they, you. They don't like seeing you downcast. You're the heart of the Hounds, Andre." Mattias nodded enthusiastically when Andre looked at him in astonishment.

He never really considered how those under his command felt about him. He always just treated them according to what they deserved. Since there was no point in mincing words or coddling them, he was as direct and honest as possible. Hearing their appreciation for his leadership touched him.

Unable to think of a response, he touched his fist to his heart in a salute.

They marched at a steady pace until their surroundings began to fade into the dream state of dusk. The clouds remained heavy and gray, hanging low in the sky. Undeterred, cooking fires sprang up surrounded by tents and pickets for animals. The noise and light of the camp would keep the wild animals away; however, sentries were assigned to watch for any loyalist scouts or spies.

Or assassins.

The thought was fresh in Andre's mind with the arrival of night. As long as the threat still loomed, he doubted he would be able to sleep.

As he settled down for the evening, Andre noticed Winston gathered with a few of the officers. He decided to stay where he was. He was long overdue to spend time with his men.

He found a campfire with Wes, Tahlia, Leana, and Caito Lazar.

"I don't believe I've introduced myself." He shook the Soothsayer's hand. "Lieutenant Andre Cordon. I'm the one who keeps this sad rabble in line." He gestured to the company around them. They laughed at his words.

"Seems more like we keep you in line," Leana Palmer contradicted, her cheeks dimpling in a smile. "You've been finding yourself in all kinds of trouble without us."

Andre shrugged ruefully. "Can't help it. You're not the only ones I have to take care of." He looked back to Caito. "I hear we've adopted you. Or rather Wes and Tahlia have. I'm glad to have you."

Caito nodded his thanks, seeming reluctant to speak.

"I won't force you to speak. So much is happening right now, it's understandable if your head is swimming. I'll have you know, though, we are due for a conversation sometime." He smiled kindly at the young man, who nodded again to acknowledge him.

Wes, sitting next to Caito, punched him the shoulder. "Don't worry; Andre may be ugly, but he doesn't bite. He's softer than a woman."

"Says you!" Leana crowed. "We all know Tahlia's the one with the balls!"

Ears red, Wes threw a stick at her amid gales of laughter, though he grinned at the same time.

The rest of the night was spent in merriment as the Crimson Hounds traded stories and sang songs. Donroe and Palmer had shot several forest fowls and roasted them over the fire, divvying up the meat throughout their group. As Andre roared with laughter at a story Mattias was telling about one of their greennoses who thought he was being hunted by a mountain lion that actually turned out to be a rabbit, he realized he couldn't recall the last time he was this relaxed and happy. Even Caito emerged from his shell a little to join them in a heated game of Pincher.

When they retired to sleep, Andre remained awake, pacing or sitting at the entrance of his tent, ears pricked and eyes roving through the heavy night. He spotted no wolves, literal or figurative.

Early the next morning, the army was moving east again. A breeze swept water from the trees, but no rain fell from the sky. In fact, the clouds broke, and a large swath of blue sky appeared to ogle down at the marching army. Pointing at the patch of color, the soldiers cheered. Andre felt his spirits lift even more at the sight, and he whistled a tune as he rode.

The army paused briefly in the afternoon, then made one more push before nightfall. The blue sky disappeared, swallowed once more by the heavy clouds that made it seem much later than it actually was.

After dinner, Andre found Caito and walked with him to a gnarled oak tree standing at the edge of camp like a wizened beggar.

"Is this a good idea?" Caito asked with a glance back at camp. "With an assassin around?"

"I'll keep an eye out if you'll do the same."

The young man seemed nervous to be alone with him, and Andre quickly tried to placate him. "What do you think of them?" he inquired with a nod back at the fires.

"I'm sorry," Caito stammered after a moment. "I've been the subject of many interviews." He looked briefly surprised at his own honesty, then quickly rearranged his expression.

Andre picked up a stone, passing it back and forth between his hands. "It's understandable to be cautious, but you're among good people, Caito. If you want to ride with the Crimson Hounds, you need to open up a little. We're a family forged by blood and trust. The things they've been through together..." Tossing the stone into the gathering darkness, he looked sidelong at the young man. "There are no dark horses among the Crimson Hounds."

Caito stared after the stone. "Wes and Tahlia told me about you. I also heard bits of tales when I was in the capital. They were only stories then, but now that I'm around you, I guess I'm a little intimidated. You have a reputation."

"I'm only a man, Caito. No more than you."

"But you're a great man—an accomplished leader and a dangerous enemy. I'd say you're more feared by Tench's soldiers than Winston."

"And you're the Soothsayer, a man of literal legend," Andre countered. "You've seen the future. You carry the weight of our fate and the hope of the people on your shoulders. Not to mention you single-handedly escaped the most secure fortress in Corynthia."

"I had help." He said this sadly, and Andre frowned sympathetically.

"Nevertheless, if you really consider it, I'm the one who should be intimidated."

Caito smiled and seemed to relax a little. When Andre invited him to tell about himself, he obliged.

He began by recounting his childhood. He grew up in a small town in Northern Corynthia. His father was a woodworker while his mother served at a little hostel in town, teaching Caito how to read and write in her spare time. She always made sure to have a full ink bottle and plenty of parchment available. Caito spent his younger years climbing trees, throwing stones at birds, and practicing his penmanship. As he grew older, he learned his father's craft, sharpening his skill with his hands as well as his attention to detail. He still preferred the quiet companionship of books to the physical labor and thus spent much of his free time reading and writing.

He was eighteen when the soldiers arrived.

"When Tench's men came," he recounted with a far away look on his face, "they quickly forced us into submission. People were starving because of their tariffs—little more than ill-disguised robbery. Many died. My aunt, Gertie, took me in after..." he trailed off.

Noticing Caito's eyes glistening, Andre hurriedly adjusted the string on his tunic.

Caito went on, telling now of his visions. His parents discovered his gift when he was only six. They noticed that he made odd comments and observations that didn't seem pertinent to anything until what he said incredibly came true later. Upon asking Caito about these strange occurrences, they learned that he received strange feelings and visions he couldn't explain. These premonitions never seemed to affect him or harm him in any way; oftentimes, he forgot about them in a day or two. Hence, his parents overcame their initial worry from this discovery. They turned their focus instead on keeping it a secret, instructing Caito to do the same.

"There was one dream my mother used to fret about. I had it every once in a while—I still do. I don't consider it quite a nightmare anymore, though there's something about it that unsettles me. It terrified me as a child."

He slipped into the same monotone as when he recounted his vision at Cappus. "There is a beautiful garden filled with the most colorful flowers and delicious fruits you could imagine. A giant tree, big as a castle, covered in hanging vines towers above it all. There's a crack at the base of the trunk with a great, fiery light emanating within. A figure stands before it, poised as though to slip through the crack and enter into what lies beyond. Something horrible will happen if they do—I know it. I try to scream, but I can't make a sound."

His eyes clearing, he looked at Andre. "I used to wake up screaming when I was little. It's been with me my whole life, yet I've never figured out what it means. Maybe it doesn't matter. Maybe its just a dream."

They continued to talk for a couple of hours. The more they did, the more Andre liked the young man. He was charming, witty, and pleasant to speak with, despite his reserved nature. Not at all the kind of person Andre expected to have alleged mystical powers. He reminded Andre of Winston, although with more humility and reserve.

Before returning to the camp, Andre reached into his pocket and produced a red dog head pin and presented it to Caito.

"I was going to give this to you anyway," he said. "Wes and Tahlia have been wringing me out to do so since they returned. However, I wanted the opportunity to meet the young man behind the Soothsayer." He smiled at Caito, who stared at the pin in his outstretched palm. "You're a good man, and I'm happy to have you. Welcome to the Crimson Hounds."

Caito could only stammer his thanks.

29

THE HOUSE OF ENDELA

THE CITY OF MARKALV was more open than Seruvia. Its streets and alleys were wider, with far more greenery in the squares. Instead of countless cobbled courtyards with market stalls, many of the streets wrapped around grassy parks or fountains that complemented the soaring, many-arched buildings very well. It couldn't quite compare to Seruvia's size and grandeur—with its towering walls, huge buildings, and Audax Keep—but as they passed orchards and elegant villas into the city center, Andre found himself marveling at his surroundings.

A misting rain fell as they walked. Because of the weather, most people were indoors. The cozy glow in the windows graced the streets with a peaceful look, as though its inhabitants had never experienced Tench's cruelty.

"Where exactly are we going?" Corence grumbled. "It's bloody miserable out."

He, Andre, and Winston were on their way to meet the leader of rebel activity in Markalv. The rebellion army was camped well outside the city limits to avoid inciting retaliation from any sulking loyalists or outrage from the citizens at their occupation. Pitt, still brooding from William's assassination, decided to remain at camp.

Winston pointed ahead to a large building with stained glass windows. It was covered in vines and surrounded by willows and seemed a noble, yet somber place. "The chapel there."

"At a church?" Corence scoffed. "This leader's not a religious loon, is he?"

"If he is, I'm sure you'll hear about it," Andre returned with a snort. Corence chuckled, though Winston gave no indication he heard him.

A single man sat near the door, presumably to guard it. It was only then that Andre realized what was missing from their venture into the city: No soldiers. Whereas Seruvia had been crawling with armed men, in Markalv, this was the first guard he had seen.

The guard wore a simple, unmarked tunic over a chainmail shirt. His hair was dark from the rain, for he wore no helmet, and outlined a pleasant face. A simple blade hung from his hip, a wooden shield across his back.

He rose, saluting as the group stopped in front of the church. "Winston Servailles. Brother Ollander is expecting you inside."

Winston thanked him and began up the steps towards the double doors.

Andre exchanged a glance with Corence before following. He wasn't a religious person. In fact, he did his best to avoid the stuff. It was difficult to understand; moreover, those well-versed in its nuances were usually insufferable. Even though he did use the the All-Mother's name (the supreme deity said to have created the world), it was merely out of an adopted habit, not based on real belief.

He shivered as he stepped into the building. It wasn't much warmer than outside, and there was a draft. At least it wasn't raining.

The lobby was a small, simple room with two tall windows on either side of the entrance. Another set of double doors frowned at them across the burgundy carpeted floor, wooden benches flanking either side. Tall candelabras at the edges of the room cast flickering light on a colored tapestry depicting the city's patron.

From what Andre understood about religion in the Corynthian and Kavalan cultures (for they were one and the same), cities claimed patrons that were supposedly lesser embodiments of a more powerful entity: The All-Mother. These patrons represented virtuous characteristics such as generosity, patience, and kindness—all bestowed upon humanity as moral guides.

Whether it was true or not, as far as Andre was concerned, neither these patrons nor the All-Mother could stop evil people from doing evil deeds. Only steel and a strong will could do that.

A man sitting on one of the benches rose as they filed in. He wore a solemn expression with just a hint of pompousness. Bowing gracefully, his dark blue robes wafting around him like river water. "Welcome to the house of Endela, friends. My name is Brother Gray. One of you is Winston Servailles, I presume?"

Winston spoke up from the head of the group. "I am. Thank you, brother, for your hospitality."

He was using a tone Andre never heard from him before, quiet and deferential—humble, almost. Winston usually conducted himself in such an authoritative manner that he took control of conversations immediately. He was certainly capable of a respectful demeanor, yet this subdued, reverent manner was disconcerting for Andre.

Suddenly, Andre realized how little personal information he knew about the man. He never discussed religion with Winston (mostly because he thought it was in bad taste), but now, he wondered what it meant to him, and what other details he had failed to consider.

"Brother Ollander speaks very highly of you. He's waiting inside."

Andre's jaw dropped as he entered the chapel. The paneled ceiling arched far above them, higher than it seemed from the outside. Ornate wooden beams spanned width-wise across the ceiling, supporting the gently curving vault. The burgundy carpet ran through the doorway all the way to the stage at the far end of the room. Rows of long pews marched down the aisle illuminated by clusters of candles on the floor and tall candelabras at the ends. Small stained-glass windows inlaid in the walls, consistent with the pews, filtered the gloomy light from outside through purple and blue glass.

The stage spanned in front of a huge stained-glass window boasting a depiction of a woman standing with her hands outstretched over a man bowing in reverence. Andre could only assume it was Endela, the church's namesake. Behind the wooden pulpit at the front of the stage, right below the window, squatted a large altar covered in countless candles. A woman, also clad blue robes, was methodically lighting them.

The doors closed behind them with a boom that echoed through the openness, making Andre jump. At the sound, three people rose from one of the pews at the front of the aisle. They turned in unison, sending shivers down Andre's spine.

Two of them, a man and a woman, were dressed in robes, his the same burgundy as the carpet, hers blue. The third was a bearded man in a tight black shirt and a sword at his hip.

"Brother Ollander!" Winston called, his voice echoing through the giant room.

The male priest raised his hand in greeting. "It's good to see you, Winston. It's been far too long"

He was a giant man, towering over even Winston, who was already an impressive height. His huge muscles, barely contained in his priest's robes, gave him the air of a mountain dripping wine. His voice matched his appearance: Deep and soothing, like thunder rumbling from the cloud of his well-groomed beard. Kind wrinkles winged his deep hazel eyes. His gaze lingered upon each of their faces before returning to Winston.

"It's difficult to visit in exile. It's good to see you, too." Winston turned to Andre and Corence. "This is Brother Ollander. He's an old friend of mine and the head priest for the House of Endela. He has been invaluable to the rebellion as the leader of resistance here in Markalv. Apart from displacing Tench's agents, he's worked tirelessly to recruit people to our cause."

Andre was taken aback at hearing this. He wouldn't have expected a religious worker to be so involved with such a thing as a civil war.

Corence apparently thought the same because he grunted, a frown on his face. "No disrespect, but aren't you supposed to be spreading peace and love, not driving out the vermin? I thought people like you would leave that to us while you sit by and condemn our actions."

Andre expected Ollander to grow angry or shout at Corence. Instead, he merely laughed. It was a deep and pleasant sound. "Aye, some of us would be happy to, especially in the House of Peace. They would groan and say your deeds are wicked even if your intentions are not. However, just because I *preach* of a peaceable kingdom, that doesn't mean I am blind to the reality we live in. Tyranny is a rot that needs to be removed and cannot be done so by sitting idly by.

"Iyala, the All-Mother, teaches that we must fight evil and keep it from swallowing good. The paradise waiting for us across the Divide is founded on the backs of her faithful: Those who stand against the darkness. And so I fight and organize resistance, and protect those who cannot protect themselves, because *that* is the true meaning of peace. Not standing back cursing those brave enough to stand up to tyranny and take back what is rightfully theirs: Freedom."

Corence nodded approvingly and gave Winston a toothy grin. "I like this man. He speaks sense and speaks it well."

Winston smiled and proceeded to introduce his companions to the priest.

Andre nodded cordially when he was introduced. At the same time, he couldn't help feeling a strange sense of betrayal. Not once had he heard of Brother Ollander, even just in passing. He considered Winston and him to be very close, yet recently that belief was being put to the test. It was obvious Winston had known Brother Ollander a long time and was partial to his religious ways, if not involved in the practice. Knowing him as he did with his sarcastic, irreverent personality and devil-may-care attitude, this new side of him made Andre unsure of who exactly he had been friends with for so many years.

With his increasingly erratic behavior and so much mystery surrounding his past, Andre could only wonder what other secrets were submerged in the murky depths of his life.

"May I introduce Sister Dell, one of our senior teachers here, and Jerard Denelsen." Ollander motioned to his companions respectively. "Jerard is our heads of operations here in Markalv—an excellent soldier and a fine cook."

Greetings were exchanged once more. When everyone shook hands and repeated names, Ollander gestured to the pews for everyone to sit. They did so and discussion began.

Ollander briefly touched on the success against the loyalists in Markalv. There had been minimal bloodshed. Much of the military presence was relocated to Seruvia; what remained was easily overwhelmed by rallying the citizens. The remainder of the talk covered strategy and troops. Apparently, Brother Ollander had been a military officer for many years in the Kavalan army, even fighting briefly in the Border Conflict, before turning his full attention to his faith. As a result, he had many insights for the siege of Seruvia.

"I can provide you with six hundred soldiers. Even so, you're grossly outnumbered no matter how many men you can find. From the information my scouts have gathered, there are close to fifty-five thousand troops mustered outside Seruvia. Unfortunately, my knowledge extends no further. Alice Jryer, my primary source within Seruvia, has stopped communicating. I fear Berling has captured her, or worse. He's completely locked down the capital. No one can enter or leave, yet the foundries billow smoke night and day, and thundering noises echo across the plains... There's no telling what he has inside those walls.

He adopted a grave expression, hands clasping in front of him. "You'll have to spread them thin if you want a chance—whittle down their numbers little by little until you can take them in a headlong fight. Only then will you be able to breach the city and attempt to move on Audax Keep." He gave Winston a dark look. "You'll need a miracle from Iyala, my friend."

"We'll make do. How soon can you be ready to march?"

"Actually, he will be staying here," Sister Dell spoke up. "He must continue Endela's teachings."

Ollander laughed, eyes twinkling like stars. "Ah, how I would love to run off with you, Winston, my friend. Sister Dell knows full well. She is here to keep me in line." With a wink at Andre, he clapped Denelsen on the shoulder. "Jerard will be my delegate."

Andre felt a pang of disappointment. After hearing Ollander speak, he felt foolish about his initial sentiment. He was a grown man; jealousy was unbecoming.

It was clear Ollander was very knowledgeable about military matters. Moreover, he held himself with obvious authority—not the overbearing kind, but rather like a father with his children. Andre found himself at ease, soothed, in his presence. Even with how little he knew about his religion, he understood why Brother Ollander was the head priest in Markalv.

"We could use your talents" he stated suddenly. "One of our officers was murdered at Cappus. It's a great loss. We would gain much from having another experienced leader such as yourself fill the gap he left."

Ollander shook his head. "My condolences to all of you, and may his blessed soul rest easy in Iyala's light. Unfortunately, I cannot leave Markalv. As Sister Dell said, my place is in the House of Endela. My work here is too important for me to abandon it even for a short time. There are people in need here. Jerard will serve you well. He has been invaluable to displacing the loyalist forces here."

"I have more than enough experience in battle, both commanding and fighting," Jerard interjected. "I won't disappoint, Servailles."

"It's settled then," Ollander declared. "Jerard and I will finish preparing the men and send them to join your camp. It shouldn't take more than a day. However, as it's already afternoon, why don't you all spend the night here, in Markalv? We have comfortable lodging and good food to satiate your appetites."

Winston agreed to stay. Andre declined. The memory of William's shrouded body lying on the bed of an inn in Cappus wavered ghostlike in his mind's eye. He also didn't want to disrupt Winston's reunion with Ollander, and they seemed capable of taking care of each other.

Jerard accompanied Andre and Corenece through the misting rain back to camp. A quick meeting was organized with Pitt and the other officers who didn't accompany them to Markalv. Andre updated them on the addition of troops and introduced Jerard. The news of more soldiers boosted the others' moods, and they welcomed Jerard enthusiastically.

Finally, Andre was able to excuse himself.

He was hungry, and the nightly vigils were starting to take a toll on him. His eyes itched, his head pounded, and his mind felt full of wool. With such an important battle on the horizon, he needed to be well-rested and refreshed. Thus, he intended to snatch a few hours of sleep before dinner.

He had just arrived at his tent when Mattias appeared beside him.

"There you are!" He was breathing heavily as though he had been running, his flushed face matching his hair. "They said you were back. I was running around looking for you."

"What is it?" Andre asked cautiously, concerned by his sergeant's urgency.

"I kept an eye on Declan while you were gone like you asked. I saw him speaking with young Lazar not too long before you returned."

"Did you catch what was said?" Andre could feel alarm swelling up inside of him, like a wineskin being filled afresh.

"No. They were out on the edge of camp, and I didn't want them to know I was watching. They both looked very serious."

Andre digested the information for a moment. He would have to talk to Caito. He didn't know what Declan Row wanted with the Soothsayer, but he knew it couldn't be anything good. Caito needed to know to be wary of the bookkeeper.

"Thank you, Mattias. Do you know where Caito is now?"

Mattias pointed him in the general direction he saw the boy last.

Andre set off, all thoughts of dinner and a good night's rest now gone from his mind.

30

A QUESTION OF TRUST

CAITO SAT HEAVILY ON the ground to catch his breath. He had been sparring with Wes and Tahlia for the last hour and a half straight and was sweating profusely as a result. He would've gone longer, but the others insisted on taking a respite for their own sakes. Even for as experienced fighters as they were, Caito was working them into the ground.

The battle at the rebel outpost stuck with Caito like mold—an unpleasant stain on his memory.

As much as he despised violence, brushing shoulders with bloody death, was a harrowing experience—one he was not willing to encounter again without being prepared. He asked Wes and Tahlia to train him, and the two eagerly agreed.

Beginning from their arrival at Cappus, they spent countless hours sparring and working on footwork every time the army halted. It became a source of entertainment for the Crimson Hounds to watch them practice. The improvements were becoming noticeable. He grew stronger and faster as the sword grew more comfortable in his hand. He started to discern patterns in his companions' fighting styles, predicting and countering their advances, becoming fluid with his movements.

As Wes and Tahlia both told him: *Combat is like dancing.*

"A dance with death. So don't get cocky," Tahlia would always add.

In fact, his improvement was rather remarkable, everyone kept telling him. He went from tripping over his own feet with his blade pointed at the dirt to matching footwork and blade strokes efficiently and quickly in only a couple of weeks.

"You're a miracle," Wes puffed for the hundredth time.

Caito had finally just bested him, a feat that hadn't even been imaginable when he began. The small ring of onlookers exploded with excitement when it happened, and were still clapping and whooping as the combatants collapsed.

Somebody passed Caito a water skin, the contents of which he greedily gulped down, handing it to Wes after he quenched his thirst. Climbing unsteadily to his feet, he made his way to the edge of the camp to relieve himself, squeezing through the back pats and congratulations from the audience. He thanked them as he went, unable to help the giddy smile plastered across his face.

He found a quiet tree to empty his bladder on and leaned against it when he finished. The adrenaline was fading now. The burning soreness from the last few days of hard training steadily engulfed his body again, freezing up his muscles with fiery aches. He was hungry, too, and his stomach let out a groan louder than his when he tried to move.

As he braced himself to make the slow, painful walk back, a voice stopped him from taking a step.

"Well done, Caito."

Caito knew who it was before he looked. The memory of the windy day in Baggot when he first heard that voice sprung into his head, then the moonlit night in his room in Audax Keep. He slowly turned to find himself looking into the emerald eyes of—

"Silarius."

It was the man called Declan Row. He had seen him around camp, but hadn't yet met him face to face.

Declan/Silarius smiled. "You're quite sharp."

"It wasn't hard to figure out."

It was true. Every time Caito saw Declan, he was lurking on the edge of meetings or slinking quietly around by himself like a prowling cat. The few times Caito heard him speak gave him the suspicion that the so-called bookkeeper was moonlighting as his mysterious counselor. Standing face-to-face made it quite obvious.

"What are you doing here?" Caito demanded a little more aggressively than he intended. "You warned me against Servailles. You told me not to trust him, but you're here helping him."

"I told you not to trust *anyone*, not just the Insurgent."

"Except you, right?"

Silarius's smile turned wolfish. "Have I let you down?"

Frustration blossomed inside Caito, an invasive flower in the meadow of his recent happiness.

Ever since he left his home, he had felt lost and scared—a child alone in a city of cutthroats. Silarius's unexpected visits had seemed like a ray of light peeking into the dark room of his circumstances—the cryptic words a tiny lifeline in the raging sea of politics Caito found himself caught up in. But seeing him now and hearing his snide words, Caito realized how useless his vague advice actually was. It made him angry.

"Now that I think about it, you never actually helped me in the first place. You told me to make my own choices. In what way is that helpful?"

"It led you here, didn't it? You made a decision and acted on it. You would've sat there dithering until the war ended or Tench quietly executed you. Now here you are, training for battle with a fire in your heart that wasn't present before. You can't say that I *haven't* helped you. It just wasn't what you thought you needed."

Caito considered this for a moment. As much as he hated to accept it, Silarius was right. Without his vague nudge, Caito would've stalled indefinitely until he was tossed aside in consequence for his uselessness. Now, here he was, just like Silarius said, his initial reluctance quickly turning to a fierce pride in his newfound abilities and a staunch resolve to help in any way he could.

Nevertheless, it didn't change the fact that the man who claimed to be his counselor was a liar and a sneak. He was playing his own game, separate from Winston and Tench, that much was certain. Caito was merely a pawn in it.

Silarius watched him, a tiny, yet maddeningly smug smile still curving his lips.

Caito forced himself to remain calm. "Why are you here, then? To brag?"

"Why the animosity, Caito?

"Why the secrecy? Why the aliases? I don't know you. You tell me not to trust the man who has been the most transparent with me while *you* run around with two names. Who are you really? Silarius, Declan, or someone else entirely? Stop with the games."

Locking green eyes to Caito's hazel, Silarius finally became serious. "You have important choices approaching. The future hangs in the balance, and you are walking a very fine line."

"I'm walking a very fine line?" Caito echoed, perplexed.

"Indeed. You are the *key*. You have the power to tip the scales and topple the first in a row of bones."

"I... don't understand."

Silarius spread his hands. "Nobody else can change the fate that comes from this war except you. Your choices affect *everything*. That's why you're so important to this war; why you can't run from your responsibilities. Not because you can see the possibilities, but because you will delegate them."

Caito tried to wrap his head around the implications of what Silarius was saying.

Noting his struggle to understand, Silarius tried to explain again.

"You're not only the lens; you're the catalyst as well. Because of your actions to come, Corynthia—the *world*—could burn. Your vision is just the beginning. A long, dark road follows."

The image of Seruvia burning wavered unbidden before his eyes. *I'm the catalyst... I could cause this?*

"Why didn't you tell me this before?"

Silarius adopted a thoughtful expression, though his eyes remained cold. "There was much I wasn't sure of. Information regarding the fate of the world is not fit to share if incomplete, no?"

"How do you know all of this?" Caito scowled at him.

"We're not too different, you and I." Silarius's eyes glinted as he said this.

Damn your riddles! Caito screamed in his head. He could have strangled him right then and there. Although, he had a feeling Silarius was more than up to the task of overpowering him. He took a deep breath to cool the anger. "Is that all?"

"I want what's best for you, Caito. You must be cautious."

Caito laughed colorlessly. "I'm not supposed to trust anyone, remember?"

"It's a wise thing to do. Just know, Berling Tench isn't the only monster. There are others with darker intentions."

"The assassin? Do you know who it is?"

Voices wafted towards them from the camp, merry and naive.

Silarius's sounded like ice in comparison. "You've made friends with some dangerous people."

"Winston has been nothing but honest with me." Caito grumbled. "Which is more than I can say about you."

"What do you know about Winston Servailles? What have you learned of him from his friends? Enough to understand and trust him?"

Caito hesitated as he realized he knew hardly anything about the rebel leader. Of course, Winston already admitted his nature as a politician and a manipulator. Aside from that, Caito had done little to learn about him, other than he was witty, rash, and lethally intelligent, rather like a hyena.

He recalled Silarius's hint back in Audax Keep about the chancellor's position—how Tench had been allowed to gain the power he did—information he hadn't taken time to consider. If that was Winston's doing, and he purposefully left a loophole in the system for his own hidden ends, it would certainly degrade his integrity.

What if Winston *was* just using him, and he was making a grave mistake?

Who, then, can I trust? All of a sudden, Caito felt helpless and afraid again, though only for a moment. He met Silarius's gaze with a staunch glare.

He must be telling me this to mess with my head. Just when he was feeling confident about his choices. He would not be frightened so easily.

All of this could be a lie fabricated for any number of reasons: To increase the pressure already squeezing the life out of him, or to give whatever parties Silarius was affiliated with more power over him. Regardless, he knew where he stood. Winston hadn't lied to him so far, at least from what Caito could tell. What was more, these people were the closest thing to a family and home since he fled his. The dog's head pin of the Crimson Hounds felt warm upon his shirt. He knew he could trust them.

Not Silarius. Not anymore.

"Thank you for your counsel, Silarius." He didn't bother hiding the coldness in his voice. "But it's no longer needed."

Silarius raised an eyebrow, hatefully calm. "You'll do well to remember my words. It would also be best to call me Declan from now on. Goodbye,

Caito." He inclined his head and turned back to the camp, vanishing amongst the tents.

Caito stood there for a moment to compose himself; he didn't want to answer any questions he knew would be asked if he looked upset. Once he was satisfied he could keep his expression neutral, he wandered back towards the smell of cooking food.

As he approached the tents, he noticed Mattias Berg sitting alone at the edge of camp, drawing in the dirt with a knife and muttering to himself. He glanced up and nodded at Caito as he walked past.

Caito returned the gesture cautiously. He liked the sergeant, but the thought of being watched released more doubts into his mind, where they ran like wild dogs.

He found his friends around a cooking fire. Sitting down, he quietly reached for one of the bowls of food set out by the spit. Leana passed him a basket of fresh strawberries, smiling at him with lips as red as the fruit. He took a handful, feigning eagerness. He wasn't hungry anymore. Still, he knew he must eat. It was almost a love language for his new friends. If he didn't, especially after a long session of training, they would know something was wrong. So he ate his fill, and smiled, and laughed with the others, until he nearly forgot his conversation with Declan.

After dinner, he extracted himself to retire to his tent. Besides the soreness setting in with a vengeance, he was feeling much better, and now wanted nothing more than a good night's sleep.

A hand laid itself on his shoulder.

Caito whirled around, grabbing the conjoined wrist, and attempted to twist his would-be assailant's arm behind him. Instead, a hand chopped into his elbow, cranking his arm sideways, and breaking his grip. At the same time, a boot slammed into the back of his knee, buckling him to the ground. Before he knew it, he was face down in the wet grass with a knee pressed into his back and his arm pinned behind him in the same way he intended to do to his attacker.

"You're quick," came Andre's voice.

"Sorry." Caito said, voice muffled by the ground.

Hands grasped him, lifted him up, and spun him around. Andre looked at him with bemusement.

Caito smiled sheepishly. "Sorry," he repeated.

"*I* should be sorry. I didn't think I left *that* bad of an impression."

Caito laughed and invited the other into his tent. Andre had a way of putting people at ease with just a few words, one of the many reasons he was such a popular officer.

"What can I do for you, Andr-lieutenant—um—sir," Caito fumbled. He was still unaccustomed to addressing people of rank.

"Andre is fine. I need to speak with you." He turned serious again.

Caito shivered subconsciously. Somehow, he knew it was about him and Declan. *Berg* was *watching*, he realized, his heart sinking. Had Winston put him up to it? Was Andre as well? Uncertainty slammed into him again, spinning his stomach in circles. Was there *anyone* he could trust completely?

They stepped into Caito's tent. "I need to be honest with you—" Andre began.

"You've been watching me," Caito interrupted. "I know."

Andre's mouth tilted, gray eyes flashing a quick apology. "You happen to be a mutual point of interest, but no, you're not the one we've been watching."

"Then who?"

Andre sighed, as if his news was heavy. "Declan, the bookkeeper. There's something sour about him, something I don't entirely trust. He's not—"

"—what he seems?"

The rebel looked at him for a moment, then slowly nodded. "Mattias—Sergeant Berg told me about your meeting. I must ask: What did you two talk about?"

His first instinct was to tell Andre about Declan's other identity. Strangely, though, he found himself holding back. Declan's words were planted in his mind like leeches despite his resolve to dismiss them. He didn't know how much he could tell Andre in confidence without him relaying his words to Winston. Until he could dispel his doubts about the rebel leader, he didn't want anything concerning Silarius to reach his ears.

Caito decided to play it safe. "He was asking me questions about my visions." It wasn't entirely a lie. "For his own ends or another reason, I don't know."

Andre's manner seemed skeptical. "What did you tell him?"

Caito thought quickly, though carefully. Declan already seemed to know so much more than him. Also, he was close to Winston. He had probably weaseled any information Caito had told the rebel leader, if Winston had not shared willingly.

"Nothing I haven't told Winston. They're close, aren't they?"

"It's... complicated. Winston trusts him well enough..." Andre seemed to be battling with himself. "I think he has something to do with William—General Draytus's murder. I can't prove anything, but I've had an ill feeling about him ever since Seruvia and the betrayal at the creek."

(A white mask with a black compass mark, keen eyes glinting behind it)

The image stabbed through Caito's head so quickly he staggered, grabbing onto Andre for support. Andre said something, but another vision drowned him out.

(Two guards stand in front of a door, their faces obscured by shadow. A figure approaches them, sword drawn)

"Caito!" Andre's voice was far, far away.

Opening his eyes, he found himself in the fetal position on the ground. His head pounded as he slowly uncurled himself. He realized he couldn't remember the last time he had a vision, which was probably why it felt like his brain had been trampled by a stallion.

Andre looked down at him with concern laced with apprehension. "Was that a vision?"

Caito nodded, unwilling speak against the wave of nausea.

"What was it? What did you see?" Andre stopped. "I'm sorry. Let me help you." He pulled Caito to his feet and supported him to his bedroll.

"Thank you," Caito said, laying himself down. "I'm going to get some rest. I'm exhausted. I think you're correct, though. Something isn't right about Declan." He looked at Andre, unable to stop the worry from showing on his face.

He wanted to tell him about Declan's words, except he had said his decisions would dictate fate. If he were right, then he would have to proceed alone. Anyone who tried to advise him or steer him in a biased direction would only complicate the situation, even if their intentions were clean.

Besides, he was his own man, not to be controlled like a puppet on strings. After all, that was why he fled from Berling Tench.

"I'm afraid for the future, sir," Caito whispered, letting his vulnerability show for a moment.

"I am too." Andre heaved a sigh. "It will work out just fine. And please"—he rose from his crouch next to Caito—"call me Andre."

He exited the tent, leaving Caito to his thoughts.

31

MASK IN THE NIGHT

ANDRE'S MIND BUZZED AS he walked through the camp. Caito's explanation for his meeting with Declan seemed weak. Of course Declan knew about the vision; Winston had shared it with him shortly after Caito revealed it. Why would he be interrogating the Soothsayer on what he had seen? Something didn't seem right. Caito had been hesitant, like he was holding something back.

Then there was the vision. After which, Caito agreed that something was off about the bookkeeper.

What did he see?

Though he wanted very badly to press Caito for answers right then and there, the boy seemed completely exhausted, as if the vision sucked the life right out of him. Andre was still a little shaken from witnessing such a thing happen.

Only a few weeks ago, he considered the Soothsayer nothing more than a hoax. Now, after everything that transpired since breaking Winston out of Seruvia—the catacombs, the Vida Imralta, finally meeting Caito face-to-face and discovering how *human* he was—Andre found himself as convinced as Winston. Even Rödfang, the knife that had killed William, was believable. Witnessing Caito collapse like he was struck and hearing the effort in his voice afterward left him wondering why he ever doubted the validity of such things.

Andre had yet to share his suspicions about the bookkeeper with Winston. Knowing his friend as he did, he would probably just be dismissed as being paranoid. However, after Caito's words, he needed to swallow his pride and talk to Winston. If the Soothsayer believed Declan had sinister intent, then Winston better heed him, especially after staking the whole rebellion and his life on the young man.

But that could be handled tomorrow.

It was completely dark now, though his path was illuminated by the warm glow of dying fires. He passed a few men still sitting around, talking and laughing. They scrambled to obey when he ordered them to bed.

Mattias was still awake when Andre entered their tent, scraping mud from his boots by lantern light. "Did you find him?"

Nodding, Andre sat down on his bedroll. He removed his own boots and reached for his pack to scrounge for something to eat. Scoring a biscuit, he took a bite.

"What did you find out?"

Andre swallowed before responding. "I don't think he was entirely truthful with me. He told me that Declan was asking about his visions, yet he was hesitant to answer." He took another bite of biscuit. "He had a vision."

Mattias's eyebrows shot up in interest. "About what?"

"I didn't ask. Well," Andre corrected himself. "I didn't press. It was short, though it hit him hard. I was sharing my suspicions about Declan, and it happened right after I mentioned the fight at the creek. He feels the same way: That there's something strange about Declan."

"Then what do we do?"

"We need to involve Winston. Since Caito agrees with me, he can't disregard both of us."

Mattias exhaled a short laugh. "I assumed that's why you didn't go to him at first. When will you tell him?"

"Tomorrow. I'll ask Caito to join me as well."

Finishing his biscuit, Andre laid down on his bed roll. The glow from the lantern faded as Mattias did the same. He stared up at the tent roof as the tapping of rain attempted to lull him to dreamland. He fought it for a moment, planning how to pitch his concerns to Winston, before submitted to sleep.

It seemed as though he just closed his eyes when he was abruptly shaken awake by Mattias.

"What is it?" Andre exclaimed, bleary-eyed and confused. He could hear shouting coming from somewhere in the camp.

Alarm flooded his body. They were under attack—Tench had sent an army to destroy them while they slept. His sense fought through the groggy panic, telling him Tench was still holed up in Seruvia.

"Trouble."

They rushed outside, knives drawn, and ran towards the source of the noise. It was pitch black outside aside from the dim embers of dead cooking fires. People stuck their heads out of their tents, shooting questions into the night. Andre's footsteps made squishing noises on the soggy ground, and he slipped on the wet grass several times.

Up ahead, people with torches moved around one tent in particular: Delvon Pitt's. Dread filled Andre as conclusions pounced into his mind.

Pushing their way through the gathering crowd, they reached the open flap to find the interior of Pitt's tent a mess. His bedroll was ripped in two. His pack lay mangled on the ground, its contents scattered like leaves after a gale. A large rip in the back of the tent fluttered languidly in the night breeze. The huge man was sprawled on the ground in the center of the chaos, shouting curses—mercifully alive.

His fears refuted, Andre let out a huge gasp of relief. "Delvon! Are you alright? What happened?"

Holding his arm, Pitt sat up, groaning. His sleeve was red and damp with blood. Mattias shouted for a medic.

"The bastard that killed William tried to put me in the ground, too." Pitt snarled, seeming more angry than shaken. "I would have returned the favor if I hadn't been half-asleep."

Andre barely heard the last statement. He stepped outside into the crowd of enthralled soldiers. "I want a detail to sweep the camp and set up a perimeter immediately! Alert the sentries! No one steps outside the camp's boundaries without me knowing! And somebody fetch Declan Row!" This last part was shouted at nobody in particular.

They immediately dispersed to carry out his orders

Crouching down next to Pitt, Andre pointed at his arm. "Does it hurt?"

"I'm not a child, Andre." When Andre raised an eyebrow at his hostility, he softened. "I'm sorry. No, I'm fine."

"Did you see what he looked like?"

"He was cloaked and wore a white mask with a mark over the eye, like a compass. He was tall, though, and fast. Very fast. He let in a draft when he entered my tent, which woke me. Thank the All-Mother, I'm a light sleeper. I was barely able to fend him off. When I started shouting, he tore through the back."

After a few minutes of waiting, they heard approaching footsteps.

"I've brought Declan Row, sir." A soldier stood outside. Declan, wearing a drab shirt and brown trousers, was next to him.

"Thank you." The soldier made to leave, but Andre stopped him with a shake of his head. "Stay here, please."

He turned his attention to Declan. "Come in, Declan."

The bookkeeper stepped in with a haughty air, as though irritated at being summoned. Taking in the state of the tent, he smirked at Pitt. "You appear to have had a rough night."

Pitt snorted. "You could say that." He looked at Andre. "Why is Row here?"

Declan spoke before Andre could answer. "Lieutenant Cordon believes I'm behind the murder of your friend, William Draytus, and the assassination that was just attempted on you. He had me brought here to interrogate me on my whereabouts tonight. That's why you're having this man stay here, isn't it? To confirm my alibi?"

Andre glanced at the soldier, who was staring straight ahead as if afraid to be called upon.

Pitt frowned at Andre. "What makes you think he's behind this?"

Andre ignored him and met Declan's eyes, which were full of amusement. "And what were you doing tonight?" he asked politely.

"Studying in my tent. I have been doing so since I spoke with the Soothsayer."

Andre couldn't stop the surprise from showing on his face. He was planning on bringing up the meeting in the hopes of catching the bookkeeper off guard. Now, the ball had been dropped unceremoniously into his court when he wasn't ready.

He tried to recover. "When did you speak with the Soothsayer?"

"Earlier this evening, shortly before you returned from Markalv. I believe your sergeant was observing us."

Andre swore silently. Declan was a step ahead of him. "You've been working at your books ever since?"

"I have." Declan flourished to the soldier, still standing and staring. "Your man can confirm; I was working very hard and am very displeased at the interruption."

The soldier nodded hurriedly. "Gave me quite the earful on the way over, sir. Said he had important information that needed notating."

"Thank you. You may go." Andre dismissed the soldier with a wave of his hand. He glanced at the pitch-dark sky. "It's very late. Not many others are up at this hour, besides the watchmen."

"Then I suggest you ask them if they saw something." He raised his eyebrows mockingly. "I daresay the ruckus you've raised will make it difficult to search the camp now that everyone is awake and on their toes. I can assure you, I haven't left my tent. Important work to be done."

"What are you working on?" Pitt queried. He was cleaning and wrapping the wound on his arm from his own medical supplies.

Andre realized a medic never arrived to treat him. It didn't ultimately matter since Pitt was quite capable of taking care of himself, but it was the principle of the thing that was important.

"As I said; it's very important, though I hope you don't mind I keep it to myself."

"Just curious." Pitt hoisted himself to his feet and turned to Andre. "Anything else you would like to ask him? I don't think he's going to tell you what you want to hear."

Pitt was right. There was no way Declan could have participated in a struggle with Pitt, escaped in the complete opposite direction from his tent, then return and adopt an equanimous manner moments before the soldier arrived at his tent. Unless the mask or some other toy in the assassin's possession gave the ability to whisk the bearer away at will, then Declan couldn't be the Wolf.

This knowledge, however, did nothing to stem Andre's suspicion or worry. In fact, it heightened it. The bookkeeper gave him a very uneasy feeling, like the metallic taste in the air before lightning struck. Moreover, he was treating the entire assassin situation with unashamed indifference and, at times, amusement. Even if he wasn't the assassin, he was certainly playing a game of his own.

Declan didn't wait for Andre to answer. "Gentlemen." The lanky man slunk like a cat back into the night.

Mattias mirrored the Andre's worried expression. "What's next, Andre? That's our main lead blown."

"We'll still meet with Winston tomorrow. We can share our suspicions after we tell him what happened."

Pitt, who had been examining his bandages, nudged Andre. "May I share a tent with you two? It's going to be bloody cold with that rip in the side, and frankly, I would rather not sleep alone anymore."

32

ANDRE'S ACCUSATION

As soon as it was light enough to see, Andre woke the others. Pitt was already awake; Andre was unsure for how long, though from the dark circles under his eyes, he assumed for most of the night.

Together, they walked towards the large tent that served as their command center. On the way, Andre stopped by Wes and Tahlia's tent to collect Caito. Then, he sent the former two to round up the officers and set a watch on Declan Row. While the rebellion's brass needed to know the new developments, Andre didn't want to risk the bookkeeper coming near. Declan was a danger to their cause; he was sure of it.

Arriving nearly all at the same time, everyone immediately began bombarding Andre, Mattias, and Pitt with questions. Word had spread quickly about the attempt on Pitt's life. As a result, people were already fabricating their own versions of it. Pitt had to discount many of the reports that were verified with him before Andre stepped in and held up his hands, annoyed at all of the noise.

"Enough. We'll explain everything when Winston arrives, so we don't have to say it all twice."

Wind blew wildly through the camp, making the flaps of the tent undulate and snap like a whip. Though it wasn't raining, the eddies of air swept water droplets from the trees, showering the canvas and making it sound as if rain was falling in torrents. It all felt very ominous to Andre: The group standing still and silent like statues as the wind raged around them.

Winston walked in not long after, soaked, yet undeterred by the building storm. He looked around before landing his gaze on Pitt, his expression deadly serious. "Are you okay?"

"Just a scratch." Pitt indicated to his bandaged arm. "I guess I'm lucky he didn't have that dagger." There was a sarcastic note in his voice.

Winston appeared to miss it. "Lucky indeed. It's in a safe place. We don't have to worry about it. Now, tell us what happened."

Pitt recounted the events in detail. He described the fight, the assassin's attire, his escape, and Andre and Mattias arriving on the scene. His arms crossed, Winston listened with a frown, occasionally interjecting with a question. He seemed especially interested in the assassin's mask, confirming the compass mark a couple of times.

When Pitt finished, the tent fell silent again. Winston scowled at the ground, his hair veiling his eyes.

Andre wondered what he was thinking. He seemed to know something. No, he *clearly* knew something. Winston was not a forgetful person; when he focused on a specific aspect of a story or report, it was because he found it to be valuable information. That meant the mask was important, and Winston knew, or at least had an inkling of, why.

"You were able to fend him off without issue?" Winston looked back to Pitt, arms still crossed.

"I don't think he expected me to wake. I certainly surprised him, but he only ran after I shouted. So, yes, I was able to. Still, he was very fast and very strong. I don't think I could have kept myself alive for long." Pitt looked nervous all of a sudden, as though he just realized how close he had brushed with death. It was a disconcerting expression to see on his face. "He's incredibly dangerous. I-I'm very lucky."

Mutters broke out among the other officers as they looked worriedly at each other. Corence ground out a curse.

Andre shared the sentiment without showing it. A deadly assassin in itself was enough to make him nervous—one with the ability to best an accomplished fighter like Pitt made his throat tighten in fear when he thought about it.

In his years in the Border Conflict, he had run into his fair share of assassins. They were different: Scared, desperate people caught between a lion and a cliff, just looking to strike and make an opening to wriggle through to freedom. Pitt's encounter was far different. It chilled him to the bone in the same inconclusive way that Declan did. There was something uncharacteristically menacing about the assassin, something he couldn't put a finger on.

Andre thought back to Declan's alibi, how there was no way he could have attacked Pitt without the aid of magic, what he now accepted as possible. If Winston knew something about the assassin's mask that tied into his suspicions, then he could bring them to light. Thereafter, Winston would have to consider.

"What do you know?" All eyes turned to Andre. "About the mask?"

"It's not important. We need to focus on keeping everyone safe."

"Discussing security is all well and fine, but addressing the root of the problem is more important."

"More important than protecting the officers?" Jerard Denelsen asked.

Andre thought that was a little disingenuous, considering Denelsen had been with the army for less than twenty-four hours. Nevertheless, he ignored him. "I have suspicions about the identity of the assassin."

There was a collective breath, and Caito's eyes snapped onto him.

Andre kept his gaze on Winston. "But I need to know what you know."

Pitt scoffed. "You're still holding onto that notion?"

"What notion?" Winston's eyes flicked between the two of them. "What are you talking about?"

Andre waved his hand to dismiss Pitt's interruption. "What's so important about the mask?"

"Andre, tell me what you know."

Pitt chimed in, trying to explain to Winston, until Andre cut him off. "The mask, Winston! Blast it! What do you know?"

Winston looked like he had been slapped. He was seldom put in his place, especially not by Andre, who gave him a lot of lenience. Usually, it was Winston who took control of the conversation by withholding his information until he was given what he wanted. Andre had been on the receiving end of such treatment time and time again. He wouldn't fold this time. He didn't enjoy the his friend's sometimes arrogant manner, though he had never felt inclined step in and address it. Thus, Winston's shock gave him a small rush of satisfaction. It felt good to finally shut him down.

Everyone stood motionless and wide-eyed.

"You're withholding vital information, Andre."

"I could say you're doing the same."

Winston glowered at him, shoulders rounded vulture-like. Andre stood his ground, knowing that if he showed any sign of weakness, Winston, rather like a wild dog, would attack. He was a politician after all.

Winston finally relaxed. "It doesn't matter. Just a bad memory. That's all."

Andre finally understood why he was so reluctant to share. Winston never talked about his past and always alluded to how troubled it was whenever it came up. Feeling slightly ashamed of himself for forcing the topic onto him, he strengthened his resolve. Winston was a grown man. He could handle his ghosts, especially around his friends.

"A bad memory?" he prodded gently. Everyone was still frozen as if time had stopped in anticipation of Winston's answer.

With a great sigh, Winston spoke, "When I began my campaign for Corynthia, I did so publicly, standing in the squares and speaking to passersby, inviting them to sit and listen to me. I made no effort to hide my opinions. In hindsight, it was not my brightest idea to openly challenge the sovereign rule of Kaval, even if their ruler is a half-wit. It gained me supporters, and quickly; however, it also captured the attention of many opponents. A madman by himself was no threat, but one who could speak sense to the people and convince them to follow him? That was dangerous.

"You all may remember Corynthia being secured without violence. That was not entirely true. There was another side many"—he faltered as a quick flash of confusion crossed his face—"you all don't know of.

"One of my biggest allies was Brother Ollander, and with him, the church. I didn't fight in the Border Conflict, though I heard the stories of the atrocities that happened." His gaze lingered on Andre for the briefest of moments, who felt a wave of shame wash through him as he recalled those dark times.

"Brother Ollander had just left the army and begun his life as a priest. He passed me one day as I debated in the streets and sat down to listen to me. He'd seen first-hand the horrible things happening in the south and told me it was against everything the All-Mother commissioned—to stand by, even prevent the persecuted from reaching freedom as death bore down on them. The church had already condemned the war. Brother Ollander gave me his word that they would spread my idea through the land.

"Alas, even with the church's support, I still had very few allies who could help make a difference: People with money and influence. My proposition was outlandish. What's more, those in power considered it unwise, even dangerous, to stand in open opposition to Kaval despite countless innocent lives at stake. While people came and listened to me in the streets, the estates remained shut. Their inhabitants were far too afraid to risk their stature to stand behind me. Thus, I was vulnerable, without protection, and someone decided to take advantage of it and silence me.

"No soldiers came to arrest me. Lord Artreus probably didn't know what I was up to, or care. It might have been someone from the court. Regardless, I found myself hunted by assassins. Obviously, I knew how to fight and defend myself—my aspirations relied on it. I couldn't oppose an emperor without consequences. Most of the assassins I was able to dispatch myself, yet there was one..."

The wind howled, filling the gap in Winston's story. His hair tumbled as the flaps waved open and closed. There was a haunted look on his face eerily similar to the one Caito often wore. A chill ran through Andre's body that had nothing to do with the draft.

"He was dangerous and relentless. We killed him in the end, William and I. He had a mask to cover his face exactly as Pitt described: Blank white, save for a black compass over the eye. He never spoke, but he was fast, cunning, and gifted in many forms of murder. Many people died merely because they were in the way. He hunted me for over a month until we managed to throw him off one of the towers of Audax Keep. I was meeting Berling Tench, who was Seruvia's administrator, as it was." Winston shrugged. "Maybe it *was* Tench the entire time. I wouldn't put it past that snake..."

He looked up at Andre as though defying him. Andre waited for him to make a comment to downplay his story, but all he said was, "Your turn."

Words escaped him. He floundered for a second before managing to say, "I... have suspicions about Declan."

Corence chuckled darkly, "I'm not surprised. He's a damn strange bird."

"Why?"

Andre didn't like this quiet, direct Winston. Without the constant wit, he seemed like a completely different person.

"He's-I have a bad feeling about him. There's something unsettling about him, and he sneaks around. I don't trust him. Besides, he fits Pitt's profile. He's tall, lightning-quick—you've seen him fight—and he has extensive knowledge on magical items. The dagger that killed William, Rödfang, could have easily been his."

"So you think he killed William?"

Everyone was staring at him with rapt attention, making him want to crawl away and hide. He didn't like being the center of attention, especially if he was debating. It made his hands sweaty and his mind slow. Taking a moment to collect his thoughts, he spoke slowly, silently willing Caito to chime in at any time to support.

"I know it sounds far-fetched, but it can't be out of the question—at least his involvement. He seems to know about everything that's happening. He's also an outlier. He's made it clear that he does not intend to befriend anyone here except you. Who's to say he's not an agent, and all of this is Tench's grand scheme to whittle us down one at a time? You said it yourself: Tench might have easily orchestrated the attempts on your life then, too!"

"Yet, we're all still here and alive. Andre, you've seen Declan at work. There is no doubt in my mind that if he wanted us all dead we would be. Even if he was merely overseeing the assassin, he's had plenty of time to observe and track our habits. I highly doubt Declan would be working with an amateur."

Winston spread his hands. "Besides, how would Tench even orchestrate such an elaborate scheme? If he planted Declan, that means he knew you were coming to save me, when you would show up, where we would run from the square, and countless other tiny details! His head almost burst when I was captured! On top of that, you're completely disregarding Declan, who left his home, books, and risked his *life* to help us escape the most heavily fortified city in Corynthia. If your only issues are his tendencies to keep to himself and a hunch, then I have to disregard your concerns. We must take a practical route to prevent more attacks, not point fingers."

Face burning from Winston's admonishment, Andre stepped back, frustration and embarrassment rising inside of him. None of this surprised him. He predicted that Winston would reject his suspicions. Still, it hurt that his friend didn't even try to humor him.

"If I may." Raising his hand to speak, Caito did so hesitantly, "Andre's fears... aren't completely without cause. I have an uncomfortable feeling about him, too. I can sense he's connected to all of this. He plays a part in the bigger picture, in my vision. He's not what he seems."

For a moment, it looked as though he wanted to add something else, then he merely shrugged. "For your consideration."

"Is that enough validation for you?" Andre demanded quietly. "From the Soothsayer himself?"

Pitt growled like a bear whose cub was being threatened. "Was this why you've adopted Lazar into your company? To use him to your advantage? We all know Winston is hooked on the idea of the Soothsayer!"

Andre bristled at the huge man's accusation. Before he could retaliate, Winston held up his hands.

"Enough!" he snapped, voice cracking. "I will not have my officers at each others' necks! Need I remind you that we have the most important battle of our lives on the horizon? I don't need you fighting like schoolyard brats!"

Pitt stepped back, still wearing a resolute scowl. Andre glared at him. Caito stood like a statue, his expression unreadable.

Winston fixed Pitt in a hard stare, "Delvon, I know what you think about the Soothsayer; regardless, you *damn* well need to respect Caito for the man that he is. As for Declan, I hear your concerns, Andre. But until I have a reason to distrust him, I will continue to do the opposite, as irritating as he may be. I think he's done enough for us that he deserves our faith at least."

He caught the look on Andre's face. "You can do what you need to feel safe. I won't stop you. However, if I begin distrusting those around me now, I'll be of no help when we reach Seruvia. I suggest you keep that in mind as well. I need you sharp when we start our assault, understood?"

Andre nodded.

A particularly strong gust of wind rattled the tent, startling everyone back to their senses.

Winston's face softened into a smile, which he shared with each of them. "On a lighter note, I nearly forgot to introduce our newest officer," he announced cheerfully with a grand flourish at Denelsen. "This is Jerard Denelsen. He was a captain of the guard in Markalv and assisted Brother Ollander in the liberation of the city. He shall be commanding six hundred additional troops joining our forces."

There were a couple of nods and awkward acknowledgments. Almost everyone met Denelsen the previous night.

Winston continued without skipping a beat. "The men should be ready to move out by tomorrow. We just need to stay off of each other's throats for another night." He gave Andre and Pitt a stern look. "Can we do that, my sweets?"

Everyone else chuckled, and Andre forced a smile. With a look at Pitt, he ducked out of the tent as Winston dismissed everyone. Pitt took the hint, joining him a moment later.

"What a bloody condescending fool," Pitt grumbled as they walked.

Andre laughed, feeling relieved. Though Pitt could be a bear, his heart was kind. Andre felt a little better knowing he wasn't holding anything against him.

Finding a cedar tree to shield them against the worst of the wind, they took shelter beneath it.

"Winston's right, though," Andre admitted as they huddled against the trunk. "We need to be working together."

He looked at his companion expectantly, waiting for him to begin complaining. To his surprise, Pitt's shoulders visibly slumped, and he let out a sigh quickly snatched away by a gust of air.

Rain began to fall, playing a chaotic percussion in harmony with the wind. Pitt pulled the hood of his cloak over his bare head. Andre, in too much of a hurry earlier to don his own cloak, stood and shivered.

"I'm just picking fights now that I think about it," Pitt uttered. "William was always my equalizer. He kept me reigned in. Now I'm just... angry. At all of this. The war, the risks, the bloody damn fairy-tales. Maybe I'm blowing things out of proportion, but the Soothsayer... It's a *myth*! Visions of the future? That's magic! It's not real! He's a boy who has nightmares! Yet Winston is completely enthralled.

"Then there's your problem with Row. Accusing him seems like you're jumping to conclusions, and I feel... It's disrespectful to William's memory.

I know that's not your intention, and I know you wouldn't make accusations without justification, but it's not viable. Declan has done nothing except help us, yet you cannot seem to accept that. While the real killer is still out there, you're wasting time and men chasing a blasted ghost! Hell, Andre, it's..." He stopped and wiped his eyes.

Andre watched him silently. He felt remarkably calm considering Pitt just accused him of disrespecting William's memory. William was his friend too, and for longer. However, he knew Pitt had grown the closest to him, so he remained composed and listened.

"You don't trust him. That's fine, but this is your crusade, Andre. Leave the rest of us out of it. Drive those words into Winston's head as well." Falling silent, Pitt slid down to sit at the base of the trunk and pulled his cloak tight to protect himself from the storm.

Soaked through by this time, Andre shivered violently as he processed Pitt's words.

It unsettled him how heavily he was being opposed. It seemed foolish to dismiss such a hunch without a second thought (he couldn't recall how many times Winston carried out plans based simply on a feeling); however, with so much on their minds—William's death, the upcoming siege, and the assassin on the loose—he couldn't blame them. Nevertheless, he was not exempt from the effects of recent events, which frustrated him even more. All the same, he knew arguing would be of no use: Their minds were made up. He would have to watch the bookkeeper himself and hope he was, indeed, wrong.

Andre was now shivering so much he could barely stand straight against the wind. The rain poured with a vengeance, and the cedar was now about as protective as parchment.

Laying a hand on Pitt's shoulder, he bent down to speak to him, raising his voice to be heard before the roaring wind swept his words away. "I'm sorry, Delvon."

There was no response.

Andre stepped out from under the tree with his head down to begin the dreadful walk back to his tent to attempt to dry off and warm himself up. At one point, he paused to look back at the lonely, hunched figure under the cedar and felt a deep sadness overcome him. This civil war had already cost so much for everyone, and he had a dreadful feeling it was only going to grow worse.

33

RIDE AND RUIN

Once again, Andre stood before Seruvia. This time, the feeling of urgency that fueled him during his rescue mission over a month ago was replaced by a sense of dull anticipation mixed with dread. He couldn't help but feel their doom awaited them within that somber collection of towers, and it wasn't because of the bristling army blanketing the field.

Winston stood next to him, a hungry gleam in his eye as he looked at the city. "We're close, Andre. I can feel it."

Andre merely nodded. He knew the look on his angular face. It was tempered obsession, intensified by days of dwelling on the upcoming battle.

They waited for Tench's delegates to emerge from the sea of soldiers before them. Winston swayed slightly in the saddle from the middle of their small formation. Andre was directly to his right, with Delvon Pitt beside him. Declan and Corence were lined up on Winston's left.

Andre wasn't quite sure why Declan was with them. Winston claimed it was because of his extensive knowledge of the city; Andre suspected it was to prove a point. Winston could be spiteful like that. Whatever the reason, he made sure to stay on the opposite side of the bookkeeper to avoid cutting remarks.

The field was soggy, which could prove treacherous for their horses, but the pearly gray clouds above withheld their rain. The air was cool, and a light breeze invigorated Andre as he silently waited.

It was a good day for battle.

All of a sudden, a loud cry rose from the mass of loyalists, and there was a flurry of movement as a column of soldiers split. Five riders appeared from the ranks and slowly rode across the field towards them.

Winston flicked his reins and trotted forwards, the others following.

As they drew closer to the loyalist party, Andre was able to make out the riders. The two on the outside were Rose Soldiers wearing the golden insignias of their position on their chestplates. He recognized Tench's rat-faced sycophant, Pilkley, and there was a dark man he didn't. The man in the middle was none other than Berling Tench himself, wearing a gaudy blue tunic, mustache impeccably groomed.

"Winston!" Tench called out as soon as they were in earshot. "Welcome back, my friend!"

Both parties stopped a respectful distance apart, close enough that they could see and hear each other clearly, but out of stabbing distance, which was a good thing because it looked as though Pilkley wanted to do nothing more. Andre certainly would have been willing to return the favor.

Tench turned his attention to Corence and Pitt, giving them nods. "Samuel, Delvon. I see you're still hanging around this rabble." He completely ignored Andre and Declan.

"Better company than the rodents you keep," Corence returned with a sneer at Pilkley.

The man tried to sputter an insult back, his face tomato red, but all that came out were unintelligible words. Corence laughed at him in response. Tench smiled indulgently.

Winston waved Corence quiet. "Berling, I'd like to offer you an accord."

"Do tell."

"We'll dissolve the rebellion and forgo our attack. We'll halt all conflict and revolt to your heinous regime. In return, we'd like your complete, unconditional surrender."

Tench's companions shared bemused looks. Then, Pilkley burst into shrill laughter, while the other man snorted and shook his head. Tench, however, peered directly back into Winston's icy stare. His twitching mustache was the only indicator of his mirth.

When Pilkley's laughter finally died down, Tench leaned over his horse to give Winston his answer.

"I'm afraid I'm going to have to refuse your offer. I have an inclination to believe it wouldn't be in my best interest. So by all means"—Tench smiled coldly—"give us everything you've got."

"In that case, Berling"—Winston began to swing his horse around—"I'll see you in hell."

The army of blue looked even larger as they rode away.

Andre joined Mattias at the head of the Crimson Hounds.

"How did it go?" Mattias inquired.

"About as well as you'd expect."

"So they're not going to surrender?"

Andre laughed and turned to face his soldiers. He took a second to look over the faces of the men and women under his command. They were pale, but set and alert. As before, he noticed just how young most of them were; except now, there was something different about them. They were tense, though less frightened. It was apparent that their experiences had ripened them from fresh, timid greennoses to soldiers prepared to accept the cost of war, to pay its greedy price.

Andre felt proud.

His horse fidgeted, excited from the charged atmosphere. "Listen up! A long and exhausting process awaits both sides. They're not here to destroy us; they're here to protect Tench. Even so, they'll be eager to lash out and end it. We can use that to our advantage. Split them up, isolating them from the main force so we can destroy them and melt back before they can recover. It will be brutal, but you've faced these odds before."

He glanced down the line where the other officers were shouting last minute instructions and encouragement to their own men. "Many people are praying for a miracle. Now, I don't believe in miracles. I think looking to a higher power to save us from taking responsibility for our own mess is foolish and impractical. However, I do believe in people like you. I believe in this army, these people who left their families and homes behind to fight against the forces oppressing their lives with the knowledge that they may pay the ultimate price. People like you. You've proved yourselves over and over again as soldiers, strategists, and as good, hard-working men and *women*."

Andre found Leana and Tahlia. Their eyes were glued to him, glowing with pride. "I never thought I would be fighting alongside mothers, sisters, or daughters, but you've made a name for yourselves throughout Corynthia. We don't need a miracle, not when we have you. For this is hardly new—the odds have been stacked against us since the beginning."

The Crimson Hounds shifted, grumbling in agreement. They were restless, a hard glint in their eyes. Ready for blood.

Andre noticed Caito next to Wes and Tahlia and met his gaze.

The Soothsayer had insisted on joining them in battle, even though Winston adamantly refused, saying he was too important to risk. Andre, impressed by the young man's determination, supported Caito. If he wanted to fight, they couldn't stop him.

Caito gave him a single nod.

Winston's voice cut through the air, crisp, clear, and carrying, like a noble hero in a story of valor.

"Champions of Corynthia! Bloodshed and glory await, for today begins your legacy of freedom! Today shall be a bloody day, but a great day! Fear no man nor blade! Let the fire of redemption rise inside of you and fight like the legends you will become! Today, we shout a message to the world: Corynthia will not be silenced, will not be oppressed, will not be subjugated to the tyrants who try to take what is rightfully ours! For if we fall, our fire will spread until the legions of hell awake and raze what is left! Then will your songs be sung and names remembered for generations to come! Ride now! Ride for death! Ride for glory! Ride for freedom!"

Winston turned towards Seruvia, raising his sword and snapping the reins of his horse, urging it into a canter.

A huge roar rose up from the rebel soldiers, and together they rolled into motion.

The rest of the world faded away as Andre accelerated until it was only the rumbling sound of hooves, pounding like a heartbeat. The walls of Seruvia seemed small and far away, while the soldiers amassed before him looked as puny as insects. A feeling of immense power filled every ounce of his being as he galloped toward the enemy, a feeling he had not experienced in a long time. Raising his blade, he let out a cry lost in the thundering charge.

There was a flash of motion from the top of the wall and a large object spun into the air, blurred from the speed of its ascent, like it had been launched—

From a catapult.

The sudden realization snapped Andre back to the present as the whistling objects fell towards the charging soldiers. Nobody else seemed to notice.

"Catapults! Scatter!" Andre screamed and jerked his reins to the right, nearly crashing into another rider next to him.

There was a dull crunching sound as the first projectile smashed into the spongy turf, followed by another and another. One landed twenty yards in front of him, and he swerved to avoid it.

It was a sphere of dark metal, a meter and a half in circumference, made of curved plates fused together, black spikes lining the seams. Scores of them thumped into the field, forming a haphazard border halfway between Seruvia and the rebel camp.

Andre glanced back over his shoulder and was relieved to see the Hounds unscathed by the strange projectiles. However, they were now scattered and out of formation, still rushing towards the enemy. There would be no time to reform.

Oddly enough, no other volleys were launched from the catapults after the first, though Andre had little time to dwell on why.

The loyalists were mere yards away. He closed the distance to the enemy, swinging his sword and knocking aside spearheads as his horse crashed into the front line. Screams rent the air, and the noise of combat swelled up around him.

Andre's steed trampled and kicked anyone within reach, rending armor and crushing bones while he cut them down from above. He rampaged through the enemy, sword whirling from side to side, dealing death with every flash of steel. Spears, swords, and halberds jabbed at him, each trying to claim a prize, but his shield absorbed the blows as a child eagerly consumed sweets. However, despite felling loyalists as quickly as he could, those killed were replaced with fresh soldiers eager for blood at an alarming rate, faster than he could keep up.

They would have to start their tactical retreat soon before they were overwhelmed.

Suddenly, a cry rang out. "The fields! There's fire in the fields!"

Andre turned to see the plain they had charged across was ablaze despite its saturation from the rain. The acrid smell of oil stung his nostrils as it wafted over the battle, and he could faintly feel the heat emanating across the distance. The fire was traveling steadily, consuming their path of escape. Before long, they would be trapped between the loyalist army and the blaze. They needed to break off the fight or they would be decimated.

Andre whistled as loud as he could. "Retreat! Fall back!"

The other company leaders echoed his cry, and the rebels wheeled their horses around, plunging towards their narrowing gap to freedom.

Holding back, Andre shepherded stragglers like a sheepdog. As they pulled away from Seruvia, he noticed that the defenders, rather than pursuing them, held formation—even shrinking further from the fire. He slowed, mind racing as he assessed the battlefield.

His horsemen were faster than the fire, the lead riders reaching the spiked metal spheres dropped from the catapults at the same time as the flames...

The foundries billow smoke night and day, and thundering noises echo across the plains... There's no telling what he has inside those walls. Ollander's words echoed in Andre's ears, a harbinger of disaster.

Why did they only launch one volley?

His eyes followed the line of flames to where they enveloped the closest of the spheres, the flickering tongues warping the dark metal. Then, it was violently replaced by a blinding flash of white light.

The ensuing boom ripped through Andre's head, crushing his eardrums. It was followed by another, then more in quick succession as the rest of the capsules discharged, buffeting his senses each time. Plumes of dirt geysered twenty meters into the air, and the ground shook from the blasts, making Andre's horse stumble.

Finally, the world stilled. The lingering sound of the detonations crackled back and forth across the plains, echoing off of Seruvia, fading with each ricochet. Dust and smoke drifted through the air, clogging Andre's throat as a muffled silence descended upon his ears.

He could barely hear the screams.

The battlefield had been ripped apart. Black craters pockmarked the ground, and fire greedily licked up the remaining grass. Body parts of both men and horses littered the bloody field. Those not torn apart by the explosions stirred feebly on the ground. There were plenty of rebels who had not been caught directly in the detonation; those furthest from the blast were still upright on their horses. Dazed and rattled, they looked stupidly around at Andre for direction.

As he struggled to collect his senses, he registered the sound of tramping feet under a wave of muted shouts. Fighting the pounding in his brain, he rolled his head around to see a riptide of loyalists flooding in to sweep away the flotsam of the rebel cavalry.

The sluggishness fled his mind, chased away by cutting fear. He snapped the reins, urging his horse into a gallop towards the carnage. Those with their wits still about them also spurred into motion to escape the killing field, some of them collecting their companions who had fallen from their steeds. Andre shouted at those still standing aimlessly, startling them out of their stupor. Soon, the survivors were fleeing the oncoming flood of enemy soldiers as fast as they could.

Too slow. Still lethargic from the trap, many of the rebels were swallowed mercilessly by the sea of blue.

Desperation and anger pumped through Andre—the primal need to reach safety, and furious disgust for leaving so many lives behind. But there was no way he could save those caught in the trap. Their wails grew clearer in his ears as he passed through the thin line of flames crackling between him and freedom. He knew those cries would haunt him for the rest of his life.

Finally, he slowed, well beyond the desecrated battle field. The loyalists were already drawing back to Seruvia, their grisly work completed.

"Lieutenant!" Donroe trotted towards him on a roan horse, Leana Palmer hanging onto his waist. Both of them were covered in dirt and blood.

Coming to a halt, Andre slowly slid off of his horse. His face felt numb as he took in the horror he had escaped. He swayed as squads of rebel medics rushed past him, carrying stretchers and bags of supplies.

"You're bleeding."

Turning, he saw Leana standing next to him. She was holding the reins to his horse, which had fallen from his limp hands. Donroe was still saddled; Andre could see tears making paths through the grime on his face.

"What?"

"Your ears are bleeding."

Andre's fingers came away red when he lifted them to the side of his head. He stared at them. His blood seemed strange to him—so insignificant compared to the carnage before him. His own life felt inconsequential when so many others just lost theirs.

How many?

"Have you seen Mattias?" he asked. His voice sounded raspy. "Did he make it?"

"He made it out." Leana wiped away blood from a cut on her cheek left by shrapnel. She looked as dead inside as he felt.

Some of the medics were returning, carrying bodies. As they passed, Andre found himself staring at the lifeless face of a young rebel soldier, barely out of his teens. Somewhere, his mother was probably waiting for him to come home, afraid that he might never, and unknowingly right.

Clenching his fists, he shook his head violently to dispel the depression. He couldn't fall apart now, not after such a debilitating defeat. The rebellion needed him sharp as ever if they were to salvage this.

As soon as he arrived at the camp, Andre pulled his unit leaders (thankfully all alive and whole) aside. After a quick inquiry, he learned that the casualties for their one-hundred-fifty-strong company had amounted to over two-thirds of their force and counting, with roughly eighty dead and dying. No one escaped unscathed.

The information hit Andre like a battering ram, and he had to fight to keep from diving back into despair.

"Get everyone taken care of," he ordered. His hands were shaking, but at least his voice wasn't. "Make sure everyone who needs medical attention receives it. Mattias, let's find Winston to report."

Tahlia caught his arm. "Andre, wait." Both she and Wes wore stricken looks on their faces.

Andre's heart sank even more, if that was possible. He looked at them expectantly, waiting for the bad news.

"It's Caito. We lost him."

Andre involuntarily bit the inside of his cheek, feeling like he'd been stabbed in the stomach. Mattias swore, and Leana clapped a hand to her mouth.

"We don't know if he's dead, captured, or wounded somewhere, but we were separated after the charge and weren't able to find him again."

Spitting out a wad of blood, Andre took a breath, grateful for the clarification. Missing was better than dead. Even so, his gut twisted painfully.

He took Tahlia's hand in both of his. "I'm sure he's alright. He's a bright boy. We'll find him." The worry in her eyes was plain, and he knew his words did nothing to reassure her. "Make sure you two see to yourselves. And stay at camp. That's an order. We'll find him," he repeated, more forcefully this time.

Once they were out of earshot, Mattias turned to Andre with a serious look on his face. "This isn't good, Andre. There's no way we can sustain an assault now."

"Let's find Winston," was all Andre said in response.

Unfortunately, Mattias was correct. Their already vastly outnumbered army had taken too large a blow to maintain a siege. Furthermore, there was no way they could defend against an offensive should Tench decided to suddenly launch one. As much as Andre hated to think it, the rebellion was probably finished. What fools they had been to rise so unprepared against such a brutal man.

Unless we turned to drastic measures, came the nagging thought in the back of his mind.

When they found Winston at the command tent, the rebel leader was already in a heated debate with the other officers. He was in a foul mood. His eyes blazed, and his pale skin looked sallow in the lantern light.

At his appearance, Winston waved jerkily for everyone to be quiet before turning his wild eyes onto him. "Report."

Andre replied with little emotion, "There isn't much to report. You saw it. We were wiped out in the blink of an eye. They're still counting casualties. What's more, Caito is missing."

Everyone began speaking at once. Winston ignored them, keeping his hard stare on Andre's face, like a hawk locating its prey.

Andre held his gaze, trying to see through his eyes and into his thoughts. *We could use William's calm right now*, he thought sorrowfully.

This time, it was Pitt who shouted for silence. "QUIET! Can we stop behaving like children? Winston, we lost our cavalry, and now your magic boy is likely dead or in enemy hands. Tench has been toying with us!"

"I'm aware, Delvon."

"What's our next move?" someone else asked.

"We barely made a *dent* out there!" Denelsen cried. "This is a fool's errand!"

Order dissolved again. Winston closed his eyes, and Andre saw his lips move in what looked like a prayer. Suddenly, his eyes snapped back open, and he held up both hands commandingly.

"Gentlemen! I am *painfully* aware of our plight. I would like to point out that it wasn't for naught. We managed to elimate roughly three thousand soldiers before they sprung their trap."

"Of course," Corence growled sarcastically. "That just leaves forty-seven thousand remaining."

Andre glared at him. "That's not helping, Samuel."

"But he's right!" Denelsen exclaimed. "We cannot continue this madness. We'll be wiped out!"

Winston dropped his hands. "Jerard, if you're thinking about deserting, just say it. Don't infect the rest of my officers with your cowardice."

Denelsen turned pink. "No—sir-that's—" He stammered for a moment before finding his words. "I just want to suggest that we pull back and regroup. Try to find more men before striking again. We need to regain our strength."

"And where do you suggest we look for more men?" Winston assumed a look of polite interest, his hands clasped behind his back.

Andre could see the veiled frustration beneath his calm demeanor and knew he probably already thought of, considered, and then discarded any solutions they could offer.

"We could send messengers throughout Corynthia. Gather additional forces."

"Your men were the additional forces," Corence commented dryly.

"Then we appeal to another nation! Tench has acted threateningly enough towards our neighbors. I'm sure they'd be pleased to remove him from the picture."

Andre opened his mouth to tell him they already had this discussion, but Winston beat him to it.

"We've already talked about this. I will not give Kaval a foothold into this mess, and I'm sure you can understand why the holy land of Salamoa is reluctant to send aid after we robbed them of their genocide."

"What about Cedaline? They would have to cross the pass, but are they willing?"

Pitt scoffed. "The Celds? Those cowards aren't willing to take the risk. They're too frightened of Tench. Too frightened of everyone, really."

"Besides," Mattias added from Andre's side, "finding aid would take too long. If we fall back and waste time trying to recruit, that allows Tench to mobilize his army and pursue us. Everything we've built would be destroyed in an instant."

Winston acknowledged him with a nod, but Denelsen wasn't placated.

"Then why are we still within striking distance? We should move now, in case he does decide to attack. We're vulnerable right here."

Andre saw his point, but he also knew why Winston was opposed. They had made impressive progress with their small army—taking Cappus was a huge victory for the rebellion. Now Tench had his back to Seruvia (more by his own choice than pressure from them), which gave the rest of Corynthia a moment to gasp for breath. To retreat now would essentially be to accept defeat. It would take years for them to reach another point where they had their enemy so dead to rights.

"We can't just give up all of our progress," Andre voiced his thoughts aloud. "We've come too far to retreat and accept defeat. We would have to start over. And I feel Tench wouldn't be so lenient a second time."

"So, we... what?" Keppen Bailer asked from the back of the tent. Mud was caked in his straw-colored hair, and he was squinting through a black eye. "Continue to throw stones at a mountain and hope it doesn't avalanche on top of us?"

Everyone turned to Winston, who was staring at the canvas wall with a faraway look on his face, hands still clasped behind his back.

"Winston?" Andre prodded gently, hesitant to disturb his thoughts.

He seemed to return to them from a great distance. His gaze roved over each of their faces before landing on Pitt's. "Delvon, I want you to pull the army back a little. Allow us some more room to breathe. Post sentries and report any suspicious movements from the loyalists. I'm sure Tench will be more than happy to let us stew; nevertheless, I don't want any surprises. Any sign of an advance and you retreat."

Pitt nodded. "What are you going to do?"

"I need some time to think." Winston beckoned to Andre. "Andre, come. Mattias you can too, if you would like."

Andre raised his eyebrow at Mattias, who shrugged. Together, they followed Winston to the edge of the camp where he stopped, staring out at the flags flapping above Seruvia. They stood a few feet behind him and waited apprehensively for him to speak.

The silence stretched long; neither Andre nor Berg dared to break it. Wind swirled around them, flicking Andre's hair pulled back in ponytail as he looked out at the battlefield. The craters from the explosions were stark against the brown-green grass, and smoke drifted like mist over the ruined earth.

"I was hoping the All-Mother would grace us with a miracle. I guess I was wrong," Winston spoke without turning around. His tall figure was silhouetted impressively on the hill, hair fluttering about his sharp face.

"I've never put much stock in those kinds of things," Andre replied cautiously.

"I'm not letting this slip away."

"Of course not. We've come too far. But we can't achieve victory with a standard siege or assault now. We've suffered too much loss." *We never really had a chance anyway,* he added silently.

"The rest of Corynthia is under my control. Berling isn't beating me now." Winston whipped around, lightning flashing in his eyes. Andre and Mattias took a step back at the intensity in his expression.

"He won't," Andre cautioned. "We need to find another way, and we need to think of one quickly. Tench won't wait forever."

"We have another way. And Berling just gave me permission. Fetch Wes, Tahlia, and some of your best scouts."

Andre grabbed him by the arm as he started to storm off. "What are we doing?" he asked, already dreading the answer. Winston's words from Cappus returned to him: *Drastic times call for drastic measures.*

These certainly were drastic times.

"What we should have done at the beginning. What we *could* have done to avoid this massacre." Winston snatched his arm back and marched back to the camp.

Mattias looked at Andre worriedly. He knew Winston well enough to be concerned about the young leader's mood. "What should we have done at the beginning?"

Andre grimaced, realizing he had never shared Winston's reckless plan with his friend. "He wants to blow up Audax Keep."

34

NIGHTMARE UNDER SERUVIA

THE FARMHOUSE WAS STILL there, lonely and abandoned, looking like a dog left out in the rain. Andre involuntarily winced as he looked at it. His ribs seemed to ache again, as if remembering their old trauma. Thinking back to his struggle with the Rose Soldier, he felt a flash of gratification for the Vida Imralta. He could have died without its healing powers.

Andre had selected a group of seven Hounds for the mission. Wes and Tahlia were there, of course; Palmer was also present, along with a few other veterans. Mattias stayed behind to maintain command in Andre's absence.

After gathering his team, Andre met back with Winston, who was having an animated argument with Pitt while Corence stood by. Pitt had discovered their intentions and was furious. He had shouted himself hoarse by the time Andre arrived and stormed off at his appearance. Corence, assuring Winston that he would stall any forthcoming violence until they returned, hurried after him.

Winston then instructed Andre's soldiers to collect the barrels of explosive powder he smuggled from Cappus and load them into a wagon, while he went to find Declan.

Finally, with fifteen containers of highly flammable powder packed into a cart, they stood before the ramshackle house. To Andre, it felt like standing on the edge of a cliff he was about to leap from.

He knew there was no arguing with Winston—his friend's mind was set. He also realized the legitimate necessity of such a plan as he looked back out at the army defying them. Their's was a daunting number of soldiers, while their own army had taken a dangerous amount of casualties. Additionally, Tench had shown that he had no intentions of playing nice and preferred to decimate them as gruesomely as he could.

Still, that didn't mean he felt good about the plan. Thus, to help ease his conscience, he decided he was only there to keep Winston alive. At least he didn't need to worry about Pitt trying to strangle him until they were back.

Winston said precious little on the trek to the farmhouse, instead walking with his eyes on the ground and a brooding expression on his face. When Andre tried to approach him with his concern for Caito, he had snapped, "Well, whose fault is that?"

Andre decided to give him some distance afterwards.

As the rest of the squad began to unpack the barrels and take apart the wagon, Andre entered the building. The floorboards creaked underfoot as he stepped inside. The interior was destroyed, even more so than he remembered, and the walls were covered in cracks and mold. Someone had come through and moved the bodies of the soldiers they killed, although dark stains on the rotting floorboards showed where they had lain. The basement was untouched. The entrance to the tunnels looked innocently normal.

"I hate this place," Andre grumbled as Wes joined him at the top of the stairs.

"What is it exactly?" Wes peeked curiously around the load in his arms.

"It's an ancient network of tunnels that was constructed beneath the city a long time ago," explained Declan, appearing behind them. He wasn't carrying anything. "It was used to move quickly around the city. Now they lie vacant."

"Why?" asked Wes, frowning. "It seems quite useful, especially since it extends out so far beyond the city."

"You'll see," Andre promised.

He descended the stairs and slid the cover off, peeking down the hole. The pale light seeping through the thin windows failed to illuminate past the lip, and the ladder disappeared into seething darkness just a couple of feet down.

Wes dropped his load and passed him a lantern.

Lighting it, Andre slid the shield close as the wick sprang to life. He grabbed the handle with his teeth and swung his legs into the hole, shuddering as he did so. He groped with his feet for a moment, finding the stone ledges, then began to climb down. He descended slowly and carefully, gripping the lantern tightly in his jaw. Before he knew it, he reached the bottom, where he stepped away from the wall, looking around with distaste.

It was the same sensation as last time. The darkness writhed—malevolent, dangerous, alive. Unsettling whispers tickled his ears.

Transferring the lantern back to his hand, he opened the shield to release its full illumination, before shaking his head and growling quietly to himself. Every hair on his body stood on end as he called back up to the others, "All clear down here!"

A rope tumbled down, landing with a soft thump. It was quickly followed by Wes, who climbed halfway down, then dropped the rest of the way. He shivered as he looked around, face slowly losing its color.

"I understand what you mean now," he muttered to Andre, as though afraid the tunnel would hear him. "It's horrible down here."

The process of moving the barrels down the hole ended up being a much simpler process than they had initially figured. Using the rope and some basic tools, they fashioned a simple winch to lower the containers. Once everything was down the hole, they built a sled using the parts from the wagon and lashed the barrels to it.

At last, the group set off into the darkness with Declan at the head. Even though half of them held lights, they instinctively bunched together close enough that they only needed a few lanterns for a perimeter of light around everyone. Declan, of course, strode out in front of the huddle, holding his own light and acting as though he didn't have a care in the world.

Andre had no idea how he could remain so composed in this hellscape.

Even though he considered himself a strong-willed man and knew what to expect from the tunnels, Andre found that no amount of mental preparation helped. He was quickly becoming as much of a nervous wreck as the others. Things were, if possible, worse than the first time. There was no break to the slithering whispers, and Andre kept thinking he saw movement just out of their circle of light.

It was clear the others were also seeing things: More than once, a sword was drawn from its sheath with a dry hiss.

However, despite his paranoia, their journey was uneventful, albeit excruciatingly long; it felt like they had been navigating the maze for hours. Andre knew it was pointless to ask Declan how much longer, and everyone else was too preoccupied with their own imagination to inquire for themselves. He hoped they hadn't been gone as long as it felt. The risk of Tench resuming the battle increased every minute they were away.

Finally, Declan stopped and held up a hand.

Andre had been helping drag the sled and slung the rope off his shoulder. He bent over with his hands on his knees to catch his breath.

Even with four people pulling the sled, it was still hard work. The barrels, although small, weighed easily forty to fifty pounds each. The nice part about the strenuous work was that it helped keep his mind occupied from the whispers.

The lantern-light flickered on the yellow walls as they watched Declan. He stood like a statue, staring into the darkness ahead of them, his hand still raised. Andre looked into his face, trying to read it to no avail: His expression was blank.

Winston joined him, peering down the tunnel as well. "What is it?"

Without responding, Declan stepped forward into the darkness, narrowing his eyes.

Andre felt a cold finger slide down his spine as he realized it was completely silent. The whispers had ceased, though he wasn't sure if that was better or not.

All of a sudden, a rushing sound filled the tunnel from behind them, and a cold draft blew through the group, ruffling their hair and causing the flames inside of the lanterns to flicker violently.

Spinning around, Andre drew his blade, breath coming in short, fast gasps. He could hear the jingle of equipment as the others moved around behind him, but it was a secondary concern to him. He strained his eyes at the blackness following them, sure that something horrible would emerge at any moment.

Declan's voice broke through his trepidation. "We need to move faster." His tone was no longer his normal, quiet drone. It was commanding, urgent.

Andre looked at him. The bookkeeper's bored expression was gone, succeeded by a one of alarm. A knife had appeared in his hand. Andre felt his apprehension melt into legitimate fear at the sight.

The bookkeeper began moving again without another word. Winston and Andre shared a worried look as they followed.

Straining his ears for any sound over the scuff of their footsteps and the grinding of the sled, he heard nothing—not even the whispers. His mind wandered back to the story Declan told them about the farmers who found this place, how they vanished wandering the tunnels. Dread filled him as they advanced deeper into the yellow belly of the maze.

They continued in silence, for nobody dared to speak. They were moving faster now, fueled by the fear of an unknown threat hunting them down. Andre no longer felt the burning in his legs or shoulders from pulling the sled and refused to stop when Tahlia offered to take a turn. If they paused, even for a moment, whatever Declan was afraid of would catch up to them. And if Declan was afraid of something, Andre was petrified.

Declan brought them to a halt at a patch of wall identical to the rest and instructed them to unload a third of the barrels without touching the yellow brick.

"We're under Audax Keep now," he explained. "There are three points under the fortress that are built on weaker foundations, sections that rest almost directly on top of these tunnels. If those are damaged, the weight of the Keep will cause the tunnels to collapse, destroying the fortress, and also burying a timeless and unique artifact from an ancient time." He glared at them as they stacked containers where he indicated.

Having heard Declan's instructions on the surface, Andre ignored him.

Winston, however, gave Declan a thin smile. "Well then, let's hope Berling surrenders."

Once they finished stacking the barrels and ensured the rest were secured to the sled, they continued, Declan setting their pace. When they reached the second spot, he pointed out where they should set the next load with another begrudging comment.

Andre had completely lost all sense of direction. The tunnels looked exactly the same, and they had made so many turns that he felt slightly dizzy. Yet, despite all of his misgivings about Declan, he found it hard not to trust him down in the darkness. Especially with the horrible feeling that they were being stalked.

He's led us out of here once; he'll do it again, he thought fervently.

Finally, they arrived at the final location.

Before they reached it, Andre noticed something was different. A narrow shaft of light sliced down through the darkness from the ceiling. Part of the tunnel was aged and rough. The magic here had been disturbed.

As the rest of the squad began to unload the last of the containers, Andre stepped into the dusty beam, squinting up at its source. There was a grate set into the stone, and through it, he could make out a room lit by flickering torches with stairs leading up and up. Notably, it was the one place where the lack of whispers felt normal, a spike of the ordinary world piercing like a spear through the hellish one they were in.

Declan stood next to him. "We're under the bell towers, the highest point in Audax Keep, and the lowest."

Andre recalled Caito's vision of the two people fighting on the towers and felt a flash of apprehension at the knowledge he was standing in the very same spot. He dismissed the uneasiness with some difficulty. He already acknowledged that they were taking a necessary step in their fight against Tench, a cautionary measure to give them the upper hand. That didn't mean the explosives would detonate. That would have to be done deliberately.

Which I won't let happen.

When the barrels were finally stacked, Winston drew a thick spool of sticky twine from a bag he had over his shoulder. Feeding the end into one of the kegs, he started wrapping it around the explosives.

Andre frowned at it a moment before realizing it was a fuse. "Are you going to have enough?" he inquired as Winston tied off a knot.

"I should. I have miles of it." He indicated to half a dozen similar bags piled on the sled.

"But to reach all the way to the farmhouse? Will it even carry a flame that far?"

Winston straightened up with a look. "We're hoping we *don't* have to light it, remember?"

"Uhh," Leana interrupted loudly. She was looking around frantically. "Has anyone seen Ian?"

Andre conducted a quick headcount, then a second, slower one. They were missing a man. He cursed himself for not doing a better job of keeping an eye on the others. He was so on edge, he hadn't even considered the thought.

"I took over pulling the sled from him," Wes offered. "In between the last two stops."

"Did he have a light?"

"I don't remember."

"Well if that boy has any sense, he'll know to stay where he is, and we'll find him on our way back."

"I'm sure we will," declared Declan. The light from his lantern only illuminated part of his face, leaving the rest in shadow and giving him an ominous, almost monstrous appearance. "Though it may not be in a state you'll like."

"What does that mean?" Leana's face was completely white.

Declan faced back the way they came. His knife was still in his hand. "Come along. We have a long way to go and little time."

"*What does that mean?*" Leana yelled, her voice echoing into the darkness, but Declan was already walking away.

Fear gripped Andre in earnest now. Heart pounding, he kept his hand on the pommel of his sword, ready to draw it at any moment. They went at a steady pace, with Winston lingering slightly behind while he unraveled his fuse. Andre, now hyper-aware of everyone, kept glancing back at him to make sure he was still there. After Declan's cryptic statement, he kept expecting the next time he looked back, Winston would be gone, taken by the darkness to whatever horrible fate awaited him among the yellow tunnels.

All of a sudden, the temperature plummeted, as though they had run into a snowstorm. The lantern light flickered violently. At the same time, someone let out a shout, stopping everyone in their tracks.

One of the men was pointing at a section of wall, just at the edge of the light's influence, his face white as flour.

Andre stepped past him, raising his lantern. The light slid over a sight that made his stomach flip.

The base of the yellow wall was painted in blood—shiny, red, fresh blood—an absurd amount of it. Swallowing, Andre lifted the lantern higher, afraid to come any closer, yet needing to see if there was more. There were no signs of a struggle, no body parts or bits of clothing and gear, just a horrible, red stain on the wall.

As everyone stared in horror, there came out of the darkness another terrible rushing sound, like a thousand breaths at once and a gust of air blew over them. It was stagnant, dead, rotting.

Andre immediately drew his sword. The bright metallic ring of the blade leaving its sheath gave him a momentary surge of courage. He stepped forward, holding his weapon at the ready. As he raised the light once again, a bipedal shape appeared from the black and leaped at him.

He swung without a second thought. His sword passed cleanly and easily through the form, cutting it in two. That didn't to stop it, however. The upper half scrabbled after him, flailing its lanky arms and making horrible wheezing noises. Andre drove his sword into the thing's head and stepped back as it finally went limp.

It was humanoid and naked. Its wrinkled skin sheened with a phlegm-like substance and hung loosely around its skeleton, the same yellow hue as the tunnel walls. Its legs were stunted, squat things, and its arms looked stretched, like putty. The upper half lay face down. Andre left it that way. He had no desire to see its face. A thick brown substance slowly oozed from its wounds, and he took another step backwards to avoid it touching his boots.

He looked up at Declan with a mixture of disgust and horror. "What is that?"

"We need to go, now," Declan answered in an infuriatingly calm voice.

"Not until you tell me what we're dealing with."

"It's a husk, a once-was. There will be more." He swept his gaze to Winston. "I believe the catacombs are aware of our intentions. We must leave as soon as possible."

Andre glanced back down at the body, then at the bloodstain on the wall. He dispatched the monster so easily, it was hard to believe they were in serious danger. What was left of Ian spoke an entirely different message.

He looked at the group—all of them still frozen, staring at the husk—and raised his voice, catching their attention. "You heard him. We need to move." He gestured at Declan. "Lead the way."

They ran now, fear driving them faster and faster. The air was still bitterly cold, and the darkness grinned silently. Andre figured they were still in danger, though no more of the yellow creatures made an appearance.

When they reached the second location of explosives, Declan tried to take them right past it. Winston insisted they stop, stating that the rebellion was as good as finished if they didn't complete their mission. Privately, Andre agreed with Declan. Nonetheless, he circled up around Winston with the others as he prepped the twine and tied it off.

Before he finished, more shapes stepped into their circle of light. Three more husks shambled towards them, wheezing and groaning, their fingers dragging on the ground.

Andre had made the right decision not to turn the first one over. The husks' faces were a horrifying mass of sagging skin with dark, gaping holes where its mouth and eyes should be. Combined with their sunken, wrinkled bodies and discordant movements, they were the stuff of nightmares.

One of them lurched for Andre, raising its arms to envelope him and turn him into just another bloodstain. With one swing, he detached both arms at the elbows before driving the point of his blade into its face. It collapsed like its bones were made of jelly and began leaking brown fluid.

A shout rang out behind him.

He turned to see Leana wrestling another husk off of her. One lay puddled at her feet, even as four more appeared to take its place. Wes was hacking at its limbs and chopping it apart, but its grasp seemed to be fused to her. She screamed, tearing at the disembodied hands still gripping her until Wes managed to bat them off.

"Run!" shouted Andre. "Go! Follow Declan!"

More husks were appearing, stumbling out of the shadows towards them. The group didn't need to be told twice. They all ran, except for Winston, who continued to lag behind with his fuse.

"Winston, leave it! We'll be overrun!"

"It's fine. They're slow."

No sooner did the words leave his mouth than one of the yellow monsters jumped at him, using its long arms to propel itself forward. Andre intercepted it, piercing it through the throat and separating its head from its body, but not before its fingers grabbed his face.

The thing's grip was clammy and sticky at the same time, and caused an uncomfortable prickling sensation that very quickly grew into an unbearable burning. It felt as though the skin on his cheeks was being shaved off and the insides seared with a red-hot iron. It was agony.

He cried out, wrenching desperately at the hands to no avail.

Winston hurried to help him until he smacked him away. "Don't touch them!"

Finally, he managed to tear the husk off of him and stumbled backwards, barely able to see from the pain.

Feeling arms wrap around him, he struggled before realizing they were trying to help him, not hurt him. He heard shouting echoing through the tunnel, accompanied by the moaning and huffing of the husks. The burning of his face was so intense he was unable to concentrate on anything happening around him. Instead, he focused on moving his legs, staying in pace with whoever was supporting. Gradually, the sound of the husks faded, and his own ragged breathing grew to the forefront of his senses.

They stopped once. Andre heard angry voices and Winston say something back before they were on the move again. The pain finally reached a point where he could feel himself losing touch with reality. What little he could see was unfocused, slipping in and out of shadow. His legs failed until he was being dragged.

At one point, hands brushed his head as something was placed around his neck. Shortly after, the intensity of the pain became unbearable, and he succumbed to darkness's call.

Andre came to abruptly. He was lying on his back, staring at the ceiling of the farmhouse. The wind whistled through cracks in the walls, and light fingers of rainfall tapped on the roof. He felt surprisingly awake and refreshed considering his recent ordeal; his face only stung a little.

He lightly touched his cheek to find it covered in welts. He grimaced at the thought of his appearance, then shuddered at the memory of the husks.

As he sat up, something shifted underneath his shirt, and he paused as a realization hit him. Reaching into his collar, he pulled out the Vida Imralta. He stared at the amulet a moment, the warm stone in the center capturing his eyes, before pulling it over his head and curling his fingers around it.

He was going to give it back to Winston, side effects be damned. He didn't feel comfortable having the amulet on his person. He cautiously slipped it into his trousers pocket and was relived when he wasn't barraged with a wave of pain. Though his face certainly burned a little more, most of it felt numb, which he could handle.

He wandered through the building, looking for someone from their excursion group. He finally found Wes and Tahlia sitting outside on the porch, talking quietly with their heads close together. They started as the floorboards creaked.

"How are you feeling, sir?" Wes inquired, standing and saluting him. Tahlia joined him.

He waved at them to relax. "I've been worse. How's my face?"

"I think it's an improvement," Tahlia grinned.

Andre laughed, then winced as pain flooded his cheeks. He was grateful for these two and their bottomless cheer. They were a gift not many people were lucky enough to have. "What of the others? Are they alright?"

"All fine... besides Ian. Leana has some nasty wounds on her arms from those monsters, but you know her. She'll be boasting about those to anyone who will listen. They're all back at camp. Winston will be sending a message to Tench for a parley. We were ordered to stay here to wait for you to wake and keep an eye on the fuse. There's a horse out back for you in case you wanted to head back."

Andre stepped off the porch. "I probably should." A thought came to him and he turned back. "Whatever Winston says, that fuse does not light."

Wes grinned. "Over our dead bodies."

35

CROSSROADS

C AITO WOKE TO FIND his body a single, aching bruise. His head pounded like a blacksmith striking his anvil while his limbs groaned. Breathing came with effort, as though heavy weights were stacked on his chest. Even his feet protested when he shifted them. He looked down to see that the leather brace he had worn into the charge had been replaced by white gauze, damp with his blood. He could feel the gash underneath burning and pulsing as blood swelled determinedly beneath the pressure of the dressing. His Crimson Hound pin was gone.

The charge to Seruvia had been exhilarating, he remembered. Riding at breakneck speed towards a thicket of bloodthirsty spears was easily the most terrifying thing that Caito had ever done. However, the high from that headlong rush was unmatched.

Unfortunately, it had also been brief.

Caito's horse was killed under him, and he was thrown mercilessly into the ravenous bloodbath, though there were plenty of other rebels on foot around him. Fighting only to incapacitate, he was pleased to find himself able to proficiently match those who contested him, though he received a nasty cut on his forearm after his shield broke.

When the retreat was called, one of the Hounds, named Joshua, pulled him onto the back of his horse. They were near the front of the retreating rebels, which meant they were closer to the capsules when they detonated. The last thing he remembered was the shock wave hitting them so violently that it snapped Joshua's neck and flung Caito into the air. He hit the ground so hard he blacked out on impact.

He glanced up from the dressings to find himself in a room appearing to belong to an inn, except all of the furniture besides the bed was absent.

A window gleamed next to the headboard, and he sat up to peek through it, wincing as his head sallied a complaint.

He was in the second-story of an inn just inside the city wall. The window faced the street, and he could see the line of buildings extending back towards Audax Keep. Dozens of armed soldiers milled about on the flagstones below.

Panic set in as the memory of his last imprisonment in Seruvia resurfaced. If he were back in Tench's grasp, that could only bode ill for him. The chancellor had been intent on killing him, and he wasn't optimistic that anything had changed since he escaped and joined the rebellion. Although he was alive and even bandaged up, so maybe he was wrong. He hoped he was.

He rose from his bed and slowly made his way to the closed door, keeping his hand on the wall for support. His side ached, his head thundered like an angry bull, and every step came with the sensation of having hiked over the entire Argos Mountain range in a day.

The door handle turned easily when he reached it, and he cautiously pushed it open, the hinges creaking slightly. Poking his head around the frame, he looked up and down the hall.

To his right was the rest of the hallway, stretching five more doors down; to the left lay the stairwell. A loyalist guard sat on the top landing against the wall. Caito could tell from the slump in his shoulders and the nodding of his head that he was fast asleep.

Realizing this could be the one moment he would have to escape, he stepped out, swallowing back his nervousness. He ventured towards the stairs, doing his best to avoid creaking floorboards. At the top of the stairwell, he gingerly peeked over the guard.

There was a landing eleven steps down before the stairs disappeared down to the right, to where he assumed the lobby was. Conversations floated up to him with an occasional burst of laughter. All of the voices he heard were men, which probably meant that the room was full of soldiers.

Caito stepped back to assess his position.

The sleeping guard was snoring like a hacksaw, but the way he was sprawled out promised a difficult sequence for Caito to move past without waking him. His shoulder was pressed against the wall, one leg bent on the top step. The other was stretched out, hanging down the rest of the stairs. His halberd (strange, considering the close-quarters setting) sat loosely in his hand, only remaining upright because it was propped against the opposite wall. To make it past the guard, Caito would have to duck under the weapon and step over the man's outstretched leg, three steps down. As he currently felt like he had been trampled by a herd of deer, he knew there was no way he would be able to accomplish such a maneuver.

Instead, he decided on another solution.

Kicking the sleeping man hard in the shoulder, Caito sent him crashing head-over-heels down the stairs.

All sound from below died.

Caito rushed down the steps as quickly as he could after the guard and scooped up the halberd. He'd never used anything other than a sword; the long weapon felt clumsy and awkward, especially with his injured arm.

Straightening, he froze in shock. He was right: The stairs led to the lobby, and it was indeed full of soldiers, dozens of them, all staring at him. At least none of them were Roses.

Caito glared back while simultaneously fighting the urge to run back up the stairs two at a time. Holding the halberd in front of him, he slowly started down the steps. He knew he couldn't fight them all. He hoped that because he was still alive, it meant Tench wanted him that way.

Every single one of the soldiers stood as he reached the bottom. The slithering sound of swords rasping across leather hummed a dry chorus as weapons were drawn. Caito held his breath, waiting to be charged.

All of a sudden the door slammed open, letting in a blast of the elements.

Tench stood in the doorway flanked by two Rose Soldiers. The men inside the inn immediately snapped to attention and stepped aside, leaving a clear path between the chancellor and Caito.

Tench looked at the guard crumpled at the bottom of the stairs, then appraised Caito. "I see you made a remarkable recovery."

It seemed an insinuation that Caito won a fight with the man. He felt he would gain more satisfaction from pointing out the incompetence from Tench's guard, so he did. "He was sleeping on the job."

"Well then, it looks like he was dealt what he deserved." Tench stepped into the building. "Clear the room," he ordered.

One of the men who looked to be an officer started barking orders at the rest of the soldiers, and they filed out into the rain, grumbling as they left the warm inn.

Tench pulled out a chair and offered it to Caito, who walked over and sat warily. The chancellor then motioned for the two Rose Soldiers to collect the unconscious man in the stairwell. They dragged him outside, closing the door behind them.

The chancellor drummed his fingers on the wooden surface of the table and smiled.

Catio stared at him. "What do you want?"

Tench sighed dramatically. "Look, I understand you may still feel upset about how our last interaction ended, and I assure you, you have every right to be. I feel that I grossly overreacted when I..." He licked his lips as he considered his next words.

"Tried to kill me?" Caito finished for him.

He bowed his head as if ashamed. "I'll admit it. My frustration clouded my judgment. I acted rashly, and I am truly sorry for that." He donned a solemn look. "Yet fate has been gracious enough to let us meet again. I ask you to listen to me, for time is short, and there are important matters to discuss."

"Such as?"

"Your insurgent friends are vastly outnumbered and hurting terribly. Their first assault was as devastating as could be. You know this. Any further attempts to attack the city shall only propel them towards their inevitable demise."

Caito had forgotten how much Tench loved using big words. He felt his distaste deepen. Still, he forced himself to keep a neutral expression. He didn't want to give Tench another motive to murder him.

"You've aligned yourself on the wrong side of this war, Caito—on the wrong side of *history*. If you keep your allegiance to them, you'll be destroyed. Therefore, I'm giving you another chance to make the right decision. Join me, and you will have a very high position among my advisers."

"Until I end up on your bad side again. I may not be experienced with politics, but I know enough. It's about conflicting ideas and compromise, challenging each other for the betterment of a greater whole. I have a funny feeling that people who challenge you find themselves absent from your good graces and afraid for their lives."

Leaning forward, Caito stared at Tench with all of the fire he could muster. Tench dropped his gaze, and he felt a bloom of satisfaction. He knew the effect he had on people and didn't often enjoy utilizing it on purpose. It felt good to make this pompous bully squirm.

"Face it, Berling; if you were to allow me into your circle, I would be challenging you *all* the time. And that wouldn't be a good look for your regime. I have strong influence with the people, as I'm sure you're aware."

A hard look came over the chancellor as he studied the table. Abruptly, he pushed his chair back and stood. "Think about it, Caito." He glared at Caito's forehead, still unable to meet his eyes. "Think about it very carefully."

So much for not giving him a motive to kill me, Caito thought ruefully. He needed to learn to keep his mouth in check around powerful people. It was so easy to lose himself in the intensity of emotion and dig a hole. The holes could easily turn into a grave if he wasn't more careful.

Marching over to the door, Tench ripped it open and called for his men. The two Rose Soldiers reappeared. Tench gave them orders to escort Caito back to his room and keep him there on penalty of their lives. They took him silently up to the room, posting themselves on either end of the hallway. They didn't bother closing the door, which Caito felt was a little insulting. They obviously weren't worried about him attempting another escape and seemed completely confident they could incapacitate him if he did.

Unfortunately, they were right.

Caito closed the door himself, stopping by the window to contemplate his situation. From any angle, it didn't end well.

The rebels were at a disadvantage from the beginning. After the first assault, which ended in a roar of fire and dirt, they were in absolutely no shape to continue the "siege", if that's what one could even call it. And if the rebellion went under, Caito's future was very bleak. He would be executed as an insurgent for helping the enemies of the nation, or if he accepted Tench's offer to join his senate, he would ultimately end up hanged when the chancellor grew tired of his antics, for he did not plan to sit idly by while the tyrant continued to abuse the people. After the taste of fighting for freedom had teased his palate, Caito was determined to do whatever he could to help, even if that meant dying for the cause. Winston had proved to him there was merit even in that.

He sat in his room for nearly two hours before his dilemma was interrupted by a knock on the door. He opened it to see a new Rose Soldier standing before him.

Unlike the others, he was not wearing armor, and his long brown hair flowed free and unkempt. A scowl on his clean-shaven face adorned his otherwise handsome features. Dark eyes peered imperiously down a strong nose—uncaring, almost bored. He stood at a casual slouch that seemed uncustomary for a soldier, especially one as elite as his status.

"Chancellor Tench has requested your presence," the man drawled.

"I respectfully decline," Caito returned, fixing his stare on the man.

The other held his gaze callously. "I was told you might say something like that, so I was given orders to forcefully escort you should you resist. Now step outside before I beat you black and blue and send you to the chancellor on a stretcher."

Narrowing his eyes, Caito channeled as much ferocity into his glare as he could. The man stared right back, surprising him and breaking his focus. Not even Winston could withstand his scrutiny.

"What's your name?" he asked, curious.

"Unimportant. Are you coming with me or not?" The guard's hand slipped down to the sword on his hip.

Caito nodded his head for the guard to lead the way, but the other laughed dryly.

"No, no, after you. Please," the man said mockingly.

As they passed the other soldier posted at the top of the stairs, Caito's guard lifted his hand in a lazy salute. The other snapped off a crisp one in return, followed by a sharp nod. It seemed as though the mystery man was someone highly respected, which only made Caito more curious.

Exiting the building, the man took him by elbow and began to pull him along, obviously not trusting him to stay by his side on his own. It was wet and cold, and Caito's injuries were already causing him a great deal of discomfort. In an effort to keep his mind off of his current condition, he attempted to strike up another conversation.

"Where are we going?"

"Chancellor Tench has requested your presence at the city gate."

"Why there?"

"You can ask him when you see him."

"Why won't you tell me your name?"

"I already said: It's unimportant."

"Is it?" Caito challenged. "We all have a crucial part to play in the future."

The man stopped short and jerked Caito to face him, sending a starburst of pain to streak from his torso to his head.

"Let me tell you something, *Soothsayer*," the Rose Soldier snapped. "I don't give a damn about you or your mystical horseshit, so do me a favor and shut your mouth, before I do so for you." Without waiting for an answer, he grabbed Caito roughly by the elbow, increasing their speed, as though he could flee from his attempts at conversation.

"You don't like your job, do you?" Caito growled, gritting his teeth against his discomfort.

The crowd of soldiers thickened the closer they drew to the front gates, until Caito's escort had to shove people aside to make a way through, which he did mercilessly. Just past the gates, the crowd abruptly vanished.

In the middle of the clearing on the brown trampled grass was a large, circular white tent with blue stripes running top to bottom along the entire circumference. The Corynthian flag fluttered in the wind on the finial rising from the center of the tent.

The Rose Soldier brought Caito to the tent entrance and left him there without a word. The two guards standing on either side stepped forward, preventing him from going anywhere except into the tent.

Caito stalled for a moment, watching his original escort disappear back into the city, before taking a deep breath and entering.

It felt like he had crashed a party. A long table garnished in twisting garlands of flowers and covered in gleaming bowls of meats, fruits, and pastries commanded the scene. Plush chairs dotted the interior of the tent, sitting on top of colorful carpets. Silk tapestries with golden roses fluttered from the roof, while a pair of musicians played a lively tune at the fringe.

Important-looking officials and pompous politicians lounged throughout, talking and laughing loudly. The sight made Caito nauseas.

The sound stalled as he entered, a short gust of air alerting them to a newcomer's presence.

Tench strode forward from a conversation with a dark-skinned man in a glittering turban, a shark-tooth grin on his face. "Here he is! Welcome, Caito! Where's Carter? He didn't want to stay?"

Carter. So that's his name. Caito wondered if he'd see him again. He found himself intrigued by the man who was so unperturbed by him, so careless about everything going on.

Tench gestured boisterously for him to approach. "Come in, come in!"

Caito stood obstinately in the entryway. "Is this another demand for me to join you? Because the answer is still no."

Tench laughed jubilantly, as though Caito had told a joke. The sycophants around him joined in, though their chortles seemed forced. A couple of them exchanged looks of poorly veiled concern.

He wondered if they knew the truth of his and Tench's relationship, or if the chancellor had fed them lies, making them believe Caito was simply a confused child that he was trying to gently guide in the right direction. Whatever the case, if Tench's lackeys were like their master (power-hungry vultures continuously looking for a way to stab each other in the back), they should all be concerned if he joined their ranks. Whether they realized it or not, he would be a significant threat to them.

Caito suddenly realized he could make a real difference in the political realm. He knew he made many people uncomfortable and probably scared plenty of the chancellor's advisers. Furthermore, his influence over the people was already huge. He could change things for the better...

If it wasn't for him, Caito amended as he looked at Tench. Such fantasies were hopeless. He knew the chancellor wasn't afraid of removing his opponents by whatever means necessary. He would put an end to his crusade very quickly.

"I'm not, actually," said Tench in response to Caito's jab. "Servailles has requested a parley. Knowing him, it won't be to surrender. Likely, it will be some ridiculous threat to convince me to turn myself over, instead. I wanted you to join me and try to speak sense to him."

Perplexed by his request, Caito frowned. "Why would I do that?"

Tench adopted a softer visage, clearly attempting to look fatherly. Instead, it came off condescending. "Caito, there's no point to any more death. The rebellion has lost. However, I know Winston Servailles. He won't surrender. He'll continue to sacrifice the lives of his soldiers until the very end. He thinks it noble; in reality, it's only senseless violence. *I* can't convince him to lay down arms, but he'll listen to you. He walked alone into my city to speak to you. Directly into my open arms and..."

Tench grimaced before recovering and smiling again. "All of this could have been avoided had you simply shared your visions with me. That cannot be helped now, but you can still end this. Will you help? You're a reasonable person. I know you see the foolhardiness of all of this. Help me stop the bloodshed, Caito. The needless death and loss of loved ones."

As much as Caito hated to admit it, Tench's words resonated with him—almost like he actually desired to end the war for the sake of the people, and not for his own selfish reasons. Caito hated the fighting and death and wanted nothing more than for it to end. Almost as much as he wanted the people of Corynthia to be free of Tench's rule. But war wasn't freedom.

He opened his mouth, but found himself struggling to form words. He wanted to spit in Tench's face, reject his offer and walk out of the tent, yet his conscience tugged at him, a desperately whispering voice. Here was an opportunity to stop the war that he hated. He would never forgive himself if he didn't at least try.

Maybe this is what Silarius meant. The image of Seruvia burning flashed before him, vivid and horrible. Maybe the only way to prevent such a disaster from becoming reality was to convince Winston to stop the war and surrender. What if there was no winning for the rebellion? What if it *was* just surrender or ruin?

Your choices will affect everything.

Caito could feel the pressure of his decision crushing him, just as he could feel everyone's eyes watching him expectantly. As much as he hated the thought, he would have to try and convince Winston to end the war. The rebellion was far outnumbered and outmatched. Any more fighting, and the people he counted as his friends would surely be killed. He couldn't live with himself if he let that happen.

It was for the greater good. They would have to find another way to topple Tench.

He looked up with such intensity that the chancellor flinched. "I'll try."

36

THE STAKES ARE SET

WINSTON'S CLOAK FLAPPED INCESSANTLY as the wind tried to yank him from his horse. Stinging rain lashed his face. Ignoring it, he squinted at the riders approaching from the city. The bodies had been removed from the battlefield, but the black craters stared at him despite his efforts to ignore them. Darkness dripped inside of him.

As Tench approached, Winston tugged at the chain holding the Vida Imralta around his neck, feeling uncharacteristically nervous. So much depended on this.

He was joined by the same people as before. Andre, face scarred and blistered from the husks; Pitt still furious with Winston; Corence, and Declan, who, much to Winston's relief, seemed to have regained a little bit of Andre's trust after their escapade. More than ever, he needed his friends allied rather than divided—the future of Corynthia depended on it.

He could make out the faces of Tench's party now. Most of the others were Rose Soldiers, yet one face shocked him into dropping his commanding posture.

"Caito?"

The Soothsayer looked even more tired and battered than he usually did. One arm was wrapped in bloody bandages, and he held it close to his body. His breaths seemed to come with effort as he hunched over his horse.

Anger erupted inside Winston at the sight of his young ally. "What did they do to you?" He was gripping his reins so tight that his knuckles were white as snow.

"Relax, Winston," Tench pontificated coolly. "This was all voluntary. He was out on the battlefield, after all. I seem to remember you offering him the opportunity to fight and die for your pointless insurgency."

"I'm alright, Winston." Caito's voice was meek. He didn't meet Winston's eyes.

Tench laughed. "See? He's a brave lad. I'm glad he's on the right side now."

"*What?*" Andre shouted incredulously.

The others echoed his words, and Winston felt a hard knot form in his stomach.

There was a look of deep sadness on the Soothsayer's face as he surveyed them. "I didn't want this, but I must do the right thing in the end. The rebel army is in no state to keep fighting. Any attempt to continue the siege will be futile. Enough people have lost their lives in this war. I can't let it continue." His face turned pleading. "The fighting needs to stop, Winston. Anymore bloodshed is foolish."

Tench's words coming from Caito's mouth. The chancellor sat gloating astride his horse.

Winston felt a malicious sense of joy at how he was about to shatter the smile from his face.

He glanced at his companions. Pitt and Corence were glowering at the Soothsayer. Andre still looked to be in shock. Declan's face was indiscernible.

Turning back to Tench, he smiled broadly. "I agree."

Nobody had been ready for his response. Pitt spluttered something behind him, but he was too focused on Tench's flabbergasted face to hear his words.

Winston spread his arms, happily back in control. "But only on *my* terms."

"Oh, this *again*," Tench yawned, rolling his eyes. "How shall you convince me to surrender this time?"

"Let me explain. Under this city, there is an ancient network of tunnels. I have been told they were used as some sort of underground highway—personally, I still think they're sewers." He imagined Declan's annoyance at his disrespect of the historical origins, and his smile widened.

"Now, Seruvia was built over these tunnels—or maybe they were built under." He shrugged carelessly. "It doesn't matter. What *does* matter is that in some places, the city—specifically Audax Keep—sits directly on top with nothing except a few yards of rock between them. The structural integrity of these locations is... weak. With that being said, if something were to happen to alter that integrity, say a powerful explosion..." He let the implications hang in the air for a moment before continuing. "To simplify things, Audax Keep is a very heavy building, and there would no longer be anything holding it up.

"I've been told that you're afraid to venture into these tunnels. That's very, very wise of you. We barely made it out alive." Winston saw everyone's eyes shift to Andre and his torn face before settling back on him. "I'm quite certain you haven't the foggiest clue where those weak points could be. Furthermore, sending men down into that cursed darkness shall gain you nothing and lose you a whole lot of soldiers. SO!" He clapped his hands, making everyone start. "Berling Tench. Here are my terms."

He began to list out his conditions for surrender, relishing the look of bafflement growing in his enemy's eyes.

"You will cease all hostilities towards me, my army, and any affiliated parties. You will step down from office immediately. After which, justice for your crimes shall be dealt accordingly. Your army shall disband and travel back to their appropriate designations, or back to their homes and families if they wish. You and your... friends shall vacate Audax Keep to an appropriate prison where you shall wait for your judgment to be decided. Are there any questions?"

Even the weather seemed stunned into a momentary lull. Caito was looking at Winston as though he had done something incredible, which he supposed he had.

Tench, however, released a clear, booming laugh that anchored itself against the wind. "You really expect me to believe all of that? Such a brash fool you are!" He grinned fiercely at Winston. "Now would you like to hear my terms?"

Winston looked at Caito again. Expression rearranged, the Soothsayer gave him an almost imperceptible jerk of his head.

"May I speak with Caito?" He asked only out of satirical politeness and gestured for Caito to follow before Tench could answer.

"No, you may not," Tench snapped.

Caito urged his horse forward anyway. Tench motioned his soldiers forward to apprehend the Soothsayer. Andre, Corence, and Pitt reached for their swords.

Before anyone could do anything more, Caito stopped and twisted around to face Tench, who immediately became very interested in his horse's mane.

"Enough." Authority dripped from the young man's voice, daring the portly chancellor to protest, while leaving him no permission to do so. "Berling, I can assure you, I will return. But I'm *not* your possession, and I will not tolerate being treated as such." He turned his glare over to Winston, challenging him to speak also.

Suddenly nervous, Winston swallowed. Such menace coming from Caito was frightening.

Yet at the same time, he felt like laughing. All of Tench's power and authority—all of his efforts to control the Soothsayer—and when he finally had him in his grasp willingly, Caito put him in his place effortlessly. He could only imagine how infuriated Tench was at being chastised like a child, how small Caito made him look. The thought brought him much joy.

Twitching the reins, Caito cantered towards Winston. The guards looked to Tench, unsure of how to act. At a wave from the chancellor, they resumed their original positions.

Winston's companions made to join them, but Caito shook his head, stopping them. Andre looked at Winston, with alarm, as though silently begging him not to leave them. He understood: He would hate to be stuck with Berling Tench for any period of time.

He gave Andre a smile to console him. "You'll be fine. We won't take long."

"Any longer than ten minutes, and I'll slaughter them all," warned Tench, voice dripping in loathing.

"You're more likely to fall off your horse, you pudgy bastard," Corence shot back.

Once they were out of earshot, Winston halted and studied Caito, noting again how battered he was, how tired he looked. He felt bad for the burden he was about to lay on him.

"Berling? Are you two on a first name basis now?"

"I'm doing what I have to, Winston. Even if I don't want to." Caito didn't meet Winston's eyes. He stared out at the city instead, at the cratered killing field. Deep sadness flowed from him. "I can't allow the fighting to continue, not when I have the opportunity to end it. While it hurts me to attempt to convince you to give up, I must try. You offered me the opportunity to fight, to really, *truly* make a difference, and I am grateful for that, but we've arrived at the end of the road. The rebellion doesn't have enough soldiers to best Tench's army, and I won't condone another assault in good conscience. Not when there's already been so much loss.

"Corynthia needs more than what the rebellion has to offer. Tench is strong and ruthless, but his power is built on a weak foundation. His intimidation encompasses the people he surrounds himself with, those in his shadow. They're all power-hungry, though none of them are as bold as he is. If there was someone on the inside, someone who could further weaken the pillars of his power, his government would eat him and itself alive. He's already made me offers to join him. If I could convince him to keep you and the others alive, I could do it."

Winston laughed coldly. "That's incredibly naive, Caito. Do you really believe he'll keep me alive at your word? He doesn't care what you think—he doesn't care what anyone but himself thinks. If I surrender, he'll execute me, then kill every single man and woman who fought against him. He wants to send a message to Corynthia that insurgence will not be tolerated, just as I want to send a message that Corynthia will not tolerate tyrants. You may be able to defeat him from the inside, but I and mine will be long gone by the time you do."

"Then flee! Go back into exile until Tench is gone! It doesn't have to be all or nothing." Caito spread his hands pleadingly. "You don't have to pull everyone down with you!"

Winston slowly shook his head, knowing his answer left him poised to step over a divide in which there was only hurt. It was selfish, but they had made it too far to stop. There were plenty of soldiers willing to fight with him until the end, willing to die trying to topple the tyrant. It was something he was ready to sacrifice to take Corythina back from Tench, to right what had been wronged.

Still, he couldn't blame Caito. War was an ugly thing. He understood why he wanted it to end, both for his own sake and for the people's. Regardless, it wasn't his decision to make. His visions didn't make him master over this war. Winston wasn't about to throw his own life away because the boy was no longer able to stomach it. If that caused Caito to shift his alliance to Tench, so be it—Winston wouldn't let him stand in his way.

"I can't do that, Caito."

A look of realization dawned on Caito's face, then morphed into horror. "This has nothing to do with Corynthia, does it? Your war is with Tench, not his tyranny. This whole time it hasn't been about freedom, it's been about revenge!"

Winston didn't deny it. "Caito, we both want the same thing. Maybe my fight is a little more personal, but we're on the same side."

Caito folded his arms, face weary, yet determined. "That's where you're wrong. I'm fighting for the people; this is just a contest for you. Whoever can spit in the other's face hardest, right? Well, Berling Tench has bested you in every facet except foolishness! How many people have *died* in your crusade? How many more are going to because of your *pride?*"

Feeling his face flush from anger, Winston fought back the urge to strike the young man. Who was Caito to adopt a stance of righteousness after betraying them to ally with Tench? He had no idea what Winston had been through, what he had suffered to rally the nation against the tyrant, what he had sacrificed for the sake of victory and a free land. The risks he had taken, the friends he had lost. This boy knew nothing of his burden.

He shut his eyes, forcing a deep breath. Caito's fickleness betrayed his naivety. He couldn't blame him; the boy believed he was doing what was right. But he had far more experience than him.

"I understand why you would call this foolishness, but you seem to be forgetting that I have a plan."

Caito blinked. "You do?"

Winston laughed. "Of course I do. You didn't think I would rush into such odds without contingencies, would you?"

"You mean your threat to destroy Audax Keep? You really believe Tench will fall for that?"

"I don't make empty threats, Caito. They're too easy to tear apart. You must have substance behind your promise, or they'll call your bluff and conquer you wholly."

"But you heard my vision!" Caito cried, aghast. "Surely you realize this plays directly into it?"

"You think we didn't consider that? I came up with the idea *because* of your vision. Everyone else was against it, and they're right: It's very risky. If Berling refuses to surrender, then..." He didn't finish the sentence.

"Even if Tench surrenders and something still goes wrong, people will *die*, Winston. Surely you didn't."

"And why not? Berling wasn't afraid to use the same tactic on us."

"You can be better!"

"I *am* better!" Winston yelled. Something inside him snapped like a rope frayed too thin. "I'm standing against him, fighting for all the little people! People like you!"

Caito flinched at that, something akin to betrayal in his eyes. Winston continued regardless, too agitated to amend his words.

"Your parents were killed because of his greed. Wes's family was torn apart, and Berling wouldn't bat an eye if he knew. How many other people have lost loved ones to his selfishness? *I* am their revenge! *I* am the righteous judgment they would cast upon his head had they the opportunity! *I* am the avenging spirit for everyone who has been hurt, beaten, or trodden under the loyalist heel! I *am* better!"

"But at risk of so many lives? You can channel this same zeal down a different path! One that doesn't have the possibility of razing a city!"

Leveling his eyes gravely at the young man, Winston found himself finally able to hold his ground against that alien gaze. Desperation was etched into every premature line on Caito's face. Winston hardened his resolve. He wasn't about to be defeated by guilt.

"I don't make empty threats," he repeated. "People are already dying. Sacrifices need to be made for the greater good. Just like you, I'm doing what I have to, even if I don't want to."

The resentment at throwing Caito's words thrown back into his face washed over him, hot and tangible. He found that he didn't care. If the boy was going to oppose him, Winston wouldn't hold back. He was too close for anyone to stand in his way.

"Winston, the risk you're taking—"

He interrupted him. "It's funny how everything worked out perfectly. I'll admit, when you didn't make it back from the battlefield I had doubts. But when I saw you beside Tench, I realized that the All-Mother is indeed with us."

"What do you mean?"

"I've set the stakes. What you have seen will come to pass, unless..." He trailed off to let Caito make the conclusion himself.

The Soothsayer's jaw tightened. "I tell Tench my vision and convince him you're speaking the truth." He looked back at the negotiation party.

Bright boy.

"I understand the damage and death that will occur should Tench refuse to surrender"—Winston spoke gently, doing his best to cauterize the wound he had opened—"but countless more people will suffer for longer if he is not defeated. This is war." He pointed towards Seruvia. "A sacrifice like theirs to end tyranny is the lesser evil, and the quickest way to peace and order."

Caito stared at him, his expression dead.

As he looked back at the young man, Winston saw a shadow of pain and disbelief in his hazel eyes that hadn't been there before and instinctively knew Caito's trust in him had been broken. No matter. He would find a way to regain it after all of this was over. When Tench was gone and everything was made right.

The Soothsayer finally turned to look at walled city, flags flicking animatedly like wagging tongues. "I suppose I can't fail, then."

37

CAITO'S MALAISE

U PON RETURN TO SERUVIA, Caito was immediately escorted back to his room at the inn, where he waited patiently, albeit a little confused. He thought that Tench would have demanded to hear his conversation with Winston as soon as they were out of earshot.

Nearly two hours passed before there was a knock on the door. He opened it to find another Rose Soldier waiting to take him from the inn. This man was much friendlier than Carter and was more than happy to chat with him on the way to their destination. While reluctant to discuss any topics relating to the war, he cheerfully pointed out his favorite alehouses and shops as they walked, going on and on about his sweetheart who could play the mandolin better than most minstrels. It made Caito realize that soldiers were just regular people also caught up in the war, not a breed of human grown from dirt with the sole purpose of sowing death.

The guard led to a grand courthouse, where he was barely able to take in the building face before he was ushered inside.

The lobby was huge. White marble pillars held up balconies on either side of the room. A cathedral ceiling gilded gold and silver curved high above them. A winged staircase split into opposite directions at the top of the first landing, and a huge Corynthian banner hung down in the center of the wall. The upper level ringed the outer edge of the lobby, with the tops of doors peeking curiously over the railing. Their footsteps echoed on the polished granite tiling as they crossed the foyer to an ornate door to the left of the staircase.

A short hallway waited for them, with another door at the end. Opening it for him, the guard waved Caito inside, closing it again as soon as he was through.

He stood at the fringes of a large, elegant courtroom. Rows of benches were sectioned off for spectators, and an upper level ran down either side of the room, large windows glaring behind them. More pillars held up the balconies, these made of black marble. Each pillar bore sconces for torches, though all were currently empty. Two crystal chandeliers hung from the ceiling, throwing pricks of sparkling light into the shadows that lay over the room like bedsheets hung to dry.

It was a grand show of stately strength with a touch of menace. In Tench's regime, it was a place where the rich ate the poor.

"Caito," a voice rang out, "please, come in."

Five people sat at the judges bench, which was raised above the floor and shaped like a crescent curving inward. Tench resided gravely in the center.

Walking down the aisle, Caito opened the gate at the end and stepped through. The entire section of the courtroom before the judges' bench had been cleared, except for a single chair. Despite this, he felt disinclined to sit down. It felt too much like he was on trial, which he suspected was the point.

"Is this really necessary?" He took a quick glance around, noting the lack of guards. They were likely waiting outside. Tench always had guards.

"Important matters must be discussed in important places."

"Your office would have been just fine. Who are you trying to impress here?"

Tench forced a smile. "You used to be such a polite boy, albeit maddeningly cautious. What happened?"

"I guess I grew up."

It was true. The last few months had changed him from the scared young man he was when he fled his home. He hadn't exactly been hardened (although there was definitely a small part of him now desensitized), but he had learned how to see the world in a new way—how to tell the difference between what was ugly and what was bad, and how to separate the immoral from the necessary. There was very little redeeming about war, especially a civil one, yet Caito now realized that some things must be done to move forward.

Evil would always seek to gain control; its success would be assured without resistance. The tyrants, power-hungry, and greedy, would rip and tear unashamedly for their desires, and words weren't enough to hold them back. Sometimes fire had to be fought with fire because there was no other way.

Caito finally understood Winston as he looked up at the stocky, pompous chancellor.

Tench was a man used to having his way, whether it was given to him freely or he took it by nefarious means. Winston *had* to keep the pressure on him, punishing and enforcing consequences for Tench's mistakes at every opportunity. Sometimes that meant taking risks and toeing lines his enemy might be too cautious to cross. Even though Caito was astounded by Winston's plan and felt hurt and betrayed by the way he had been shamelessly manipulated, he could appreciate that the rebel leader was using all of his resources in order to defeat Tench.

On the other hand, Caito also understood that this wasn't just about winning the war for Winston: It was about utterly humiliating Tench. He wasn't just fighting to remove the tyrant from power, he was trying to crush him entirely. It explained every crazy, unnecessary risk that Winston had taken, along with his unwillingness to back down. It was a power struggle. And in a war seemingly for freedom, that realization deeply unsettled Caito.

It also made his job here all the more crucial. Who knew what lengths Winston would resort to gain an upper hand on Tench? If he did indeed destroy Audax Keep, and Tench still refused to surrender, how far would Winston strive for his goal? That was the thought that scared Caito the most.

"Yes, you're very mature now, aren't you," Tench mocked.

I could just let you burn.

The thought surprised Caito. He closed his eyes, stomach turning as the image of Seruvia burning flashed before him, followed by a myriad of others. He gripped the chair in front of him to steady himself until the vision passed.

"Winston's not lying," he stated without opening his eyes. "About the explosives."

"And how do we know *you're* not lying?"

The nausea finally faded, and Caito reopened his eyes to find the speaker: A ruddy-faced man with red hair combed in a center-part. His long, spindly fingers were pressed together into a steeple, and he leaned forward menacingly.

Caito calmly met his gaze, planning his answer carefully. So many people's lives depended on the words he chose.

Surprisingly, Tench came to his rescue. "Bertran, you wouldn't be able to fathom the amount of pressure young Lazar is under. Keep your conniving to yourself." The chancellor indicated for Caito to speak, almost graciously.

With a deep breath, he began, staring directly into Tench's face as he described his vision. He went into vicious detail about the burning city and the bell towers collapsing, the death and destruction wreaked. He shared his conversation with Winston back on the battlefield, how the rebel leader was more than willing to sacrifice his soldiers and even the city to gain victory. As he talked, he saw the faces of his audience take on expressions of worry or incredulity. Most importantly and unfortunately, the chancellor appeared unmoved.

"So," Tench declared when Caito finished, "my options are to surrender or suffer the fiery consequences? And if I call his bluff? Servailles is a showman, much like me. Something like this is extreme, even for him."

"You don't understand," Caito pleaded. "This isn't just about removing you from power. He wants to utterly destroy you, no matter the cost. Why else would he have come to Seruvia *alone* and steal me directly from under your nose? Why else would he threaten to destroy the Keep unless you surrender? I saw the look in his eyes when we spoke. This is personal. Surely you must realize that! The war is a front; his real objective is *you*."

Tench chewed the end of his mustache. His companions whispered around him, sounding like dry reeds in the wind.

"You're at a crossroads, Berling. I've seen the future, but that doesn't mean it has to end that way. The future is fluid; it changes with every choice people make—I've seen it before. Right now, the lives of thousands of people are held in your hands. I can't see what will happen to you if you surrender, but this is a chance to be something more than you are now.

This is a chance to make a sacrifice for the people, to show the leadership you've wasted."

He paused to let his words sink in before continuing softly, "A chance for you to break the cycle of violence you've created. I know you, Berling. You want power. You want to be invincible, immortalized forever. Yet the path you've chosen to reach that goal has been through selfishness and greed. Nobody would expect you to surrender to this threat. After all, haven't you caused enough damage to Corynthia?"

He had been hesitant to bring up the unfortunate relationship between Tench and the people of Corynthia because he was afraid of how the chancellor would react. But now, he knew what was at stake. Now that he finally understood the game being played, he threw his caution to the wind and spoke from the heart, trying to reach Tench's buried humanity.

"Winston doesn't care how high you climb. All that matters to him is that you fall—the further and harder, the better. Your lack of compassion gives him the justification to make such threats. He's relying on pattern. By refusing to surrender your power, you become the initiator and cause of any consequences henceforth."

Tench sat back in his seat and studied Caito for a moment. He seemed contemplative, rather than angry as Caito thought he would be. "Did you *see* him set the trap?" he finally asked.

Heart sinking, Caito slowly shook his head. If Tench refused to take him at his word and instead insisted that it was nothing more than a ruse, he was out of options.

"Then what if I call his bluff? He wouldn't have the gall to detonate them, not when it could damage his prize."

Caito shook his head again, more vigorously. "You don't get it! This has nothing to do with Corynthia—I don't know if it ever did! This is about revenge! He has *one* objective in mind! Removing the nation from your rule is just an added bonus. Berling, please," he pleaded, "Winston doesn't give a damn if the city burns as long as you burn with it!"

Tench's advisers all started speaking at once, their words creating non-sensical noise as they bombarded the chancellor. Caito almost felt bad for him as he watched Tench shout back.

Finally, Tench stood, slamming his hands down and bellowing in a voice that rattled the windows, "ENOUGH!"

The room rang as the word hung in the air a moment longer, but it was more than enough for Tench's advisers to finally cease their prattle.

Breathing heavily, Tench looked down at Caito and forced a smile. "Young Lazar, can you excuse us? I must convene with my associates. A guard will escort you to the lobby."

Caito bowed his head and exited the room. At the door, he glanced back and saw the five men already in animated conversation. The door shut, cutting off the frantic buzz of their voices. A guard led him back to the lobby, where he took a seat on a couch to wait.

It wasn't long before the sound of a door slamming echoed through the room, and footsteps approached. Caito, staring absentmindedly up at the ceiling, looked around to see Tench walking towards him with a dark scowl visible from across the room. He stood up and waited nervously.

Waving away the guard, Tench crossed his arms. "It seems your testimony was enough to awaken their cowardice. They begged me to surrender *for the people's safety*." He scoffed. "They don't give a pig's ass about them. They just want to save their own skins."

As do you. "Do you think I'm lying?"

"While it's not above Servailles to do such a thing, I can't see it coming from you. You're right. We've been at odds with each other since the beginning, and I know he has a healthy hatred for me as I do for him. I would probably do much the same if our roles were switched." He smirked for a moment, then his smile faded.

"But *you*. You've cared only for the truth and what's right. It was enough to flee when I became admittedly bloodthirsty. It was also enough for you to turn back later when the rebellion's dream went sour. You're a good man—one who understands the world and can see through the distractions and lies. Thus, I want to hear your counsel again without those chattering crows in my ear."

It was like Caito was speaking to a completely different man. Gone was the exuberant jolliness and sadistic sarcasm. Tench was quiet, serious; his eyes now carrying a hint of uncertainty as he spoke with cutting honesty.

He hesitated. This new development in Tench's behavior left him confused. He was prepared for a raging refusal or open contempt for his vision, along with accusations that he was conspiring with Winston. It was the expected reaction, although unwelcome. Caito was entirely unprepared for the grave attitude the chancellor now wore.

Maybe if I had spoken to him sooner, Caito thought, *so much more could have been avoided.* "You're not going to like my answer."

"I understand." Tench heaved a sigh, ruffling his mustache. "Nevertheless, I need honesty. I'm no fool; I know what I've done to the people and how they feel about me consequently. I enjoy comfort and power, and that comes with costs—costs I can make others pay. But believe me when I tell you that this isn't all my fault. The system was broken from the beginning. I merely took the opportunity to step into it and reap the spoils. You may have forgotten, but the people voted for me. They *chose* me as their leader."

"That justifies beating and robbing them?"

Tench spread his hands, as though his thought process seemed obvious. "People who cross me or disregard my laws are punished accordingly and immediately. I have no tolerance for rebels or those who don't give me what I am owed."

Caito gave Tench a piercing look. "The price of which you have set yourself. How does that seem fair?"

"Caito, again, I stepped into an already broken system. One that had no safeguards to stop me. If you were given the opportunity to live in leisure with nobody to oppose you, would you honestly tell me you would turn that down? I have riches and power that few can dream of! Even the Lord Artreus must deviate to the senate! Although in his case, he's not fit to rule fully."

"Not at the behest of others. My happiness for theirs would be crooked and low."

"And that's where we are different, Caito. I took the opportunity and stepped readily into the role of the villain. Who could stand up to me?"

"Except you made a mistake. You let Winston live."

Tench curled his lip, eyes flashing coldly. "The final remnants of a flawed dream. His *democracy.* The judges were partial. I had to let him go. I made necessary changes soon after that."

"And now, the reparations of your actions have caught up to you."

"Yes, it would seem that everyone has turned against me," Tench sighed. "Which is why I seek your counsel. You've always been direct and truthful with me, as far as I know."

Caito accepted the compliment graciously, then sighed wearily, feeling decades older than he was. "Winston's not bluffing. I know I have no way to prove it besides what he's told me and what's in my head, but..." He trailed off and looked away from Tench, out a window.

Hanging flower pots rocked wildly in the wind as rain drummed on the glass. The gray sky above churned hungrily, reflecting how he felt inside himself. Tumultuous thoughts and conflicting feelings rolled through his mind. He sorted through them, picking out the words he wanted to use, trying unsuccessfully to discard the others.

"I told you I would try to convince Winston to surrender, and I did. However, my ultimate goal is to help the people of Seruvia. That's the side I chose. Not the rebellion, not you, but the people. That led me to join Winston, and now it's taken me back to you. I fear that if you do not surrender, he *will* follow through with his threat. If that doesn't work, he'll find something else—something more extreme. I'm afraid that if you don't give yourself up... I know far more innocents are going to die."

Caito's throat tightened as he thought of his vision. "Winston won't stop. And you won't be able to hide from the mob that will chase you down after he's spun his tale of how it's your fault."

"You know what will happen if I surrender?" Tench's voice was blunt, emotionless.

Caito watched him sadly, sensing the chancellor's internal struggle. In front of him was a frustrated and defeated man who knew he was out of time, not the powerful tyrant who had been terrorizing the Corynthian people for years. He was simply a wicked man whose consequences to his actions had caught up to him and now loomed darkly over him. All of the power and wealth in the world, and none of it could help him out of the hole he had dug for himself.

"Winston will have you executed, I'm sure. I will try to make sure you're given a fair trial. It's the least I can do."

To his surprise, Tench laughed mirthlessly. "Spare me with a quick death. That should be the least of your concerns."

"What do you mean?"

"You're a smart lad. You've learned a little about how our mutual friend operates, but do you really know Winston Servailles, young Lazar? What drives him besides revenge? Have his *friends* filled you in on anything about his past? His reasonings behind this *experiment*?" He laughed again, jackal-like. "They're all probably as in the dark as you are."

"What are you talking about?" Caito pressed again. He felt his face flush to mirror the dull panic rising inside of him.

An unpleasant smile plastered on Tench's face, like mold on a wall. His shoulders shook with suppressed laughter, yet he held his tongue.

"Berling, what are you talking about?"

He felt sick. Tench's words swirled like poisoned honey, unraveling everything, even as he gained a step closer to victory over the lurid fate in his mind. What did Tench know? What wasn't he telling him?

Regaining his composure, Tench puffed out his chest, that awful smile persisting. "I'll surrender and accept the consequences. Those snakes in the other room were going to kill me anyway if I didn't. At least I can torment Servailles one more time before I die. But remember this, Caito: I was just a man—a wicked man, they'll say, a cruel man—but just a man, nevertheless. I'll have you escorted back to your room."

Tench turned and walked back towards the courtroom, leaving Caito standing fixed to his spot.

His vision swam in and out of focus. Bile rose in his throat, then the images hit him like a hammer to the head, and he collapsed.

(A body slumped in a chair, blood pooling on the floor. A door guarded by two soldiers. A figure in a white mask with a compass mark approaches them. A crackle of lightning illuminates the bell towers, tall, dark, and sullen. The silver amulet gleams in darkness. Red flames waver in the shining silver as the amulet falls through the air. Fire fills his vision)

Caito snapped back to the present. He was curled into a ball on the floor and could feel the coldness of the granite through his tunic. The chill helped him regain his senses, and he sat up, wincing as his palms made contact with the stone. Any part of his body that wasn't already in pain ached from his fall. Using the couch to pull himself up, he hobbled to the door, praying there would be no soldiers to stop him.

He needed to get back to the rebel camp, back to Wes, Tahlia, and Leana. He didn't know who else to go to. He no longer trusted the rebel leader, even before Tench's cryptic words. Winston had shattered his trust as brutally as he would crush an egg, and as coldly as a cat plays with a mouse. He didn't know any of the officers well enough to confide in them.

Except Andre. He trusted Andre.

Tench was surrendering, yet everything still felt wrong. There was something sinister at work, something involving the amulet in his visions and the assassin, who seemed to have disappeared since his last attack on Pitt. Both needed to be found, and time was running out.

38

THE SOOTHSAYER'S WARNING

"CAITO'S HERE TO SEE you, sir."

"Caito?" Andre glanced up from the mirror he was using to lather salve on his face.

The ravaged skin still stung like hell. The medics had instructed him to cover the wounds with the healing concoction twice a day. He wasn't sure if it was working, but the cool lotion felt nice on his face. It hurt to make any sort of expression, and he winced as he involuntarily frowned at the announcement.

"Yes, sir."

"Thank you, Donroe."

Andre barely had enough time to ponder how Caito managed to escape from Tench when the young man stepped through, a frantic look about him. His eyes found Andre's face, and he stopped short.

"How's your face?"

Andre grinned, stopping when his wounds protested. "It's been better. I don't think anyone will be able to call me a handsome bastard anymore. What about you?" he inquired. "You went back to Seruvia with Tench. Did he just let you leave? That doesn't seem—"

"Can I trust you?" Caito looked close to tears.

Andre stuttered for a moment, completely thrown off by the question. "What do you mean?"

Caito was staring at him with a vehemence that scared him. "Can I trust you, Andre?"

"Of course you can. What's all of this about?" Andre asked, now significantly worried.

The Soothsayer hesitated, then opened his mouth to speak, looking reluctant to do so. "Tench has agreed to surrender."

Andre broke into a painful smile, still confused about Caito's manner. "Well, that's wonderful news! Does Winston know? Have you told him? What's the problem?"

The young man was looking more and more distressed with each question, so Andre stopped. "I'm sorry. There's more to it, isn't there?"

Caito began to talk very fast. "Something else is wrong; I can feel it. There's so much to decipher, but I think I'm beginning to understand now. Tench isn't the real problem. I think all of this has to do with the assassin... and the body—he's going to kill again!" He brandished his hands as he spoke. "And then the key—it's connected to all of this. I think that if we find the amulet, we find the assassin, then we can put a stop to it."

Andre held up his hands to halt Caito's ramblings. "Slow down. What do you mean Tench isn't the problem? What key are you talking about?"

Drawing a shaky breath, Caito burst out. "My vision hasn't changed! Berling is surrendering, but I saw the images again!" He pointed to his temple, his eyes wild. "I see them right now! The assassin is going to kill again, and he's somehow connected to the amulet that I keep seeing—the one I described back in Cappus. It's silver, with a red jewel. I-I think the assassin is going to somehow use it to set off the explosives, or maybe—I don't know!"

Andre shook his head. "That's impossible."

Now it was Caito's turn to look confused. "What?"

"The amulet you've been seeing, it's called the Vida Imralta. I found it when we broke Winston out of Seruvia. Took it off a brute of a Rose. According to Declan, it has magical healing powers. But it's safe. The men who came with us to the capital tried to kill me over it. Afterwards, I gave it to Winston to hold on to it. The only other person who knows about it is..." Andre trailed off as the realization hit him.

Declan.

The bookkeeper was the only person besides himself and Winston who knew about the existence of the Imralta. Andre still held his suspicions in the back of his mind, pushed aside because of the siege, but not forgotten. This new insight from Caito made sense. If the Imralta was connected to the assassin, that would place Declan at the top of the list of suspects. Maybe it was the whole reason for his appearance and all of his help. He was trying to get his hands on the magical amulet. And he obviously knew about the explosives and where to find them.

Another thought popped into Andre's head. "Why did you come to me first? Winston needs to know this information as soon as possible."

"I don't know if I can trust him," Caito confessed softly. He looked miserable.

Andre waited silently for him to explain.

"Berling said some things that gave me pause when he agreed to surrender. Besides, I've realized that all of this has been a personal vendetta for him. He's waged this war to exact revenge against Tench, putting lives needlessly in danger and using the All-Mother knows how many people with the sole purpose to strike a blow to his enemy's dignity. Surely you've come to this realization. With all of the risks he's taken, his judgment and integrity have been questionable at best. You would know even better than I!"

Relief washed through Andre. He had been waiting for Caito to say something incriminating against Winston that he had heard or seen in a premonition. There were plenty of things he didn't know about Winston (he wondered what dark secrets Tench thought he knew about the rebel leader), but he had yet to let Andre down in all the years he had known him, even through the risky and outlandish moments.

"Caito, you can trust Winston. I would have to agree, much of this movement and this war has been personal for him, but he's always been a rash and emotional person. Even so, he's made huge strides for the rebellion and given us the opportunity to take back Corynthia from oppression. And yes, right now, he's putting a lot of people at risk, and I don't agree with his plan..." he bit the inside of his cheek as he tried to think of how to word his next statement. Any way he spoke it in his head seemed like a weak excuse. "It was necessary."

Caito's gaze intensified, and Andre threw up a hand as though to ward off a blow. "We are outnumbered and stand no chance. Tench blew a quarter of our forces into bits! We needed to level the playing field."

"That's not justification for—"

"Caito, it's alright! Tench surrendered!"

"And what if I hadn't been there to convince him to?"

Andre stepped back in shock. He had never heard Caito yell before.

The Soothsayer's eyes were blazing with anger, his face drained of all its color. His hands, balled into fists, shook against his thighs. An otherworldly aura emanated from him—ancient, powerful, beyond Andre's understanding. There he was: The Soothsayer of Corynthia, terrible under the pain of his burden.

"What if I had died on that battlefield, and Winston never had the opportunity to *throw everything on my shoulders?* When I spoke with him, there was no discussion, no choice! I do things his way, or he lights the fuse! Did you know that? I've tried all I can to help the people of Corynthia, assisting *your friend* in breaking them free from this wicked regime! I've learned, and lost, and gone farther than I ever wanted to, only for your *fearless leader* to spit in my face and treat me like a dog! And you tell me to trust him!"

Andre stared at his feet, unable to look into Caito's wrathful face. He knew how the lad felt. Winston had done much the same thing to him when he disappeared to Seruvia without telling anyone. But the sense of betrayal that Caito was feeling was far greater than any frustration Andre had experienced in that moment.

He spoke softly, calm in his empathy. "I'm sorry. I didn't know he did that to you. That wasn't right, and your anger is justified. I know you don't want to hear me defend him for his actions, but please just listen to me.

"Winston is a good person. He's not without faults. He can act irrationally and compulsively, but he cares about his people. He's a good leader and has the best of intentions, even if the execution is flawed. I've known him and worked with him for years, and he hasn't let me down yet. I know he wouldn't light the fuse. That calamity..." He shook his head. "He wouldn't be able to live with it. He has a human heart, even if it doesn't always seem that way.

"His biggest strength is his ability to direct situations to his desired outcome. He does that by selling his act and manipulating people. I'm very sorry you found yourself on the receiving end—I've been there a few times. However, he needed it to be real, or Tench wouldn't surrender. Winston is a good man and a man of integrity." He placed a hand on Caito's shoulder, forcing himself to look into his hollow eyes. They were another world. "You *can* trust him. I've learned the hard way."

"And yet, Seruvia still burns in my vision."

"Caito, I won't let those explosives detonate. I give you *my* word. Wes and Tahlia are there now, guarding the fuse. Not even Winston is allowed near it. We need to focus on the other things you've seen in your visions. We need to find the assassin, and I think I know where to start."

Caito finally relaxed. "Declan."

Andre clapped him on the shoulder, yet as he looked away from the young man's eyes, he saw that the anger hadn't fully dissipated and still glowed faintly in the hazel irises. It was set aside, but not forgotten, and Andre knew he hadn't convinced Caito about Winston.

For some reason, that made him afraid.

PART FOUR: RED DAWN

39

SERVAILLES VICTORIOUS

T HE CROWDS FILLED THE streets of Seruvia again.

The gray blanket of clouds finally lifted, and the sky was clear except for a scattering of fluffy, white remnants like sheep separated from the flock. The streets were packed with people in celebration garb. Brightly colored flags marked the numerous vendors that had reemerged with the return of the masses. Smiles lit up the faces of the Corynthians, and laughter and song swelled through the air, bringing as much life as the sun shining merrily in the sky.

Tench had issued his surrender three days prior, much to the utter shock of the entirety of Corynthia.

Rumors circled like hawks. Some said that Winston Servailles used magic to convince him to give in, while others said that Tench had been blackmailed or forced by his own allies. While most were inclined to believe the latter, everyone happily speculated about the former. Tench's army was far too big to be overpowered, and nobody understood why he would give up such a huge advantage so suddenly. Magic or not, everyone was overjoyed when Winston Servailles marched into the city and announced the war was over.

The celebrations commenced immediately and were still in full swing.

The loyalist army was given the choice to head back to their homes and families, or at least to where they were originally stationed. Since most of the soldiers had been away at the border for months before being ordered back to Seruvia, they gladly took the opportunity, and the army disbanded. Those still loyal to Tench were locked up until appropriate measures could be decided upon for their future.

On the day of the surrender, Winston and a large number of men, including Andre, went to Audax Keep to arrest Tench and his incumbents. After a brief altercation with some Rose Soldiers, they found the chancellor waiting patiently in his office for them.

Tench greeted them candidly. "Hello, Servailles, Cordon. I think you'll find my associates cowering in their estates with the doors locked and curtains drawn. Ironic, since they were so adamant that I place them in this position. You'd think they would have greeted you at the gate."

Winston smirked as two rebel soldiers walked around the desk to stand on either side of Tench. "Don't worry Berling; we'll bring them out, too. They can't avoid their fate."

"And that's to be the same as mine?"

"That's for the judge and jury to decide."

Tench laughed softly. "I assume I don't have the luxury?"

"You're lucky you'll have a hearing at all," Winston sneered. "Caito requested we hold one for you. I'll humor him, but I already have my mind made up." He nodded to the guards, and they escorted Tench out of the room.

Winston turned to Andre, an ugly look on his face. "He'll get a trial. It's a waste of damn time, but believe you me, he'll be tried."

Andre didn't like the sound of that.

Their next order of business was to detain Declan.

Andre and Caito went to Winston immediately after their discussion to tell him of Tench's surrender and their epiphany about the bookkeeper. Thankfully, Winston had been alone when they found him, poring over maps of Seruvia.

"Well done," he told Caito when they relayed the first news. "I knew you would do it."

Caito didn't acknowledge his praise. Instead, he described the vision he saw in the courthouse after talking to Tench and what he had already told

Andre. He spoke quickly and bluntly, as though to be finished as soon as possible.

Winston listened intently, his eyes never leaving the Soothsayer's face. "What does this—" he started to say when Caito concluded.

Andre interrupted him. "I told him about the Vida Imralta, Winston."

Winston had suddenly looked nervous and reached into the front of his shirt, pulling out the silver pendant. Slipping it over his head, he held it out to Caito, who took it dubiously.

Caito's eyes widened as his fingers closed around the amulet, and he inhaled shakily. "That's—"

"Dangerous," Andre finished.

"And you're sure that it's connected to the assassin?"

"Yes," Caito answered quietly, still transfixed. "This is it." He abruptly let the pendant slip through his fingers, catching it by the chain, and offered it back to Winston.

Hanging it back around his neck, Winston tucked it out of sight again.

"There's only one other person who knows about the Vida Imralta," Andre stated.

Winston raised an eyebrow at him. "You're still accusing Declan?"

"Yes, I am. You don't have to believe me, but something must be done sooner or later. We haven't seen a trace of the assassin, and if we continue to just pretend like nothing happened, he will strike again. I'm not asking for an official arrest, just to hold him somewhere we can keep an eye on him. It's better than doing nothing, and Declan is our only suspect."

"He's your only suspect, you mean."

"Winston, please. He's *the* only suspect—unless you've been keeping something from the rest of us. Just until we can conduct a full investigation." Andre didn't understand why Winston was fighting him so hard. Did he want an assassin on the loose?

Winston looked at Caito, who was watching impassively. "What is your opinion, Caito?"

"For the sake of transparency," Caito said frostily, "there's something else about Declan I haven't told you. He's not who he says he is. I've met him before under a different name: Silarius. He came to me before I joined the rebellion to offer me advice. I think it's safe to say he has ulterior motives."

Winston pursed his lips in disapproval. "Why didn't you tell us this sooner?"

Caito lifted his chin. "It's amusing how that makes you feel, isn't it? When someone hasn't been honest with you."

Andre, feeling the air become charged, stepped forward. "Stop it. Both of you. Why didn't you tell us, Caito?"

"I didn't realize it at first," Caito explained, his eyes still locked with Winston's. "I hadn't been around him much. However, when he spoke with me at Markalv, it was obvious. Assassin or not, he needs to be apprehended until we can figure out who he is and what his agenda is."

Now, they stood at the front door to Declan's bookstore with a detachment of six guards. Andre didn't know for certain that he would be here, but Declan had disappeared once the rebellion took over the city, and he felt it was a safe assumption considering he had been absent from his books for two months.

He grabbed the brass knocker, rapped three times, then retreated back with the others to wait.

Winston stepped up to one of the dark, lifeless windows and tried to peek inside. "I don't think he's here, Andre. I don't want to waste more time than we have to. There are still important matters to attend."

Saying nothing, Andre tried the door. It was unlocked, and he opened it.

"Now that's just—" Winston protested, but Andre hushed him and stepped into the building.

He made his way through the darkness to the dim outline of the windows, throwing aside the curtains to let the natural light fill the space. The room looked the same as last except dustier. The curved bookshelves stood tall and forlorn, and books were everywhere. Besides the furniture, the room was empty.

Winston entered behind him. "He's not here. Don't worry, I'll have people look for him. Come on."

Andre reluctantly followed Winston back out of the bookstore, feeling like he was missing something important. He felt uneasy that Declan had just suddenly vanished. It was too convenient. He had been so involved in the rebellion's operations since he joined—always lurking at the edges of meetings and staying close to Winston—but now that the fight was over, he was nowhere to be found.

However, Winston was right: There was still much to take care of. Andre just had to trust that Declan would be found.

Thus began the meetings with the members of the senate who hadn't been directly in Tench's pocket. They discussed the upcoming trials for the chancellor and the various members of the senate who had merely acted as bodies so Tench could "legally" push through his laws. The tyrant kept the farce of a democracy throughout his regime, even though it was as transparent a lie as glass. The half-honest politicians who sat uselessly like aging cheese, too afraid to speak out against Tench, were very eager to be involved with the condemnation of the former chancellor. Andre knew Winston nursed a special kind of disdain for those who failed to act, even if they didn't side with the enemy. He expected that many of them wouldn't hold their position much longer.

The future of the Corynthian government was discussed extensively. With Tench awaiting his fate, the country would need new leaders. Tench's laws would need to be reversed or altered, while the justice system and senate required a total reevaluation. There was plenty of work to go around.

Winston, of course, offered to take over as interim leader while all of the wrinkles were flattened out. He was vetoed immediately by Pitt and Caito, who was surprisingly eager to take part in the politics.

"That's going to cause a storm, Winston," Pitt warned darkly. "It needs to be a fair election."

"If we're to fill the office, we have to do it right," Caito agreed adamantly. "Until then, we'll have to work together to find solutions." It was readily apparent that he much preferred the hours of debate rather than the sound of steel and the smell of blood and sweat.

Andre, on the other hand, hated politics. The long, weighty discussions and incessant arguing made him tired and irritable. In a matter of an hour, he had lost track of the number of fingers pointed and pontificating speeches that fizzled into the air like gaudy smoke while he sat there wishing he was down among the celebrating citizens.

I don't even know why I'm here, he thought peevishly as two men he didn't know spoke at the same time. Neither looked like they had ever missed a meal. The only times Andre opened his mouth was to yawn widely and pointedly. He knew Winston had him there because he valued his opinion, but Andre was more than happy to trust his friend to do what was best.

When a reprieve was finally called for lunch, he was the first one out of his seat and through the door, gasping gratefully when he stepped out of the stuffy room. After the meal, however, they went right back to it and worked until dusk. Although Andre did his best to stay present, when they finally adjourned for the day, he had no idea if they actually made any progress. He was just glad to be done.

To his immense relief, he was omitted from participating the next day and spent it happily wandering Seruvia with Mattias, Donroe, and some of the other men. They hopped from tavern to tavern, where they downed pint after pint of ale and recounted stories to other customers, mostly attractive young women who were very interested in the rebel soldiers. Andre received special attention due to the damage done to his face, though this kind he welcomed. The tavern keepers received them cheerfully; the men brought good business with them.

Andre went to bed late that night, exhausted and drunk, but feeling content for the first time in a long time. The hangover the next morning left him decidedly less so, especially when he was once again summoned to Audax Keep by Winston.

Having claimed Tench's office as his own, Winston was sitting reading documents when Andre approached the open door. His head was pounding like a battering ram, and he pressed a palm to his temple as he knocked on the frame.

Winston looked up and snorted. "Enjoy yourself last night?"

"What do you want?"

"Well, my cranky friend," Winston chuckled, "you may or may not remember that Berling Tench's execution is scheduled for later today in Dominus Square. I was going to ask if you and your company would act as security, although I don't think you're in the right state for that."

Andre vaguely recalled seeing fliers with Tench's face and large bold letters hung up in the many taverns they went to. "No, I can have them ready by then." Winston's words registered a moment later, and he held up a hand to stop him from responding. "Wait, execution? I thought it's supposed to be a trial."

His friend leaned back in his chair. "Andre, you know how it's going to end. I've only organized a hearing because Caito requested it. Since I'm doing him this courtesy, I might as well enjoy it. He will be tried."

Andre felt his stomach twist. The glint in Winston's brown eyes and the sly smile on his sharp face did not bode well. Knowing his flair for dramatics and his malicious nature towards his adversaries, Andre had a very bad feeling that the "hearing" would be much uglier than it should. He suddenly wished Caito hadn't let his compassion get the best of him.

"You're going to turn this into a spectacle, aren't you?" He already knew the answer.

"I've been waiting for this moment for a long, long time, my friend. I'm sure there are many others who have been as well. It's an opportunity to show the world what we do to tyrants—to people that try to force us into submission. We'll make a statement to the other lands: Corynthia will not be compliant."

"Winston, you're walking a dangerous line. Right now, you're Corynthia's hero. If you do this, it could sully the people's view of you."

Smiling, Winston indicated to the window. "Do you not hear them? Were you not down there with them last night? They are *reveling* in our victory. They've been held under curfew with their backs buckling from the weight of taxes and abuse, while people were taken from their homes every day for the slightest toe out of line. And now all of that frustration and fear has been lifted. They're going to enjoy seeing their enemy receive the punishment he deserves."

Vacating his seat, Winston went to stand at the window, looking down on the city. He turned. "Do you trust me, Andre?"

"Of course I do. But you're planning on running for chancellor aren't you? This may put a stain on your chances when people reflect back on it. You know how fickle they are. I'm just trying to look out for you."

"I appreciate that. Let me worry about my public image. I just need to know if you're with me."

"Of course I am."

His stomach still felt a little queasy, though he attributed that to his hangover. Winston was excellent at overcoming adversity, and Andre knew he had contingencies in the back of his mind as he always did. He still didn't feel great about the trial, but he had to admit it *was* forthcoming after everything that Tench had done.

"Good." Winston gave him an easy grin, brushing hair out of his eyes. "I already have workers clearing and preparing the square. I would be grateful if I could get a detail to secure it as soon as possible."

"Right away." Andre turned towards the door.

"One more thing before you leave."

Glancing back, Andre saw that the smile had slipped from Winston's face, replaced by an expression of deadly seriousness.

"Caito may... react. I need you to make sure he doesn't do something stupid. That boy doesn't need to be hurt anymore."

Andre left the office, feeling more uneasy than ever. He knew how important and personal the whole ordeal was to Winston. Still, something about the conversation made him second-guess his assurance to his friend. He shivered, though it had nothing to do with the drafty corridor. He considered warning Caito to stay away from the trial, then figured it could incite the Soothsayer to make an act in desperation and behave even more rashly than he might in the moment. The boy was benevolent almost to a fault.

Returning to the inn that he and his men had slept at, Andre found them wallowing in misery from the night before as they ate breakfast. He acquired two hangover remedies (the lemon juice and ginger mixture was believed to dissipate headaches and replenish cognizance) and pulled Mattias aside.

"Let me finish my eggs first," Mattias complained when Andre thrust the drink at him.

"Relax, you have time. Tench's execution isn't until later today."

Mattias downed the glass in one gulp and made a face. "I must have missed that."

"I did too." Andre shared his conversation with Winston. "I don't know for sure what he has planned, but I can guarantee you he's going to rile up the crowd. I need everyone awake and ready as soon as possible. Riot detail."

Mattias nodded, and Andre knew he understood exactly what was expected.

They had done plenty of crowd control together during the Border Conflict. Ideally, the soldiers wouldn't have to do much today, just stand and hold back the masses. Nevertheless, it was better to be prepared for something unexpected than be caught with their pants down. Besides, with all the important people who were bound to be present, it was a prime opportunity for the assassin to strike. They needed plenty of space between the event area and the crowd, and plenty of eyes on the lookout. It promised to be a long day and a lot of work.

His men were tired and grumpy already, and he knew they wouldn't be pleased with the assignment, but he also knew they would rather suffer through the discomfort than let him down.

They went to work as the day progressed, directing foot traffic, setting up barriers, and planning out where they would assign posts to overlook the square. Some carpenters and other craftsmen were building a stage almost identical to the one built for Winston's own trial. People were beginning to gather in droves to watch the proceedings, and Andre felt an innate sense of irony as he scrutinized the scene.

After a couple of hours, the workers finished and left the square to return their tools and tidy up before joining their fellow citizens in the crowd.

Dominus square was packed, and Andre's guards already had their work cut out for them as people jostled them, and children tried to clamber onto the stage. It appeared the crowd didn't feel nearly as threatened by the soldiers now that they weren't all uniformed in blue.

Andre was walking around the edge of the square, pointing out spots of interest and barking orders, when the crowd suddenly erupted into wild cheers. Glancing around, he saw Winston striding onto the platform wearing a crisp, black formal tunic with a gold rose on the lapel. A handsome steel sword was strapped to his waist. It looked ornamental, but Andre knew better. His friend looked every part of a royal prince.

Behind Winston, two Rose Soldiers with shiny halberds dragged up a man with a hood covering his face.

Andre grimaced as he looked at Berling Tench, finally brought to justice.

Delvon Pitt and Samuel Corence were at the back of the stage with their arms crossed. A few robed officials stood next to them. A little further back at the foot of the steps to the Keep, Caito stood alone, wearing a hooded cloak.

Seeing Andre down on the floor, Winston jerked his head for him to join. Pulling himself up, he went to greet his friend.

Winston grasped him by the arm and pulled him into an embrace, holding him there for a moment as he spoke into Andre's ear. "Stay with Caito. He's there by the steps. He didn't want to be down on the stage to avoid agitating the crowd. That could change. Make sure he stays there."

Andre pulled back to look Winston in the face. "Are you sure about this?"

"Berling's time is at an end." Suddenly he smiled widely and clapped him on the back.

Andre joined Caito as Winston began to address the crowd. "How are you doing?"

"I can feel them," Caito murmured.

Andre glanced at the young man. He was staring out at the sea of faces with a distant look. "What do you mean?"

"It's a little hard to explain. I can sort of tune into people's emotions. Right now, there's a lot of pent-up frustration and a lot of anger at their leaders. Not just Tench, but anyone who would assume authority over them. It feels like a dam waiting to burst. As though one crack—one small chip—and the pressure will be too much." He turned his haunted gaze onto Andre, who suddenly felt cold as if a shadow passed over him. "They're dangerous right now."

Andre looked at Winston speaking animatedly to the crowd that clapped and cheered back at him.

Be careful, Winston. The last thing they needed was for him to be hung by an angry mob.

"—been forced to live under lock and key as poverty slowly consumes you," Winston was saying. "While your *leaders* enjoy the fruits of your labor!"

He paused as the crowd shouted retorts, angry and excited.

"Most of them, of course, were merely lackeys. Spineless puppets ordered to carry out the commands of their master. Their master"—he pointed at Tench—"who kneels, vanquished before you!"

Insults and hisses rang out. Several objects, mainly fruits and vegetables with some more unsavory items, were launched from the crowd and exploded on the stage. Winston stood still, undeterred. A couple of the guards shouted warnings at the throwers, but more produce was thrown in response, accompanied by cheers.

Caito looked pointedly at Andre and mouthed *dangerous*.

Winston held up his hands and waited for the commotion to die down. When he was satisfied with the silence, he began again, his words oddly reminiscent of Tench's during his own trial.

"Today marks the day you cease to become his subjects. Today you become free again, as Corynthia is supposed to be. And furthermore, today, *you* are the voice of justice. You shall act as judge and jury to decide the punishment for the crimes of this tyrant who has controlled and belittled you for so long! You will decide his fate!"

The crowd cheered wildly, and Andre understood. Winston wasn't going to allow any of the blame to even touch him. He knew the crowd's temperament and was playing it to his advantage. They would *give* him the authority to carry out his wishes without him having to compromise his character. It was genius.

"Bring him forward!"

The cheering quieted as Tench was brought to the front of the stage.

"On your knees, dog," Andre heard Winston whisper to Tench as he was forced into a kneeling position.

Winston grabbed the top of the hood and ripped it from the prisoner's head, revealing a flushed, whiskered face. To Andre's surprise, Tench was smiling.

The crowd erupted into jeers and shouts for his head. More produce was thrown, splattering on and around their target. A tomato soared through the air and struck Tench directly in the face, exploding its juices into his mustache. His head snapped back from the impact, yet the gruesome smile never left his face.

Pitt and Corence watched stonily. Caito was shaking his head, looking sick.

Andre understood. It was difficult to see this sort of treatment upon anyone. "Keep your stomach, Caito. I've seen much worse."

"This isn't right," Caito muttered.

Winston held his arms up again to still the clamor. "Now speak! Let us hear your voices of reason and justice! Tell us what shall become of the enemy of your freedom! This man has chained you, beaten you, and robbed you! He's torn apart your families and sentenced them to unjust punishment for merely trying to survive! How many of your loved ones have *died* because of his greed? Too many! Tell me, you righteous people, does this man deserve your mercy?"

"NO!" came the single unified cry, echoing through the streets to storm the stage once more.

"Then what say you for his punishment?"

"DEATH!" the crowd chanted as one. "DEATH!"

Winston basked in the sound, the moral shackles now gone from his wrists. His hand slipped down to the hilt of his blade almost casually. It twitched on the pommel like the tip of cat's tail before it pounces.

"This isn't right," Caito repeated more urgently. He looked at Andre as though expecting him to jump in between and put a stop to it. "He's using them. This isn't a trial! This is heinous! Andre, I can't let this happen!" He advanced, but Andre grabbed him by the elbow.

"You can't. I don't know what he'll do to you if you interfere."

"That's the least of my worries!"

"And it's *my* biggest concern," Andre snapped back. "So stand down!"

Caito growled, and for a moment it seemed like he was going to strike Andre. Instead, he curled his hands into fists and wrenched his arm back. He resumed his original place, breathing heavily.

Harsh laughter rang out, stunning the crowd back into silence. Tench was doubled over, his shoulders shaking with mirth as peals of mad cackles cascaded from his mouth.

Winston turned towards him, looking uncertain for the first time. Recovering quickly, he sneered at the hapless man. "What's so amusing?"

Tench smiled broadly up at Winston. "All of this, and it's still for naught. You'll never have what you want if you continue to dance around it, dipping your toes in and pretending you aren't interested. You have to *take it*, Winston. You have to seize it by the throat and wring it for all your worth. That's the secret to power, my friend. Until you learn that, you will *never* succeed."

Winston's hand came up so quickly, it took Andre a second to realize it was empty. His backhand flew across Tench's face with a crash nearly as loud as the crowd's cries moments before. Tench sprawled hard on the wooden planks.

Nobody breathed.

"*Silence you cur!*" Winston screamed, face lit up in his fury. His lanky form looked like a scarecrow in formal garb as he hunched over his enemy. He was shaking with rage. "*Your time to speak is over!*"

Tench began laughing again, the sound muffled against the platform.

Winston grabbed him by the hair, yanking him upright. With his free hand, he removed his blade from its scabbard and pressed the edge firmly against Tench's neck. A thin line of blood welled and trickled unsteadily down the doomed man's collar.

Tench continued to laugh. "You won't win!" he taunted, punctuating the statement with a series of coughs. "There will always be people standing in your way, for good or for ill, and you'll continue to dance around them like the frightened insect you are!" He exploded into a fit of coughing, shaking violently in Winston's iron grip. "You'll keep losing, Servailles!"

Letting out a terrifying roar, Winston brought his sword up with a powerful sweep. Blood sparkled as it sprayed into the air. For a moment, he stood there motionless, bloodied weapon in one white-knuckled fist, and the head of his enemy in the other.

Finally, he turned to the crowd, raising both in the air.

"The tyrant is dead!"

As the square erupted into celebration, Andre turned to Caito, but the Soothsayer was long gone.

40

STORM OVER SERUVIA

I N THE DAYS FOLLOWING Tench's horrific execution, Caito's nightmares worsened. After he escaped Seruvia, they had been nearly nonexistent. He supposed that running and fighting for survival kept his mind occupied enough to hold them at bay. However, now that Tench was dead and the war was finished, they returned with a vengeance, stealing his sleep and his happiness.

Worse yet, the visions remained unchanged. Seruvia still burned brightly, with every nightmare bringing more images of carnage. He was irritable from lack of sleep, as well as frustrated and confused about his premonitions. His friends, Wes, Tahlia, and Leana, noticed his descent into misery and expressed their concern. Unfortunately, there was little they could do to help him. Declan's words still nagged at him, making him feel solely responsible for finding a solution to his vision. So, he lied to them, claiming it was merely a mixture of politics and nightmares leading to poor sleep that left him so ornery.

They commiserated and did their best to cheer him up, to no avail.

Finally, after a week of sleepless nights and dead ends, he swallowed his pride and reluctantly approached Winston.

He still hadn't forgiven the man for lying to him. After Tench's horrifying execution, he trusted him even less. Still, he knew if he went to Andre, it would be reported anyway, so he decided to eliminate the middleman.

Winston gave him a strange look. "You're still concerned about that? We won. Reform is in full swing. All is well."

"All is *not* well, Winston," Caito snapped back. "My nightmares are becoming worse again."

"The same ones?"

"The same ones."

Lacing his fingers together, Winston fixed him in a hawkish stare. "We're doing everything we can to find Declan. What else do you suggest?"

"Remove the explosives. The city can't be destroyed if there's nothing there to destroy it."

Winston smiled comfortably. "Already taken care of, my friend. We cut the fuse and sealed the hole. No one can enter."

"But you didn't remove them?"

"No, of course we didn't."

"Of course—" Caito shook his head adamantly. "If someone were to find a way down there—"

"Caito, trust me when I tell you that nobody would descend into that hell hole of their own freewill. Besides, if they did, they'd still have to navigate their way through a maze of identical tunnels in the dark. Along with monsters worse than nightmares."

"That's my concern," Caito retorted, gritting his teeth in frustration. The dismissal deepened the wound. It felt like Winston had thrown him away after his victory. Did he ever care about what Caito had to offer? "You said Declan led you through the tunnels. He knows how to navigate them, which means he can find the fuse. If he's the Wolf—"

"And we have people keeping an eye out for him." Winston smiled almost the same condescending smirk that Tench had so often thrown his way. "If you would like to venture down there and remove the kegs yourself, I won't stop you. However, I can assure you that we have everything as secure as we can make it. The last thing I want is for your vision to come true. All we can do is watch and wait."

Caito shifted in his chair. Part of him wanted to press harder, to force Winston to bend to his will as Winston had forced him. Reason protested against his resentment. He didn't like it, but Winston probably did everything in his power to alleviate the danger. Now that Tench was gone, the threat was no longer necessary.

Besides, spite was Winston's domain. Caito would not become him.

"Fine," he consented. "But you'll have to forgive me if I'm not fully convinced."

Sympathy overcame Winston's expression, and he sighed. "I understand. I'm not trying to fight you, Caito. I know how much trouble your visions cause you, and I *am* doing my best to keep it from a reality. Nobody wants it to happen." He paused. "Have you maybe considered they're nothing more than—"

"Nightmares?" Caito finished bitterly. "Yes, I have." He stood up to leave, then stopped when a thought struck him. "What about the amulet?"

"The Vida Imralta? What about it?"

"We know it's an object of interest, and that it's connected to the assassin. It needs to be kept safe."

Pulling the amulet from under his collar, Winston dangled it from his fingers. "It is."

"I mean lock it up. What if it's what the assassin is after, and he tries to kill you to acquire it?" Winston opened his mouth, but Caito cut across him. "What if he has more magical items like Rödfang? We don't know what he's capable of."

"The dagger is safe as well." Winston indicated to his desk. "Caito, we don't even know if this assassin is still a threat. I mean, he only struck a couple of times. Most likely, he was hired by Tench and now has no interest since his commissioner is dead. Besides, I can take care of myself." He sighed again. "Look, I understand your concern, but everything is well in hand."

Caito felt like screaming. What was the point of being the Soothsayer, if nobody listened to his counsel?

"Winston," he said calmly, speaking not as Caito Lazar, the young man wrapped up in a problem too big for him, but as the Soothsayer—wise and commanding, with authority passed down from forces incomprehensible by human reason. "I have had a vision of death and destruction. It *will* come to pass unless you do as I tell you. I can feel the world teetering on the brink, on a ledge that separates life from death and freedom from chains. If you will not help me, I will take matters into my own hands."

Winston held his glare for a moment, the shadow of defiance in his eyes.

"You forced me to trust you," Caito reminded him. "Now I'm asking you to trust *me*."

Eyes dropping from his face, Winston consented somewhat reluctantly to lock away the Vida Imralta with a guard detail. Certain conditions were set as well: Nobody could know what it was they were guarding, and nobody was allowed to enter the room without Caito's express permission, not even Winston.

After some complaining, Winston finally agreed and suggested one of the libraries on the second floor. It was a good idea. There would be plenty of nooks and crannies to hide a small object like the Vida Imralta. Even if someone did break past the guards, they would likely have to destroy the entire room to find it.

Caito made Winston wait outside while he hid it, then locked the door and pocketed the key. He found the perfect place, somewhere even he wasn't sure he could find again, given enough time had passed.

"Is this all really necessary?" Winston asked as they walked back down the hall. "I still think it would be safer keeping it on one's person."

"People can be killed, Winston. Even with the Imralta."

A rotating guard detail was assigned, though Caito went privately to Wes and Tahlia, since they were the two people he trusted the most. After explaining the situation as much as he could without giving away incriminating details, they agreed, assuring him they would guard that door with their lives. Their eager affirmation made Caito a little more confident that everything would be resolved.

Alas, those feelings had long since dissipated. Nightmares assaulted him nightly, leaving him exhausted and defeated. With the war over, people seemed to have forgotten or stopped caring about his visions. He couldn't blame them; there was so much to do.

He himself was playing no small part in the restoration of the Corynthian government. It was hard to believe that any more destruction could happen in the midst of the progress they were making, yet the burning city and Vida Imralta continued to pester hm. He found himself wishing for Silarius's advice again, as frustrating as it was.

But Silarius (or Declan, as Caito knew him now) had vanished, while Andre, Winston, and the others were swamped with work, much to Andre's obvious displeasure. Caito saw Wes and Tahlia as often as he could, though he couldn't confide in them, not with the uncertainty surrounding his visions.

He also spent plenty of time with Leana, finding her surprisingly girlish now that she wasn't involved in war, though she still boasted about the scars on her arms from the husks to anyone who would listen. She loved flowers and jewelry, and taught him how to dance so they could participate in weekly nighttime festivals. He found himself looking forward to the time they spent wandering the markets together or talking on the balconies of Audax Keep.

But even with her, he felt horribly alone.

Caito lay on his side, staring at the curtained window. The wind rose and fell behind the panes. Every now and then there was a tap on the glass from the occasional raindrop. The storm had been brewing for about two hours; Caito had been awake for much longer.

As a faint image danced in front of his eyes, he found himself wishing for release from his hell. Minutes stretched into hours as he lay unmoving, listening to the wind. In his exhaustion, his imagination made up unintelligible voices—calling, crying, and moaning in the rush outside. He felt lost in a sea of hopelessness. Forty foot waves swelled and crashed around him, sweeping him closer to the edge of the lifeboat of sanity. There was no rescue, only darkness waiting for him to finally slip into the fullness of its melancholy.

And still, Seruvia burned.

The rain was hammering incessantly on the window now, so when there came a knock on his door, it took him a moment to register it for what it was. When his fatigued mind made the connection, he bolted upright. It was pitch black outside, for sunrise was still a few hours away. He jumped out of bed, exhaustion giving way to wired adrenaline as he threw open the door.

No one was there.

He peeked up and down the hallway as a flash of lightning printed the shape of the windows on the wall. A clap of thunder followed just a few seconds later, making him flinch even though he was expecting it.

Maybe it was just my imagination, he thought, starting to close the door. As he did, he glanced down and stopped.

A piece of parchment rolled and tied with twine sat innocently on the threshold. He bent down to pick it up and undid the knot, unfurling the paper to reveal words in fluid, unfamiliar cursive.

I hope this letter finds you, Soothsayer, and not some other unfortunate soul. I wanted to thank you for all that you've done for me and give you a chance to reach your full potential. Tonight, I will finish the work I've started, and nobody, not even Winston Servailles, will stand in my way. I want you to be there as the bells ring out my victory.

Meet me at the towers, Soothsayer.

His blood ran cold as he finished reading; a spiky black compass marked the bottom of the page.

Not even Winston Servailles will stand in my way.

As though summoned by the words, an image of a figure slumped in a chair stabbed into Caito's mind.

He immediately broke into a run towards the chancellor's office, barefoot and still in his nightclothes. He didn't know where Winston's quarters were, but it wasn't uncommon for him to stay up late into the night in his office while he worked. Oftentimes, he was found asleep at his desk in the morning, having been too tired drag himself to his quarters.

Lightning crackled and thunder roared as Caito ran. Whenever the sky lit up as he was passing a window, he caught a glimpse of the roiling clouds and torrential rain outside. The lightning was nearly the only light he had to guide himself through the Keep. Despite an occasional sputtering torch or dim lantern, most of the corridors dripped in darkness. Multiple times, he skidded into a wall or tripped on the carpet because he was unable to accurately gauge his surroundings.

He was bruised and out of breath when he arrived at the office door; Audax Keep seemed much bigger when he needed to be somewhere quickly. He knocked with shaking hands. He didn't even know what he would say if Winston was there. He supposed the note would speak for itself. Even if he didn't believe in impending doom anymore, Winston certainly couldn't ignore a blatant threat.

Unless I'm already too late.

He knocked again. There was no answer. He pressed his ear to the door to listen for activity inside. It was silent, so he tried the doorknob gingerly. It turned, and he pushed the door wide. The note dropped from his hand as he revealed the ghastly scene inside.

The room was completely destroyed. Papers were strewn everywhere, furniture was overturned and broken to bits, and the various instruments and decorations were shattered on the ground. The tapestries on the wall were all ripped to shreds, while the curtains had been yanked from the windows. In the center of all of the wreckage, the large wooden desk sulked intact and uncaring, ink dripping off of its surface. A straight-backed chair sat before it, facing away from Caito. A circle of blood pooled around the legs of the chair, soaking the mess underneath it red—his vision brought to life.

Careful to step around glass shards and bits of jagged ceramic, Caito moved slowly into the room. He paused with his foot in the air as he reached the edge of the pool of blood. Taking a deep breath, he lowered his foot, gagging as it made contact with the wet, sticky papers. The blood was still warm. Holding bile in his throat, he slipped and slid his way to the chair, grabbing the back of it to steady himself.

With his stomach tied in knots, and his breath coming in short, shaky bursts, he braced himself and peeked around the chair to see who was sitting in it.

He turned away, heaving violently as vomit shot from his throat. Retching, he fell to his knees. He stayed there for a moment, trying to calm himself. Shock lurked like a wolf waiting to pounce. After a moment, he pulled himself back to his feet and forced himself to look at the victim.

Delvon Pitt was slumped over in the chair, clothes drenched in his own blood. His head lolled to one side with a bloody hand-print on his cheek, opposite the tattooed fist. His eyes were open in deathly fascination with the mess below him. He had been sliced from his sternum to his belly button, and blood still oozed grotesquely from the wound.

Such a gruesome death for someone so strong and proud—the first in an inexorable march to the undoing of peace. Fate seemed to be laughing at Caito.

He slid Pitt's eyelids closed with his blood covered fingers, his own eyes averted from the horrifying sight. Glancing around the room, he desperately looked for any clue of what to do next. Nothing stood out in the chaos, no sign of Winston.

Maybe he made it to bed tonight, he hoped.

Or the assassin took him with him, came another voice in his head. Maybe that was the assassin's plan: To kill Winston, one of the most powerful men in the world, in front of him.

He really hoped Winston made it to bed.

A realization hit him. The room hadn't been torn apart in a fight, but rather as though someone was searching for something.

The Imralta. He was right. The assassin was after the amulet that granted immortality. There was no time to fetch anyone now. If the Wolf was looking for the Vida Imralta, Caito needed to reach it first.

He was about to dash out of the room when another thought struck him. Bounding around to Winston's desk, he began rifling through its drawers until he found what he was looking for. He let out a gasp of relief as Rödfang glinted at him from a jumble of papers and scrolls all soaked in ink. Snatching it up, he sprinted out of the office.

Caito's feet thumped on the carpeted floor as he tried to remember the way to the library. A flash of lightning helped him recognize where he was.

He knew something was wrong before he turned the corner. A faint light flickered from the corridor, yet it was silent besides the clattering of rain on the windows. He entered the hall and stopped.

Tahlia sat against the wall next to the library door, holding Wes's lifeless body in her lap, their weapons discarded. Caito broke into a run, numbness flooding through his body.

She looked up as he fell to his knees beside them, tears tracing lines through blood on her face. "Caito..."

He stared into Wes's face. His friend looked peaceful like he was sleeping, his handsome features unconcerned by blood stains on his cheeks. Caito's eyes traveled down to the bloody wound in his chest. He wasn't wearing mail.

He met Tahlia's wavering eyes, tears beginning to pour out of his own. "What... happened?"

"He was too fast. Wes didn't wait for me, the idiot. He charged him as soon as—" Her breath hitched, and she squeezed her eyes shut in pain.

"Tahlia, are you—?" Caito stopped as he noticed the side of her tunic was darkened with blood. He sprang to his feet. "I'll find help."

She snatched his hand. "No. You have to find the Wolf and stop him. There's too much at stake. I know why you haven't been sleeping well. Your visions haven't left you."

Caito shook his head wildly, reeling desperately. "I should have told you. I'm sorry. I let this happen to you!"

She smiled a smile so full of affection that the world brightened just for a moment. "No, Caito. It isn't your fault. We would have followed you willingly into the fire, whether you told us or not. There is no better sacrifice than to lay your life down for your friends."

"Not like this!"

Caito gritted his teeth against the lump traveling up his throat, threatening to choke him as he gasped. Everything was turned upside down. First Pitt, now his two best friends. The end was marching closer, despite all of his efforts, taking the people he cared about on the way. *This can't be happening.*

"I'm going where I need to be going. To be with him." Shaking her head, Tahlia let out a weak chuckle. She looked down and traced a finger softly along Wes's jaw. "He was too scared to admit there was more between us. Imagine that, Caito—Wes, scared of a girl."

He let out a sound halfway between a sob and a laugh, remembering Wes's spurts of awkwardness around Tahlia—only Tahlia, the girl he loved, yet was too bashful to tell—the secret glances they shared, thinking no one else noticed.

Tahlia fixed her tear-stained gaze on Caito again, her breath coming with more and more effort. "Go. Go now. Don't let him win, Caito."

Caito began to back away. "I'll come back, Tahlia. Just hold on." Just before he turned, he saw her lean over and kiss Wes's forehead.

He felt as though his insides had shriveled up. Breath catching in his throat, he gasped for air as he ran. He stumbled to a stop at a window, eyes squeezing shut. His friends' laughing faces wavered in his mind, and he screamed against the storm raging outside. They faded away as he opened his eyes again, leaving him alone in a nightmare.

I want you to be there as the bells ring out my victory. Meet me at the towers, Soothsayer.

The Wolf was waiting for him at the bell towers. His vision was taking shape like a swarm of locusts to consume the fresh shoots of growth being established. After killing Winston, the Wolf, with the Vida Imralta in his possession, would be able to venture fearlessly into the catacombs and detonate the explosives.

Seruvia was doomed. Caito had failed.

No, he resolved. *Not yet.*

The killer was waiting for him. He would have to fight the Wolf himself, or the city would burn. Thinking again of Wes's still face and Tahlia's tears, his jaw tightened, raw anger lighting up his limbs. He could do it. He had to.

He set off again, a white-knuckled grip on Rödfang. He knew where to go. He had wandered past the entrance to the towers many times. His anger persisted, stronger than the fear and grief trying to convince him to collapse and give up.

Before he knew it, he stood at the door. A torch flickered in the hall outside. He grabbed it, unsure if the room on the other side would be illuminated and unwilling to take the chance of being ambushed in the dark.

The bell towers were the tallest part of the fortress. There were two of them, except there was only one access point. The door before Caito led to a staircase that spiraled up to the top of the first tower. From there, a bridge spanned the gap between the second. There was no other way down besides flinging one's self from the towers. Caito would have the Wolf cornered.

With a deep breath, he threw open the door. Swinging open easily, it slammed into the wall, creating a gust of air that swirled through the hall and snuffed Caito's torch. Thankfully, the inner room was full of light from hanging braziers.

He tossed the torch to the side and advanced towards the figure standing before him.

The Wolf wore fitted, black leather armor with a cowl pulled up over his head. A long handsome blade hung at his hip, and around his neck glittered a silver chain with a pendant: The Vida Imralta. He was tall with a slim but muscular build. Intelligent eyes glinted behind the white mask on his face, a killer's eyes. The jagged, black compass mark seemed to absorb the orange light.

The eyes settled on Caito as he entered. "Hello, Caito," the Wolf said in a muffled, yet strangely familiar voice.

Caito pointed the dagger at him, his arm shaking so much from his fury that he was barely able to hold it steady. He quickly scanned the room, looking for any sign of Winston, but besides a few barrels stacked under the stairs and a grate in the middle of the floor, the room was empty.

He felt a brief sense of relief. Maybe Winston was out of harm's way.

"Who are you?" His voice shook almost as much as the knife. "Where's Winston?"

The Wolf raised his hand to his face and removed the mask.

41

THE MADNESS OF WINSTON SERVAILLES

C AITO FELT THE BLOOD drain from his face. Lowering his weapon, he stumbled back a step. "I don't understand."

With a smile, Winston Servailles spread his hands in front of him. "I know this is probably very confusing."

Caito shook his head violently, as if doing so hard enough would transform the person in front of him into someone else. It must be an illusion, some evil magic affecting his brain and making him believe the killer before him was Winston. Everything he had accomplished, all of his friends who had been killed, it couldn't be him. There was no sense to it.

"I don't understand," Caito repeated stupidly.

"Then I will explain," Winston said. "I had a vision for Corynthia, a vision of a strong, independent country. I wanted Corynthia to be a place where anyone could come and feel safe. I thought that democracy was the right option, but it appears I was mistaken. It seemed like a wonderful idea at first. The people united, deciding how they are governed. The nation's power is their voice. It keeps them happy and content because they control their lives, not the bureaucrats in their mansions."

Walking to one of the braziers, he traced his finger around the brass rim, creating a low hum. "Until they decide it's not enough, and they're not happy with their leader. And therein lies the problem. I understand the sentiment. It keeps things *fresh,* allows diversity, and gives them a sense of control. Yet I've realized for a strong nation, it's a shackle. A nation can't grow if change and conflicting ideas constantly plague it. It will stall and start to move backwards until it falls apart on itself.

"Berling Tench was a perfect example of this: A cruel, selfish man who was given an opportunity to take advantage of the people, given to him by the people. They dug their own grave. If we hadn't overthrown Tench by force, he would have been their lord and master *permanently*."

Caito frowned. "But you said change is a shackle." His point seemed contradictory.

"In his case. His concern was to grow fat and rich, whereas mine is to create a strong and united nation. I've realized that democracy is not the right tool for such a vision. Placing the power in thousands of people's hands—there is far too much room for error. Thus, I've decided I must do what's necessary and take control before any other blood-sucking tyrant can do so. As much as I disagreed with Berling, he was right in one aspect: I must grab what I want by the throat, otherwise I'm standing in my own way."

Caito grew more and more horrified by what he was hearing. Though he always saw Winston as headstrong and ambitious, often making question- able decisions, the words coming out of his mouth went against everything he and the rebellion had worked towards for months.

Winston took a step towards him. Caito raised the dagger again, and he stopped.

"Caito, I know what you're thinking. My vision is different than the chaos that Tench sowed. He was powered by greed, taking what he wanted and using the system to justify it. *I* shall turn Corynthia into what it was supposed to be from the start. A place of peace and protection; somewhere to run to when in danger; a *free* land where people can live as they choose. And I will watch over everything, making sure those ideals are upheld"—he tapped the Imralta on his chest—"forever."

"But you've killed people!" Caito cried. "Winston, you've killed your *friends*. They followed you, fought with you, and trusted you! You killed them like that meant nothing! How can you justify that? Do you not realize what you've done?"

An odd smile crept onto Winston's face as he answered. It was frayed at the edges, a ragged masquerade of his normal one. "I had to. They were in the way of progress. William, may the All-Mother bless his soul, was against me from the start. He said if I tried to assume leadership again, he would oppose me. On top of that, he refused to take the risks I knew were necessary to defeat Tench. He weighed us down. And Delvon—well, he was just a problem. Too headstrong, too fiery. He was a match in a haystack and far too unpredictable, especially after William's death. I tried to convince him, though. I was willing to give him a chance. He threatened to kill me himself."

Caito clenched his teeth against the retorts fighting to be spat at Servailles. He hadn't included how he butchered Wes and left Tahlia for dead. They were just another obstacle, whatever friendship they had blown away like leaves in the wind. His head swam with the insanity of it all.

"Sacrifices had to be made, Caito! For the sake of Corynthia! They wouldn't stand with me, which meant I had to remove them before they stood against me! I can't wait for the perfect opportunity to present itself because it never will! I'm sure Kaval has been licking its lips while we've been fighting this war, waiting for any chance to take Corynthia back! Then there are the people like Tench who live in our borders! I had to take action or everything I've built was going to fall apart!"

All of a sudden, he stopped and looked at Caito, gray eyes manic. "I digress. Caito, I called you here to thank you. Your visions lit up the path we needed to take to defeat Tench. Your involvement was crucial to our victory, and I am very grateful for all you've done. Without you, Tench never would have surrendered. You won us the war, Caito!"

He spread his arms and laughed gleefully. "Now we can build a fortress that will stand against the evil in this world forever! Corynthia will be a shield for the weak and a spear against the proud!"

Caito was doing everything in his power not to lash out at his old ally. His confusion had vanished entirely. Now, he only felt disgust mixed with a deep sadness—sadness at seeing how far Servailles had fallen and at what he knew he must do to stop him.

"You're sick. I won't help you." He lifted Rödfang.

Face hardening, Servailles drew his sword. "I was going to ask you to be my guide. You were to be my adviser through this new age, our seer through the unknown. Your visions were to guide us to glory that would last forever."

His words stunned Caito. How did Servailles think the gruesome path he took to reach his goal would entice Caito to join him?

He remembered how Tench had threatened him, trying to use fear to take what he wanted, and realized how much more dangerous Servailles was. Tench was just a bully thinking of material gain; Servailles's vision was bigger with undertones of a darker reality. If he had his way, it wouldn't just be the people of Corynthia in danger; it would be every nation on the continent in a way war simply couldn't fabricate. The entire land would be razed by his madness.

Another obvious flaw revealed itself, and he poked at it. "How do you plan on sharing your immortality and keeping your *servant* alive? I wouldn't want to anyway. You can keep all the blood on your hands." He spat at him, knowing it would throw him into a rage.

Servailles lunged at Caito without warning. Caito just barely spun out of the way. Still, the hot bite of the steel opened his arm, spilling blood.

He was immediately at a disadvantage. The room was large enough for Servailles to maneuver his longer weapon with full reach, which meant he could keep Caito with his smaller weapon, at a comfortable distance.

Servailles redirected his blade with lightning speed towards his neck. Caito threw himself aside, rolling back to his feet. They began circling, eyeing each other warily.

Caito had never seen Servailles fight, though he had heard from some of the rebels that the man had lost his touch. Yet in those first few seconds, Servailles moved faster than anyone else Caito had sparred with, even Wes or Tahlia. He needed to find a way to close distance and strike him with Rödfang, or he was a dead man.

He glanced around to a brazier hanging beside him. It was still burning brightly with plenty of glowing coals inside. Unhooking it from its chain, he swung it at Servailles before leaping after him. Servailles brought his blade up, smacking the brazier out of the air. The vessel crashed to the floor in front of Caito, sending sparks and burning embers everywhere.

Caito sprang back, covering his face to avoid being burned. When he looked up, he saw Servailles was frozen, staring at the grate in the middle of the floor upon which the brazier rocked back and forth. He followed his gaze to the grate, confused.

"What have you done?" Servailles growled.

The realization hit Caito like the flat of a blade across his face. Audax Keep was built on top of the catacombs. There was only one place that grate led.

Servailles's words from the battlefield came back to him. *I don't make empty threats.*

As he met Servailles's eyes with a horrified look of his own, there was a deafening noise, and the room turned inside out.

Caito flew back, smacking the wall, then dropping to the ground, where he covered his head as he was pelted by bits of stone. When the room settled, he dragged himself up, shaking his head to clear the ringing in his ears. His back ached from slamming into the wall. The air was thick with dust, and he coughed as he tried to inhale. Putting an arm over his mouth, he waved his knife in front of him to clear the air.

The room was still intact, but the wall separating it from the corridor outside had been pulverized. The floor beneath had been blown outward, leaving a dark hole between Caito and the way out. Another low rumble sounded, and the tower shook, sending dust and small pieces of rubble falling into the hole.

There was the sound of shifting debris, and Caito swung around to see Servailles pulling himself to his feet. The mask was now cracked and brown with dust. Eyes glinted angrily through the slits.

"You couldn't have just died quietly, Caito?" Servailles shouted, his voice cracking. "Do you realize what you've done?" His sword was up as he circled around, blocking Caito from making an attempt to jump to safety.

Caito stepped backwards instead, finding the first step leading up through the bell tower with his heel. "You knew the risk you were taking. Consider it a monument to your sins."

Servailles advanced, swishing his sword back and forth threateningly.

Holding the dagger in front of him, Caito mounted the stairs. He didn't feel particularly brave anymore. He also didn't feel much fear. Just sadness.

Lightning flashed and thunder roared, echoed by another large boom. The Keep shuddered violently, and Caito nearly fell. Seizing the opening, Servailles sprang at him, but he was able to regain his balance and retreat further up the stairs. His opponent's slash skipped harmlessly at his feet.

"You can't run from me, Caito." Servailles spoke as though there were a shred of reason left inside of him. Caito knew there was only madness in his mind. "You're cornered. There's nowhere to go from here."

Except up. This is how it ended.

He remembered his vision: The two combatants on the bridge high above; the bridge crumbling. It was he and Servailles. They would fight until they fell. Maybe he wouldn't have to kill his old friend after all. That thought heartened him as he turned and began to make the long climb to the top.

The room at the top was dim, though not entirely dark. The braziers were cold. Even so, an orange glow filtered in through the large, barred arches in the wall. Wind whistled mocking laughter through the metal bars, and rain sprayed through the openings. A huge brass bell, the bottom rim about two feet higher than Caito's head, hung down from the ceiling. A thick rope attached to the clapper trailed back and forth on the floor as the bell swung gently.

Caito crossed quickly to the door at the other end of the room, glancing out of one of the arches as he passed. He wasn't able to see to the ground, but he knew with a heavy heart the source of the glow. Opening the door, he was almost blown over by an onrush of the storm raging around the tower.

The bridge from his nightmares stretched out before him. It was narrow with waist-height stone barriers on either side. Caito wasn't sure if they would help if a large eddy of wind tried to send him over the edge, and he did not want to find out.

He shut the door again, turning back just as Servailles appeared at the top of the steps.

"End of the line, Caito." He was out of breath, which Caito found strangely comical.

He stepped away from the door towards his enemy. He didn't want to fight Servailles. He was outmatched and ill-prepared, but he wanted to venture onto the bridge even less. He held Rödfang up in what he hoped seemed a threatening manner.

"You're finally going to stand your ground, then? You know you can't kill me." Servailles tapped the Vida Imralta on his chest.

Caito's heart sank. He forgot about the amulet.

Lightning crackled around them, and the dagger sheened red. *Unless...*

"Remind me how this dagger works? Something about draining its victim's life-force? I think I have more of a chance than you believe. All it takes is one cut, right?" He took another step towards Servailles.

Servailles scoffed, though he shifted his weight. Caito couldn't tell for certain, but he thought the gray eyes looked nervous behind the mask. "The Imralta will protect me from its effects. I have nothing to fear from you." He began to close the space between them.

"Why now?" Caito burst out, stalling for time he didn't have. "Why here?"

Faltering, Servailles lowered his sword. "What?"

"Why did you wait so long to turn on everyone? Why did you allow me to hide the Imralta if you were just going to take it back later?"

"Because I'm not the monster you're making me out to be!" Servailles cried. "I tried to exhaust all of my options. I tried to change their minds, to make them see reason! Tonight was my last attempt. That's why I called Pitt to my office. I wanted to try to convince him one more time. He refused my offers, saying it was the path to tyranny. He told me he'd kill me if I tried, so I put him out of his misery."

He turned to one of the windows, looking out at the city. "As for this place..." He heaved a sigh that almost seemed remorseful. "It was ironic. The place where it was all supposed to end in flames was to be where the glory of Corynthia began. I wanted to show you that we had beaten your vision."

Caito circled around him, trying to come between him and the stairs. Maybe he could trap Servailles up here.

"I guess I was wrong." Servailles's head snapped around with all the ferocity of a demon. "Going somewhere?"

Caito froze automatically, giving his enemy the split-second to lash out with his sword. He brought the knife up, deflecting the sword up and over himself. Servailles stepped deftly to the side and slashed at him again, forcing him back to the center of the room, directly underneath the bell.

Thinking quickly, Caito grabbed the rope and pulled it as hard as he could before diving for the door to the bridge. He wrenched the door back open, stepped out, and slammed it shut behind him just as the clapper collided with the interior. A huge clang rang out like a giant's hammer striking a monolithic shield. It vibrated the stone underneath Caito's feet and drowned out the sound of the storm for a moment.

The rain soaked him through in seconds while the wind grabbed him with violent hands, trying to throw him over the side of the bridge. He held tightly onto the railing as he backed away from the door, glancing down at the ground.

The city was in flames. Destruction spread outwards from the Keep as the tunnels under Seruvia collapsed. One mistake had ravaged the proud city in minutes, catastrophe springing forth as fast as a rabid rat from a cage.

Caito felt his breath catch, shock threatening to shut him down, as the door opened.

Servailles stalked towards him, loose ends of his tunic snapping in the storm. A piece of the mask had broken off completely, and Caito could see the corner of his mouth twitching angrily. He could imagine how loud the bell must have been inside the room.

No more time was wasted in talking. Servailles struck at him aggressively and wildly, swinging in wide, sweeping arcs that left him exposed. With his shorter weapon, Caito was unable to take advantage of his carelessness. Once again, he was on the retreat, dodging and parrying for his life. He tried multiple techniques designed to lock their blades so he could close the space between them, but Servailles countered all of them.

They were halfway across the bridge now, and Caito was quickly growing tired. Realizing he couldn't fend off his enemy much longer, he desperately sent out a mental prayer for help to the All-Mother.

As if in answer to his request, the bridge suddenly shook, knocking both of them off-balance. The dagger almost flew out of Caito's hand as he slammed against the stone banister. Breath fled his lungs, and he hung over the barrier gasping for air.

His eyes roved over the wreckage below, landing on the base of the first bell tower. It was quickly disintegrating. With a terrified gasp, he pushed himself back, trying to put as much distance as possible between him and the deteriorating tower.

Servailles hadn't noticed. Balance regained, he approached at the same ominous speed, probably assuming Caito was just trying to give himself more of a reprieve.

All of a sudden, there was a sound like a whip amplified a thousand times over as a giant crack appeared just behind Servailles's heels. The back half of the bridge disappeared, pulled down by the collapsing tower. Servailles lurched backwards, windmilling his arms, trying to gain enough momentum to throw himself forward, but it was already too late. His center of gravity was over the edge, and a gust of wind was enough to break his moment of limbo.

"NO!"

Tossing aside his dagger, Caito lunged for him, trying to grab the front of Servailles's tunic. His hand tangled in the chain around his neck, offering the briefest moment of resistance before it snapped.

It seemed to happen in slow-motion. Winston's eyes widened as he fell. Pure, unfiltered fear filled them, chasing out the fires of madness. In that moment, all of his power, influence, and authority was gone. He was just a man about to die. Those eyes found Caito's.

And then he was gone.

Caito fell to his knees, staring down at the Vida Imralta in his hand. The red jewel glowed as though fueled by the fires below. He numbly held it out over the edge. As he let go of the amulet, all of the fear, despair, and anger in him released, breaking through the dam of adrenaline and shock. He began to weep uncontrollably.

He wept for his peaceful life that was broken, and the months of fear and uncertainty that followed. He wept for the friends made and lost; for the people of Corynthia and the hardships they had endured. He wept for everyone who lost their life during the war and the families that would never again be whole. He wept for Winston—for the madness he succumbed to and the horrible deeds he committed. And he wept for the future.

Because as he wept, he saw as if through the eyes of an eagle high in the sky a shadow creeping across the land, snuffing out light and withering life, leaving nothing but bitter husks—shells of the beauty that had once been.

A shadow cast by a malevolent force playing a game in which they were nothing more than pawns.

Caito saw the future, and he wept because of it.

Lightning flashed around him, blinding him. A huge gong resonated through the air, and everything went black. The darkness squeezed him, suffocating him, pulling him deeper. Voices and whispers swirled around him. Suddenly, he was engulfed in excruciating pain. Then, all was silent and still.

The darkness lightened in front of him, and wind ruffled his hair. He opened his eyes to find himself lying on a grassy cliff under a sky of clouds. Except rather than dark and menacing thunderheads or dreary, gray rainclouds, they were soft and white, as if full of snow. Sitting up, he saw gray water far below him. He was so high that it seemed glassy and smooth like a marble floor. The sea stretched out before him until it curved out of sight at the horizon. To his left sat huge, snow-covered mountains with peaks shrouded in clouds. Birds circled below him, their cries piercing like mourners at a funeral.

He inhaled deeply, breathing in crisp air that, despite the goosebumps it left on his skin, was no cooler than a glass of water. Gone were his body's aches and pains; his wounds were healed, his skin unblemished by scars. His mind was quiet and calm. He had been plagued for so long by the visions and headaches, he had forgotten what it was like to just be able to think.

Caito exhaled and relaxed. He was finally at peace.

42

THE LORD ARTREUS

A ROLL OF THUNDER shook Andre awake. He opened his eyes, grimacing when he saw it was still pitch black outside. Rain drummed dully, while a draft circled through the room from his partially open window.

Pulling the sheets over himself again, he rolled over. It had been another long, boring day full of stuffy politics, and he was exhausted. Lightning flashed, followed by another peal of thunder. He growled as he realized that sleep had escaped him.

Throwing the covers off, he rolled out of bed, shivering slightly. After wrapping a cloak around himself, he ventured silently out into the hall to search for a drink of water. The corridor was very dark, and he swore as he fumbled through his pockets for a match.

He didn't like sleeping in the Keep. It was too big, too drafty, and there were too many rooms. Furthermore, when night fell, most of the lighting was neglected. As he shuffled down the hall, he thought wistfully of the inn he had stayed in the night before Tench's execution. He much preferred the coziness of an inn. The smaller, simpler bedrooms and warm fireplaces were far more comfortable.

He found what looked to be a washroom and peeked inside. The little flame from the match revealed a latrine and a basin with a small pump. Smiling with satisfaction, he entered. Once he had quenched his thirst, he shuffled back out to the hall.

Another peal of thunder rumbled through the halls. A moment later, the floor underneath Andre's feet trembled. He stopped with a frown.

That's odd.

Audax Keep shook again. The match fell from Andre's hand and extinguished on the floor.

He was running before it landed.

Tearing full tilt through the fortress, he banged on doors, yelling at the top of his voice to wake as many people as possible. Some poked their heads out blearily, confused by the ruckus, and he screamed at them to flee the Keep. Many of them realized immediately what was happening as the fortress shuddered. They scrambled around, collecting belongings and pulling on clothes. Others didn't understand until a huge explosion echoed through the halls, and Audax Keep shook so hard it seemed like it would collapse in on itself.

Reaching the door to his room, Andre wrenched it open. He threw a tunic and trousers over a chainmail shirt, then grabbed his sword. Though he didn't know what had detonated the explosives, it most certainly meant there was trouble. As he fumbled with his belt strap, he grimly figured that Declan had returned to finish his job and kill everyone all at once. He cursed himself for following Winston's plan, even though it *had* been the only way.

It didn't matter now. What was important was evacuating as many people out of the fortress as possible.

Footsteps and panicked shouts were passing by his room at a steady rate now. Someone skidded through the open door, slamming into the frame. It was Mattias.

"What the *hell* is happening?"

"The explosives were set off somehow," Andre snapped back, finally managing to secure his buckle. "The Keep's falling apart! Find the Hounds and tell them to help as many civilians out of here as they can, then get out themselves!"

"Where are you going?"

Already sprinting in the direction of Winston's quarters, he shouted over his shoulder, "To find Winston! He might be in trouble! Go! I'll meet you outside!"

He cursed at how big the fortress was as he ran. He was going to be lucky to even make it to his friend's room in time, much less out of the Keep.

The fortress shook again. Dust fell from the ceiling as lightning flashed outside. Involuntarily, he glanced out a window and stopped to gape.

An orange glow emanated from another section of Audax Keep, and smoke billowed into the sky. Heart sinking, his eyes traveled downward towards the city. Huge cracks ripped through the streets; buildings crumbled as the tunnels underneath caved in. People were running or cowering, and he shook his head to dispel the thought of their screams. As he watched, a multi-storied house crumbled, sending a plume of flame curling into the black night.

Wiping away the tears in his eyes, he continued on his way, fearing that it was already too late.

Andre raced up a flight of stairs, heading for the next floor. A few of the corridors he wanted to use were already caved in; hence, he resorted to using a longer, roundabout route to reach Winston's room, though his options were quickly thinning. He turned a corner, and the little hope he had remaining evaporated.

The way ahead of him was engulfed in flames. He could feel the heat from the inferno blistering his already ragged face. Beams cracked and splintered from the ceiling as the paintings on the wall wept, shriveling from the heat.

Andre stood for a moment staring into the blaze, fighting the sense of helplessness filling him. There was no way he could make it across. Winston was on his own.

Damn it!

He stepped back just as the Keep lurched like a drunken soldier. He was thrown flat on his back. The terrifying crunching sound of monstrous teeth reverberated in front of him as a huge crack appeared in the floor. It snaked towards him, ravenous. Digging his palms and heels into the floor, Andre scrambled his limbs as quickly as he could. It was pointless: The crumbling corridor gained on him.

Right when it was about to swallow him whole, it shivered to a halt, leaving him with his feet hanging over ruin and his heart racing.

Realizing he was holding his breath, Andre exhaled, though it did nothing to release the tightness in his chest. He scooted backwards on his rear until he was a respectable distance away, then stood up trembling.

The trip out was as harrowing as the one deeper into the decaying fortress. More than one wall tried to collapse on him. At one point a flight of stairs crumbled beneath his feet, forcing him to dive for safety and twisting his ankle in the process. The fire became more of an obstacle as well. It was spreading fast, nearly as fast as Andre could hobble. Finally, after what seemed like hours of racing destruction, he mercifully found himself in the main entrance hall.

It still seemed structurally sound despite the piles of ruin on the margins; thus, he paused to catch his breath. The doors were wide open. He could see people running around outside through sheets of rain.

Another rumble passed through Audax Keep, and there was a sharp crack as a chunk of stone fell from the ceiling, shattering against the ground. Andre wasted no more time in rushing out of the building into the ruins of Dominus Square.

The city burned. Smoke billowed into the sky from the crumbling shops and houses, and the night was filled with sounds of destruction. The falling rain did nothing to stop the roaring flames and merely sizzled against the heat. Blood, dust, and rain water trickled between the paving stones, dripping into the cracks and rents in the road. Screams and wails pierced the air as Andre limped away from the Keep.

It was like a layer of reality had been stripped away to reveal the underworld itself.

Hearing someone crying for help from one of the collapsed buildings, he noticed a man trapped under a beam of wood, halfway to freedom. He went to him and strained against the debris until the man was able to wriggle out. He was caked in dust and his own blood, and his leg was bent at an unnatural angle.

Shaking his sopping hair out of his eyes, Andre saw a Corynthian guard tending to an unconscious woman and waved for his attention. The guard nodded his understanding, shouting at a few others nearby. Andre rose as men ran over to the injured citizen and continued his way down the ruined street, keeping his eye out for any of the Crimsons Hounds.

All of a sudden, over the sound of thunder and destruction there came the great ring of a bell.

Freezing in his tracks, Andre slowly turned towards the bell towers.

Lightning flashed, illuminating two figures locked in combat on the bridge. As he watched, a fireball erupted from the base of the towers.

Moments later, the sound of the explosion pummeled his ears. The right tower began to crumble from the bottom up as he looked on. Gravity took hold, accelerating the collapse. The two combatants moved along the bridge, inching away from the threat.

All of a sudden, the bridge snapped.

Andre cried out in horror as one of the figures teetered on the edge, arms flailing, then fell into open air. The survivor stood for a moment, silhouetted against the red and orange sky, before falling to their knees. A crackle of lightning lit up the sky, streaking toward the remaining tower. It struck, and the bell inside let out a final, gigantic crash before the room at the top exploded outwards.

Andre broke into a hobbling run towards the scene of the disaster. He climbed over and around wreckage as best he could, trying not to get lost in the maze of ruin. He passed hundreds of distressed civilians, screaming, crying, or wandering aimlessly in shock. Corynthian soldiers rushed around, clearing piles of debris and helping the injured. There were far too few of them to tend to the sheer amount of hurt and helpless.

A familiar voice rang out. "Andre!" It was Leana Palmer, her face pale underneath a layer of dust and blood. She was in a nightdress, elbow-deep in a mound of broken boards. "Give me a hand!"

He looked, but didn't stop. He couldn't.

Other voices accosted him as he ran, asking, begging, pleading for his help. Hands reached for him, and sobs followed him as he passed by. He blocked out all of it, shunning the horror around him—solely focused on his destination, yet terrified at what waited.

He passed through a demolished section of the Keep wall and climbed over a large mound of wreckage, dropping over the other side. Buckling as he landed on his bad foot, he gritted his teeth and picked himself back up. Wincing from the throb in his ankle, he began to carefully climb the pile of rubble that was the remains of the bell towers. As he neared the top, he fell to his hands and knees, partly from exhaustion, partly from despair, and crawled the rest of the way.

There were two bodies among the shattered stone and rent wood. He pulled himself to the first.

It was clad in nightclothes so soiled and bloody that the original creamy color was virtually indistinguishable. The body itself lay broken from the fall, limbs crooked like the branches of a tree.

Andre felt the air leave his lungs. It was Caito, his face a gross parody of surprise. His glassy eyes reflected the flames of the burning fortress, and his mouth sat open, collecting rainwater.

Reaching over his lifeless body, Andre closed his eyelids with a shaking hand. Then he sat back on his heels and buried his face in his hands. Tears welled up behind his eyelids as he squeezed them shut.

Caito was one of the kindest people he had ever met. His thoughtful, grounded attitude had been a calming presence amid of a group of so many reactive personalities. His compassion and determination for doing the right thing had been matched by none other. Seeing his broken body shook Andre to his core.

He cursed at the All-Mother he didn't believe in for unfairly taking such a good and virtuous soul. There had been so much potential for his life, for the good he could do. Now, that was stolen, and the world had lost a treasure.

He wiped his eyes fruitlessly. The rain was still sheeting down, soaking him thoroughly. He stumbled to his feet, gritting his teeth in pain, and hobbled toward the other body. He stood over it, chest heaving from physical and emotional turmoil. The Wolf's mask stared back at him, streams of water running along the chips and cracks. A chunk of the mask had broken off; through it, Andre could see the corner of the killer's mouth.

He reached down and peeled the mask off of the dead man's face.

The world melted away. The sound of the rain and rumbling city faded, becoming obsolete as though he passed into the eye of the storm. His breathing slowed almost to a complete stop. Legs giving way, he fell to his knees again, staring numbly, transfixed in horror. The face before him was unmistakable.

It was the face of Winston Servailles.

"Tragic, isn't it?"

It took a moment for the words to penetrate through the fog in his horrified brain, and another for the voice to register. Andre tore his eyes away with difficulty, unsure if it was tears or rainwater running down his face.

Declan stood in front of him, turning rocks over with his foot.

"What did you say?"

Somehow, he wasn't surprised the bookkeeper was there. He had probably been there the entire time, lurking in the shadows at the edge of this cyclone of ruin.

Declan didn't look at him. "I said it's tragic. The one who created Corynthia, who fought *so* hard for it, was the one who brought it all crashing down."

Reaching down, he collected something from the debris. The object glittered in the firelight as the bookkeeper held it up for scrutiny. A smile spread across his thin face. "Ironic, too."

Andre shook his head, refusing to believe that what he was seeing was true. His vision blurred, and he wiped his eyes again. "It's a trick. A spell. I know magic is real now. That's what it is." He wasn't sure who he was reasoning with. Declan was the only other one there, and it bloody well wasn't him.

Declan laughed. It was a cold, harsh laugh, different from his normal, soft one, akin to a jagged mountain peak about to release an avalanche. Ice slid down Andre's back at it.

The bookkeeper pocketed the object he found, though not before Andre recognized the silver flash of the Vida Imralta. His heart jolted, and he rose slowly to his feet.

Casually flicking water from his fingertips, Declan finally looked at Andre. His face was alight with cold, mocking amusement. "Not that kind of magic. Those with powers to enchant died out a long time ago. All that is left are the shadows of spells cast, while even those are slowly dwindling. No, what you see is real, and so *very* tragic. He was so brilliant and at such a young age."

"I don't understand."

"People like you never do. The concept of *trust* and *brotherhood* is so deeply ingrained that you cannot fathom how someone you thought you knew would betray you. It's what makes you weak. Ironically, it's what ultimately led to Winston's own downfall. He thought he could convince the Soothsayer to join him. He trusted the young man to see his side of things. That trust let him down."

"But why would he do this? Why would he kill his friends? It doesn't make sense!"

"Again, Andre, you're the trusting type. I wouldn't expect it to make sense to you." He turned Winston's head with his foot and clicked his tongue.

Rage sprang up inside of Andre like a wild beast. He had to force himself not to draw his sword and attack Declan. Who did this cruel sadist think he was that he could dance on the misery around them? What gave him the privilege to commentate so icily on the downfall of such a great man? This was all just a joke to him. It always had been.

"Winston wanted more than he was given. By whatever justifications he told himself, he wanted complete control. He managed a taste when he succeeded in taking Corynthia from Kaval, yet a taste wasn't enough for him. Then, of course, Berling stepped in, and, well, you know how that ended. As for his friends"—Declan smirked as lightning flashed above—"I assume they stood in his path in one way or another. He never took kindly to being told no, did he?"

"You're wrong," Andre growled in tandem with the thunder.

"Am I? Look around you. Look who's laying at our feet." Declan cocked his head to look at Caito's face, so young in death. "He could have prevented this. I warned him that his decisions would effect the outcome, that he would be the reason Corynthia burned if he chose wrong." He made another clicking noise. "What a shame."

Suddenly feeling that he was missing some vitally important information, Andre scrutinized Declan. Something about him wasn't making sense. He still stood tall and relaxed, but his reserved air was gone, replaced by something proud, almost regal. He was watching Andre in turn, a lopsided smile on his sharp features, green eyes gleaming with malicious fire. No longer an insufferable scholar, he was something more—his true self.

Andre felt small and powerless in the presence of it.

"Who are you?"

"I've been waiting so long for this moment, Andre," Declan whispered, just loud enough to hear over the storm. "And now it's here. Your precious *Corynthia*"—he spat the word out like poison—"broken and vulnerable. Ripe for the plucking."

Andre thought fast, trying to piece together his words and connect them to a valid explanation. Even as he did, he couldn't help but feel he was running out of time, as if something horrible would happen if he didn't land right answer.

"I can't even begin to tell you how frustrating all of this has been. Waiting and watching through a fog as the senate let Servailles run away with his foolish dream, as they tried to throw away everything I inherited."

He paused, looking serene. Then, his face twitched into something monstrous, and he shouted into the storm. "MY BIRTHRIGHT!"

The blood drained from Andre's face as he finally made the connection. The Lord Artreus, the mysterious emperor of Kaval, was standing before him.

There were many rumors surrounding the ruler, though nobody truly knew anything about him. Most people said he was a half-wit, and the actual ruling was done by the royal senate while he stayed confined in his palace. As Andre stood feeling the malice emanating from him, he realized that everything he knew about Artreus was false.

"Ten long years, they kept me drugged and imprisoned in my own mind. I wandered in a fog while they squandered my wealth and land in *my* name! Do you know what my crime was, Andre? Ambition. They knew the plans I had once my father passed; I'm sure they suspected I was behind his death. They were afraid of how great I was going to make Kaval, afraid of the glory I was going to bring to my name!

"So they created a jail inside my head. I could still walk and talk, though only where they let me with the words they gave me. I was incapable of thinking my own thoughts, incapable of living my own life. I was left to the will of those weak, cowardly insects *for a decade!*"

Andre wanted to shrink back from the rage radiating from Artreus. He wanted to cringe and hide from the emerald fire pouring from his eyes. Nevertheless, he stood his ground, unwilling to back down from this new threat.

It all made sense now. The reason Declan treated everything with amusement was because all of their strings were being pulled by Artreus. And nobody had a clue.

"I learned to fight it. It took me far too long—the drug they used was extremely potent—but with the help of a secret ally, I began to take back control of my mind. I was cunning; I didn't let them know I was regaining consciousness. I began to notice the damage they wreaked during my sleep. I heard of the Border Conflict and what was becoming of my land to the south because of it. I heard of a young man named Winston Servailles who was pushing for a solution to Salamoa's holy war—a solution that would cost me what was rightfully mine.

"I couldn't have that happen. I'm sure you understand, Andre. My birthright had already shrunk so much. I was still recovering my strength, too weak to lash out at my jailers and destroy them. Instead, with the aid of my ally, I sent my Seethers against Servailles. I didn't know how fortuitous he was then.

"What was more, the senate heard of the attempts on Servailles's life and correctly deduced who was behind it. As weak as they were, they were not stupid. They realized I had found a way to break through the cage in my mind and was regaining strength. They decided to take action before it was too late and kill me. What they didn't know was that I had an ally. With his help, I escaped and fled." Falling silent, Artreus stared at Winston.

The rain had slowed to a mist, the wind to a languid breeze. A boom shook the air, and the ground trembled, small pieces of rubble shifting and skipping down the pile they stood on.

Artreus emerged from his reverie, turning his green eyes back onto Andre. "I came down to this... Corynthia to see for myself. I had no money for a room at an inn, but a bookkeeper in Seruvia was kind enough to give me lodging for the night. He told me all that had taken place since Corynthia was ripped from its rightful ruler. He told me of the unrest around the presidency and how Servailles had been exiled by the new leader. He shared his own struggles, how he had no money because of the increased taxes and could barely afford food each day. I gave him the help he needed." His eyes glinted, and Andre had a feeling he knew what Artreus meant by help.

"In return, I acquired a hiding place where I could regain my strength and bide my time. As I watched, Corynthia began to fall apart—a broken nation that never really had a chance to breathe." He spread his arms, a smile growing on his face. "It's beautiful."

Andre felt a fiery resolve ignite inside of him. There was already so much pain and conflict in Corynthia's short history. So much struggle just to achieve the freedom it was made for. He would be damned before he let another tyrant take advantage of the ruins they stood amongst.

Drawing his sword, he held it in front of him with both hands. It shimmered orange in the night.

"I think you'll find that Corynthia isn't as broken as you'd like."

Artreus laughed, clear and cold. "Andre, we may have had our differences, but I have no intention to harm you. In fact, you would be a welcome ally. I've been watching you for a while, ever since you took the outpost. You've proved yourself to be smart, resourceful, and courageous many times over, and you have a heart for your soldiers. If you join me, I can give you all of the riches you would like. After Corynthia, I shall take my conquest to the whole of the continent, and *you* can lead my armies."

"I appreciate the compliments, except you left out a few important details."

Artreus raised his eyebrows. "Those are?"

"*Trust and brotherhood,*" Andre spat. "We made this nation for people to live outside of the shadow of those like you. You will have to take it back over my dead body."

Green fire smoldered in the emperor's eyes. They held no remorse, no pity, just sick pleasure. "Very well, I will."

Artreus's sword was out before Andre had time to blink. He whipped it around with deadly speed. Andre barely brought his own up to waylay the strike. He caught the blade with his hilt and tried to twist the weapon away from Artreus's hands. Artreus pulled back and lunged. Andre parried again and sidestepped, sliding the weapon past him harmlessly.

He would have to be very careful. With his sprained ankle, one wrong step on the untrustworthy, slippery footing, and he would be dead.

Andre struck back, trying to flip the momentum around. Artreus dodged with ease and laughed again.

"Such a sorry sight you are," he ridiculed as he started to circle around Andre. "How long do you think you'll be able to keep this up?"

Andre shook his head, flinging his wet hair out of his face. "As long as it takes."

They engaged again, exchanging blows furiously. Artreus was frighteningly fast, faster than anyone Andre had fought; he found himself struggling to keep up. A bad feeling he was being toyed with settled in his gut, like the emperor was a cat playing with its food before eating it. The memory of how quickly Artreus dispatched Thomilson's men at the creek after breaking Winston out of Seruvia lit up his mind. He shoved it determinedly back down again. Doubt could kill him as easily as a careless step right now.

They fought and fought, dancing up and down the pile of rubble. The storm had passed over them, rolling away to terrify distant towns. Thunder rumbled faintly while the rain petered to a stop. Even the fires began to falter and dwindle.

There were a few moments when Andre stumbled on an unstable chunk of debris or his ankle simply buckled, yet he was able to recover just quickly enough to stay alive as Artreus pressed him harder and harder. He was exhausted, aching everywhere, but every time he felt like giving up, he remembered Caito and Winston's faces and was fueled with new rage. They fought until his arms were numb, until he was soaked with more of his own sweat than rainwater. And still, Andre refused to quit.

Artreus *had* been toying with him in the beginning. Now, his arrogance turned to determination, then frustration as Andre matched him blow for blow. His attacks came faster and harder, the sick smile on his face fading to intense concentration.

Then, without warning, he stepped back and lowered his sword.

Too tired to seize the unexpected opening, Andre waited, chest heaving, for his next move. He became aware that a ring of people had gathered. Looking around at their grave faces, he recognized the members of the Crimson Hounds. They watched silently, but he could feel their support.

"You have my respect," Artreus announced, wiping his forehead with the back of his hand. He sheathed his sword.

Andre watched him, panting and confused. "What are you doing?"

"I have important matters to attend to. People to hang." He smiled coldly. "I'm not going to waste any more time with you. My main concern has been taken care of." He began to walk away.

Andre watched him leave, too weary to do anything else.

As the ring of spectators parted hurriedly for Artreus, the emperor stopped at the edge and looked back. "But don't fret. I'm not finished with Corynthia. I'll be back."

"Then we'll be waiting," Andre returned savagely.

Artreus laughed and saluted mockingly before vanishing into the blackened shell of Audax Keep. The laugh lingered spitefully in the thick air.

As soon as he was out of sight, Andre swayed and collapsed. Strong arms caught him.

"I've got you, Andre." It was Mattias. "Are you okay? You were right, huh? That bastard Declan was the killer?"

Andre shook his head. "It's worse." He was hardly able to let the words out. Tears streamed down his face as the reality set in.

Young Caito Lazar was dead. He had laid down his life for the people of Corynthia. Winston had betrayed them horribly and was now dead as well. And Artreus, the cruel emperor of Kaval, had personally vowed to punish them for daring to walk to free.

Andre could hold himself up no longer. He leaned all of his weight against his friend and sobbed quietly.

"It's so much worse."

EPILOGUE

Andre ran a hand through his freshly trimmed hair, heart pounding frantically as he stood in front of the crowd of hundreds of people.

The storm blew its course three days ago, yet the wreckage left behind was many weeks from being cleared. Victims of the disaster were still being found buried under the rubble. More than a few were Andre's own soldiers. Pitt, Wes, Tahlia were still missing, and he dreaded the day that they were found. Better to hold the belief that they were crushed and died quickly rather than buried alive, suffering as they went. Corence and Keppen were both safe, but many of the other rebellion officers were confirmed dead.

It took nearly all three of those days for Andre to wrestle his grief back into check. He hadn't eaten or slept, and any attempts to console him fell on deaf ears. The thought of what Winston had done plagued him day and night, accompanied by the heavy question of what Winston would have done had it been Andre standing in his way. He had killed William, the best man Andre knew. Would he have killed Andre, too?

The thought that his friend he had known for years had committed such a monstrosity made him question even the assurance of his own identity. What had he been fighting for? And for whom?

Finally, he pulled himself together, forcing himself back to the realm of the living. Artreus was still out there, planning on taking advantage of Corynthia's wounds. Someone needed to take charge amongst the fragments, and he wasn't about to sit idly by.

He sent search parties (one of them led by Mattias) out to capture Artreus before he could leave Corynthia. Next, he issued an announcement to the people, letting them know he would be speaking publicly, whereat questions and concerns were welcome.

He stood before them now.

A breeze blew over the ruins of Dominus square, ruffling the hair and hoods of those looking on. Nobody spoke. Every eye pinned Andre to the spot.

Taking a deep breath, he began, "Hello, all." He faltered, unsure of what to say. There were a lot of faces in the crowd. A lot of sad and hurting faces.

"I understand that many of you may not know me. My name is Andre Cordon. I was an officer in the rebel army and a close friend and adviser to Winston Servailles."

"Where is he?" called a man in the crowd. "Why isn't he here?"

Winston's betrayal and death were not public yet. Andre and the others decided to withhold its details for fear of the crowds' reaction. Though he didn't feel good about keeping the information from them, until they could figure out how this catastrophe came to be, it was for the best.

He glanced at Keppen, who gave him a sad shrug in return.

"Winston perished in the destruction of the city. As did Caito Lazar, the Soothsayer."

Gasps escaped from the crowd, and questions began to shower him from all sides.

Andre held up his hands to stem the clamor. "One at a time please."

A women spoke up from the front row. Her face was still grimy from helping clear the city, and tear tracks ran down her cheeks. "My family was killed, and my home destroyed. I have nothing left. Please, how did this happen? I thought the war ended."

They deserve to know, Andre decided. They had lost so much. He at least owed them the truth.

"There was an assassin. A saboteur working against Corynthia, fighting against the freedom it represented. He set up a trap underneath the city to use to his advantage."

"Andre..." warned Corence's voice, cautioning him against what he was about to say.

No more lies.

He spoke quickly like he was ripping off a bandage. "That saboteur was Winston Servailles."

There was shocked silence.

"Winston was a good man. He was kind and caring, and he was proud. It was his pride that caused him to fall." Even as the words left him, he found himself having trouble believing them.

Did he care? he wondered to himself. *What if it had been me instead of William or Caito? Would he have killed me, too?*

He continued to speak, doing his best to weave a tale that justified the man Andre thought he knew; to honor him, even when he had lost every right to be honored. "He lost sight of his morals and lost his way in his fantasies. He turned the rebellion into a personal vendetta, disguised as something being done for the greater good. In that vision, he no longer recognized his friends and could no longer see the consequences of his actions. As long as he accomplished what he set out to do, it didn't matter who stood in his way."

A single tear slid down his cheek. He wiped it away. "Caito Lazar stopped him before he could take complete control. In doing so, he met his own demise. The Soothsayer died as he lived: Working and fighting for the people. For what was right.

"I know how dark these last few days have been. I want to implore you, for those of you struggling with grief, do not be afraid to reach out to others. And if someone asks you for aid or comfort, don't turn them away, please. Use each other to rise out of this shadow, because in these times especially, we need to be there for each other. If we are not unified, Corynthia will be destroyed."

He took a deep breath. "The Lord Artreus has been among us. He is not a half-wit, but wholly cunning and malicious. Right now, he feasts his hungry eyes on our nation. He does not feel sympathy for us. He enjoys the violence we have been struggling with and is eagerly planning to strike us in our plight. Today, you can mourn; tomorrow, you must find a way to rise up. There is another storm coming, and the only way we can weather it is together—as one unified nation. Corynthia as it is meant to be."

As Andre looked out over the sea of stricken faces, a woman with black hair tied in a ponytail and a posture like a shorebird slowly raised her fist into the air in a salute. A large, bearded man with ferocious eyebrows next to her joined. One by one, the rest of them followed suit until every last man, woman, and child in the square stood fists held high.

He glanced back at Corence and Keppen. They were doing the same. Corence gave him a grave nod.

Raising his fist in the air, Andre let his eyes rove to the city wall, then to the sky above, hope blossoming in his chest like a mountain flower in winter.

Whatever was out there, whatever Artreus had in store for them, they would survive it.

Together.

Dear reader, if you enjoyed Vision of Fire, consider leaving a review and suggesting it to a friend!
Want more? Follow me on Instagram @yourhomesliceeph to stay in the loop!

ACKNOWLEDGEMENTS

Writing *Vision of Fire* was a long and sometimes arduous process, and would have been even more so without the support and eager anticipation of some wonderful people.

I began writing the book in my junior year of high school in 2020, the start of "the Dark Years." COVID impacted a lot of things in my life, and would have killed my passion for writing this story if my Mom hadn't allowed me to drop my English class and work instead on my book. As a homeschooling mom of three, she was more than capable of taking the rough chunk of marble I started with and helping shape it into a statue rivaling Michelangelo's David! Well, maybe not quite. But her hard work and countless hours sacrificed poring over my manuscript are the reason I still have hair on my head, and why I am a significantly better writer than I was when I began.

In my opinion, a book isn't complete without beautiful illustrations, and I would be dead in the water if it weren't for my sister Felicity. From character concepts for social media to the cover art and map, and even an animation, her careful work was the proverbial frosting on the cake. Her outrage at me using an AI-generated image for a cover concept is well-deserved.

Two heads are better than one, and many heads are better than two. Hence, my deepest appreciation to all of those heads. Those who plodded through my earlier drafts: Salena Sikorski for always explaining how she sees the world and for pointing out copyediting errors I never would have found; Mary Aleksandruk for enduring a roller coaster of emotion (I'm sorry), and inspiring deeper character development; Ron Whitley for pointing out that a simple innkeeper in a far northern village probably wouldn't know the inner machinations of an entire nation; and my brother, Gavin, for challenging me to make a prologue and being wonderfully delighted by my plot twists. And of course, those who politely engaged in my long-winded tangents about my stories: Sean Spencer, who shares ideas with me just as eagerly as I do with him; my Dad, who has as deep a love for fantasy as anyone I know; Benjamin Bullock, for the prayers and promises of blackmailing his own friends to buy my book; and so many others for always asking me how much longer until I'm done: Namely, anyone who has ever had the pleasure of being my coworker, and of course, my homies at *Thug Shaker Central* (a more excellent group of friends I could never find). Thank you for all of the prayers, patience, questions, and encouragement!

I'm also extremely grateful to Jeremiah Laselle for walking alongside me during this process. Not only did he save me from the horror of Word and Google Docs by introducing me to Scrivener, but his pioneering into authorship paved the way for my own. For technicalities and nuances, he's the man. Likewise, a thank you to Kelson Brewer, author of *Flowers of the Far Fields*, for encouraging me and helping me see that publishing *isn't* as scary as I thought.

Also, OODLES of love for everyone who has supported me and expressed their excitement! While it's been a long, impatient era of hearing me say, "It's so close," for years, your enthusiasm have been my motivator, especially during times of lethargy and writer's block (gross). My dream has always been to take the stories in my head and turn them into something tangible that others can enjoy, so THANK YOU for sticking around!

Lastly, but most importantly, thank you to the Lord for the desire and determination to stick through five long years of hard work to make my dream a reality. "Give thanks to the God of heaven, for his faithfulness is everlasting." Psalm 136:26

Ad multas plures adventuras!
Ephraim Wright

ABOUT THE AUTHOR

As a homeschooler, Ephraim Wright had plenty of opportunity to cultivate his fire for the fantastic. The countless soundbites and elaborate LEGO scenarios with his siblings eventually led him to start writing *Vision of Fire* in 2020. He lives in Washington State, where he is continuing to develop *The Atheralyn Legacy's* universe, along with other works.

www.ingramcontent.com/pod-product-compliance
Lightning Source LLC
Chambersburg PA
CBHW070158120726
47909CB00001B/156